Ex-National Hunt Champion Jockey, ~~~~ ~ancome is a broadcaster on racing for Channel 4 and has established himself as one of the front runners in the racing thrillers stakes. He lives in Lambourn, Berkshire.

His previous bestsellers have all been highly praised:

'Francome provides a vivid panorama of the racing world . . . and handles the story's twist deftly' *The Times*

'Francome can spin a darn good yarn' *Racing Post*

'Thrills, twists and turns on and off the racecourse. Convincing and beguiling' *Irish Independent*

'Move over Dick Francis, here's competition' *Me* magazine

'A thoroughly convincing and entertaining tale' *Daily Mail*

'The racing feel is authentic and it's a pacy, entertaining read' *Evening Standard*

'Irresistibly reminiscent of the master . . . a most readable yarn' *Mail on Sunday*

'Thrills to the final furlong . . . Francome knows how to write a good racing thriller' *Daily Express*

'Mr Francome adeptly teases to the very end and cleverly keeps a few twists up his sleeve until the closing chapters' *Country Life*

*Also by John Francome*

Tip Off
Safe Bet
High Flyer
False Start
Dead Ringer
Break Neck
Outsider
Rough Ride
Stud Poker
Stone Cold

*Also by John Francome and James McGregor*

Eavesdropper
Riding High
Declared Dead
Blood Stock

# Lifeline

John Francome

**HEADLINE**

Copyright © 2000 John Francome and Mike Bailey

The right of John Francome to be identified as the Author of
the Work has been asserted by him in accordance with
the Copyright, Designs and Patents Act 1988.

First published in 2000
by HEADLINE BOOK PUBLISHING

First published in paperback in 2001
by HEADLINE BOOK PUBLISHING

10 9 8 7 6 5 4 3 2 1

ISBN 0 7472 6607 7

Typeset by Avon Dataset Ltd, Bidford-on-Avon, Warks

Printed and bound in Great Britain by
Clays Ltd, St Ives plc

HEADLINE BOOK PUBLISHING
A division of Hodder Headline
338 Euston Road
London NW1 3BH

www.headline.co.uk
www.hodderheadline.com

With thanks to John Selby for his advice

# Before

On the last morning of his life Jeff Collins woke from a deep sleep feeling fully rested for the first time in weeks. He reached for his watch on the tea chest that passed for a bedside table. He'd slept for six hours straight. He couldn't remember when he'd last done that. Not recently, that was for sure. Not since he'd stolen four million Hong Kong dollars from Bernard Shen.

He got dressed and made breakfast. That took all of five minutes. The one-roomed shack an hour out of Melbourne, where he'd been camping for the last few days, offered few amenities. Of course he could have parked himself up at the house with Tim, luxuriating in his own private bathroom and enjoying slap-up meals cooked by Sharon. In fact it had been hard work convincing his former employers that he wanted to rough it out here. He'd made up a load of hooey about getting back to nature which he knew they hadn't fallen for. They probably thought he was still cocking his leg over the barmaid from the hotel and wanted a bit of privacy. Which was fine by Jeff.

He swallowed the last of his roll – it was stale – and washed it down with a mouthful of instant coffee. He shaved using the cracked mirror over the sink and stepped outside to relieve himself. The day was cool but dry and the rolling green country stretching to the horizon looked inviting. Time for one last ride out and then he could head for the airport. Another twelve hours and he'd be on the way to England and safety. He couldn't wait.

Glory Days was an uncooperative animal unless you knew him well but Jeff had a soft spot for him. The pair of them had come second in the Ampol Stakes at Flemington two years back – a result that Jeff rated above any of the wins in his career to date. He reckoned he would soon put that minor triumph in the shade, however, once he got a few rides under his belt in England.

As he mounted the big brown gelding and walked him out of the yard, Jeff had a brief vision of what his life was going to be like from now on. He imagined strolling the parade ring at Newmarket, riding a finish at Goodwood, leaping victorious from the saddle at Epsom. He could taste it already. Did all the Pommy women sport crazy hats at the races or was that just on the television? What the hell – it was going to be great. He'd make a name for himself in England and come back to Oz when all this had blown over.

He put a stop to this train of thought. He wasn't out of the woods yet. The whole of the Far East was Mr Shen's fiefdom and the Triad hand extended from Hong Kong to Australia with ease. Jeff wouldn't feel safe till he was on that plane to London.

Nevertheless, as he hacked Glory Days across the field of sheep that backed on to Tim's yard, he wondered if he wasn't being paranoid. The fact that he'd slept undisturbed by fear and had dreamt of riding winners in England – maybe this was telling him something. Perhaps Mr Shen hadn't put the missing Pick Six ticket down to Jeff. Maybe he had simply written off the loss. Shen was running a high-risk business after all – even if laundering drug money on the racecourse wasn't exactly legitimate.

Jeff dismounted to open the barbed-wire gate at the bottom of the field. He made sure he'd fastened it behind him after he'd led the horse through. Tim would get it in the neck from the farmer if he let any of the sheep escape.

He allowed Glory Days to amble at his own pace along the unmade track. Underfoot was just compressed earth and rock, full of holes where man or beast could turn an ankle. It was best to let the old horse find his own way. Fortunately the dirt track only ran for half a mile, between a bramble-filled ditch and the barbed-wire fence, before leading to another gate and open country where he could enjoy a canter.

Just before they reached the second gate the track curved round to the right and Jeff was surprised to see a four-wheel-drive vehicle barring the way. A small guy in a golf cap was peering into the boot.

Jeff brought Glory Days to a halt. 'Got a problem?' he asked.

The guy in the cap looked up, a jack in his hand. Jeff was alarmed to see that he looked Chinese. 'Nothing serious,' he said affably. 'Just changing a wheel.'

Jeff suppressed his fear. He couldn't spend the rest of his life avoiding everyone of an Oriental appearance.

He climbed off Glory Days, leading the horse to the gate on the other side of the 4WD.

'Shall I hold him for you?' offered the guy with the cap as Jeff reached out to open the gate.

'Sure.'

'Nice horse.' The other man took the reins. He was still holding the jack. 'You must be Jeff Collins.'

*What?*

'Not me, mate,' Jeff said quickly.

'Yeah. Sure you are,' said the other, grinning now. 'It's him, isn't it, Mickey?'

*Mickey!*

A familiar figure appeared from nowhere. Had he been behind a tree? Crouching in the back of the 4WD? What did it matter?

Mickey Lee was short and stocky; muscles strained against his pastel blue polo shirt and his face was twisted by a bad skin-graft. He didn't have an official job title in Mr Shen's organisation. Unofficially, 'fixer', 'enforcer' and, sometimes, 'executioner' summed up his function.

'Hello, Jeff,' said Mickey and held out his hand in greeting.

Jeff took it – what else could he do?

'You left Hong Kong in rather a hurry.'

'I had to get back to my folks. My mother was ill.'

'I'm sorry to hear that.' Mickey was still holding Jeff's hand, like he'd forgotten to let go. 'She looked well enough yesterday.'

'You've seen my mother?' He was shocked.

'How do you think I found out where you were?'

Jeff's bowels turned to water. 'You didn't . . . I mean, she's OK, isn't she?'

'Absolutely fine. Your father, too. Charming people. They said I could go back any time and visit. I might just do that.'

Jeff was shaking, his fingers sweaty in Mickey's steely grip.

'No, you mustn't! Please leave them alone.'

'Just give me back the Pick Six ticket, Jeff, and there'll be no need.'

'I haven't got it.'

'Give me the money then. It was worth about four million HK, wasn't it?'

'I haven't got it, I swear.'

Mickey sighed. 'Don't make this difficult, Jeff. I don't enjoy killing respectable retired folk. Or stupid little flat jockeys either. But I will.'

Jeff whimpered. He tugged at his hand but Mickey's fingers were round his wrist like a handcuff. The other fellow was watching them with a smile on his face, still holding the horse and the jack.

There was nowhere to run.

'I mean, I've sent the ticket to England.'

'England?' Mickey sounded surprised.

'Yes. It's in my trunk. I've sent all my stuff on ahead.'

Mickey thought for moment. 'Where are you staying in England?'

'At Freddy's.'

'Freddy Montague?'

'Yes. I put the ticket with all my things. It's safe. When I get over there I'll send it back to you, I swear.'

'Does Freddy know about this?'

'It was his idea. He was going back to Hong Kong later to cash it in.'

Mickey laughed. 'You've got some nerve.'

'Let me go now, Mickey. Please. I thought we were mates.' Jeff jerked his arm frantically, trying to free his hand. Mickey did not appear to notice. He seemed lost in thought. Finally he spoke.

'Listen to me carefully, Jeff. What I'm going to say to you is degrading for both of us but it is necessary. I have to be convinced you are telling me the truth.'

Then he told Jeff, in explicit detail, what he would do to his mother and father if he were forced to return to their home.

Jeff was in tears long before he had finished.

*

Mickey had hung out with Jeff and the English rider, Freddy Montague, once or twice in Hong Kong. He'd shown them some hot bars and taken them to Kowloon for the best Chinese meal in the city. They'd been good company and everyone had had a laugh.

He reflected on this now as he ordered Jeff to get back on the horse. The fact that Mickey had bought the jockey drinks, laughed at his smart remarks and checked out the bar-room pussy with him didn't make what he had to do any easier. This was work and it had to be done. But he didn't like it. He had a heart just like the next guy.

He could see that Jeff was surprised to be allowed back into the saddle. He probably thought Mickey had taken pity on him for old time's sake. Well, Mickey couldn't help that.

As he seized Jeff's right boot, he checked that Pete had the horse securely by the bridle. They'd positioned the animal facing back up the track, the way he'd come.

'What are you doing?' cried Jeff.

Mickey said nothing but yanked hard on the stirrup iron, pulling the jockey's foot right through. Jeff sprawled half on and half off the horse's back, his boot jammed fast.

'Let him go, Pete,' Mickey said.

Pete released the reins and gave the horse a hard smack on the rump with the flat of his hand. Glory Days shot ahead along the track, obviously unhappy at the way Jeff was dragging him down.

Mickey started the 4WD behind him.

Jeff shouted in terror as he frantically tried to free his right leg from the stirrup.

Mickey put his hand on the horn and drove forward, closing

on the horse. Glory Days took off again.

'Help me!' screamed Jeff.

The horse stumbled on the uneven surface and Jeff slipped from his back, hands flailing for purchase as he fell between the animal's legs. His shoulder smashed against a rock and his body convulsed in pain. As Jeff was dragged along behind the horse, his head tipped back and Mickey stared directly into his eyes. They were filled with helpless fear. Mickey had seen that look before. Poor bastard.

Mickey accelerated.

Glory Days plunged on in blind panic, heading back up the track for home, lengthening his stride to get away from the roaring machine behind him.

Jeff jolted and bumped along behind the pounding hooves, helpless to save himself. His back scraped over every rock and pebble on the track, and his head bounced and slammed with every stride.

Mickey put his foot down harder and Glory Days hit top speed. They were flying now, all the way along the rocky track, with Jeff flopping and jerking beneath the runaway horse like a doll.

Glory Days leapt the barbed-wire gate at the end of the track as if he were a seasoned jumper. Jeff was not so lucky. His bruised and broken body smashed into the four strands of wire, uprooting the poles on either side. The horse was dragged off his feet and crashed to the ground with the snap of a fetlock. By the time Mickey reached him, the animal was squealing and whinnying in agony. Someone would hear him soon enough.

Mickey quickly checked on Jeff. He was glassy-eyed and bloody. And stone dead – probably a broken neck.

Mickey jumped back into the vehicle, relieved that it was over.

Shame about the horse.

Twenty-four hours later it was Mickey, not Jeff, who was on a plane to England – and a rendezvous with Freddy Montague.

# PART ONE

# Chapter One

The June sun beat down mercilessly on the first afternoon of Royal Ascot. The heat hit Tony Byrne like a hammer as he emerged from the weighing room and made his way to the parade ground ahead of the 4.20 race. He was sweating already and his silks were sticking to his back – he'd been out of the sauna for less than thirty minutes. Making eight stone twelve had been a nightmare and he'd only just squeaked it. Now he felt as weak as a kitten. How the hell he was going to impose his will on half a ton of racehorse in the next few minutes he wasn't sure. He only knew he had to. This was his big chance and, if he screwed up, maybe his last.

Just in front of him, Freddy Montague strode into the parade ring, raising his whip to acknowledge a small gathering of fans. Nobody took any notice of Tony but that didn't bother him. As far as he was concerned, the spectators were irrelevant. He made an effort to shut them all out – the Hoorays in their toppers, the lads in their rented suits, even the women exposing more flesh than was wise to the scorching sun. He hoped his mount, Lifeline, was ignoring them too. This was by far the largest and most boisterous crowd the colt had ever experienced and Tony had no idea how he would react. He could see the big chestnut on the far side of the ring being led round by Neil Kelly, a sixteen-year-old apprentice.

He made for a slender figure standing on her own in the

centre where the runners' connections were gathering. She wore a long skirt in navy blue with a light summer jacket and – in concession, he guessed, to the Royal-ness of the occasion – a straw hat with a matching band of blue. Somewhere in Tony's mind he registered that his trainer, Kate, looked a sight more desirable than any of the more extravagantly dressed women on show. He had more important things to worry about than female desirability, however.

'How's he doing?' he demanded, noting that her eyes, too, were on Lifeline.

'Fine – touch wood.' She turned to Tony. 'He wouldn't go in the saddling-stalls, though. We had to saddle him up outside.'

'Oh?'

'There was a shadow across the stall. You know Lifeline – gives anything suspicious a wide berth.'

'I don't like the sound of that.'

He saw her taking in the beads of sweat on his lip, the tension in his jaw. 'Are you all right?'

'I can look after myself, Kate,' he snapped, 'just you worry about the horse.'

Her clear grey eyes regarded him with surprise.

'I'm sorry,' he muttered. Being rude to your trainer wasn't smart, as Tony knew to his cost. His CV was littered with burnt bridges and he couldn't afford any more.

'All right, get back in your pram,' she said. 'I was the one who didn't think Lifeline should run at this meeting.'

'That's just because you want your brother to win.' The words were out before Tony could stop them. 'Just joking,' he added hastily. Not far off, Freddy – the brother in question – was listening intently to a small Oriental woman in a daft hat. 'I see Mrs Lim's giving him an ear-bashing.'

Freddy saw them look over and rolled his eyes. Kate smiled. 'I'd better rescue him.'

'No last-minute instructions for me then?'

'Where Lifeline's concerned, Tony, you don't need instructions. But if you want my advice, you should concentrate on keeping calm yourself.'

She gave him a leg up into the saddle.

'Who knows? You might even win,' she added as she walked away.

Tony tried to dismiss her remarks from his mind. As it happened, she was right. He didn't need instructions about Lifeline, a foal he'd helped raise after the excruciating birth that had killed his dam. The loss of the mare had been a blow to Tony's father – she'd been the darling among the few horses he kept on his Yorkshire farm. The old man fancied himself a judge of horseflesh and though Wishful Thinking had been a neurotic beast, with a fear of confined spaces, her elegant lines and turn of foot had always excited him. He claimed there was some fine breeding in her ancestry somewhere and had laid out more than he could afford to send her to stud. Along with the neuroses, Lifeline had inherited Wishful Thinking's talent but Tony's father had been diagnosed with cancer soon after the foal's birth and had not lived to see his investment bear fruit.

So here they were, about to take part in the Group 3 Coventry Stakes at Royal Ascot, the best two-year-old race of the season so far and a step up from the five-furlong maiden and a conditions race at Salisbury, Lifeline's only previous outings. Tony reflected that the old man would be proud of the pair of them – wherever he was. He stroked the horse's neck and Lifeline lowered his head, long ears flopping forward. Tony tried to read his mood: was Lifeline ready for his greatest test –

or about to fall apart? As the sweat trickled down his spine, Tony wasn't sure how he'd answer that question himself.

'A right bloody pair we are,' he muttered.

What did Tony mean by that? Neil wondered as he led Lifeline on a circuit of the ring.

The lad was feeling pretty nervous himself even in his minor role. He'd never been to Ascot before and the occasion was overwhelming. He knew how anxious Tony was about Lifeline but Neil had no doubt the horse would do them all proud. There was a spring in the colt's step and a sparkle in his big caramel eyes that suggested he was up for the race. Neil wanted to tell Tony as much but he held his tongue. He wasn't one for volunteering unsolicited remarks, especially at a moment like this.

Tony caught his eye. 'What price is he?'

Neil glanced up at the huge Tote screen above the champagne bar. 'Lifeline sixteen to one. Pay Back Time evens. The favourite.'

Pay Back Time belonged to Mrs Lim's horse. Son of Cash Back. Winner of the Belmont Stakes in New York. Freddy Montague was riding him.

It dawned upon Neil what he really wanted to say to Tony. 'Please finish in front of Freddy. Go and stuff the little bastard, just for me.'

But all he managed to mutter as Tony left the parade ring was, 'Good luck.'

Lunch in Ascot's Pavilion restaurant can be a lengthy activity, stretching from pre-prandial cocktails to a last-race Monte Cristo, taking in four courses, a full tea-time spread and, if your host's generosity holds out, as much fine wine as you can guzzle. And, while stuffing your face, you can even watch the racing on television, restricting any other physical exertion to the unavoidable – such as strolling to the nearest Tote window to place a bet. If this is your idea of a day at the races, it takes some beating. But, on the other hand, if it's not . . .

Greta Somerville was having a loathsome time. At the present moment an indulgent afternoon surrounded by happy hedonists with their snouts in the trough was the last thing she needed. She had fled the company of Gavin Marshall and the balding banker who sat on her other side as frequently as she could, on the justifiable pretext of getting some fresh air. But she couldn't desert her post at the table for long or Laurie would get suspicious – and Laurie's suspicions had to be kept in check till she figured out exactly what she was going to do about her problem. Fortunately, when it came to Greta's personal concerns, her husband was not inclined to be perceptive. Provided she looked like she was doing her bit – laughing at Gavin's off-colour witticisms, keeping the men's glasses charged and allowing the banker to gawp at her cleavage without protest – then Laurie would be satisfied. The effort was killing her.

The Somervilles' syndicate lunch at Ascot was an annual affair – a thank you, so called, to the eight-strong team of backers who let Laurie wheel and deal in horseflesh with their money. In fact, the relaxed and bibulous atmosphere provided fertile ground for an accomplished operator like him. It was amazing the number of other enterprises which sprang from that soil, germs of ideas planted at the yearly Pavilion lunch. And Greta was expected to do her share of weeding and tilling – or stroking and massaging, as she referred to it. As the only woman present – this being a recognised business meeting and she being Laurie's official PA – it was an unspoken part of the deal that she put on her glad rags and spread the feel-good factor. If she was in the mood, it could be a laugh. This year, despite her fixed grin, laughter was the last thing on her mind.

'What do you fancy in the Coventry, Mrs S?' murmured Gavin Marshall in her ear, his voice heavy with innuendo as usual. It particularly irritated her when he called her Mrs S, calling to mind an image of herself as a tweed-skirted chattel of her husband. Of course, he knew it irritated her – that's why he did it.

'Pay Back Time's strong for his age,' she replied. 'I haven't seen anything so far this season that can beat him.'

'Hmm.' Marshall sounded unimpressed. 'I can't bring myself to put money on a nag with Fly Freddy aboard.'

Greta looked surprised.

Marshall leaned closer. 'He's such a monkey, you never know what game he's playing. Maybe he wants to win today – or maybe he doesn't. And even if he doesn't win he won't lose out, if you know what I mean.'

'Freddy Montague's a bloody good jockey,' she protested.

'Exactly.' Marshall was amused by her defence. 'And it's not just horses, is it? I'm told he's keen to get his leg over anything in knickers. No stablegirl in Lambourn need ever pass a lonely night when he's in town. That's what they say.'

He reached for his brandy glass, his inquisitive eyes on Greta as he sipped, gauging her reaction. She made an effort to keep her smile in place as he continued.

'Fact is, I'm thinking of setting up one of those porno websites' – internet companies featured heavily in Marshall's business interests – 'call it FreddyCam or something like that.

Plaster it with nude totty. Get a load of stupid oiks to send in pictures of their girlfriends with their kit off. Run regular features – Who's Fast Freddy riding this week? – that kind of stuff. You'd get a load of hits, I bet. Might even link it up with some tipster lines. What do you think?'

Try to laugh it off. 'Gavin, you're a hoot!'

'I'm not joking. Sex, betting and the internet – there's money to be made, my girl.'

'Don't "my girl" me, you smug sod!'

It came out much louder than it should have. Laurie froze in the middle of his conversation with Charlie Hargreaves, a mail-order millionaire, and shot Greta a look of panic and reproach.

Time to backtrack fast.

'I'm sorry, Gavin, I didn't mean to be rude but' – she laid a hand on his shirt-sleeved arm, felt the rough hair through the cotton – 'you know Kate's very upset about it.'

'About what?' Marshall's voice was curt. He wasn't used to being put down in any situation, let alone in public and by a woman.

'The rumours about Freddy and all these girls. She doesn't see her brother as a heart-throb.'

'She can take a joke, can't she?'

'Not on this subject. It's really got to her recently. I've been a bit of a shoulder for her to cry on.'

'I didn't realise you two were such bosom buddies. I'd better watch my tongue in future, I suppose.'

'That's not an apology, is it, Mr Marshall?'

A bit of a risk, but worth it because his thin pink lips stretched into a grin.

'It's the closest you're going to bloody well get. Now' – he picked up a race card from the table – 'since you're such pals

17

with Kate Montague, tell me about this other runner she's got in the next race.'

'Lifeline? Kate says he's a bag of nerves but runs like the wind.'

'Why's Tony Byrne on him? I heard he couldn't do the weight.'

'Tony's mother owns the horse. He's starved himself to ride.'

'A proper gamble then.'

'You could put it like that.'

Marshall smacked the card hard against the table top. 'That's the kind of gamble I like.' He stood up and held out his hand. 'Come and watch a smug sod like me clean up, Mrs S.'

Greta, God help her, took his hand and said, 'My pleasure.'

Lifeline bounded down to the start. The colt was obviously in fine fettle and eager to run. Tony wished the same could be said for himself. The days of dry toast and milkless tea and the past few hours in the sauna had taken their toll. His head felt stuffed with cotton wool, as if he had a heavy cold and the rest of the world only existed through a pane of glass. But out here on the course the breeze was fresh in his face, clearing some of the fog from his brain. He reined Lifeline in, keen to preserve his energy now he'd had a feel of the ground, and the colt responded at once. Suddenly Tony found himself grinning. Lifeline was a fantastic horse and he was a lucky bastard to be aboard with a chance to prove it.

He forced himself to focus on the race ahead. Though it wasn't his habit to worry about other runners, if he were honest he'd have to say Pay Back Time, Freddy's horse, had the beating of Lifeline. Tony had seen plenty of Pay Back Time out on the gallops and he looked a rare prospect: strong, handsome and well-bred. Nevertheless, Tony had every confidence in his own horse. One thing was for sure: if Pay Back Time was evens, Lifeline was better than 16-1.

Except, that is, for Factor X – the unknown ingredient in Lifeline's mental composition – the gremlin that had made the colt shy away from the saddling enclosure.

Tony had delayed bringing the horse down from Yorkshire for as long as possible but had finally bitten the bullet the previous winter. After a long and difficult journey, Lifeline had arrived at Beechwood Lodge, Kate's yard, with a marked disinclination to be cooped up – his mother's old trouble – and an aversion to motor vehicles.

Lifeline had finally conquered his fear of enclosed spaces but getting him accustomed to travelling had taken a little longer. It had caused Tony many a sleepless night. What, after all, was the use of a racehorse who wouldn't go in a horse box? Unless he could get over it, Lifeline would not be able to race. But with Kate's help and, later, Neil's, Tony had won this battle too. In the end all it took was patience – a limitless supply of it. He'd started by getting the horse into a stationary horse box, then taking him on short journeys and, after that, longer ones. Thankfully it had worked and nowadays Lifeline was able to travel with no obvious ill effects.

And so for the colt now to revert to old habits and refuse to enter the saddling-stall was irritating. Unless it was just a blip, of significance only to those who knew his history. Tony reminded himself that Kate, who was almost as familiar with Lifeline as he was, had not seemed that concerned.

As the runners began to load into the starting stalls, Tony urged Lifeline forward and the horse obeyed, heading for his allotted position without protest. Tony breathed a sigh of relief. It was going to be all right.

Then a horse down the line suddenly reared up with a snort of protest and his rider pulled the animal away. 'Sodding wasp,' he said to no one in particular.

Lifeline stuck his toes in at once, a yard from the mouth of the stall.

'In you go, sunshine,' yelled one of the stall-handlers, nudging the colt from behind with the rubber butterfly-wings designed to urge the reluctant into place. Lifeline bucked and shied away.

'Give us the hood, Charlie,' the handler shouted to his mate.

'No!' cried Tony. A hood was sometimes placed over the head of an obstinate horse to get it into the starting-stall – a good trick in some cases but, with Lifeline, it would be a disaster.

Tony turned the horse away from the gates, taking him on a short circuit to calm him down. As he did so he stroked Lifeline's neck and murmured into his ear. It occurred to him that he probably had just one more chance to get his unpredictable mount into place or else he'd be left behind at the start.

'It's OK, old fellow,' he muttered. 'There's nothing to worry about.'

All the other horses had now loaded. Only Lifeline remained.

A voice rang out clearly. One of the other jockeys, eager for the off.

'Come on, Byrne, you dozy bastard. We haven't got all bleedin' day.'

Tony didn't respond. He took his feet out of the irons and relaxed his body to give the horse more confidence. The starter wouldn't wait much longer.

\*

The crush on the rails hadn't lessened Greta's discomfort but at least she was in the fresh air. She'd been amused by Marshall's flamboyant display as he'd worked the line of bookies hunting for the best odds on Lifeline and wagering what seemed to her reckless sums of money. He'd been followed by the banker – Hartley – who'd tagged after the pair of them and now stood pressed up behind her with his binoculars jammed against his brow.

'One of them won't go in,' he announced. 'Number fourteen.'

'That's Lifeline,' said Greta.

'Damn it,' muttered Marshall, glaring at her.

'Well, I did warn you.'

'He's off on a bit of a walkabout,' said Hartley.

'Oh, for Christ's sake,' Marshall growled.

Greta kept her mouth shut, though not for the first time she wondered at a grown man's sense-of-humour failure when it came to having a bet.

'That's it, my lad, that's it.' Tony's voice kept up the gentle words of reassurance, like a steady drip of rain, as he turned Lifeline back towards the starting-stalls.

'Time's running out, Mr Byrne,' called the starter but Tony didn't acknowledge him.

'Come on, my lovely fellow.' They were two yards away now. 'Come on, lad – let's *run*.' The last word seemed to galvanise the horse. He pricked up his ears and stepped smartly between the jaws of the gate as Tony popped his feet back into the irons. Lifeline liked running.

'Nice of you to show up,' came Freddy's voice from the next stall. 'I should be in the winner's enclosure by now.'

Before Tony could reply the gates were open and all was lost in the shouts of encouragement and creaking of tack and drumming of hooves as fifteen sleek and powerful racehorses hurled themselves forward.

'Go on, Tony! Go on, my son!'

As Marshall's voice boomed in her ear Greta wondered why punters were so predictable in their choice of language.

'Go on, Tony! Give it some!'

Marshall looked like he might burst a blood vessel as his voice climbed the octaves, his face the colour of the boiled lobster he'd polished off for lunch.

'What's happening?' Greta yelled to Hartley.

From their cramped position on the rails it wasn't easy to see much as the pack of horses thundered towards them and the gabble of the on-course commentary was swallowed up by the crowd. Hartley concentrated on the huge TV screen in the middle of the course, struggling to match the jockeys' colours with his race card.

'Driving Force in the lead, I'd say,' he shouted. 'Pay Back Time's breathing down his neck, though.'

'Go on, Tony,' screamed Marshall. 'Where the fuck are you?'

Greta grinned, the buzz getting to her now, despite everything. She clutched her ticket tight. She had her money on Freddy.

Tony no longer felt weak and woolly-headed; he was as high as a kite, wired up to the beast beneath him as they pelted over the springy turf. Half the race was gone already and nearly a dozen horses were abreast of them. It was a flat-out cavalry charge with little time for tactics or a change of pace.

Lifeline had been drawn on the stand side with only Pay Back Time inside him. But Driving Force, the colt on the other side, had shot off like a bullet and found himself in the lead – at which point he'd made for the rails where he now ran three lengths clear of the field.

Freddy was cruising, Tony could see that. With a furlong left, the rest of the field was going backwards but Pay Back Time was eating up the turf, poised to pick off Driving Force and take the race. Unless, Tony thought, Lifeline had more to give. They were in unknown territory now – the colt had never gone further than five furlongs. It was time to see what he was made of.

Whip in the right hand, Tony gave his horse a flick. *Come on, feller*. Then another. *Go, go, go!*

And suddenly Lifeline went.

Tony saw Freddy give Pay Back Time a crack, switching him out to take Driving Force before the line. But there was no room. Tony was up alongside, holding his ground, boxing Freddy in behind the fast-fading Driving Force. For a timeless moment, Lifeline and Pay Back Time were neck and neck, eyeball to eyeball.

'Get out of my fucking way!' screamed Freddy but the sound was lost in Tony's slipstream as, at another touch of the whip, Lifeline moved into overdrive, flashing past Driving Force.

As they crossed the line the blood was singing in Tony's veins. The thought flashed into his head that he'd never been this fast on a horse before.

'You beauty!' he shouted into the wind even as he wondered how to get Lifeline to stop.

The smoky fug of the Great Portland Street bookie's seemed to isolate Derek Pearson from the shouts of the men around him. There were only half a dozen punters in the shop but they made enough noise for twice that number. The climax to the 4.20 at Ascot had provided the best sport of the afternoon so far – not that any of these spectators cared a hoot for sport.

'Bloody Freddy Montague,' spat a man in overalls as, on the bank of TV screens ahead, Lifeline beat Driving Force and Pay Back Time to the winning post. He turned to Derek. 'What was the silly arse doing on the inside, eh?'

Derek said nothing. The man's pink face was less than a foot away yet, to Derek, the fellow could have been on the moon. With a mutter of disgust, the punter turned away to find a more sympathetic reception elsewhere.

Derek fumbled in his pocket for his ticket. A clock on the wall told him it was 4.28 – the Tuesday afternoon video conference with New York would be in full swing by now. Today's was the first he'd missed since he'd sold out for a fistful of dollars last autumn. Funny, but he didn't feel anything.

All he could think about were his cardiologist's words, uttered just an hour before in the cool of the Regency-striped consulting room in Harley Street. In fact, Derek had known the worst before Mr Digby even opened his mouth. He could tell by the expression on the heart specialist's face as he looked up from Derek's latest set of results.

Derek fished out his betting slip. Bloody hell, he'd won again. A tenner to win at sixteens. In normal circumstances he'd have been bursting with excitement, the kind of two-large-Scotches-and-a-smoke excitement that, according to Digby, must be forever in his past – if he was to have a future, that is.

Of course, it was thanks to Digby that Derek was on his winning streak. Breathless in the 3.30 had started it – that was how he felt as he'd tumbled in out of the heat, the old ticker hammering away nineteen to the dozen. In the next, Side Effect had romped home by five lengths – another easy choice of name. Derek's discovery that a diuretic could make you impotent had been a turning point in his condition. If only there'd been just the wife to think about at the time . . .

Which brought him to the 4.20 – a more difficult choice since he'd liked the look of both Night Nurse and Last Chance Saloon. In a moment of inspiration, however, he'd plumped for the one thing he desperately needed. And though he still didn't have a lifeline he did have £160 less tax in his pocket.

Now he put all his winnings on his selection in the next race. An easy decision. The other runners didn't stand a chance against a horse called Defibrillator.

After the race, Marshall made just the kind of song and dance Greta would have predicted. Back at the syndicate table in the restaurant, champagne and brandy took their place beside the fruitcake and scones and Marshall tipped the waitresses with twenties – though only the young pretty ones. He'd obviously cleaned up.

She herself didn't feel so chipper. Her nausea was back with a vengeance, not helped by the clouds of cigar smoke that now wreathed the table.

Marshall favoured her with a smile of self-satisfaction. 'Cheer up, sweetheart. You must have won enough to buy yourself a new outfit.'

'Actually, no.'

'Come on, I saw you having a bet.'

'I was on Pay Back Time.'

'I don't believe it.'

'He'd have won if he hadn't got boxed in.'

Marshall laughed like a drain, then pulled a bank roll out of his pocket. 'Look, I owe you for the tip. Go and buy yourself a pair of fancy knickers.'

Greta was tempted to tear the fifty-pound note into pieces but had a better idea. She caught the eye of a middle-aged waitress who was clearing away the tea cups.

'We've had a bit of luck on this table. Here's a little present in appreciation of your marvellous service.'

The woman looked at the money Greta pressed into her hand. Suspicion flickered for a moment across her tired face, then she smiled.

'Ooh, thank you, madam.'

'That's just for you – we've already settled with the other girls.'

The waitress was beaming now. 'That's very generous of you, my dear.'

Greta got to her feet. 'Don't thank me, thank this gentleman here,' she said and left Marshall to his new admirer.

Laurie caught up with her before she could leave the room.

'Where are you off to now, Greta?'

'I'm going to the loo.'

'You've been up and down like a jack-in-the-box all afternoon. I want you to come and work your magic on Charlie.'

'Do I have to? I'm beginning to feel like the company whore.'

The words came out with more force than she'd intended. His face registered the impact.

'Are you feeling all right, Greta? You don't seem yourself.'

'I'm sorry. But if you don't let me go now, Laurie, I'm going to throw up over both of us.' And she fled for the Ladies.

*

Freddy stood under a cold shower for a minute then changed briskly. Not normally one to dwell on run races – what was the point in that? – the ride on Pay Back Time had left him annoyed with himself. The win had been there for the taking, in fact the taste of it was already in his mouth when Lifeline had shut the door on him. That the victor was his stablemate, trained by his sister, was no comfort – in fact it made the result all the more unpalatable. Now he'd have to pretend that Tony Byrne and his flakey horse were worthy winners on the day. That kind of sporting bullshit made him sick.

There was another reason for his ill humour and the explanation for his quick-change routine – Gladys Lim. He knew Pay Back Time's owner would be outside gunning for him and he couldn't face the thought of being polite to her. Not that politeness came high on Mrs Lim's own list of virtues. She wouldn't be happy with finishing third. She'd be bound to ask him if he'd not been aware of Lifeline coming up like a train on his outside – and Freddy didn't want to answer that. The truth was he hadn't had a clue. Fuck you, Tony Byrne.

But – and his mood suddenly lifted – one flukey victory was neither here nor there. Tony might have screwed him today but, in the long term, Freddy knew who was really getting shafted.

'Oy, Fred.'

Freddy looked up to find a half-stripped jockey, Jonno Simpson, at his side. Freddy bent to lace his shoes.

'I'm in a rush, Jonno.'

'Just a quick word, eh?'

'I don't think we should be having any words at all.'

Jonno looked crestfallen. He was a tiny lad of twenty with a ruddy weather-beaten face and a skinny white torso.

'Look, after York, I think they're on to me.'

'Crap. You're still riding, aren't you?'

Freddy gave his thick brown curls a last rub with a towel.

'Yeah, but I can't get away with nothin' right now. D'you see?'

Freddy dropped the towel on the bench and gave Jonno his full attention. For the moment they were alone in the changing room.

'What are you saying?'

'I can't make the last.'

'You're joking.'

'I daren't, Freddy. They'll do me – I know it.'

Freddy glared at him. Christ, this really made his day.

'Look, you little twat, there's others will do you long before the Jockey Club if you don't hold your end up.' Speaking quietly he prodded Jonno's pale pigeon chest with one finger for emphasis. 'A lot of things can happen in a race if you ride smart. Just make it look good – OK?'

Jonno opened his mouth to reply but at that moment a string of riders entered the room.

'Good luck,' said Freddy, picking up his bag and heading for the car park.

The first thing he did when he got outside was to reach for his mobile phone.

Hartley the banker discovered Greta in the crush around the parade ring.

'You're hiding from me,' he said, his eyes darting to her chest as usual. 'Just when I need you most.'

She gave him a rueful smile. He wasn't as big a boor as Marshall, and it wasn't exactly his fault if the top button of her blouse kept coming undone – one of the drawbacks of her current predicament.

'I need your advice on the last,' he continued, turning to the runners circling the ring. 'Another little tip like Lifeline would put me ahead for the day.'

She turned back to the ring. 'I know precious little about this lot. I like the look of that one, though,' she added, indicating a dainty black horse just in front of them. 'He's got nice sloping shoulders – means he's got good shock absorbers.'

Hartley looked suitably impressed. He consulted his race card.

'I see Simpson's on board.' He leaned closer and spoke directly into her ear. 'I've got a pal in the Jockey Club Security Department. He says they've got their eye on him.'

'I thought they had their eye on everybody?'

'They think he might have stopped one at York over the weekend.'

Greta nodded, feigning interest. This kind of gossip was standard fare at the races. Everyone pretended to have some kind of inside information. 'So you're not going to back him then?'

'Of course I am – now I know about the shock absorbers.'

Tony made his way to the car park, having seen Lifeline safely settled in the racecourse stables. The horse wouldn't travel back till later with Pay Back Time and two runners in the last from a neighbouring yard. Tony was due to drive Kate back to Lambourn.

He was still buzzing. Funny how a win could wipe away all the things that were bringing you down. Or maybe the experience of riding out of your skin was so intense it simply drove everything else from your mind.

Like Sarah, for instance. He'd drawn the line at begging her to come today but he'd made it pretty clear how important this race was to him. At the end of last season, when they'd first started going out, Sarah used to follow him to the furthest-flung meetings in the land, seemingly happy to watch him lose on all sorts of dismal beasts. But now she couldn't even be bothered to see him ride a winner on the first day of Royal Ascot on a horse he practically owned. Tony knew there was a message there somewhere but he was reluctant to read it just yet.

He spotted Kate making her way towards him through the parked cars.

A late afternoon breeze had sprung up, whipping her long, loose summer skirt above her knees and, for a second, revealing a glimpse of well-formed thigh. She controlled the errant garment as if by magic, which was typical of her, he thought. Typical, too, that her beauty should be elusive, seen only in a snatched glance, quite the opposite of the many other handsome women on hand at the racecourse who brazenly flaunted their looks. An outsider would not have taken Kate for a trainer of racehorses. She looked too young and too feminine – just not tough enough to impose her will on a headstrong thoroughbred over ten times her weight. But Tony knew better – Kate Montague was more than a match for any horse liable to give her trouble.

Kate was already a well-known figure on the racing scene and frequently mentioned in the press. The sports journalists loved her, not only because she was a rising female star in a man's world, but because she always spoke her mind. She was also good copy for the gossip columnists, who had promptly dubbed her the 'Goddess of the Gallops' and ran photos showing off her high cheekbones and wide-set eyes, next to a few lines of speculation about her love life. To date they'd not been able to unearth any substantial rumours, so they'd begun to refer to her as the 'Ice Queen of Lambourn', which appeared to amuse her.

Tony was less pleased to see Kate's companion, who marched by her side, jabbing the air with one hand as she spoke and hanging on to her hat with the other. Mrs Lim was in full flow and Tony guessed she had been bending Kate's ear ever since Pay Back Time had been beaten.

'It's you!' shouted Mrs Lim, pointing at Tony as they approached. 'You're a bad boy – you don't ride fair!'

'What do you mean?' he said indignantly.

Mrs Lim was next to him, glaring into his face. 'You boxed me in! You stole my race!'

Tony felt the blood rush into his cheeks. 'Now, look —'

'Come off it, Gladys.' Kate's voice was low, tinged with amusement. 'You can hardly blame Tony for Pay Back Time getting boxed in. He rode brilliantly.'

'Ha!' The sound was like a pistol shot, taking Tony by surprise. 'Ha, ha, ha!' Mrs Lim's round face was contorted by her ebullient laughter. 'Of course he did. Freddy fouled up but you rode great, Tony. But next time, you do it on my horse – OK?'

'Well . . . I suppose.'

'Good show,' she cried and pointed to a Mercedes whose chauffeur leaned against the bonnet, reading a newspaper. 'That's my car. I'll be calling you soon, Kate.'

They watched her go, Tony with considerable relief, aware he'd been close to the kind of rudeness that is not forgotten.

'She'll be calling me the minute I step through the door,' said Kate.

'I don't know how you put up with her. I couldn't.'

Kate turned her serene grey eyes on him and smiled. 'You would if she had over twenty horses in your yard and paid her bills on time.'

The bookie's had filled up with office workers making a swift escape from their desks. In the circumstances the last race at Ascot was something of an anticlimax, Celestial Dance romping home for the easiest victory of the afternoon with his jockey, Jonno Simpson, looking over his shoulder.

After the action was over, Derek lit a cigarette and waited for the crowd to thin out before making his way to the counter. The bored girl on pay-out duties looked straight through him, even though he'd been her most regular customer throughout the afternoon. But as she read his betting slip a flicker of interest stole across her face.

'Would you wait a sec? I've gotta ask the manager.' She disappeared into a back office.

A moment later a spruce fellow in a suit was beaming at Derek through the security glass. 'Will you take a cheque, sir?'

Those magic words. All his life Derek had longed to hear them.

'Cash, please,' he said, as he'd always planned should he find himself taking a bookmaker to the cleaners. But it was a hollow victory just the same.

Greta tugged Laurie's sleeve. Even though the racing was over for the day, their party showed no signs of breaking up.

'A toast to a winning afternoon!' brayed Hartley, tipping champagne into his glass.

'How soon can we get out of here? I've had it,' Greta whispered.

'We can hardly cut and run at this point.'

'Let's not stay till the bitter end, please.'

Laurie sighed heavily. 'Gavin's got some proposition he wants to discuss.'

'Why couldn't he have done it before? We've been here all afternoon.'

'Quite. But you didn't favour him with your racing expertise till the fourth race.'

'What's that got to do with it?'

But her husband had turned away to clap Marshall on the back. Greta slumped into a chair and removed a shoe. It looked like a long wait.


Tony and Kate crawled out of Ascot towards the M4. Even though they'd beaten the rush, traffic was heavy all along the route – not that Tony was bothered. He had a few things on his mind.

'Do you think Mrs Lim was serious about me riding for her?'

'Maybe,' said Kate.

'And how about you? Can I expect a few decent rides from you now?'

'After your brilliant performance today, you mean?'

'Well . . .' Now was no time for false modesty – though he wasn't good at blowing his own trumpet. 'Lifeline was fantastic, of course. But I think I did OK.'

She nodded. 'You always do OK.'

'But . . .?'

'But you half starved yourself to make the weight.'

'So?'

'You were a wreck before the race. You didn't look strong enough to carry your whip.'

33

'Appearances can deceive, Kate.'

'They count for a lot where owners are concerned. An owner doesn't want a jockey on board who looks as if he's about to faint when he gets a leg-up.'

Tony overtook a coach and put his foot down for a hundred yards before the next bottleneck forced him to slow. This conversation wasn't going as he'd intended.

'Maybe I was a bit hyped up because it was Lifeline,' he said.

'How do you feel now?'

'I feel just great.'

'*Hungry*' would have been the honest answer. Like many jockeys operating at a couple of stone below his natural weight, Tony was used to the familiar nagging in the pit of his stomach. Grapefruit for breakfast, plain chicken breast for lunch and clear soup for supper – these were the staples of his diet.

'I suppose Sarah's a help in organising your regime.'

Tony shot Kate a swift sideways glance. It appeared to be a straight question.

'A great help,' he said. Was she hell! Having Sarah in the house for the last few months had doubled the intensity of his daily fight against temptation. It was one thing to deny yourself at mealtimes; it was ten times worse to share those mealtimes with someone who had no intention of participating in your sacrifice.

'So the answer to your question,' Kate said, 'is, *if* I can rely on you to make the weight, I'd love to give you some better rides.'

'That's great.' Tony was still grinning as the shrill beep of a mobile phone filled the car.

\*

The late-afternoon sun was blinding as Freddy pushed through the crowded West End street and ducked into the casino. Inside it was cool and gloomy. There were no windows and no clocks. It could have been any stage of the day or night. Gamblers lived in a world outside time.

Even on a day like this the place was busy. Freddy pushed through the crush surrounding a roulette table. Though his was a well-known face in the gambling world no one gave him a second glance. All eyes were on the spinning wheel.

He found Herbert Gibbs playing blackjack – a burly, shaven-headed figure shuffling a pile of low-denomination chips. He did not look like the chairman of a fast-growing leisure and property company with fancy offices in the City and an outstanding portfolio of Millennial developments. Herbert more closely resembled what he had started out as fifteen years before – a hard-man rails bookie with an eye on every punter's last fiver.

The bookmaker gave Freddy a sullen stare and jabbed his thumb at the empty chair next to his.

'Siddown.'

'I don't want to play.'

'You think I do?'

The dealer, drawing to a 3, turned over a 9 then a jack and pushed a pile of chips in Herbert's direction. Herbert slid half of them to Freddy.

'You told me Simpson was solid,' he muttered.

'Sorry, H. I'm as pissed off as you are.'

The bookie's shaven head swivelled in his direction. 'Is that a fact?'

'Sir – are you playing?'

'Your shout,' grumbled Herbert.

Freddy looked at his cards – 16 in total – said, 'Hit me.' He grinned at his companion. 'That's what they say in the movies, isn't it?'

The croupier dealt him a 5 and, a moment or so later, a bigger pile of chips.

Freddy turned to Herbert. 'I think he got the wind up after last week. He's scared of the Jockey Club.'

'Jesus.' The bookmaker looked aggrieved. 'I'm a damn sight more scary than that lot. Aren't I?'

'Sir?' The croupier was talking to Freddy again.

He turned his cards over: an ace and a king.

Herbert began to chuckle. 'I heard you were a lucky little bleeder. Unlike your pal Simpson.'

Kate took the call, retrieving the phone from Tony's hold-all on the back seat.

'It's Laurie,' she said.

Tony assumed he wanted to speak to Kate; he'd known they were travelling together. Laurie and Kate's association went back many years to when he used to ride for her father. Now Laurie was Kate's partner in the yard, with the Somerville family living in the other half of the large house next to the stables.

But Laurie was not calling for Kate.

'He wants to make you an offer on behalf of some business-men.'

'Me?'

'Technically, your mother.'

Tony was lost. Why would Laurie want to talk to his mother? Then the penny dropped.

'It's Lifeline, isn't it?'

'Yes.'

'Tell Laurie he's not for sale.'

Kate spoke into the phone. 'Look, he'll call you later. He needs a chance to discuss it.'

She rang off.

'Why didn't you tell him it was no? I don't need to speak to my mother. I know what she'll say. Everything to do with Lifeline is in my hands. And I'm not selling.'

'You might want to think about this, Tony.'

'Oh, yeah? Why?'

'He's offering three hundred thousand pounds.'

# Chapter Two

Derek squeezed his BMW between a tatty Mondeo and a Land Rover and surveyed the terraced house across the street. It had been tarted up since he'd last seen it: a brick screen hid the dustbin from view and the front door had received a lick of paint. He guessed Diane was at home because a freshly watered hanging basket of geraniums still dripped on to the path. And that was her battered black Golf parked three cars down.

He hadn't planned to be here. When he'd collected the car from the Cavendish Square car park he'd intended to slog out through West London to the M4 as usual, heading for the marital home in Berkshire. At some point, he supposed, he'd call Vivian, though he wasn't sure what he was going to say.

However, when he reached Hammersmith some old instinct took over and he found himself driving round the familiar roads of Brook Green. It was, after all, just a short detour from his route – an excuse he'd used often in the past. He and Diane had joked that stopping at her place was a quickie in every sense. But that had been at the beginning.

He rang the doorbell with no idea in his head of what he would say. In the few seconds it took for footsteps to advance down the hall and the door to swing open, panic and shame seized him together.

Diane looked different. Her black hair was bobbed to jaw length and there was an unfamiliar sharpness about her features.

Or maybe that was due to alarm caused by his unexpected appearance.

'Derek.' The voice was the same, though, low and throaty. 'You can't come in,' she said.

'I know. I don't want to. That is, I just –'

Her face softened. 'What on earth are you doing here?'

'I saw Digby today. He says my heart's packing up.'

'I didn't know you had one.'

'That's unfair.'

She shrugged. 'I bet you still smoke, don't you? And I can see you've put on weight. You should have listened to your doctor a long time ago.'

'I just wanted you to know.'

'OK. Now you've told me.' She began to shut the door.

'Please, Diane.'

'Look, I'm sorry to hear it but you chose your wife, remember? Your business isn't mine any more.'

The door closed. Derek stood on the step, staring at the fresh navy paint just inches from his face. He put his hand in his pocket and came up with a roll of fifties. He pushed them through the letter box and turned towards his car.

Why had he come? What a bloody fool.

Tony was still on a high as he opened his front door.

'Sarah!' he called. There was no reply but from the next floor up he heard the sound of pop music.

He tore open the letter on the hall table addressed to him. He recognised the franking on the envelope and thought that a cheque from his house insurers would cap his day. But there was no cheque, just another note nit-picking over the details of his claim. He chucked it on the table and headed up the stairs past the empty alcove which had once housed his grandfather's carriage clock – before it was stolen. At least the insurers weren't disputing *that*.

The music was coming from the bathroom.

'Hi, darling,' he called and stepped inside.

'Tony – for God's sake!' squealed the woman in the bath, sliding down beneath the foam, sending a wave of water crashing against the taps.

'The conquering hero returns!' he announced and pulled his shirt from his waistband.

'What are you doing?' she cried.

'What does it look like? I'm getting in with you.'

'No, Tony, please.' She sat up. 'Not now. This is a serious bath.'

He stopped in the act of stepping out of his trousers.

'A serious bath?'

'I've got to shave my legs.'

'I'll help you,' he offered.

'No. If you really want to help, bring me a gin and tonic in about ten minutes. Please.'

He made for the door. So much for the spontaneous gestures of love.

'Congratulations on the race.'

Tony turned back.

'So you watched it?'

'It was very exciting. You were a bit mean to Freddy, though, blocking him in like that.'

As usual, Derek ordered a half then converted it to a pint with a large Bell's on the side. Not much point in being abstemious now, was there? If Karen behind the bar registered the change of habit she chose to say nothing. Though Derek was a regular at this time of night, stopping off for a swift one most evenings before the last leg home, Karen was not the inquisitive sort.

He lit a cigarette and made his way to the pay phone beside the front door. It rang for a while before Vivian answered.

'I'm running a bit late,' he said.

'What a surprise.' The indifference in her tone was chilling.

'I'm sorry, darling.'

'Is that all, Derek? I'm missing *Coronation Street*.'

'Aren't you going to ask me about Digby?'

'Just tell me.'

But he couldn't. Later – maybe.

Tony half filled two tumblers with ice and added a wedge of lemon. He splashed gin into one glass and, for a moment, his hand hovered over the other. If ever he deserved a drink it was today. Just one, in honour of his victory. But Kate's words of caution were still uppermost in his mind and, besides, maybe a celebratory glass of wine with Sarah later would be more fun. Especially if they drank it in bed.

He topped her glass up with tonic and added mineral water to his own. He returned the bottles to the fridge, trying to ignore the shelves of seductive fat-filled food that called to him: a dish of mayonnaise-rich potato salad, tubs of taramasalata and houmous, two pouting chocolate eclairs oozing cream. How a snake-hipped woman like Sarah managed on such a diet without turning into a balloon amazed him. He slammed the fridge door shut.

Upstairs in the bath Sarah raised her glass and sipped with all the rigid concentration required of someone wearing a face pack. Her hair was bundled out of sight beneath a shower cap and her features were now smothered in lime-green ointment that had dried solid. From the neck up she looked alien and unapproachable yet her breasts peeked through the rapidly fading foam, round, tempting and clearly off limits.

'I thought we might have a bit of a celebration. Go out for dinner.'

'Huh,' she muttered through clenched teeth.

'Well, you can eat and I can watch. I like to watch you.'

'Sorry, Tony. I'm going out.'

The words were clear enough and so was the message. He left the room.


On the last leg into Lambourn, Vicky made Neil sit in the front of the horse box between her and Pat, the driver. She knew the lad would rather return to the bench on the inside, facing the horses, but she didn't think it was good for him to hide away. One of these days he was going to have to make an effort to get on with people, not just animals.

Vicky was a tireless young woman who combined the duties of head lad at Beechwood with much of the travelling that, in most yards, was taken on by another senior lad. Though she was only twenty-seven she'd been around a bit, working in equine establishments of all sorts, and she knew her job back to front. She was first into the yard in the morning and last out of it at night. The welfare of all the horses and lads – some hundred creatures all told – was down to her. And just as she was concerned that the horses were properly fed, watered and comfortably housed, so she cared about the staff who ministered to them. She had a particularly sharp eye for a new lad who was having trouble fitting in. In her opinion, young Neil

Kelly needed a bit of jollying along.

They'd spent the last twenty minutes dropping off the two horses from the other yard and it was now past eight. They waved goodbye to the lads they'd travelled back with and started up the drive. They'd be home in ten minutes.

'How you doing, Neil?' said Vicky. 'Worked out how you'll spend your money, then?'

As Lifeline's lad, Neil was up for a 'present' of £100 after the horse's win.

'I expect he'll blow it down the pub like the rest of you lot,' said Pat as he manoeuvred the big horse box on to the Lambourn road.

'He would if he could, wouldn't you, Midget?' said Vicky. 'Except he can hardly pass for twelve, let alone eighteen.'

Pat joined in with her laughter as Neil stared sullenly ahead.

'Whoops, I think I've hurt his feelings. I'd better be nice to him or his dad'll send the boys round.' Vicky leaned towards Pat. 'His dad's a gangster. Big time.'

'Is that right, son?' said Pat but Neil didn't reply.

Vicky wondered if she'd been a bit insensitive in mentioning Neil's big bad dad – though in truth having a father who'd been convicted of manslaughter did him no harm in the eyes of the other lads. She decided to change tack and put a comforting arm around his shoulders. 'Cheer up, Midget. I'll get the drinks in for you tonight.'

Neil shied away from Vicky's embrace. She was unfazed. 'Don't worry, I'm not after your body.' Maybe that wasn't strictly true, he was a handsome boy. Too young, of course.

'Don't 'e like girls, then?' said Pat.

'There is one girl he likes. You wouldn't say no to sitting up front with Sarah Cooper, would you, Neil?'

Neil continued to stare through the windscreen, his face a blazing red.

Derek debated whether to have another whisky but decided against. Best to get home and tell Viv the truth. Get it over with quick and then he could hammer the decent malt he'd picked up last week.

As he drove off he realised he was scared. Whenever he saw Digby he came away with a picture of his heart clanking away in his chest like some clapped-out, furred-up piece of machinery, teetering on the verge of complete breakdown. He'd remind himself to relax, calm down, take it easy – all those stupid mantras Digby was so fond of and which were impossible to put into practice. Derek's way of dealing with a crisis was to get worked up about something else, the office as a rule, though for a time it had been the affair with Diane and a good standby was his running feud with his wife. He blamed her for everything that was wrong with his life just as, no doubt, she blamed him. That was one of the reasons for being married, wasn't it? So he'd not said much to Viv about his visits to the cardiologist. It had been a long time since he'd been honest with her about anything. And what he was scared of, he realised as he crested the hill to the south-east of Lambourn, was that, when he told her the truth, she wouldn't give a stuff.

Halfway down the hill, on his side of the carriageway, a horse box lumbered along. He put his foot down and pulled out.

With the road clear ahead of him, Derek knew he had time to overtake and tuck back in before the bend at the bottom of the hill. Then a car rounded the curve on the road ahead.

Acting on reflex, Derek eased off the accelerator. He was a safe driver, no points on the licence, unblemished record and all that but – where the fuck had it got him? What was the point of caution now? He stamped down hard on the gas.

As he sped past the horse box, the car ahead flashing its headlights in alarm, the machine that was his heart really began to tank along. But not with fear, with a rush of adrenaline and the thrill of the moment as – *yes!* – he shot in front of the horse box, a bare ten feet away from the car, its horn loud in his ear as he took his foot off the gas and turned into the bend . . . and that was the moment the engine in his chest seized up. As the coronary ripped through him, Derek's hands froze on the wheel and the car kept on going. Off the road and through the fringe of trees and over and over, bouncing down the rutted hillside above the village.

He was dead long before the BMW came to a halt.

In the seconds before the crash, Neil remembered Pat saying, 'There's a right clot behind us,' and feeling the lorry decelerate as the brakes were applied. Suddenly a dark saloon materialised out of nowhere in front of them and a car on the other side of the road veered out of its path, then over-steered towards them. Vicky screamed and Pat swore and Neil sat petrified as they swerved to avoid a collision, the nearside wheels of the horse box running up on to the grass verge.

The car ahead had vanished and now they were rumbling and bumping along with the bend in the road coming up to meet them as the driver fought to keep the lorry on an even keel. But the ground was falling away as they careered into the thin screen of hawthorn and bramble along the verge. Then came a sudden bang and a lurch and, in horrible slow motion, the horse box toppled over to the left and crashed on to its side.

For a moment there was silence. Pat had cut the engine. Neil's weight was on Vicky. He thought, We're OK. Then came a fearful, inhuman sound from behind him, so loud it felt as if his head was gripped in a vice.

The horses.

Tony had just got off the phone to his mother when Sarah came downstairs. The old girl had been low key about events at Ascot – she hadn't even watched the race on television. All the same, he could tell she was pleased for him.

'They said on the wireless you'd won, son. Your father would have been so proud.'

Tony had previously tried to get his mother to come down for the event but had soon realised she would only do it under sufferance, to please him, so he'd dropped it.

The fact of the matter was that she hated horseracing and had seen Tony's father's obsession as divisive and expensive. In the early days of their marriage he'd been a gambler, punting with money they could ill afford. Later he'd entertained illusions of training winners and she'd been forced to tolerate his love of horses as a politician's wife tolerates his mistress. She'd put up with it but she hadn't liked it. It had been naïve of Tony to expect her suddenly to turn into an enthusiastic race-goer. Eighteen months after Archie's death, it was still too raw a subject.

'What will you do with the prize money, Mum?'

'I don't want it. You have it.'

'I'll take my ten per cent for the ride and so will Kate. There's something owing to the lad, too, but that still leaves over twenty thousand.'

'Well, I never.' Then there'd been a silence on the line before she'd added, 'It doesn't seem right, your dad not being here when this happens.'

After that they'd barely even discussed the offer to buy Lifeline.

'What would you rather have, Tony,' she'd said, 'the money or the horse?'

Which settled the matter as far as he was concerned.

Then Sarah had appeared, looking delicious, and he'd made a mistake. Two, in fact. First he told her about the bid for Lifeline.

'Three hundred thousand pounds!' she exclaimed. 'That's fantastic.'

'We're not going to accept.'

'You think you'll get more?'

'I just don't want to sell. Lifeline's going to be a champion.'

'You're mad.' Her walnut-brown eyes flashed with anger – or maybe contempt. 'That horse is a neurotic liability. You've slaved over him all year. Will he go in the stalls? Will he go in the horse box? Will he say boo to a fucking goose? He gets more attention than I do. And now you won't cash in when you've got the chance. I just don't understand you, Tony.'

She turned for the door – which was when he made his second mistake.

'Where did you say you were going?'

She whirled round, the hem of her brief summer dress kissing the caramel skin of her thigh. 'I didn't but, since you're so curious, I've a meeting at the shop. I promised Dad I'd cast an eye over the new lease.'

Sarah's father owned a chain of jewellers, one of which was situated in Swindon.

'I don't know when I'll be back. I imagine Jean and I will

discuss it over a meal. With your permission, of course.'

And Sarah had gone, leaving him to wonder how come a middle-aged branch manager called Jean merited a major cleansing session in the bath, Sarah's skimpiest summer outfit from Prada, and a cloud of Paloma Picasso.

Then the telephone rang and drove the matter from his mind.

The road out of Lambourn had been closed off so Tony abandoned the car and made a plea to the WPC on sentry duty to let him proceed on foot.

'My horse is in the accident,' he explained and, after a moment's reflection, she allowed him to pass.

As he strode up the hill he could see that all the emergency services were in attendance. An ambulance passed him on the way down and, when he reached the bend in the road, he could see a fire engine and a police car. He also recognised an estate car belonging to one of the vets at the equine hospital.

From what Kate had said on the phone he'd expected a scene of carnage. He saw at once the gap in the roadside bushes and through it, fifty yards down the hillside, the inverted shape of a big, powerful car. The driver had died in the crash, so he'd been told – he wasn't surprised. The others were OK, Kate had said, but she'd not heard about the horses.

Tony's heart was in his mouth. If you worked with animals you had to be able to bear their loss. But Lifeline was not just another horse. He was like a member of his family.

Further up the hill, the horse box lay on its side half on the verge, the metal ramp at the rear sticking out into the road, its back doors splayed open. Tony presumed the fire brigade had wrenched them apart – with the lorry in that position it would have required some force. So at least the horses were out.

A few feet away, two blankets were spread out on the grass. He recognised their grey-and-white weave – they came from Kate's yard. He also recognised the shape beneath them and their purpose. He swallowed hard as he bent to lift a corner. For a moment his future hung in the balance.

'Excuse me, sir,' called a voice.

He pulled back the blanket. Pay Back Time's great head stared up at him unseeing, his eye dull and dark.

A policeman in shirtsleeves was standing next to him. 'I'm sorry, sir, you'll have to leave.' He didn't sound sorry.

'Where's Lifeline?'

'I must insist, sir –'

'It's all right, officer.' Vicky appeared looking grubby and dishevelled but, Tony was relieved to see, uninjured. She added, 'We need him to catch the horse.'

The policeman backed off and she turned to Tony. 'When they got the doors open Lifeline bolted. Neil's gone after him but . . .' She shrugged and pointed beyond the overturned horse box. Tony looked over the hillside where the fields of corn made a pretty patchwork of greens and yellows in the evening sun. He could see no sign of horse or boy.

'What on earth happened, Vicky?'

She told him briefly, in phrases that already sounded well used – some nutter had screamed past them downhill and Pat had been forced to drive off the road to avoid another car. The horse box had turned over but they'd all climbed out in one piece, thank God. She'd called for help on her mobile and Pat and Neil had gone to see what could be done for the car driver. So she'd been left with the horses, trapped in the back of the upturned box, bellowing and screaming, until the fire brigade had arrived. Pay Back Time had broken both front legs and the vet had had no option but to put him down. As for Lifeline . . .

'I'll go after him,' said Tony.

Tony set off across the field, following the path cut through the crop by the fleeing horse. He strode on for half a mile with no sign of Lifeline. At the bottom of a large sloping field of barley he came to a stand of birch and hawthorn and a thin line of hedgerow marking one field from another. Neil was sitting on a log. He raised a hand as Tony approached.

'Are you all right?'

Neil put a finger to his lips then pointed through a gap in the hedge. Tony took a pace forward. Lifeline was standing in the next field, his legs planted four square on the trampled ground.

'I can't get no closer,' whispered Neil. 'Every time I try and get near he runs off.'

Tony could see the tremors running through Lifeline's body and noted the way he rocked his head from side to side, his ears pricked. Tony knew the signs of old. The horse was spooked.

'At least he looks like he's in one piece,' he said in a low voice.

The lad nodded.

'You go on back, Neil. Get yourself checked out.'

'I landed on Vicky.' The boy grinned. 'It was like falling on a feather bed. Anyhow don't you need a hand?'

The wine bar was filling up fast and Freddy fought his way through the crush at the door. He spotted his date in the far corner with an empty plate and a bottle of wine in front of her. She pulled a face as he approached.

'You're late,' she grumbled but her eyes danced with delight as he bent to kiss her on the lips.

'You've been eating that garlic bread.'

'Let's have some more, I'm starving. And don't you dare tell me you're not allowed to.'

He chuckled. 'I can have what I like.'

He put his hand on her leg under the table, then slid it upwards.

She stared into his eyes and bit her lip.

'Perhaps we can skip the food.'

'Thought you were starving?'

She squeezed her thighs together, trapping his fingers.

'Oh, I am.'

They left in a hurry.

The light was fading by the time they had Lifeline under control. Tony had talked to him softly for ages, half an hour or more, till the horse had stopped the strange head-rocking, the nervous tic that Tony knew so well.

He'd picked some juicy dandelions, Lifeline's favourite, and showed them to the colt once he had his full attention. It had been easy after that to take his bridle and stroke that big trunk of a neck just the way he liked it.

Then Neil held him while Tony made as thorough a physical inspection as he could.

'He's got some swelling on the near hind leg. And there's scratches on his flanks, probably caused by scraping through a few hedges. That's all I can find. He's been lucky.'

Neither of them made any reference to Pay Back Time – they didn't have to.

Tony and Neil walked Lifeline around the fields, down to the bottom of the hill and on to the road in the village, avoiding a return to the scene of the accident. The sun had set by the time they started up the lane on the last leg of the journey back to Kate's yard but the summer night was far from dark as they picked their way along. It was slow going. Every time a car came by the horse reacted, whinnying in fear and pulling away. Tony and Neil would shield Lifeline as best they could, stopping in driveways and leading him up on to the pavement as they saw headlights approaching. But there was nothing they could do to protect him from the growl of engines as vehicles passed. Each time the horse became more agitated and, when one driver failed to slow down as he shot by in a swirl of dust, Lifeline froze, taking root on the narrow carriageway.

At that moment a bicycle came down the hill. Tony didn't see it till it was on them.

'Hey, Neil!' said a boy's voice.

'It's Paul,' Neil murmured to Tony. Paul Somerville – Laurie and Greta's fourteen-year-old son.

'They're all wondering where you are.'

Tony was pleased to see the boy. From the moment he'd found Neil and Lifeline he'd regretted leaving his mobile phone in the car. He wanted to report to the yard that the pair of them were in one piece.

'Paul, do us a favour?'

'Yeah, sure.'

'Get back to the house and tell Kate we're on our way. Say we might need a bit of help. Would you do that?'

'No sweat.' And he was off into the night. No wonder Tony hadn't seen him coming. His bike didn't have any lights.

Jonno Simpson made a night of it with some old pals at the Rack and Manger. Strictly vodka and slimline tonics and a chicken sandwich, no butter – he knew enough these days to watch his weight even when on the piss. He'd not been down the Rack for a year and he got a bit of a ribbing for forgetting his old friends now he was making a name for himself. Of course they'd seen him bringing home Celestial Dance and that made him feel better about the whole thing. Positively noble about it, in fact.

By refusing to stop the horse he'd dropped around seven grand – the difference between the ten Freddy Montague's boys would have bunged him and his percentage of the prize money. Turning down ready money was a novel experience for Jonno – up to this point in his career he'd grabbed every bean offered and not given a hoot where it came from. But things were different now he was riding for Jem Hutton. Good rides were coming his way and so was legit money. If he just did an honest job he'd be in clover anyway.

On reflection, the business at York had been a timely warning. He'd thought that by pushing his mount wide at the turn he'd done enough to prevent Stickleback getting up in time. But the bloody horse had been quicker than he'd thought and he'd been forced to flourish his whip in one hand while putting the brakes on with the other. He'd had a hard time explaining it to the stewards, who'd given him a fair old chin-wagging one way and another. Which, in the circumstances, made the loss of today's cash seem like a prudent investment in his long-term future.

Such were Jonno's thoughts at the beginning of the evening but by the time the taxi deposited him at his front door at eleven-thirty he wasn't able to get his brain round much at all. Except the barmaid maybe. She'd been there, like always, and he reckoned she'd have been up for it too – like always. But getting his leg over wouldn't have been fair on Jackie and there was no guarantee one of the others wouldn't have told on him. As with the Jockey Club Security Department, he didn't need his fiancée on his case. Especially the week before he was due to move in with her.

He stumbled along the hall and into the kitchen. He needed water – a lot of it. As he drank he ignored the scummy plates in the sink, the takeaway boxes on the table and the overflowing swingbin by the door – he'd be done with this shitheap forever on Saturday. He couldn't wait.

Kate was standing by the top of the drive that led off the road to the Beechwood yard, her face deeply shadowed in the half-light.

'I'm sorry about Pay Back Time,' Tony said.

She nodded and they began the long plod up to the house in silence. Two older lads, Dermot and Josh, were waiting. Laurie stood a little way off, observing, but there was no sign of Paul.

As Neil walked Lifeline under the arch the horse jerked on the rein and swished his tail.

'Steady,' the lad muttered, trying to make for the colt's stall. Lifeline moved reluctantly.

The stall door was open, a single overhead bulb shining light on to a deep bed of fresh straw. It looked inviting but the colt planted his feet and stood immobile in the doorway.

Tony laid a comforting hand on his flank. 'Come on, feller. Don't go all moody on us now.'

Neil tugged on the rein, Lifeline shook his head. Just as if he was saying no to something, Tony thought. Which, of course, he was.

Dermot and Josh were watching.

'We'll get him in if you like,' said Josh.

'It's not worth having an argument with Lifeline,' said Tony. He'd learned that the hard way. 'If he doesn't want to go in the stall there's nothing you can do about it.'

'Oh, yeah?' Josh had never been known to duck a challenge. These days, now his chances of making it as a rider had gone, he spent a lot of time in the gym developing his muscles. He picked up a broom and, without warning, rammed the bristles into Lifeline's rear quarters.

The intent was obvious – to frighten the horse forward into the stall – but the result was disaster. Lifeline lashed out with both hind feet and whipped around, yanking the rein from Neil's grasp. He veered sharply sideways, knocking Josh to the floor, and galloped across the courtyard and beneath the arch, out into the night.

The man with the shotgun stood motionless in the shadows of the garden. He watched as Jonno made his painstaking preparations for bed. The man was patient. He had been waiting for some while already and a few more minutes made no difference to him. He'd seen Jonno's stumbling arrival. Now he watched though the kitchen window as the jockey downed glass after glass of water – a hangover precaution he himself swore by. Unfortunately for Jonno, the man reflected, it wouldn't just be his head hurting tomorrow morning.

A light went on upstairs behind the frosted glass of the bathroom, then in the next window along – the bedroom. The man needed no clues to the geography as he'd already had a good look round while he waited for Jonno to return. He'd sussed out which steps creaked on the stair (the third and fourth from the top), the direction Jonno lay in bed (head to the wall, just behind the door) and his own getaway (out the back and along the alley by the dustbins – the car was in the next street). It was the kind of job he enjoyed – made him feel like a real hit man.

Dermot and Josh had dashed after Lifeline with Tony's curses ringing in their ears. Neil and Laurie had followed but Tony had been restrained by Kate.

'Let them catch him. You look done in.'

'Speak for yourself.' The words had a cutting edge that he hadn't intended. 'Sorry. I mean, you've had a tough day too.'

She ignored his remarks, her mind on more practical matters. 'We'd better put Lifeline back in the barn.'

When the colt had first arrived at Beechwood he'd refused to go in a stall, either in the old stables or the big new American barn. So Kate had cleared one of the out-buildings on the side of a barn used to store feed and hay. It had a high roof and two sides open to the elements which could be blocked off to make a home suitable for a claustrophobic animal like Lifeline. Gradually Tony had enclosed the area until the colt had become used to a more confined space and could be transferred to the stable. But it had been a long haul – Lifeline had spent the first three months of the year there – and the thought of returning him to the barn was a depressing one.

Tony nodded miserably. There didn't seem to be any alternative.

Neil appeared under the arch. 'They've got him,' he shouted breathlessly.

'Let's get on with it then,' murmured Kate.

This time Lifeline made no fuss as Tony coaxed him into his old space. Dermot rigged up a light as Josh and Neil fetched water and hay.

Laurie appeared out of the dark, his face grim as he peered closely at the horse. 'This puts a spanner in the works, doesn't it?'

'What do you mean?' Tony knew perfectly well but the remark irritated him.

'I mean, he's obviously had a nervous breakdown – like before.'

'I bet your nerves would be shaken up if you'd just been bulldozed off the road in a horse box.'

Laurie sighed, exasperated. 'I'm sorry, Tony. It's a damn shame but no one's going to cough up good money for damaged goods.' He strode off.

Kate watched him go. 'Sounds like the deal for Lifeline's off.'

Tony shrugged. 'It was never on.'

Half a mile away, in Freddy's cottage, a woman was complaining – though in affectionate tones.

'Do we always have to have the light on?'

Freddy moved his body on top of hers, bent his head to nibble the lobe of her ear.

'That's because I like to see what I'm doing.'

She wriggled as his hot breath sent a shiver through her body.

'Do you have to be so crude?'

'Don't tell me you don't like it.' He moved back and swatted her bare rump.

'Freddy!' As before, there was no substance to her protest.

'Anyhow, isn't it about time you got going, Lady Muck? Else you'll be in trouble.'

'Who cares?' She sat up, the long curve of her mouth now

set in a straight line. 'I'm getting fed up with things as they are. I might just stay all night.'

'I don't know about that. I need my beauty sleep.'

'Honestly! You're such a little sod.'

'That's why you like me though, isn't it?'

Sarah didn't disagree.

Beechwood Lodge was a big sprawling house, its core erected in the late-nineteenth century with many additions and alterations since. Kate's father had trained there and, when he'd retired, had divided the living quarters into two so she could take over the business without ousting her parents from their home. As it turned out, neither Kate's father nor mother had enjoyed a long retirement, dying within three months of each other five years previously.

Rather than occupy the big house on her own, Kate had suggested the Somervilles move in to share the Lodge. It had seemed a sensible arrangement, providing company and security. Laurie ran his bloodstock business from next door, frequently stabling syndicate horses at Beechwood. Though he had a small financial stake in the yard he played no part in Kate's training operation. However, as he sometimes reminded her, his door was always open should she need advice. These days she rarely did.

Right now, Laurie was sitting on the bed in the first-floor room he shared with Greta. Like everyone else, they'd been consumed by the drama of the road accident and had only just succeeded in heading upstairs for bed. In Greta's case this was a matter of deep regret – she'd intended getting to sleep at least three hours previously.

Laurie considered the prone form of his wife beneath the

covers, her back towards him, the swell of her hip a few inches from his hand.

'Did I tell you how gorgeous you looked today?' he said.

She mumbled something that might have been the word no.

He placed his hand on that beckoning arch of hip. 'It's true. You get even better looking as you grow older, darling.'

She turned her head irritably. 'Not now, Laurie.'

He lay down beside her, his arm curling round, his hand exploring beneath the bedclothes. He grunted with satisfaction as he found what he wanted.

'Mmm, I swear these have got bigger –'

'Get off me!'

She pushed him away with such force that he slammed against the bedside table, knocking a pile of paperbacks to the floor.

'For God's sake, Greta, what's got into you?'

She was sitting with the sheet pulled up to her neck, her face flushed with anger.

'Just sod off, will you? I've had men letching over me all day.'

'But I'm your husband!'

'So what?' She lay down again, facing away from him. 'Good night, Laurie.' Her tone was final.

The man in Jonno's garden waited twenty minutes after the bedroom light had gone out. The shotgun stock was warm in his hand. He was well aware that the gun was the least professional element of the affair. Shotguns made a lot of noise and they weren't easy to hide. On the other hand they did a bloody good job. Bloody being about the size of it.

The man glanced at his watch. Time to move. He opened the

kitchen door (still unlocked – pathetic security) and glided into the hall. He stood at the foot of the stairs, running through his mind the sequence of events which would follow.

From above came a noise and the intruder froze. The sound came again, a booming, ragged expulsion of breath. The man shook his head in disbelief. For a little fellow, the jockey snored like a brass band.

The man slipped silently up the stairs and into the bedroom. Keeping his eyes on the dark shape of Jonno's head on the pillow, he gently eased the covers back off the bed. In the half light he could see that the jockey was still wearing his socks. The man smiled as he raised his gun. Wasn't there an expression about having your socks blown off? He squeezed the trigger.

By the time Jonno's screams had roused the neighbours the man and his gun were on the dual carriageway. Easy.

Out in the barn, Tony watched over the restless horse. Lifeline prowled the perimeter of his new space – up and down, back and forth, just as he'd done when first lodged here all those months ago. It was incredible to think of what they'd been through together since then. And incredible to think of having to do it all again.

On the other hand, at least this time he had some idea of the problems. He forced himself to focus on the situation at hand. There must be something he had learned from their past experience. One thing struck him: Lifeline might benefit from the company of another animal. On the other hand, he couldn't think of any horse in the yard that might be suitable. He didn't want to risk putting another racehorse in with him – they might end up kicking each other.

A sound came from behind him. Neil's pale face emerged from the dark.

'What are you doing here?' Tony asked.

The boy held up a sleeping bag. 'Thought I'd keep an eye on him.'

'Well, there's no need. You get yourself off to bed.' Tony spoke sharply but the lad didn't move.

'Neil, you've been in a car crash, you've been tramping the countryside half the night, you probably haven't eaten – '

Neil was grinning. 'You sound just like Vicky.' He began to pull things from his pockets. 'I got into the pantry. It's a bloody useless lock.' He held out a packet of ham, Ryvita, some apples. 'I tried to bring stuff you could eat. You know, with watching the weight and everything.'

Tony was touched. The boy was not as gormless as he looked.

'Thanks, Neil.'

The lad beamed and produced a bottle of lager.

'We can share it.'

Tony shook his head. 'I'd better not.'

'Come on. One swig. To celebrate.'

'Celebrate what?'

Neil looked at him in amazement. 'Lifeline's win, of course. Don't tell me you forgot?'

But he had. In all the gloom and doom of the past few hours, the fact that Lifeline had won had completely slipped from Tony's mind. Neil offered him the bottle and he took it.

As the cold fizzy liquid slipped down his throat, Lifeline continued to pace the barn like a caged tiger. Or a racehorse whose nerve was completely shot.

Tony handed back the bottle. It was going to be a long night.

# Chapter Three

DC Annie James was on her knees beneath her desk when she heard the door to the CID office slam back on its hinges.

'Where is every bugger then?' moaned a familiar voice. DS Keith Hunter – she'd had more than enough of him recently. Annie decided to stay where she was.

'I'd rather they were out on the ground, Keith. You don't catch too many villains sitting on your bum.' That was DI Jack Fletcher which put a different complexion on things. Perhaps she should show herself.

'I've just seen Jim Henderson in the canteen. He'll do.'

'I'd prefer someone less abrasive,' said Fletcher. 'How about Annie James?'

'Do me a favour, guv. She'll want to mother the kid. Anyway, she's skiving off somewhere.'

That settled it.

'No, I'm not!' Annie stuck her head above the desk. 'I've dropped a contact lens, guv,' she explained.

Fletcher grinned. He was an overweight flirt but Annie didn't mind him. At least he had a heart – unlike Hunter.

'Keith here needs someone with a sympathetic bedside manner,' Fletcher said. 'Naturally, you sprang to mind.'

'Oh?' Annie spotted the tiny transparent disc next to the wastepaper bin. She picked it up carefully.

'There's a jockey in the Radcliffe with a gunshot wound,'

Hunter said, keen as ever to get down to business.

He had Annie's full attention. 'Which jockey?' she asked.

'Jonathan Simpson. Heard of him?'

'Sure have. Jonno Simpson rode the winner in the last at Ascot yesterday.'

Fletcher beamed. 'Very impressive, Annie. I didn't realise you followed the horses.'

'It's an interest of my father's.'

'Fascinating. You must give me a few tips sometime.'

Hunter looked peeved. 'Perhaps that can wait till we've interviewed Simpson. If DC James is ready –'

'I've found my lens,' said Annie, getting to her feet.

'We'll get on with it then, guv.' Hunter was already halfway out of the door.

'An interest of your father's, eh?' he added as Annie rushed after him down the corridor. 'I suppose he's one of the hard-luck fraternity who keeps the bookies in business. It's a mug's game.'

'Actually he used to be a trainer.'

'Used to be?'

'The yard went bust.'

They were in the car park now. Hunter grinned at her as he fished in his pocket for keys. 'My point exactly, Annie. A mug's game.'

She got into the passenger seat without a murmur. She wasn't going to argue about that.

Kate dashed into the office after second lot, as ever a million things on her mind. She had no runners today but the rest of the week was busy, particularly in the wake of last night's road accident and the death of Pay Back Time. She'd worked with horses all her life and had never succeeded in hardening herself to the casualties that were part of the job. She'd even stopped training jumpers because of the constant injuries. However, accidents to horses on the racecourse were one thing – to lose one in a road accident was even worse. She felt a twinge of guilt. A man had died but her feelings were for the animal.

A list of callers lay on her desk. Predictably, the first name was that of Mrs Lim.

Kate dialled the number. She'd talked to Pay Back Time's owner for an hour the night before and once already this morning. Her need, however, was understandable.

Gladys Lim answered on the first ring. 'Don't worry, Kate. I've dried my tears.'

Kate smiled to herself. There had been no tears the night before, just howls of anger.

'Now I'm looking forward to tomorrow. Have we got a chance?'

Mrs Lim's No Ill Will was a contender for the King George V, the last race on the card at Ascot the next day.

'Every chance,' said Kate. 'He's in great shape. He had a good pipe-opener this morning.'

'Excellent. A winner on Ladies Day would cheer me up. But I have a change of plan.'

Warning bells went off in Kate's mind. Last-minute changes of racing plan weren't necessarily welcome – particularly Mrs Lim's. However, she was easily Kate's most important owner.

'I don't want Freddy to ride.'

Kate digested this news. 'Why's that?'

'I was not impressed by him yesterday.'

'He was boxed in. There wasn't much he could do about it.'

'He could have thought ahead. Poor positioning. I don't want him on my horse.'

'But—'

'No, Kate. I understand you stick up for your brother but this is business. I want Tony. OK?'

Kate was silent for a moment. Tony would jump at the chance but there was the question of weight. She knew the problem he had had in doing eight stone twelve for Lifeline and this was a tougher ask. However, she said nothing to Mrs Lim. Given the circumstances, she had no choice.

'OK,' she murmured into the phone.

She was still turning the issue over in her mind when Vicky stuck her head around the door.

'Have you heard about Jonno Simpson?'

The young doctor wasn't overjoyed to see the two police officers and not just because he'd obviously been up half the night.

'Mr Simpson's not in very good shape, you know. We only just saved his foot.'

'Will he be able to ride again?' asked Annie.

'It's a bit early to say.' The doctor frowned. 'That's not why you're here though, is it?'

He left them in the corridor outside Jonno's room while he checked on the patient's condition.

'Why were you so keen to rush over here, Sarge? I mean, if he's just had an operation he probably won't make much sense.'

Hunter grinned, not a pleasant sight. 'I always like to catch people at their weakest, Annie. When they haven't got the strength to cover up.'

'So we're going to interrogate him while he's half out of his head?'

'Well, you're not. Like the DI said, you provide the sympathy while I try and find out exactly who your jockey friend has managed to upset.'

The doctor emerged from the room and walked towards them. He cleared his throat preparatory, Annie guessed, to delivering a lengthy account of Jonno's condition.

'Mr Simpson is in a very delicate state . . .'

But Hunter had already walked past him and had his hand on the door.

'Thanks, doctor. Five minutes will be great. Come on, Annie.' He vanished inside.

The doctor gaped after him.

Annie squeezed his arm as she slipped by. 'Don't worry, we'll be gentle.'

Kate had a hard time with Freddy who sounded like he'd just woken up.

'She can't do that to me,' he complained.

'Of course she can, it's her horse.'

'I have all her rides. We agreed at the start of the season.'

Kate sighed. 'So what are you going to do, Fred? Sue?'

'Very funny. Who's she going to use?'

'She wants Tony.'

'He'll never do the weight!'

'Well . . .' Kate didn't want to get into that. 'Have you heard about Jonno Simpson?'

'What about him?'

'He's been shot.'

'What do you mean?'

'Someone broke into his house and shot him in the foot. It's on the news.'

There was silence on the line.

'Freddy?'

'I'll catch you later, Kate.' And he hung up.

Jonno Simpson looked tiny in the big hospital bed, propped up on a bank of pillows, his wounded leg hidden beneath a foot cage which kept the weight of the covers off his injury. His mouth hung open and a string of spittle glistened on his chin. The pupils of his eyes were like tiny peepholes into his misery. Hunter had been correct – Annie did want to mother him.

So far, the DS hadn't made much headway.

'So when you woke up, you were alone?'

'Yes. I reckon.'

Jonno's voice was faint.

Hunter spoke louder. 'Are you sure you didn't see anyone?' No response. 'Did you hear anybody?'

'I could hear screaming.' Jonno's face began to crumple. 'It was me.' He began to sob gently.

Annie took his hand and shot Hunter a leave-it-to-me look. He leaned back in his chair, disgruntled.

She let Jonno grizzle for a bit before she spoke.

'What a dreadful way for the day to end. After your marvellous win, too.'

The sobs stopped.

'Did you see it?'

'My dad told me about it. Said you walked it.'

The lad managed a small grin.

'Yeah. He's a cut above, that horse.'

Hunter had had enough.

'Mr Simpson, can you think of any good reason why someone would want to blow your foot off?'

Jonno's face crumpled again.

'No. 'Course not.'

'Are you sure you haven't been doing people favours? Losing when you should be winning – or the other way round?'

Jonno turned his head and stared at the wall as Hunter continued.

'Somebody has gone to a lot of trouble to give you a message, Mr Simpson. I suggest you pass it on to us quick so we can help you. Or maybe next time they'll take a pot shot at something more vital than your foot.'

Jonno shifted his gaze back to Hunter.

'Just fuck off.' He yanked his hand from Annie's grasp. 'And you too.'

In the corridor, she caught Hunter's eye.

'That went well, Sarge.'

But her sarcasm was lost on him.

'The little bastard's hiding something,' he said grimly.

Kate caught up with the third lot as they rode out towards the gallops. She drove her dusty Volvo estate with the windows rolled down, keeping an eye on the horses as they moved steadily uphill, Vicky at their head. This string were some way from racing fitness and their work was designed accordingly. Kate ran a critical eye over the dozen or so horses as she drove. She knew them all well, their foibles and weaknesses, both mental and physical. She'd heard married couples say they were as familiar with their partner's ailments as their own. That was how she felt about her horses. And, she reflected, for all the excitement she currently enjoyed in her personal life she might as well be married to them too.

It wasn't that Kate didn't have admirers. She knew many

men who, given the slightest encouragement, would have wined her and dined her every night of the week, which would have been fun. And they'd have bedded her too, which would also have been fun but that was where the danger lay. She knew from painful experience there was a price to be paid for too much fun. Right now she didn't trust any man enough to let him into her heart. At least you know where you are with a horse, she thought to herself.

She caught sight of another rider back down the slope and pulled over when she realised it was Tony on Lifeline. Obviously he was trying to get the horse back into his regular routine.

'How is he?' she called out.

Tony stopped as he reached the car.

'He seems sound. Just the odd scratch and bump.'

'So why aren't you looking more cheerful?'

'He's not eating. He had nothing last night and nothing this morning. And, of course, there's being in the barn.' He scratched the horse's ear and Lifeline rolled his big head at his rider's touch. Tony smiled at Kate. 'Actually, I'm grateful he's all in one piece.'

'I've got more good news for you. Mrs Lim would like you to ride No Ill Will in the King George tomorrow.'

'Bloody hell.' He looked shocked.

'That's what you wanted, isn't it? A ride for Mrs Lim.'

'Of course. Yeah – that's great.'

'So I take it you'll be able to do eight stone nine?'

Tony thought about it for a second. 'Sure. No problem.'

She hoped to God there wouldn't be.

Freddy stared at the phone in the phone box, willing it to ring. He felt vulnerable standing out here on the road into the village.

His fire-red Porsche Boxster stood out like a sore thumb. He rarely used phone boxes these days. Give a medal to the guy who'd invented mobiles. But he could see why Herbert insisted on using an untraceable line in certain circumstances. Like now.

At last the bloody thing rang. He snatched up the receiver.

'Hello?' He knew Herbert Gibbs was on the other end but he wasn't supposed to say his name. As far as he was concerned this cloak-and-dagger stuff was a right pain in the arse.

Herbert launched right in without a greeting. 'I hope you're not going to give me any grief about your little pal.'

'You might have warned me.'

'Just call him Hopalong Cassidy from now on, eh?'

The bookie laughed. Freddy didn't join in.

'Look, it's not about that. It's the King George tomorrow. I'm not riding.'

'You're joking!' Herbert did not sound amused.

'I wish I wasn't.'

'You mean, your sister's jocked you off?'

'No, the owner. Sodding Gladys Lim.'

'You told me you had an agreement with her. Cast iron.'

'She's backed out of it. There's nothing I can do.'

'Shit.'

Freddy said nothing. Waited for Herbert.

'There's a lot depending on that horse. This is down to you, you know.'

Freddy took a deep breath. 'I've been thinking. Tony Byrne's on it . . . I could have a word with him.'

'I didn't think that was possible.'

'Well . . . he might go for a sweetener. He's probably going to put up overweight anyway.'

There was a heavy sigh on the other end of the line.

'You'd better sort him out then, Freddy.'

'Hey, no names.'

'Bit late for that. I'll give you another name and you tell your pal Tony.'

'What's that?'

'Hopalong Cassidy.'

Freddy got back into his car with some relief. He had no intention of talking to Tony. In a race with eighteen runners, he'd take the chance that No Ill Will would find something too quick for him.


'Ain't you hungry, feller?' Neil said as he jabbed the pitchfork into the straw bedding of Lifeline's barn.

The horse took no notice of him, just stared moodily out into the yard over the lad's head.

'I know you're upset but you've got to keep body and soul together. That's what my mum says.'

'Oy, Neil.'

The lad looked round. Paul was leaning his bike against the wall. He wore the white shirt and grey trousers of his school uniform – he must have just cycled back.

'You talking to yourself these days?' Paul scaled the metal five-bar gate and came over. 'That crash must have loosened your screws.'

Though Neil didn't react he was pleased to see Paul. He was easier to get on with than the lads in the hostel who, for the most part, ignored Neil or pushed him around. As the youngest apprentice, he was painfully aware of his position at the bottom of the pecking order.

Paul, by contrast, had latched on to Neil and helped him out in the stables whenever he could. The pair of them had things in common. Horses, for one.

'Is he OK?' Paul patted Lifeline's flank. The big horse permitted it – he knew Paul well.

'He's off his feed still. And he won't go back in the stall. Tony tried again after third lot and he wouldn't have it.'

'What you gonna do about it?'

'There's this pony on Tony's mother's farm up in Yorkshire. When Lifeline was a foal the pony used to keep him company. So Tony's getting the pony sent down.'

'And that's going to sort him out, is it?' Paul didn't look convinced. He spoke to Lifeline. 'Your mate's coming down for a visit. What d'you reckon?'

The horse continued to stare out into the yard then suddenly stiffened and stamped his foot.

'It's the cars,' said Neil. 'He does it all the time.' He took hold of Lifeline's head collar. 'It's OK, feller.'

The engine noise echoed off the walls as a silver Renault turned into the forecourt and parked just opposite them.

As the engine cut out, Lifeline relaxed. Neil kept a comforting hand on his neck.

'See, he's OK now.'

But Paul was no longer interested in the horse. His eyes were on the woman with tumbling, copper-coloured hair who was getting out of the car. He leaned over the gate and called to her.

'Hi, Sarah.'

She turned. For a moment it looked as though she would simply wave and walk on, then she crossed the track towards the barn.

'Not bunking off school again, are you, Paul?'

'Would I do that?' He grinned, his eyes admiring her frankly.

She cut quite a dash in jodhpurs and boots.

Sarah looked past him to Neil who had resumed mucking out.

'Hello, Neil. I heard you were in a car crash.'

He looked up at her, his cheeks reddening. 'Yeah,' he mumbled.

'Are you all right?'

'Yeah.' Another mumble.

'Great. Well, I'm off for a ride. See you.'

She turned and walked away.

'See you,' Paul called after her. 'You bet I'll see you,' he muttered for Neil's benefit. 'Just look at that arse.'

'Don't,' said Neil but his eyes, like Paul's were glued to Sarah's apple-cheeked rear displayed in her skintight jodhpurs.

'You really missed out last night, mate,' Paul added.

'Shut up.'

'Got the full treatment. X-rated.'

'She didn't even ask about Lifeline.'

'She's not interested in horses, dumbo. She prefers jockeys.'

Kate was sorting through unpaid invoices – hers and her suppliers'. It was funny how the second pile was always bigger than the first.

The office was situated at one end of the American barn, next to a tack room and a feed store. Through the internal window Kate could look down the row of stalls and cast a protective eye over some of the horses in her care. She could also see the door at the far end, which now opened to admit an unfamiliar figure. She couldn't remember when she'd last seen Sarah in the yard.

'Hiya,' she called through the open door.

Sarah stepped into the office.

'Vicky's going to saddle Mr Plod for me. I just fancied a ride.'

'I know. I was here when you phoned.'

Kate didn't mention the disbelief the call had been met with in the yard. Sarah had not been near a horse for months – unlike the early days of her romance with Tony when they'd not been able to keep her away.

Kate took in Sarah's riding gear. How typical of her to show up dressed like a model from *Horse and Hound*.

'A pity Tony's not around,' she said. 'You could have had some company.'

'Who's after company?'

The voice came from the doorway. Freddy had appeared from nowhere.

'Hello, Sarah. Bit of a stranger in here, aren't you?'

'I'm going for a ride.'

'I was saying it's a pity Tony's not around to ride out with her,' added Kate.

'Won't I do?' said Freddy. 'I need to do a bit of work on Cold Call.'

Sarah appeared to consider the matter.

'Don't be afraid to say no,' said Kate. 'I'm looking forward to the day when a woman tells my brother to get lost.'

But she could tell that woman wasn't going to be Sarah.

Greta surveyed the bedroom and cursed. Every surface was covered with items of clothing she'd unearthed and discarded. Ladies Day at Royal Ascot never usually caused her this sort of problem. Much as she disliked the whole rigmarole of dressing up and wearing a hat, she knew it had to be done. As a rule she decided on an outfit for the occasion weeks ahead and she'd done the same this year too. The only problem was, the stupid thing didn't fit her now.

At least she had a hat. She was thankful that her head hadn't got any bigger and wished the same could be said for the rest of her. Not that it was obvious – yet. If she breathed in, she could still get into the cream suit she'd worn two years ago and if things got too uncomfortable she could always undo the hook and eye at the back of the waist, provided she kept the jacket on. She tried it out in front of the mirror. The hat too. Wearing stuff from the year before last was an admission of defeat and it wouldn't go unremarked – but who cared about that? Actually, she did. Though it wasn't as if she had a choice, despite the confusion of garments littering the room.

She stepped into a pair of heels. Ow! She hadn't realised her feet had swollen too. It was so unfair the way your body betrayed you. She rummaged and found a flatter pair with a small grass stain she'd not been able to remove. At least they were comfortable.

She heard the bang of the front door and went out on to the landing.

'Paul?' she called.

There was no reply so she started down the stairs, thoughts of tomorrow instantly replaced by parental concern. Paul would need feeding and supervising, otherwise he'd just scoff junk and do no homework. And though the end of term was in sight, there was still work to be done – Mr Maxwell had made that clear. Especially, as he'd put it at the last parents' evening, for a boy so 'academically disinclined' as Paul.

As expected, she found him in the kitchen with a packet of chocolate digestives and a Coke.

'You're late,' she began, hating the tone of the familiar nagging words which, even as she spoke them, reminded her of her own mother. Reminded her, too, of what little effect that nagging had ever had.

Paul turned to face her.

'Oh, Mum,' he said, staring at her.

'What is it?' This was not the response she'd expected.

'You look –' and as he groped for the right word she remembered what she was wearing: the suit, the shoes, the hat '– Mum, you look brilliant.'

Greta could have hugged him. In fact, she did.

It was glorious up on the gallops. They had the sunny green uplands to themselves. Sarah enjoyed the roll of the dependable old hack beneath her and the breeze in her face as they ambled along. Freddy had explained to her she'd have to look on as he did a bit of work on his small black mount, Cold Call.

She watched as the pair of them trotted in circles, Freddy with his stirrup irons let right down like a dressage rider. He told her he was trying to get Cold Call to balance himself better, instead of leaning into the bridle the whole time.

After a quarter of an hour, Freddy pulled up beside her, seemingly satisfied. 'I'll say this for my sister, she's a bloody genius at getting horses into shape. This one was out for all last season with tendon trouble and now look at him.'

Sarah looked. With the best will in the world she couldn't tell a thing from a horse's appearance. Give or take the colour, they were all the same, weren't they? She didn't voice this sentiment, however.

'Has Tony told you then?' Freddy's voice had changed. He wasn't so satisfied now.

'Told me what?'

'He's on my ride tomorrow at Ascot. I've been jocked off.'

'Why?'

'You'd better ask his new friend, Mrs Lim. Apparently she was very impressed with his ride in the Coventry.'

Sarah thought for a moment, she wasn't familiar with the names of races. 'That's the one when he wouldn't get out of your way?'

'That's right. Still, I should worry. Gives me a day off tomorrow. Think I'll put a deck chair out in my back garden.'

She searched his eyes, bluer than the sky, for other meanings.

'Sounds good,' she said.

It was funny what some people enjoyed, Tony thought as he drove out of the health-club car park. He'd been at the end of his stint in the sauna when two pink and beefy citizens had plonked themselves on the wooden bench next to him with grunts of satisfaction. One had announced, 'This is the life!' as the other had sloshed water on the glowing coals, raising a hissing cloud of steam. Tony had grabbed his towel at once and left. He swore that when he quit race-riding he'd never endure the inside of a sauna again.

He drove back to Lambourn in a sweatsuit with the heat turned up and the windows closed on the blazing afternoon sun. Making the weight for the King George was torture but he'd do it if it killed him. He wasn't going to let anyone down, not Kate, not Mrs Lim – not himself.

He found Sarah sunning herself in the garden in a bikini. Suntan lotion gleamed on her thighs like wet paint.

She raised an indolent hand in greeting. 'Isn't this heavenly? I could sunbathe for ever.'

Tony grunted. His idea of heaven was a cold beer in the shade but he couldn't allow himself to think like that.

'Look,' he squatted next to her, 'you won't want to drive with me to Ascot tomorrow – I've got to sweat. I'll fix you a lift with one of the others.'

'Sorry?' She turned her head marginally in his direction.

He repeated himself. 'You're going to be all dolled up, aren't you? You won't want to sit in my car with the heat turned on.'

He had her full attention now. There was uncertainty in her expression though her eyes were hidden behind her dark glasses.

'I think I'll drive myself.'

'Are you sure? Laurie and Greta could give you a lift.'

'No.' She'd turned away from him now, settled back in position. 'I'll make my own way.'

For a moment he contemplated the tiny droplets of sweat beading her shoulder just where the strap of her bikini top cut into the silky skin. Right now, sweat was the name of the game.

Despite the heat, Greta cooked a hot supper and served it early as she always did. Her men were as traditional in their appetites as any working-class stereotype. Pile it high and serve it quick was the maxim she lived by. She found it worked. So at six-thirty, with the summer sun still blazing outside, Laurie and Paul sat down to chicken casserole and mashed potatoes.

'You're not eating?' Laurie said to her as she sipped a glass of mineral water.

She shook her head. It was hardly a surprise for she rarely had much at this time. Her role was to fetch and carry and make sure the boys had their fill, like a mother at toddler feeding-time. The comparison had often struck her.

But Laurie wouldn't let it lie.

'You're still feeling sick, aren't you?'

Oh, how true that was.

'A bit.'

He looked hard at her. 'This has been going on rather, hasn't it?'

'Well . . .' She could hardly deny it.

'You were a right wet blanket at lunch yesterday. I hope there's more life in you tomorrow.'

So that was the cause of his concern – the next day's syndicate gathering at Ascot at which, in honour of Ladies Day, the other wives would be present. Once more Greta was expected to be on parade.

Laurie was staring at her keenly, expecting a response. To her surprise Paul came to her aid.

'Don't worry, Dad. She's gonna look great.'

Laurie turned to him. 'Really?'

'I've seen her all dressed up. Truly excellent. Take it from me.'

Greta found herself grinning. 'Thank you, darling.'

Paul got to his feet, he'd cleared his plate. 'I'll get pudding, shall I?'

Laurie waited till he had left the room. 'So, how much did you pay him to say that?'

'Oh, piss off.' She said it with a smile, to take the edge off.

He didn't react, obviously thinking. 'What I can't figure is – I never see you eating but you're piling on the weight.'

She had to stop this fast. 'What are you complaining about, Laurie? Last night you told me I was looking better than ever.'

'Yes, but—'

'But you only said that to get what you wanted, is that it?'

He squirmed. 'Of course not.'

'Anyway,' she said, stacking plates, 'it's too hot to eat.'

Then she fled to the kitchen.

Visiting time was in full spate by the time Annie got to the Radcliffe. As she walked down the corridor to Jonno Simpson's room, she ran into the one person she'd hoped to avoid. The young doctor looked even more knackered than he had that morning. However, he wasn't too fatigued to recognise her.

'Oh, it's you,' he said, stony-faced.

She gave him her biggest smile. 'Gosh, doctor, still on duty?'

'I might ask you the same question.'

'I'm on my own time. I thought I'd see how Mr Simpson's getting on.'

The doctor's expression did not soften. 'Where's the other one?'

It took her a moment to realise what he meant. 'You mean Sergeant Hunter?'

'I mean the obnoxious officer who upset my patient. I understand that the police sometimes have to play rough, but bully-boy tactics are out of place in a hospital.'

She defended her colleague as best she could. 'That's just Sergeant Hunter's manner, doctor. His bark's worse than his bite.'

He didn't look convinced and she didn't blame him.

'I made a serious misjudgement in allowing you to interview Mr Simpson this morning. He's had an uncomfortable day.'

Annie was tempted to remark that since Jonno had almost had his foot blown off that wasn't surprising – but she held her tongue.

'In the circumstances, I'd much prefer it if you postponed your next interview with the patient until he is feeling stronger.'

Annie tried another tack.

'To be honest, doctor, I know it didn't go well this morning. I thought a personal visit, on my own, might make him feel better. I've brought grapes,' she added, holding up a carrier bag.

Down the corridor, behind the doctor, the door to Jonno's room opened. A small blonde girl in a yellow T-shirt and tight jeans stepped out. Even at this distance Annie could see she was crying.

The doctor caught sight of her then spoke urgently to Annie. 'If you have any decency, officer, you will leave any further interviews for another day.'

'Who's that?' she asked, standing her ground.

'That's Mr Simpson's fiancée. Will you leave now? Please?'

Annie went.

Neil lingered over his last duties. As an apprentice, he had to stay on after the other lads had gone to clean out the feed buckets and sweep up. He didn't rush. He had a phone call to make and he wasn't in any hurry to get to it. In fact, he didn't want to do it at all but he'd promised his mother.

He went back to check on a couple of horses stabled in the old wooden stalls in the courtyard. Like all the lads, Neil had three horses to take care of: Lifeline, Summer Storm – a big hazel-eyed bay – and Cold Call. He was fond of all three and, with Lifeline taking up a lot of his time at present, it was important not to neglect the others.

Paul turned up as he was changing the rug on Cold Call. 'Still at it?' he said, peering into the stall.

'There's always things to do, especially with this boy.' Neil cast an eye over the manger and bedding.

'Yeah? Why's that?'

Neil leaned on the door, gave Paul his full attention. ' 'Cause

Freddy Montague works him. He rode him out this afternoon.'

'So?'

'Anything not right with a horse and Freddy blames the lad.' Neil turned his back and pulled up his T-shirt to display a six-inch-long weal, the skin crimped and purple. 'He did that to me.'

Paul stared at the scar. 'Christ, what for?'

'Nothing. Said it was on account for when I cocked up. Said lads were like horses and sometimes you had to show them the whip if you wanted the right result.'

Paul digested this for a moment then flashed Neil a wicked smile. 'So – you coming out later?'

'I've got stuff to do.'

'After that. Come on. You really missed out last night.'

'You already said.'

Annie waited on the ground floor, keeping an eye on the lifts. It was a gamble but, sure enough, the girl in the yellow T-shirt emerged after ten minutes. She looked more composed. Annie guessed most of those ten minutes had been spent in the Ladies.

She stepped up to her. 'Excuse me.'

'Yes?' The girl looked startled.

Annie showed her badge. 'Can I have a word about Mr Simpson?'

The girl's cornflower blue eyes stared at her through a veil of misery. Annie was prepared for more tears but this girl was tougher than that.

'Do I have a choice?'

Annie steered her to a seat. The girl, Jackie, revealed that she was due to marry Jonno in August but *this* had changed everything. What was going on? Why had he been shot? Who had done it?

83

'That's what we're trying to find out,' Annie said. 'But we need to speak to Jonno. He might have an idea what this is all about.'

'You think he's been up to something, don't you?' The blue eyes were focused now, scrutinising Annie closely.

She played it down. 'I'm just saying he's got to be frank with us. Not now but when he's feeling better.'

Jackie shrugged and stood up. 'Jon said some bastard of a policeman tried to grill him this morning. He doesn't want to talk to that man again, I know.'

Annie gave her a card. 'He can talk to me.'

The girl took it and tucked it into her back pocket. She turned to go.

Annie held out her carrier bag.

'Do you think he might like some grapes?'

Neil spent an age shuffling coins on the shelf next to the phone. Finally he fed the pay slot and began to dial.

The receiver was lifted on the first ring, as if someone had been waiting for the call.

'Neil.'

'Hello, Dad.'

'How you doing, son? Your mum tells me you were in a car crash.'

'I'm OK. Not a scratch on me.'

'Thank God for that.'

There was a pause, filled by his father's nicotine-induced cough.

'Have you been home long?' asked Neil. Silly question. He knew to the minute when his father had come out of prison.

# Chapter Four

Tony stood on the bathroom scales stark naked. He hardly needed to look down at the little Perspex window between his feet. He was so in tune with his body he could tell his weight almost to the ounce.

In a second he'd know what he'd be eating for breakfast.

The figures read eight stone eleven pounds. All he'd be having for breakfast was a sauna.

He had two rides ahead of him today. War of Words in the fourth race wasn't a problem. But No Ill Will in the last definitely was. The handicapper had given the horse eight stone nine which meant, taking into account two and a half pounds for saddle, clothing and boots, Tony was currently four and a half pounds overweight.

He rummaged in the cupboard behind the sink. It was packed with Sarah's stuff, discarded hair products, bath oils, exfoliants and God knows what else. But at the back was a small brown bottle containing the tablets Tony only used in emergencies like this. His pee pills.

The doctor who'd written out the prescription had warned Tony that they'd keep him on his toes and he'd not been kidding. They sent him rushing to the loo like a pensioner with a prostate problem. But every fluid ounce lost helped and, in the present circumstances, what choice did he have?

He'd taken a laxative the night before and already felt like a squeezed-out sponge. But there had to be more to come. He swallowed the tiny white tablet without water. It tasted disgusting.

With Tony leaving early to have a long sweat, Kate had arranged to travel to Ascot with the Somervilles. She knocked on their door.

Greta appeared, still in her dressing-gown.

'What time are we leaving?'

'Half-eleven,' Greta replied. 'I suppose I'd better get a move on. I feel a bit of wreck.'

Kate thought she looked like one too – by Greta's standards anyway. Her naturally flawless skin was pink and puffy and there were shadows under her eyes.

'Are you feeling all right?'

'Well . . .' She hesitated. 'I could do without all the palaver again today.'

Kate had never known Greta to be reluctant to dress up and strut her stuff on occasions like Royal Ascot. Something must be up. But there'd be time enough for her to get to the bottom of it later. She wanted to see her runners safely on their way.

'See you later then,' she said and headed for the stables.

As Tony opened the kitchen door the aroma of freshly ground coffee ravished his senses. Sarah sat at the table nursing a large milky cup of the stuff. On a plate at her elbow, a half-eaten croissant sat in a thick pool of apricot jam.

'Hi, darling,' she said. She was wearing a plain cream blouse that tied at the throat and a charcoal grey business suit: the uniform of middle management – austere, respectable, strait-laced. On her it looked damned sexy.

'You're not wearing that to the races,' he said.

'Of course not. I've got to pop into the shop for Dad.'

'This morning? But you'll be late.' He hated the way his voice sounded: anxious, pleading, needy. Couldn't he at least pretend he didn't care?

'Don't worry. I've got plenty of time to get back and change and drive to Ascot. God, you'd think the world might end if I missed a horse race.'

'I didn't mean it like that.' But, of course, he did.

She stood up, popping the last morsel of croissant, dripping with jam, into her mouth and drained her coffee. How come she didn't get fat? he thought. Or maybe the extra ounces just went to flesh out her succulent frame and render it even more enticing. Standing there in her little business suit, the cloth pulled tight round the swell of her breasts and over the curve of her hips, a speck of jam on her swollen lower lip, she looked good enough to eat.

She took a step towards him, craned her neck to kiss him goodbye on the cheek and he crushed her body against his in a fierce embrace.

'Tony!' she squealed in protest but allowed him to kiss her on the lips, like she was doing him a favour.

He relaxed his grip and she stepped smartly away.

'For God's sake, Tony,' she protested. 'Save it for the race.'

He heard her footsteps in the hall, the front door closing and then the sound of her car engine. He looked at the leftovers of her breakfast on the table. His stomach was in knots and he no longer felt hungry.

He was losing her and there wasn't a damn thing he could do about it.

\*

Gavin Marshall cornered Greta on the balcony just before lunch.

'So where's your knock-out friend then?'

It was a good question. Some weeks previously Greta had sweet-talked Marshall into inviting Sarah to watch the racing from his box. At the time Sarah had been thrilled at the prospect and had splashed out on an outfit which, Greta had promised Marshall, would knock him dead. Hence the sarcastic reference. Sarah's absence was on Greta's conscience, not least because she was painfully aware of the price per head of a private box overlooking the winning post on Ladies Day at Royal Ascot.

'I wish I knew. Believe me, I'm furious with her.' Though she was laying it on for Marshall's benefit, it was no more than the truth. Sarah had landed her in it, the selfish little cow. 'I'm seriously embarrassed about it, Gavin, but she may still turn up.' In her heart, Greta doubted it, though. She'd been calling Sarah's mobile number ever since she'd arrived – without success.

Marshall savoured her discomfort for a moment then smiled. 'Never mind. You'll just have to make it up to me by giving me the benefit of your expertise in matters equine.'

'What?'

'Just a rundown of the card, for my ears only.'

Greta laughed out loud. 'I've no idea what's going to win.'

'You did pretty well the other day.'

'That was luck.'

'I don't believe in luck. I believe in inside information. So why don't you tell me about your friend Kate Montague's two runners?'

Greta had a brainwave. 'Why don't you ask her yourself? I'll give her a buzz and get her to come up.'

She could see Marshall liked the idea. 'Ask her to stay for lunch,' he said, 'since we appear to be one short.'

\*

Sarah was also on Tony's mind as he sat on the bench in the weighing room. He'd been trying not to think about her on the drive down and during his last session in the sweat box. He needed to focus his energy and concentrate on the races ahead but she kept thrusting herself into his thoughts. Was this really love? he wondered. If so, it was doomed. He recognised the feeling from his past and the one other affair with a woman who had mattered to him. That relationship had gone down the pan too.

Monica had come right out and blamed his obsession with riding and watching his weight – with his job, in fact. And he could understand it. Living with a jockey on a permanent wasting regime was a nightmare for a partner. There were few fun nights out – or none that included food or drink, at any rate. She had to cope with separate eating regimes and the unspoken disapproval that went with them. ('At least I'll be able to scoff a doughnut without feeling guilty,' Monica had said in their last painful conversation.) She also had to put up with the short temper that went hand in hand with permanent hunger. Tony could well understand Sarah's disillusion. Not that it made it any easier to bear.

'Greta,' Kate called through the closed cubicle door. From inside she could hear the sound of retching. 'Greta!' she said again, knocking on the door for emphasis.

After a moment, the toilet flushed and the door swung open. Greta smiled brightly as she emerged, though she couldn't disguise her pallor or the uncertainty in her step as she made for the row of wash basins.

'Are you all right?'

'Something I ate disagreed with me.'

'But you didn't eat anything,' Kate protested. She had been sitting opposite her friend throughout lunch.

Greta had her back to her, peering into the mirror. She obviously didn't want to pursue the matter. 'I suppose Laurie sent you.'

'You've been gone for ages. I said I'd see if you were OK.'

'I'm fine now.' Greta turned to Kate. She'd repaired her eye make-up and there was colour back in her cheeks. 'Thanks for coming to lunch. I need a bit of moral support with that lot.'

Kate sympathised. Marshall's City-slicker guests were fizzing on the limitless champagne and a long afternoon lay ahead.

'Typical of Sarah not to turn up. I thought she was going to help you shoulder the charm burden.'

Greta pulled a face. 'I guess Tony won't be happy about it either.'

Kate was only too aware of that. It was one of the reasons she had accepted Marshall's invitation – so she could monitor the Sarah situation for Tony's sake. She knew that the pair of them had hit a rocky patch which, frankly, didn't surprise her. Sarah was clearly not cut out for a life around horses and the sooner she took her designer tastes and drama-queen antics back to London the better. In Kate's opinion, Sarah wasn't worthy of Tony. On the other hand, right now it would be useful to be able to tell her anxious jockey that his girlfriend was looking forward to seeing him ride.

'What are you going to tell him?' Greta asked.

'Nothing.' Kate had already decided a white lie was in order. 'I'll say I've been busy with my owners and haven't been up here.'

Greta chuckled. 'Beneath that innocent exterior you're just a canny old boot, aren't you?'

'Tony's got a job to do. And I wouldn't be doing mine if I let a woman like Sarah Cooper stop him doing it.'

Tony felt a distinct sense of *déjà vu* as he strode into the parade ring ahead of the Cork and Orrery Stakes. As on Tuesday, the heat was intense and he was weak from the sauna and his fierce wasting regime. He knew he'd be OK once the excitement of the race kicked into his system but even forcing a smile to his lips was an effort as he shook hands with Bill Walsh, the owner of his mount, War of Words.

He'd met Walsh once before and formed the impression he was in love with the sound of his own voice. A tubby antiques-dealer with just a couple of horses, he was one of Kate's long-standing owners. Notwithstanding, War of Words, a neat black gelding with a white blaze on his face, had only just come under Kate's wing.

Unusually for an owner before a race, Walsh did not want to discuss the contest ahead.

'Nasty business, this Jonno Simpson affair,' was his opening remark.

Simpson's wounding had been the talk of the weighing room and Tony was sick of it already. He felt sorry for the lad but couldn't pretend he liked him.

'Was he on the take, do you think?' said Walsh. 'I only ask because he rode for me in one race. He came second and at the time I thought he'd ridden a blinder. Now I wonder – perhaps he should have finished first, eh?'

Tony forced a grin.

'Anyway, Tony,' the owner continued, 'I trust you're not taking a back-hander to stop my horse today.'

'What's that supposed to mean?'

Kate, who had been monitoring their exchange, flashed a warning glance at him.

'Just a joke, old boy. According to the papers, you jockeys are picking up bungs all over the shop.'

Tony flushed with anger. He ignored Kate's restraining hand on his arm. 'If you're implying I'm dishonest, Mr Walsh, you can stick this ride up your arse.'

Walsh's big toffee-coloured eyes bulged with alarm.

'Well, of course not. I said it was a joke, didn't I?'

'Don't be offended, Bill,' Kate intervened. 'Tony doesn't do jokes just before a race.'

'Oh.' Walsh did not look mollified.

'But,' Kate continued, 'if Tuesday's anything to go by, he'll probably bring your horse home in front.'

That did pacify the owner. Kate's grey eyes looked hard into Tony's as she helped him into the saddle.

'You'd better win now, hadn't you?' was all she said.

But as Tony lined up for the start of the race he doubted he had any chance of victory.

Like the Coventry, the Cork and Orrery was run over the six-furlong course in a straight gallop where runners usually ended up under the stands' rail. But this race was for fully grown horses, mature sprinters of three years and up. War of Words was seven years old and in flat racing terms could be considered a senior citizen. Walsh had moved the horse to Kate in the hope that she could get one more season of quality sprinting out of him. Tony thought that beyond even her. Though he hadn't said so, he suspected that the gelding's best racing form was behind

92

him and that these days he was running strictly on memory.

That memory, however, was based on plenty of experience and War of Words jumped smartly out of the starting stalls and into the lead. Tony was thrilled by the surge of power as the black horse seemed to scorch the grass beneath him. Maybe he'd done Kate and War of Words a disservice. Perhaps there were more glory days ahead.

Two furlongs from home War of Words was still leading. Tony had managed to get tight to the rail and the old horse loved having something solid to run beside. It was an exhilarating sensation to be ahead of the pack, streaking past cheering spectators on both sides of the course, tearing towards the seething grandstand, the winning post in sight. For a moment Tony thought he had the race in the bag, then he felt his mount's stride begin to shorten.

In less time than it took him to pull his stick into his right hand, a handful of horses came past as if the gelding was standing still.

The moment he was headed, War of Words lost his rhythm. His stride faltered and he veered to his right. Tony pulled hard to keep him running straight and gave him a fierce crack on the shoulder. There were shouts and curses from other riders as War of Words threatened their ground then they too were ahead. Suddenly it was over. They'd finished way down the field, ninth out of twelve runners.

'I thought for a moment you were going to hold on,' said Bill Walsh as he emerged and caught the horse's bridle.

'I'm sorry,' said Tony.

'There's no need to be sorry. I didn't expect you to win.'

But Tony hadn't meant that. He'd felt sorry for the horse, seeking one last victory on instinct and guts and cheated by time. But he couldn't have put that into words and he didn't try.

'He's a brave fellow,' he said. 'He just ran out of puff.'

Walsh nodded and patted his horse's flank.

'Looks like you did too,' he said.

Tony realised he was breathing hard and wondered if his legs would hold him when he climbed out of the saddle.

The race had taken just over seventy seconds. Tony felt as if he'd run a marathon.

'Your old man looks knackered,' said Freddy as the camera lingered briefly on Tony's tall thin frame hunched over War of Words. For a second his face filled the screen, his brown eyes ringed with shadow in his pale face.

'That's because he's half dead from starving himself,' replied Sarah. 'Can we turn the television off now?'

'No fear, sweetheart, this is work. Tell you what, I'll turn the sound down.'

They were in Freddy's front room, spending an indolent afternoon enjoying the racing in their preferred style. It was hot but that wasn't the only reason they weren't wearing many clothes.

Freddy pressed the mute button on the remote control and shut off the commentary. Sarah moved swiftly to position herself between him and the screen.

'Oy,' he said, motioning her out of his line of sight.

'Come on, Freddy, the race is over. I've got something much more interesting for you to look at.'

Bloody typical of a woman, thought Freddy. Wants your attention all the time, like a child. But Sarah was no child, on the contrary she was very good at grown-up games. Not that he wanted to play right now – unfortunately she hadn't got the message.

Sarah stood squarely in front of him and inched her long T-shirt up her shapely thighs. In fact, it was his T-shirt and she wore nothing beneath it – as she was in the process of reminding him.

Freddy considered the deep whorl of her navel, the smooth slope of her belly and the soft fringe of brown curls at the junction of her legs. She was offering herself on a plate but right now he wasn't hungry.

'Put it away, woman. You're making a spectacle of yourself.'

She let go of the hem and the shirt fell like a curtain. She whirled away.

'You're such a pig, Freddy.'

'Right enough,' he replied unconcerned and took a long pull on his beer, savouring the cold yeasty tang as it went down. Thank God he didn't have to deprive himself of life's little pleasures like that sad sod Tony Byrne. Though, on second thoughts, maybe the sad sod wasn't deprived in all departments.

'Here, Sarah. How come Tony has weight trouble living with a nympho like you? Can't you shag those extra pounds off him?'

She chucked a cushion at him, which would have put paid to his beer if he hadn't seen it coming. She followed it up with a punch which he caught in his fist, pulling her down on to the sofa. The struggle that followed was predictable and he let her slap him a few times to make her feel better. Naturally, this led to a clinch and somehow that T-shirt rode up again, not that he objected on this occasion, though he kept an eye on the clock, bearing in mind the next race was off in ten minutes. There wasn't time to get into anything serious.

To his surprise, she pushed him away.

'Freddy?'

The tone of her voice set alarm bells ringing – he'd heard it from many women. He thought of it as the Handcuff Voice, the one a woman uses when she's making plans to tie a man down.

He knew what Sarah was going to say next even before she opened her mouth.

Tony weighed out at a pound overweight for the King George V. He found it hard to look Kate in the eye as he got off the scales but he forced himself.

He read disappointment there and reproach and other, softer, sentiments he couldn't fathom.

'I'm sorry,' he said for the second time that afternoon. It was becoming a habit.

'Just don't lose by a length,' she said.

Horses in a handicap race were weighted according to ability so that, in theory, all of them would reach the finishing line at the same time. In practice, of course, this never happened. Nevertheless, every ounce a horse carried on its back was of significance in its efforts to reach the winning post ahead of its rivals. And for a jockey to burden his mount with additional weight to that allotted by the handicapper was sloppy and unprofessional.

Tony knew that every extra pound his horse carried represented a length lost over a mile and a half. If he were to be beaten by less than a length it would be his fault – hence Kate's remark. If that happened it would prey on his mind for weeks to come. Some jockeys were able to shrug off such things but he wasn't one of them.

Time to change the subject. 'Have you seen Sarah yet?' he asked.

Kate shook her head and took his saddle from him.

'Sorry, Tony. I haven't had time to get up to the box.'

'Freddy, I was wondering . . .'

Here it comes, he thought.

'I can't bear it at Tony's much longer. I could go back to London, of course. On the other hand . . .'

Sarah paused. It was his cue. But he wasn't reading from her script.

'Maybe I could move in here,' she continued. 'I'd pay you rent. In money and in kind.' She gave him her naughty-minx look, her fingers in his hand subtly increasing the pressure. And waited.

He did it as gently as he could. 'That sounds great, babe. But I'm sorry – I've already got someone moving in.'

'What!' The seductive smile was replaced by thin-lipped shock. Her hand was removed from his in the same instant.

'I'm expecting an Aussie pal of mine any day now.'

She was indignant. 'You never said anything about this!'

'Well, Sarah sweetheart, we've had better things to talk about.'

She wasn't to be fobbed off. 'I don't believe you,' she said angrily. 'What Aussie pal?'

He got to his feet and reached for her hand. She snatched it away.

'Follow me,' he said.

Freddy led her into the kitchen and out of the back door. Next to a lawn mower and a sack of compost was a square black trunk with reinforced metal corners. He pointed to the label

97

which was clearly marked: Jeff Collins c/o Montague, Woodside Cottage, Beechwood Lodge, Upper Lambourn, Berkshire, England.

'Jeff sent it on by sea from Hong Kong. He's back in Oz to see his family but should be here any day now. I'm waiting for his call.'

He could see she was debating whether to believe him, weighing up just how much of a rat he was. But the fact of the trunk, sitting there as tangible proof, could not be overlooked.

'Oh, shit,' she said. 'Perhaps I'd better go.'

He put his arm around her and gave her a reassuring hug. 'If that's how you feel, darling.'

Now they were reading from his script again, which was just how Freddy liked it.


The King George V Handicap for three-year-olds started by going downhill away from the stands, with the runners required to complete almost three sides of a curving triangle before reaching the winning post, a mile and a half distant. It was peaceful out here, away from the hysteria of the dandified half-drunk crowd packed into the stands and massed around the marquees and betting rings. Not that Tony was of any mind to appreciate the serenity of the scene. All his energies were now concentrated on the animal beneath him.

No Ill Will was a rangy individual who in the past three weeks had really come to himself. As a two-year-old he'd been backward, slow to grow into his big frame, and Kate had only raced him twice, over a mile, at Nottingham and Leicester. Over the winter he'd strengthened up nicely and had had a couple of successful outings, at Leicester again, and more recently in a handicap at Pontefract where, carrying nine stone four over a mile and a quarter, he'd won handily. This was his first attempt at a mile and a half. Kate was convinced he'd get the trip, especially since, given the class of the race, this time he was only carrying eight stone nine – in fact, eight stone ten since Tony had put up overweight. As she had said, he'd better not lose by a length.

The mile and a half at Ascot is tough, with every stride of the final eight furlongs being uphill. More races are lost there by going too fast early on than anywhere else in the country. But, if you don't hold your position, you can easily find yourself at the back of the pack with the impossible task of coming wide round a wall of tiring horses.

They were racing in the shadows of the trees and going at a good pace but No Ill Will was holding his own. Then they left the trees behind and began to track the white rail that ran down to Swinley Bottom.

The leaders began to pick up the pace. Tony squeezed his mount gently between his knees. The effect was instantaneous, like putting your foot down in a powerful car, and he eased up at once. A sudden elation ran through him – maybe this horse was the real thing.

They raced out of Swinley Bottom and began running uphill along the Old Mile. One of the front three began to flag and Tony cruised past before he could get boxed in. He sensed the chasing horses queuing up to make their challenge. No Ill Will was heading into unknown territory. Kate was sure the further he went the better he would be. Tony hoped she was right as he shortened his reins and settled down into the drive position.

It was now two furlongs from home. He gave the horse a crack and once more felt that satisfying thrust of power beneath him. No Ill Will closed the gap on the leader, the fleet-footed favourite Tungsten who was carrying almost a stone more. Tungsten's jockey raised his stick and the little horse responded, thrusting out his neck like a terrier straining at the leash.

They were against the far rail and Tony could hear the crowd above the thump and thunder of the horses around him going flat out.

It was nip and tuck between the two of them, with No Ill Will never quite able to head Tungsten. Both riders used their whips, seeking that extra surge that would take them to the post first.

Tony was amazed by the horse beneath him. He was deep into the unknown now, galloping further than he'd ever done before. Tony asked the horse for one final lung-bursting effort and for the first time No Ill Will got his head in front. The winning post was just fifty yards off.

Tony raised his whip again but this time the blow had no effect. Suddenly No Ill Will was going nowhere, travelling on momentum alone, out of petrol. Tony pushed with his hands but he knew his horse was spent.

He lost by a length.

Freddy was feeling extraordinarily pleased with himself as he sat down at the desk in his back room. Did he know horses or what? More to the point, did he know people?

Take that strait-laced snot Tony Byrne. From the way he'd reacted when Freddy put out the feelers when they'd first met, he knew Tony only played by the book. He had made it plain he looked down on men who were prepared to be a bit flexible when it came to riding races – men like Freddy. And where had that attitude got him? Tony would have a kitten if he knew Freddy was slipping it to his girlfriend on a regular basis. But that was nothing to the way he would react if he discovered a bent bookmaker like Herbert Gibbs thought he'd successfully bribed him to throw a race. And if the matter ever came to light that's just how it would look.

Freddy unlocked the bottom drawer of the desk. It wasn't the most secure place to keep a bit of cash but it was handy to have some spare about the place. He counted out three grand in fifties, slipped an elastic band over the roll and popped it into a square brown envelope. On a yellow post-it slip he wrote: 'You rode a great race for the King George' and left it unsigned. Then he scribbled Tony's name in capital letters on the front and sealed the envelope. In a few moments he'd drive a mile down the road to Tony's and pop the letter into the post box on the gate at the end of his drive.

The whole notion pleased him hugely. He wasn't yet sure how he might use this. An anonymous call to Gladys Lim maybe? Let Tony explain to her why three grand had been given to him after he'd come second on her horse. That would serve the bastard right for stealing Freddy's ride. At the very least, Tony would be aware that someone thought they'd bought him – and that wouldn't suit the self-righteous little prick at all. As for the money, that hardly counted. Herbert would be paying him much more than that for the fix.

Of course, once Jeff got his Aussie arse in gear and showed up with the Pick Six betting ticket, Freddy could pack in the little deals and start thinking big.

He whistled as he headed for his car.

Laurie nagged Greta all the way home.

'Why won't you see a doctor?'

'Because there's no need. It's just a tummy bug.'

'But you've had it for nearly a week. There must be something wrong when you spend half your life in the toilet.'

'Stop fussing, Laurie.'

Eventually he'd appealed to Kate in the back seat. She tried to laugh it off.

'Don't ask me. I'm sure if Greta felt bad enough she'd go.'

Kate had no desire to be dragged into their conflict. She'd had enough of other couples' disputes for the day.

After the last race and the agonising post mortem with Mrs Lim, from which the owner had finally stalked off in obvious dissatisfaction, Tony had turned to her.

'Why didn't you tell me Sarah hadn't turned up?'

So he'd finally found out. 'Why do you think? I wanted your mind on the job not on some girl.'

He'd glared at her. 'She's not "some girl". She's my partner.'

Kate had backed off with a swift apology. She had her own opinions about Sarah and Tony, just as she did about Greta and Laurie, but she had no intention of airing them.

She gazed out of the window and tried to ignore the bickering from the front seat.

'I'm sorry, darling.' Sarah looked contrite as Tony opened the front door. 'There was a new drama about the lease. The landlord refused to sign.'

'I see.' He had had plenty of time to consider how he was going to react to Sarah's no-show at Ascot and was determined not to lose his rag – to try and stay cool while retaining the moral high ground. But she'd promised she'd come and she'd disappointed him. He couldn't just let it go.

'You don't believe me, do you?'

She was keen for a fight, he could tell. He knew Sarah

well enough by now; attack was always her preferred means of defence. As it happened, he didn't believe her. After Kate had confirmed Sarah's absence, he'd rung the shop and caught Jean just as she was closing up. She'd told him she'd not seen Sarah since midday. But he didn't want to go down the where-were-you? route. It would only end up in a slanging match.

He went into the kitchen and poured himself a glass of water. She stood in the doorway, watching him, eager to plunge into battle.

'It's all gone a bit wrong, hasn't it?' said Tony.

'What do you mean?'

'You don't want to be with me any more, do you?'

The aggression seemed to leak out of her. Her shoulders slumped. Maybe with relief. 'I'm sorry, Tony,' she said.

So he hadn't been fooling himself. It was over. He didn't feel angry or upset. Just resigned. He could handle it.

'The thing is,' she said, 'I've met someone else.'

He hadn't seen *that* coming. Maybe he couldn't handle it after all.

Greta was completely whacked. She slumped in an armchair in the sitting room, drifting in and out of sleep. Distantly she was aware of Laurie and Paul talking in the kitchen. She wondered if they were capable of getting themselves supper. For once in her life she didn't care.

Now the room was darker and she was more alert. Her limbs still felt like lead weights and she was too tired even to contemplate stumbling up the stairs to bed. She still wore her Ladies Day outfit, crumpled like a rag. Her hat lay on the sofa, her shoes were beneath the glass-topped coffee table where she'd kicked them. She had no idea how much time had gone by since they'd got home.

'Laurie,' she called but her voice was faint, almost a whisper. 'Laurie!' Louder this time.

He arrived at once.

'Thanks for letting me sleep.'

'How are you feeling? Shall I ring the doctor?'

'No!' Greta's protest was too strident. She corrected herself at once. 'Honestly, Laurie, it's OK. I'm just tired and I've got a headache.'

He didn't look happy. She tried to change the subject. 'Where's Paul?'

'He's meant to be doing his homework. I was just going up to check.'

'I'll stay here for a bit, if that's OK?'

He looked at her closely. She hoped he wasn't going to raise the doctor issue again.

Eventually he said, 'I'll get you some painkillers, shall I?'

'Yes.' Anything to stop him staring at her like that.


Tony leaned on the gate of Lifeline's barn. He'd been there some time, outwardly still, his eyes resting on the horse and his new companion, the pony from Yorkshire. But inside, Tony was in turmoil.

So she'd 'met' someone else? What exactly did that mean? Well, he could guess. When he and Sarah had first run into one another, in the winner's enclosure at York, she'd been celebrating with her then-boyfriend, a Hooray Henry with a share in the winner. The boyfriend had celebrated so hard he'd slipped into an alcoholic stupor by eight that evening and Sarah had spent the night in Tony's hotel room. He'd been the someone else she'd met that night.

The knowledge that it was now his turn to be chucked aside poisoned his thoughts. He could picture Sarah in bed with her new lover. He knew how she'd excite him, how she'd please him, how she'd coax every last drop of desire from his veins – because she used to do the same for him. Used to.

He'd been jealous before, at the end with Monica when she too had found someone else. It had been living hell. He'd tortured himself over his rival, wondering who he was and why she preferred him. Until he'd encountered the man six months later, an affable balding Mr Ordinary with dodgy taste in ties. He resolved to try as hard as he could to take no interest in Sarah's new man.

He was disturbed from his thoughts by the rasp of a wet tongue on his cheek. Lifeline was being friendly.

'Sorry, old feller,' said Tony, patting the colt's muzzle, 'I didn't mean to ignore you.'

He dug into his pocket for a mint. Lifeline snaffled it and pushed into his jacket, hunting for more.

'Recovered your appetite, have you?' He'd bumped into Vicky on the way down and she'd told him the good news. From the moment Norman the pony had arrived Lifeline had been back on his feed. Well, that was one correct decision he'd made at any rate.

'Here, Norman,' he called, 'you like mints, don't you?'

The scruffy grey pony gave him a disdainful look but when Tony held up the green packet he strolled over for his share.

As the pair of them nuzzled into him, their big luminous eyes on his every move and their warm breath in his face, he wondered if it was not safer and more satisfying to put your trust in a horse.

*

'Greta.'

Laurie was back. There was something in his voice, a discordant note she couldn't place. Fatigue enveloped her like a fog.

He pulled up a chair, sat down facing her just a few feet away. There was something in his hand. He held it up in front of her.

'What's this?'

The fog cleared instantly. Illuminating her stupidity.

'I found it in your bedside drawer.'

She thought she'd thrown it away. She opened her mouth but no sound came out. Her wits had deserted her.

'It explains a lot,' he went on, his voice calm but that menacing undertone more to the fore now. 'The sickness, the tiredness, the fact that you're bulging out of your clothes.'

He prodded the little plastic stick into the swell of her left breast.

The little plastic stick with the thin blue line across its centre that indicated she was pregnant.


Sarah changed her mind and put the phone down on the second ring. After this afternoon's scene at Freddy's, now was not the time to throw herself on his mercy – if he even had any. She had no doubt that, in the long term, she could tame him but he wasn't the sort you could rush. He was like a wild dog who needed to be brought to heel.

Her mother and father would be scandalised if they knew she was planning to take up with Freddy Montague. They'd been upset enough when she'd moved in with Tony, a dedicated professional jockey sometimes referred to by journalists as Mr

Clean – not that he made the papers that often. Freddy, on the other hand, was never out of them, usually with a different woman on his arm, frequently having a dig at his rivals or a shot at the racing establishment. And nobody ever called him Mr Clean. There would be many who'd consider her mad to try and change him. But Sarah relished a challenge. The fact that her family wouldn't approve gave the whole affair added spice.

However, there was no doubt she'd got her timing wrong. That business with the trunk from Hong Kong had thrown her. Even if some man from Australia were about to turn up, he could jolly well stay somewhere else. And that's what Freddy would tell him once she'd had a chance to make him see where his best interests lay. In the meantime, she needed to let him stew for a bit. She had no doubt he'd come sniffing around in a day or two, once he realised how much he missed her.

In the meantime, she'd revealed too much of her hand to Tony. But he was a simple proposition compared to Freddy. She was confident she could keep him on hold for another week or so. That should be plenty of time.

Laurie paced the room, a big threatening shadow in the half-light. In all their marriage he'd never laid a finger on Greta. But she knew he was close to it now. And she couldn't blame him.

'Well?' he said.

Of course, it was all wrong. Telling your husband you were pregnant was meant to be a joyous moment. Especially the husband with whom you had tried so hard to have a family. And they did have a family but Paul was not their natural offspring. He'd been adopted – after they'd discovered Laurie could never father a child.

'So, whose is it?'

'Nobody's.'

'What – an immaculate conception? It's the second bloody coming, is it?'

He was closer now, looming over her.

'Nobody you know – nobody who counts.'

'I see. You've been fucking around with people who don't count?'

'Not people. Just one man and it's all over.'

His face was in hers, a mean yellow glint in his eye. She knew he wanted to hit her. She could almost feel the blows. Maybe she'd lose the baby. Maybe that would solve it all.

He turned abruptly and threw a white china vase filled with roses from the garden on to the glass top of the coffee table. The smash echoed around the room. Shards of china and glass flew around them.

In the silence that followed the thought occurred that the vase had been a wedding present from her mother.

Laurie was standing amid the chaos he'd caused, a nick of blood from a flying piece of glass crimson on one cheek.

The door opened and Paul rushed in, his eyes wide with shock.

'What's going on?'

'Just an accident,' Greta heard herself say. 'Your father dropped the vase.'

'Get out,' snarled Laurie.

Paul stared at him in disbelief.

'I'll help you clear up,' he said.

'No!' Laurie roared. 'Are you fucking deaf? Get out *now*.'

The boy vanished.

'Don't take it out on him, Laurie,' Greta pleaded. 'It's not fair.'

'And I suppose you smashing up our family *is* fair? Is that right?'

His voice was cold now. The immediate white-hot need to lash out had gone, replaced by a cold fury.

'When were you going to tell me, Greta? Or did you think I wouldn't notice? Do you think I'm that stupid?'

'I didn't know what to do.'

She put her head in her hands. It throbbed in a steady rhythm but she was anaesthetised to the pain.

'I'll tell you what to do, Greta.' He pulled her hands from her face and bent close again, forcing her once more to meet his gaze. 'You might not care for me but if your home matters – and living here with Paul matters – you will *get rid of it.*'

'I can't do that!' The words were out before she could think. All her life she'd longed for a child, her own child. She couldn't destroy her only chance of that. It was pure instinct speaking.

'I see.' He stood up. 'In that case, Greta, I suggest you find this Mr Nobody and see if he'll have you. Our marriage is over. I'm not bringing up your child by another man.'

Glass and china crunched beneath his feet as he walked to the door. 'Fortunately I know a good divorce lawyer. I'll talk to him in the morning.'

He closed the door quietly behind him.

On his way upstairs Laurie stopped outside Paul's room. He knocked on the door. There was no reply but he went in anyway.

The room was dim but he could see a figure huddled on the bed.

'Paul?' Still no reply but the boy couldn't be asleep. 'I'm sorry, son.'

He sat down on the bed, put his hand tentatively on Paul's shoulder.

'I wasn't angry with you. It's just that . . .' He stopped. He didn't know what to say.

'It's OK, Dad.'

The boy's voice was thick and in the half-light Laurie could see he'd been crying. He put his arms round him and the boy clung on tight. Neither spoke though their thoughts were racing.

It was dark by the time Tony returned. He'd not taken the car to the stables and the walk had cleared his head. He made straight for the kitchen. The emotional disturbance of the last few hours had gripped his stomach and he'd not eaten. But now his hunger was back with a vengeance. He rummaged in the fridge for something not-too-damaging and found ham, tomatoes and wheat crackers. He took grim satisfaction in reflecting that all the other high-fat junk was destined for the rubbish bin once Sarah packed her bags.

She came in wearing a scarlet kimono and sat opposite him.

'I was worried about you.'

He stared at her, noting the scanty nightwear. 'Why?'

'You were gone so long and I thought, well, after what we'd said that you must be really upset.'

He swallowed a mouthful and took a gulp of water. 'I'm pissed off, if you must know. But I'm all right. I've thought it through.'

'And?'

He shrugged. 'We're not married. These things happen. I can't say I'm happy you've fallen for someone else but I'll survive.' He took another bite.

'Oh, Tony.' She put a hand on his arm. 'I've been thinking

110

too. You're such a great guy. It's always been one of my faults, thinking the grass is greener.'

He stopped chewing. 'What are you getting at, Sarah?'

'Well, I thought' – she shifted in her seat, the kimono gaped at the neck – 'we might discuss it in bed.'

He froze.

'We don't have to do anything,' she continued, 'just hold each other. Like we used to.'

Her hand was warm on his skin through the cotton of his shirt. He pulled his arm away and stood up.

'I'm sleeping on the sofa, Sarah. You're on your own.'

He closed the door behind him, leaving her still sitting at the kitchen table, her face white with shock. He'd probably regret his petty triumph but it brought a rare smile to his face just the same.

Neil made a final check on his horses before he went to bed, Lifeline last of all. It tickled him to see the horse and the old pony rubbing along. Norman had only arrived at lunchtime but he seemed like a fixture already. And the change in Lifeline had been remarkable.

'Well, I got that wrong then.' Paul emerged like a ghost out of the dark. 'I gather the pony's done the trick.'

'Seems like it.'

They stood for a moment in silence, watching the animals. Paul had his hands sunk in his pockets, chewing on his lip.

'What you up to then?' said Neil.

'Had to get out of the house. You?'

'Not much.'

'Why aren't you out with the others?'

'Why do you think?' Neil never went out with the other lads.

He didn't like having the mickey taken out of him all night. In a town where all the men were vertically challenged, Neil was the smallest by some way.

Paul turned round and looked out over the stable roofs, the stars pin-cushion bright in the black sky.

'Brilliant night for it,' he said.

'For what?'

Paul grinned, his teeth gleaming in the dark. 'What do you think?'


Freddy was surprised to see Greta on the doorstep. He'd been half expecting Sarah to turn up but this was better, much better.

'Hello, stranger,' he said. 'I thought you'd gone off me.'

She pushed past him into the hall and in the light he saw her cheeks were wet.

'Oh, Freddy,' she cried and fell into his outstretched arms.

He held her gently and stroked her back through the silk of her blouse as she sobbed. He was used to women shedding tears and many had run through the gamut of emotions in his embrace. His technique was the same in all situations: hold the lady close and let her cry her heart out. Once the waterworks were out of the way she'd feel a hundred per cent better. Guaranteed.

For once, as he held the weeping Greta, he felt blameless. Not that guilt was a familiar sentiment but occasionally he had twinges. Not on this occasion, however. His fling with the delicious Mrs Somerville had been very sweet but regrettably short and, for once, he'd been the one who hadn't wanted it to end. He wasn't inclined to look back with romantic nostalgia on past conquests but the two afternoons he'd spent in bed with Greta featured high in his top ten of fantastic fucks. She was older than most of his girlfriends and her marriage was stale. And when she made love to him it was as if she brought all the thwarted passion of those neglected years and made him a present of it. But she'd killed off the relationship before it got out of hand. He wished she hadn't, whatever the consequences. In his book, she was worth six of a woman like Sarah.

She'd stopped shaking now and the tears had slowed. He found a paper tissue in his pocket and she blew her nose. Her face was blotchy and her short blonde hair stuck up in spikes.

'You're lovely,' he murmured and kissed the corner of her mouth.

'No, Freddy,' she said but she let him kiss the other corner, then her full pink lips which trembled beneath his for a moment before she pushed him away. 'We've got to talk.'

'I thought we'd done all that. "We had a wonderful time but my marriage comes first." That's what you said.'

'I know.'

'But maybe you've changed your mind. Is that what you want to talk about?'

She hesitated. Whatever it was, he could see she was having difficulty spitting it out. Well, they'd get there in the end. He didn't mind if they took the long way round.

'Are you still wearing your Ascot stuff?'

'Yes?' She looked bewildered at his change of tack.

'Turn round and let me look.'

'Freddy, I'm a mess.' But she did as she was told.

'You look bloody gorgeous to me,' he said and caught her by the hips, propelling her towards the stairs. 'Up you go.'

'Freddy! I haven't come round here to get laid.'

'Perish the thought,' he said, his hands on her bottom through her skirt, pushing her up the first step.

*

I must be mad, Greta thought as she climbed the stairs. Mad to get involved with him, mad to come here – mad to be doing this. She knew Freddy's reputation with women. But she also knew how he'd been with her, that her rejection of him had been a blow. Not many women, she imagined, had seen his crystal-blue eyes mist with pain as they said goodbye. But would he want her back? More to the point, would he want her when he discovered she was carrying his child?

She was at the top of the stairs now and he was right behind her, one arm around her waist as he urged her forward, through the doorway ahead. He clicked on the light and they were in his bedroom. She'd been there twice before in the daytime – the room seemed smaller at night. The bed was vast. She wondered how many other women he had entertained on it.

'No, Freddy. Let's go back downstairs.'

But his lips were on the back of her neck, at the top of her spine, teasing the nerves gently, making them tingle.

'Stop it, Freddy.' He took no notice. His fingers found the zipper of her skirt and tugged downwards, then pulled the hem of her blouse from her waistband.

She stopped protesting but did nothing to help him as he undressed her. She accepted that he was going to make love to her before she told him about the baby. Maybe that was wrong of her. Maybe she should break the spell right now and blurt out the truth. On the other hand, what real difference would it make? As she stood like a doll, his hands on her breasts, his hot sweet breath on her neck, she knew she had already given in.

'Freddy,' she murmured, 'you could at least draw the curtains.'

He chuckled in her ear.

'That's open country out there. You think we might frighten the owls and the foxes?'

But he was already moving to the window, raising his arms to draw the curtains together.

Greta turned towards the bed, stepping out of her skirt which lay in a ring on the carpet. So she didn't see the moment when Freddy died.

There was a noise, a far-off bang, and a ripping sound as Freddy swayed back, his fingers gripping the material of the curtain.

She turned to see him falling, crumpling on to the carpet, the curtain still in his fist.

'Freddy!' The word came out as a shriek.

She was on her knees beside him in a flash. There was blood on his shirt in the centre of his chest.

'What happened?' she cried.

But she was talking to herself. She looked into those crystal-blue eyes and knew by some terrible gut instinct that there was no one behind them any more.

Just before midnight Mickey parked his hired car off the main road and walked the remaining quarter of a mile to Freddy's cottage. He'd reconnoitred in daylight and knew just where he was going. He figured that an unexpected late-night visit would catch Freddy nicely off-guard.

The night was hot and airless. Not that it bothered Mickey, but wasn't England meant to be cool and fresh? The times he'd been here before he'd been so cold he'd worn an extra layer of clothing.

Lights blazed from Freddy's cottage and, as Mickey

approached, he could hear the soft mutter of voices. The front door was wide open.

He stopped in the shadows, by the garden hedge, and peered into the room. He couldn't see anybody though he spotted the source of the voices – a television was broadcasting to the empty room.

Mickey waited. The open door was a puzzle. Maybe Freddy had gone out for some reason and would be back any moment. In which case, Mickey decided, there would be an unexpected guest waiting for him on his return.

He stepped into the narrow hallway. The cottage wasn't large; downstairs there were just two small rooms and, he could see, a kitchen in the back. He began to look around – no point in wasting time. It didn't take long to see that Jeff Collins's trunk was not tucked away in a corner. Maybe it was upstairs.

Finding the corpse was a shock. Somebody had got to Freddy before he had – who the fuck could that be?

There was no time to worry about it. The dead man – the *recently* dead man, he could tell – added a degree of urgency to the situation.

Mickey pulled a pair of thin rubber gloves from his pocket, the kind a surgeon wears as he takes a scalpel to your flesh, and slipped them on. What had he touched? Nothing so far, he was sure of it.

He gave himself five minutes, tops, to find the Pick Six ticket. He couldn't take longer – it wasn't worth the risk. The last thing he wanted was to be found at the scene of a suspicious death – though that would be pretty funny, considering that this particular death had nothing to do with him.

There were three upstairs rooms, two bedrooms and a bathroom, and no trunk in any of them. Mickey quickly reevaluated the situation. Maybe Freddy had removed the ticket and put it elsewhere.

He found Freddy's wallet in a jacket lying on the front bedroom chair. He flicked through it expertly – no luck. He replaced the wallet exactly as he'd found it and quickly checked out the bedside table. Nothing.

Four minutes were left of his self-imposed deadline. The open front door worried him – maybe someone had gone to fetch help? Without a glance at the dead jockey, Mickey skirted the body and slipped downstairs. He turned off the television so he could hear the sound of approaching footsteps or the murmur of a car engine.

He searched the desk in the back room. The bottom drawer was locked but the key was in the lock. This was his best bet. But it contained just a bundle of cash and some cheque books. He ignored them – they weren't what he was looking for.

Mickey checked the undersides and backs of the drawers without success. He had no expectations now. A single slip of paper could be concealed in many places. Finding it would take time he didn't have.

One minute. He took a quick glance round the kitchen, ignoring the bachelor debris by the sink, peering along shelves and looking into dusty jugs. He'd heard the British kept items of value in teapots but not Freddy, just a couple of mouldering teabags and an inch of scummy brown water.

Mickey was out of time. He turned the television back on and stepped out of the house, leaving the door just as he'd found it. No one would ever know he'd been there.

The velvety darkness swallowed him up.

*

Greta woke in the night to the sound of rain. Next to her, Laurie breathed evenly in his sleep. She found these noises comforting. She felt secure in the cocoon of her bed. Then sleep receded further and the horror of the night before returned in full force.

Was there something she could have done for Freddy? She knew basic first aid. She could have put him in the recovery position and phoned for help. She could have tried CPR, compressing his chest and breathing into his mouth.

She could have done these things but it would have been futile – what was the point in trying to revive a dead man? He'd had no vital signs – she'd checked for those. She'd been utterly bewildered. It was as if Freddy's heart had just exploded. But she'd heard a bang and seen the neat hole in the windowpane. She'd lived in the country all her life and she knew what a gunshot sounded like. She'd seen someone shot before, on a duck shoot, though he, lucky fellow, had survived. She'd known within seconds that a bullet had left Freddy lying lifeless at her feet.

So, to her shame, she'd just abandoned him. She'd tried no emergency first-aid and made no phone call to the ambulance service. The only result would have been to reveal to the world that she'd been about to climb into Freddy's bed. So she'd gathered up her clothes and fled. Who would blame her for that?

Who wouldn't?

No one must ever find out.

Greta stared into the half-light as wide awake as she had ever been in her life.

Overnight Sarah had formulated two plans. She got up early and packed a hold-all with her essentials – that was for Plan B, in which she would make a tactical retreat to London. She still nurtured hopes for Plan A, however, which entailed a rapprochement of sorts with Tony until she was sure of Freddy.

She found Tony downstairs, opening the post.

'How was the sofa?'

He looked at her suspiciously then took her at face value. 'Fine. I could have slept anywhere.'

'I'm sorry about last night.'

'At least we cleared the air.' He picked up a brown envelope. 'So when are you off?'

'I've been thinking. About what we have together. Maybe this is just a bad spell.'

'I thought you said you'd met someone else?'

He tore open the envelope.

'Tony, it's not what you think . . .' But her carefully prepared speech froze in her mouth as she saw the roll of banknotes fall into his hand. 'What's that?'

'I don't know.'

He took the notes out of the rubber band and quickly shuffled through them as she watched.

'My God,' she said. 'There must be thousands there.'

She picked up the yellow post-it note which had become detached from the bundle and read 'You rode a great race for the King George'. Her stomach turned over. She looked at Tony through new eyes.

'It's a bribe, isn't it?'

'Sarah, this isn't what it looks like.' He sounded sincere, but so what? She suddenly felt dirty.

'I don't believe this, Tony. You turn down a small fortune for your basketcase of a horse but you'll accept a grubby little bung like this?'

'I don't know anything about this money,' he protested.

'That's your story, Tony. But in answer to your question – I'm moving out right now.'

She collected her hold-all from the bedroom and stalked to her car. It was Plan B after all.

Kate was enduring a frantic morning. Not only had Freddy failed to turn up and ride out but a couple of lads had cried off sick – hungover was Vicky's estimate – which had thrown the work schedule. Then there was a scare about Big Dee who'd become cast in his box and damaged his hip, so they'd had to call out the vet. And the usual barrage of owners had rung in to find out when their horses were going to run and, in the case of the more optimistic ones, when they were going to win.

What's more, she had a runner that afternoon at Ascot, Blue Mountain, who was inclined to put his head in the air. She needed to talk to Freddy and find out whether he wanted a neck strap on the horse – it might help take the weight off his mouth. But she couldn't raise her brother on the phone, his mobile was off and his answerphone was on – usually a sign he had overslept.

When she spotted Neil returning from the gallops she sent him down the lane to get Freddy out of bed and to ring in straightaway. Neil hadn't looked happy about it as she'd explained where the spare key was hidden. Too bad.

Now, as Kate discussed the injured horse with the vet, keeping an eye open for the horse box that was due to pick up Blue Mountain, she heard the sound of Neil shouting for her.

For an instant she'd forgotten about his errand.

He ran towards her, his face contorted with emotion.

'Whatever's the matter, Neil?' she cried.

Then he told her.

# PART TWO

PART TWO

# Chapter Five

Despite the excellence of the cuisine in the restaurant on the Île St Louis, Mickey Lee was not enjoying his meal with Mr Shen – but then he rarely enjoyed any meal.

He'd relished his food once – before the accident. He could remember the delight of a simple bowl of chilli noodles – the hot blast of spices in his nostrils as well as his throat, the breeze-borne scent of fresh sardines barbecued on a beach and the anticipatory aroma of a thick steak sizzling under the grill. He still ate these things but somehow they turned to pap in his mouth and nowadays meals were simply a refuelling operation.

In the same way, he no longer drank wine. Years ago he'd hankered after fine vintages and fancied himself a budding connoisseur. Not that he'd been able to afford good wine in those days but he'd started to develop his palate, appreciating colour and texture, refining his 'nose'. He'd given that up now. It was hard to refine your nose when it was fashioned out of a metal plate.

Mickey pushed away his half-eaten entrecôte and watched Mr Shen as he crunched and sucked his way through a vast plate of *fruits de mer*. He sat in silence. There would be no further conversation until his employer was finished and Mickey knew better than to rush him. His mind turned to those pleasures he could still enjoy despite his handicap – the other oral pleasures.

After taking leave of the rapidly cooling corpse of Freddy Montague, he'd spent ten days in Paris trawling the bars and night clubs, sampling the Parisian whores. It had been wild, exhausting and very expensive. But these days Mickey had the money and he had long ago lost any prejudices about buying a woman's favour. It was easier that way. It also ensured he got what he wanted, even if it lacked challenge. Sometimes, with women, Mickey liked a challenge.

Mr Shen laid down the last splintered crab claw and pulled a shred of flesh from his back teeth. On the instant, a waiter appeared to whisk away the debris and proffer a fingerbowl and hot towels. Mickey waited impatiently while the other man groomed himself with painstaking care. The waiter offered the dessert menu but they ordered coffee instead.

Few people in the world could make Mickey nervous but Mr Shen was one of them. The day after Freddy's murder, Mickey had called Hong Kong and been instructed to remain in Europe. And now Mr Shen had flown in from the Far East, apparently just for this meeting. No wonder Mickey was apprehensive.

He had already recounted the circumstances of his encounters with Jeff and Freddy. Then the food had arrived and business had been set aside – temporarily.

'It's unfortunate,' said Mr Shen at length, 'that neither of the two gentlemen are still with us.'

Mickey nodded. 'I might have been a little premature with Jeff. But as far as Freddy's concerned –'

'Yes?' There was something in the way he said it, his small curranty eyes staring at Mickey without blinking.

'You don't think that I . . .?'

Mr Shen's moon face split into a grin. 'No, Mickey. I don't

think you shot Freddy from outside his house and put the ticket in your own pocket.'

Well, that was a relief.

'But you think someone else killed him for it?'

Mr Shen shrugged. 'To tell you the truth, I am not so concerned about the Pick Six any more. Those responsible for the theft have been punished. Maybe that is the best I can hope for.'

Mickey nodded, taking care not to reveal his delight. The whole business had turned into a can of worms and he couldn't wait to get free of it.

'On the other hand,' Mr Shen continued, 'Freddy Montague was useful to me and I must replace him. How would you like to return to England for a while?'

Mickey thought for a moment.

'I was planning on going back to HK. I've been letting a few things slide.' This was true. His side-interests – his cousin's real-estate firm and the video rentals – had not received his attention for months.

Mr Shen brushed this aside. 'Let Rupert take care of it.' He was the cousin.

Mickey considered. He didn't want to go to England. 'I've been away from home too long,' he said finally.

Mr Shen sipped his tea, impassive. 'Do you remember a young lady called Amy Ho?'

Mickey's stomach clenched. 'No.'

'A very attractive girl, just turned nineteen. She's studying law but she helps out occasionally in the family restaurant in Kowloon. Her father came to see me.'

'She's a pushy little bitch. We had an argument.'

Mr Shen ignored him. 'She says you took her out, then

drugged and raped her. I believe they call it date-rape, don't they?'

'She's lying.' He didn't sound convincing, even to himself.

'Mickey, we have a long association. You have done difficult things for me and I value that. I can sort this matter out. Maybe the family will accept help with her college fees. A small clothes allowance.'

Mickey was annoyed. 'You don't have to do that. I can pay.'

'They would go to the police rather than take your money. They might take mine though. And a guarantee you won't be returning to Hong Kong.'

'What!'

He knocked his cup over in his agitation. The black lake of coffee was still sinking into the white linen of the cloth when the waiter appeared out of thin air to set the table to rights. It gave Mickey a moment or two to calm down.

'Wait a couple of months. The storm will blow over. In the meantime you can perform a task for me in England. I ask you as a friend as well as your chief.'

The cunning old bastard. He had Mickey both coming and going.

'In that case,' he said, inclining his head and giving in with as much grace as he could muster, 'it will be my pleasure.'

If Mr Shen was gratified he did not show it. He placed a briefcase on the table.

'In here you will find some papers on matters I was discussing with Freddy Montague. He was closely involved with my plans for England. For the present, that means a horse called Cold Call.'

'I know Cold Call.' Mickey remembered the skinny black colt from two years ago, when he'd done a stint at Mr Shen's yard in Kentucky. The horse had never been well. Mickey knew he'd missed his entire three-year-old season with a strained tendon. 'I didn't think he was racing.'

'He hasn't run yet, but he will. I sent him to a new trainer in England.'

Mickey was sceptical. 'Who?'

Mr Shen opened the briefcase and removed a newspaper cutting.

'Kate Montague,' he explained, laying the paper in front of Mickey. A half-page picture showed a sombre group of people dressed for a funeral above a headline that read: A SISTER'S FAREWELL. In the centre stood a woman in a black suit, clutching a bouquet of white lilies. Mr Shen pointed to her. 'Freddy's sister.'

Mickey looked closely at her face, at the wide-set eyes and full lips, the anguish and sorrow etched there only enhancing her appeal. Suddenly he felt more enthusiastic about the trip to England. He'd heard about Freddy's sister but he didn't know she was a beauty.

'She doesn't look like a trainer,' he said

Mr Shen chuckled. 'According to Freddy she's a miracle-worker. Her speciality is healing the sick. She can get them ready without a race.'

'Like Cold Call?'

'That's for you to decide. If the horse has improved as much as Freddy has been telling me then maybe we can do business.'

'So you want me to go and check him out?'

Mr Shen nodded. 'I have other plans for Miss Montague's yard. Maybe it's not a bad thing Freddy's out of the way. I'm sure you can get things done just as effectively.'

Mickey's eye returned to the picture of Kate. She looked like a real challenge. Things could be a lot worse.

'So I'll forget about the Pick Six ticket?' he said.

'Find it and we'll go fifty-fifty.'

Mickey was shocked. His employer was not known for spontaneous acts of generosity.

Mr Shen held out his hand to seal the bargain.

'Thank you,' said Mickey as he accepted the handshake.

For a senior citizen, Mr Shen's grip was surprisingly firm. As he hung on to Mickey's hand, he said, 'I don't suppose Freddy's murder has anything to do with his association with me, but . . .'

'Yes?'

'I wouldn't stand in front of any lighted windows, if I were you.'

Mr Shen released his hand and began to laugh. Mickey smiled politely but, to be honest, he didn't find it all that funny.

Kate knew some people thought her a cool customer. The fact was she had pretty good control over her feelings – which didn't mean she didn't have any. Right now she didn't care what others thought about her. She was determined today, ten days after the discovery of her brother's body, to focus only on the yard. Part of her was numb, frozen in shock, and she feared that when the thaw set in the tears would flow for ever. So she'd work now, while she could.

Even though there'd been a tragedy there were still horses to look after, races to run, other people's business to take care of. Up to now, Vicky had insisted Kate stayed out of the yard but today she was having none of it. What was the point? At the house, on her own, there was only time to brood. Kate had grown up in that house as one of a family of four. Now she was the only one left.

So far she'd been up on the gallops to look over the horses, quizzed her work riders on their progress and busied herself in the office. They'd been uneasy with her at first, treating her as if she was a stranger and they had to be on their best behaviour.

'Hey,' she'd said to Josh as he nodded to her and tried to walk past without another word. 'What do you expect me to do? I've got a business to run.'

So let them call her a cold fish, she didn't care. But, please God, don't let any of them start saying how sorry they were. Their sympathy was unbearable.

After a while the atmosphere improved and she felt more like her normal self. She laughed at a few jokes. The lads stopped making obvious allowances. And she managed to block out the black cloud of poor Freddy's death with the hundred and one everyday things that claimed her attention.

Then the police turned up and the black cloud settled on her once again.

The past week had been exciting for Annie James. She and Hunter had been attached to the enquiry into Freddy Montague's murder at the request of the Senior Investigating Officer, Detective Chief Inspector Ronald Orchard. Hunter said it was because they'd been handling the Jonno Simpson shooting but Annie was convinced Jack Fletcher had something to do with it. The DI had not forgotten her father had once been a trainer. In front of her, he'd complimented Orchard on adding someone with racing know-how to the team.

Not that there had been much chance for Annie to demonstrate whatever inside knowledge she might possess. So far it had been legwork all the way, much of it knocking on doors throughout Upper Lambourn, asking people if they could remember the night Freddy had died. *Did you notice anything out of the ordinary? Did you see anybody acting suspiciously? Did you observe any strange vehicles?*

It didn't help that there were no other houses within two hundred yards of Freddy's cottage and they were on the main road at the end of the lane. There'd been plenty of car movement but that was no surprise – the road was always busy. No one had seen any hooded strangers with rifles or suspiciously parked vehicles. Two reports mentioned a possible car backfire some time around eleven-thirty p.m. – which tied in with the estimated time of Freddy's death. That was it, however. Basically, the house-to-house had been a dead end.

So, too, had been the search for the murder weapon. Annie and a dozen uniformed bods had spent three days plodding through the field opposite the cottage and poking through the woods at the top of the rise. She had never been involved in a murder investigation before and at first it had been a bit of a thrill to think she was hunting for clues that might bring a murderer to justice. But after she'd been caught in a couple of downpours and bitten by horseflies the thrill had been replaced by tedium. Not to mention a certain resentment that she was the only detective amongst the foot soldiers in the field. She was the only female CID officer, too, which of course was entirely coincidental.

At least tramping the hillside in front of the cottage had given her a good insight into the crime itself. They'd located the spot from which the fatal shot has been fired, just on the fringe of the woods at the top of the field. A path ran the other side of a well-preserved four-barred metal fence. Directly opposite the cottage, a marksman with a suitable weapon could look across the meadow and into Freddy's bedroom on the first floor. The slight elevation would give him a perfect view of anyone standing in the window, especially at night with the lights on. Mind you, Annie thought, it was still a heck of a shot. 'A touch of the Lee Harvey Oswalds,' said Hunter when she'd expressed her opinion. 'I assume you know who I'm talking about,' he'd added, just in case she thought he was being unnecessarily chummy.

Annie had also managed to look around Freddy's cottage and stand in the spot where he'd been hit. That had been pretty spooky. She'd been accompanied by Russell, a Scene of Crime Officer on a final trawl, who kept an eye on her for form's sake. Not that there was much she could disrupt by that stage, anything of interest having been sent off for analysis.

Russell reckoned there'd been enough evidence of female visitors to keep Forensics busy for months.

'Like this,' he'd said, picking a long curling copper-coloured hair from the carpet near the skirting board. 'This woman left her calling-card all over.'

Annie held the hair up to the light in the window; it glinted in her fingers.

'Pretty,' she said.

'He only went out with real crackers, didn't he?' said Russell. 'He had his reputation to consider.'

Annie had been miffed to discover that, while she was tied up with the search team, Hunter had had another tilt at Jonno Simpson, taking along Jim Henderson in her place. She'd not been surprised when the pair of them had got nothing out of the lad, who was now recovering at his fiancée's house. Orchard had looked pretty miffed too, which wasn't surprising. Two jockeys shot within forty-eight hours couldn't be a coincidence.

Everyone on the investigation was already convinced that whoever had put Jonno in hospital, had gone one step further with Freddy and put him in his grave. Everyone except Annie, that is. She was trying hard to keep an open mind.

One reason for that was Kate Montague. If the murder was as a result of Freddy being knee-deep in racing corruption where did that leave his sister? The newspapers were already rife with speculation and Freddy's reputation was hardly spotless. Despite the sympathy that existed for Kate, Freddy was a legitimate target in the eyes of the tabloids. Not to mention a dead one and therefore beyond the protection of the libel laws. Unfortunately for his sister, quite apart from the pain it caused her, some of the mud flying around was bound to stick to her and her business.

The strain was evident in Kate's eyes as Annie faced her across the desk in the trainer's office. At last Annie now had a task close to the heart of the investigation – to sit in on the interview about to be conducted by the aggressive presence at her side. So far Kate had been treated with kid gloves but time was passing and Orchard was becoming anxious. He'd decided to send in the hounds. One hound to be precise – DS Keith Hunter.

'Can we make this quick, please?' Kate tried to keep the apprehension out of her voice. The sudden arrival of two police officers she had not met before was unnerving. 'I've got a bit of catching up to do here.'

The female with unruly carroty hair said, 'You've got a runner in the Northumberland Plate, haven't you?'

Kate was surprised. 'That's right. Last Ditch.'

'Is it worth a flutter?' The girl sounded genuinely interested.

'Don't go mad. He's not likely to win.'

The redhead grinned. She had treacle-brown eyes and freckles.

The other one broke his silence. 'What exactly does that mean, Miss Montague?' There was no warmth in his tone.

He was waiting for her answer.

'It means he's likely to be outclassed. There are some highly ranked runners in the field.'

'You're referring to the official ratings?'

'They're a good indicator. Last Ditch is rated seventy-five. He'll be up against horses of over a hundred.'

The fluorescent light in the office bounced off the officer's high-domed forehead and the bridge of his pencil-sharp nose. It seemed he wanted to pursue this. 'I take it this race is a handicap?'

'Yes.'

'In which case, as I understand it, the weights are adjusted to slow good horses down so second-raters like yours can catch up. Therefore, surely, every horse has an equal chance and you can't say with any certainty that your horse won't win?'

Kate felt the stirrings of irritation. She had no idea where this was going and she'd specifically asked them not to waste her time. 'You obviously don't follow the sport, officer.'

'I have recently acquired a professional interest, Miss Montague. And from what I can see, sport hasn't got much to do with it. Underprepare the horse or overtrain it before the race, go off too fast or hold it back till too late, hit it too hard or don't hit it at all. It seems to me there are many, many ways to speed the gee-gees up. Or slow them down.'

Kate's irritation was growing into anger. A thought occurred that this might be his intention. 'What point are you making?'

He smiled, annoying her further – she couldn't help it. 'Simply that where billions change hands each year on the efforts of a few dumb animals, there's going to be widespread corruption and violence. It's no surprise to me that two jockeys have been assaulted recently. The criminal fraternity has no recourse to the law – their justice is more summary. As in your brother's case.'

Kate could hardly believe what she was hearing. 'You're saying my brother was corrupt?'

The policeman said nothing, just grinned his smug grin. She wanted to put her fist through it.

'Why are you saying these things? You're meant to be catching my brother's killer not insulting his memory.' She stood up abruptly, knocking a coffee cup off the desk to smash on the stone-flagged floor. 'I want you to go – *now*.'

The detective looked surprised by her reaction. The female officer sprang to clear up the mess on the floor, no doubt to cover her embarrassment.

'Just go,' Kate repeated. The wave of anger had broken, it would soon be followed by tears, she could feel them welling inside. She fought them back, reaching for the box of paper tissues on the table. '*Please.*'

The male officer remained seated. 'Perhaps you'd feel more comfortable discussing this down at the station?' he said.

Kate began to tremble. The lads ought to see her now, she thought as she blinked back the water from her eyes.

'Why don't we leave it for now, Sarge?' said the female. 'Give Miss Montague a few days.'

Kate blew her nose and came to a decision. 'No. Let's get it over with,' she said.

The man smiled at her wolfishly. She felt limp, beaten.

He turned to the woman. 'Perhaps Annie could rustle us up a cup of tea?'

Kate nodded. Anything, just to get these two out of her yard.

Just outside the office, tucked in the corner, Annie found a sink. On the small fridge next to it stood an electric kettle and other tea-making equipment. She quickly put the kettle on and turned her attention to what really interested her – the horses.

She'd never been in one of these American barns before, with its four rows of breezeblock horse stalls on either side of two wide corridors running the length of the building. The roof was high enough to prevent claustrophobia, with see-through panels on either side of the ridge. The effect was of light and air. Underfoot it was spotless, still damp in places from a recent hose-down. The horses had more room than in an old-fashioned stall. The lucky ones, along the walls of the barn, could look out of a window on to the outside world. The others had to content themselves with gazing at their comrades through the bars of their stalls.

Annie was impressed. This was a smart and professional operation, a far cry from the ramshackle set-up of her father's which she remembered with fierce nostalgia from her youth. She walked down the first row, inspecting with longing the sleek and handsome creatures within. She'd not lived with horses for years. She missed them.

A muttering from the far corner caught her attention. She turned away from the handsome bay she'd been admiring and walked further down the row. In the far pen a child was rubbing down a compact black horse and talking to him gently as he did so. For a moment she felt as if she were intruding, the lad was talking so intimately to the horse and the animal was clearly enjoying the attention. As she caught the timbre of the voice Annie realised this was no child but a jockey-sized youth. She glimpsed his face from the side and recognised him from a photo in the incident room: Neil Kelly. He was the one who'd discovered Freddy's body. Because of that, and also because of a father with some serious form, he'd been the subject of some interest at the station.

'What a gorgeous horse,' she said, announcing her presence.

Neil jerked round in surprise. She gave him her biggest smile. 'Sorry to make you jump.'

''S OK,' he mumbled.

'What's his name?'

'Cold Call. He's a colt by Arctic Chart.' The boy wouldn't look her in the eye. The horse was eager for her attention, however. He pushed his head through the aperture in the gate and allowed her to stroke his muzzle.

'He's a friendly fellow, isn't he?'

The boy shot her a shy grin and looked quickly away, grunting something that might have been 'Yes'.

'I'm Annie.' She stuck out her hand, a tomboyish gesture she often used to good effect. Annie liked to get to grips with people. The boy's hand disappeared into her strong grasp.

'Neil,' he replied.

'Are you a jockey?'

'Apprentice.'

'Got any rides coming up?'

He was looking openly at her now, blushing. 'Yeah. One or two. Now Freddy's not . . . I mean . . . now we're a bit . . .' He stopped, not wanting to put his foot in it. 'Are you an owner?' he said.

'No, wish I was.' Time to come clean. 'I'm a policewoman.' His face was a picture.

'Are you acquainted with many bookmakers, Miss Montague?'

'Not really.'

Kate looked past her inquisitor's ear, out through the internal window into the stable area. She could see Big Dee, the horse nearest to the office, peering out of his stall. She wondered how his hip was healing. She'd check on it once this ordeal was over.

'How about your brother – was he pally with the bookies?'

'Jockeys aren't allowed to bet.'

The policeman – Hunter, she now remembered – smirked. 'That's not what I'm asking. I mean, did he socialise with the bookmaking fraternity?'

'Racing's a very sociable business. Everyone knows everyone.'

'So you won't be surprised to hear that your brother was seen in the company of a bookie called Herbert Gibbs two days before he died?'

'No.'

'They were seen together in a casino in London.'

'Freddy liked casinos,' she murmured softly.

'Mr Mitchell was observed passing gambling chips to your brother.'

Kate shrugged. 'I'm sure it was perfectly innocent.'

Hunter smirked again. 'How do you account for the money we found in your brother's cottage?'

The police had discovered just over eight thousand pounds in cash in a drawer in Freddy's desk. They'd given Kate an official receipt for it.

'Jockeys often have a lot of cash. They get presents from

owners if they're successful on their horses.'

'Is that so?' Hunter looked sceptical. 'I must be in the wrong line of work.'

'I don't think so, officer. I'd say bullying the bereaved suits you down to the ground.'

Hunter's brow furrowed and he opened his mouth to speak but was cut off by the ringing of the phone on her desk.

Kate snatched it up with relief.

'You're the one who found Freddy Montague, aren't you?'

'Yeah.' Neil looked petrified. Annie knew he'd been thoroughly interviewed on the subject. She felt a twinge of remorse at raising it again but she couldn't resist.

'Poor you. It must have been a heck of a shock.'

The boy nodded.

'Was he a good friend of yours?' Annie was just trying to establish a bond of sympathy. To her surprise, Neil's reply was uncompromising.

'You must be bloody joking!'

'Really?' Get him talking, that was the idea. He'd said very little in his statement.

'Freddy was a great bloke if he reckoned you could do him any good but he was a right sod to me. I've slaved over this horse here for him and all I've ever got is a kick up the arse.'

'So he wasn't popular?'

'Not with the lads. You won't tell Miss Montague I said that, will you?'

She shook her head. 'I promise.' He looked so small and pathetic standing there, Annie felt like giving him a hug – except that would have petrified him even more.

'Tell me, Neil – did Freddy have a girlfriend?'

The boy laughed. 'Don't you read the papers? He had hundreds.'

'I mean someone special. Maybe someone with long red hair.'

Neil's laughter shut off like a tap. He turned away. 'No.'

Annie was feeling mischievous. 'How about you? Have you got a girlfriend?' But she had obviously pushed it too far for Neil had turned his attention back to Cold Call, resuming his rub down with vigour.

'Sorry, miss,' he muttered without looking at her, 'I've got to get on.'

Kate was surprised to hear a precise, ageless voice announce himself on the line.

'Hello, Mr Shen,' she replied. She had never spoken to Bernard Shen before. All her dealings with him had been through Freddy, or by letter or fax.

'I wish to offer my sympathies, Miss Montague. I was very fond of your brother.'

Kate murmured her thanks while speculating on the real purpose of this call. She'd already received a handwritten letter of condolence from Mr Shen. Surely he wasn't about to take Cold Call away from her and place him with another trainer?

'Cold Call is working really well at last, Mr Shen,' she said quickly. 'I know it's been a long haul but he's ready to race now.'

'I'm happy I put him in your care.'

Kate breathed a small sigh of relief.

'You will shortly be hearing from an associate of mine,' Shen continued. 'Mickey Lee has agreed to represent my racing interests in England.'

'I see.' So this was why he was phoning. 'We need to find a race for Cold Call, Mr Shen.'

'Talk to Mickey. He speaks for me in everything.' And he rang off abruptly.

'Problems?'

Hunter's query took Kate off guard, she'd forgotten about the interview.

'One of my owners,' she replied.

'I imagine they're always trouble.'

Kate looked at him in surprise. He looked positively affable and she wondered what had brought about his change in mood.

At that moment the policewoman bustled in with the tea.

'About time too,' said Hunter. 'We've almost finished.'

Kate took her mug with relief. That was the best news she'd heard all morning.

'Though maybe,' he added, 'while we drink our tea, Miss Montague could give us a list of her current owners.'

Kate glared at him. 'What for?'

'Just so we can get a complete picture.'

'I don't want you upsetting my owners.'

'We'll treat them like bone china, I guarantee it.'

Kate was still not convinced.

Hunter added, 'You do want us to catch your brother's killer, don't you, Miss Montague?'

She turned reluctantly to the computer and began to do his bidding.

The incident room had been set up directly above the canteen in the Farley Road police station. Which ensured that forever afterwards the smell of a bacon sandwich would trigger off in Annie's mind the details of Freddy Montague's murder.

It wasn't a large space and it was crammed with desks, phones and computer terminals. On the wall were blown-up maps of Lambourn and similarly enlarged aerial photographs of Kate's yard, with Freddy's cottage and the location of the shooting clearly marked.

So far, Annie thought, the investigation was stalled on the grid with everybody running round trying to get the damn thing on the road. The first stumbling block was the absence of a murder weapon. To date, extensive searches of the fields and roadside ditches had failed to yield anything more threatening than a bust umbrella. Most likely, the killer had taken the gun away with him and disposed of it elsewhere.

At least they had the bullet, which had passed straight through Freddy's chest and lodged in the plaster of the bedroom wall. So they knew the kind of weapon they were looking for – a .22 rifle. A couple of officers had been detailed to conduct an inspection of all licensed .22s in the area.

The bullet was by far the most significant piece of physical evidence they possessed. Officers had examined every blade of grass on the spot where the shot had been fired but had discovered nothing of interest. The path along the edge of the wood was popular with dog walkers so the turf was well worn. By way of incriminating clues they'd found a few ancient cigarette butts, two Walkers crisp packets (salt and vinegar) and plenty of dog turds. They'd kept the butts and the packets and left the turds where they lay.

The SOCO team who had arrived at Freddy's cottage had at first been excited by the clear tyre prints left by a vehicle on the lay-by opposite the cottage. Though it seemed unlikely that a killer would park directly outside his victim's home and then walk a hundred yards up a field to shoot him, the marks obviously bore investigating. Then some bright spark pointed out that the dry spell had broken in the early hours of Friday, the day the body had been discovered, which meant that the vehicle must have left its muddy tyre print some hours after the crime had been committed. Possibly someone had dropped by to see Freddy early on Friday morning and, getting no answer, had driven off again.

Alternatively, maybe the driver had simply pulled over to let another car pass – or stopped for some other, unconnected reason. Since Freddy's lane was used principally as a back route to Beechwood, the police had spent a lot of time quizzing the yard's workers about traffic movements that morning – without success. Nobody remembered anything at all helpful. As for the tyre print itself, it came from a newish set of common-or-garden Firestones. Its precise origin, together with that of the car's driver, was one of the mysteries of the investigation.

The forensic examination inside the house had yielded plenty of material, as the SOCO investigator Russell had already indicated to Annie. Evidently Freddy had entertained on a regular basis and cleaned with no regularity at all. They discovered fingerprints and stray hairs all over the place; and rogue items, such as a single earring, a plum-coloured lipstick and a pair of dusty tights balled up behind the sofa, where they had doubtless been since the winter.

Most of the dead jockey's visitors appeared to have been women, though his male visitors had included Laurie Somerville and a couple of jockey pals from a neighbouring yard. Of the 'female spoor', as Hunter put it, not all of the hairs and prints had been identified. They'd been unofficially divided into 'non-combatants' – women who had innocuous reasons for visiting, including Kate, Laurie's wife, Greta, and Vicky, the head lad –

and 'live ones': Colette, a stable girl from Limerick; Irene, a trainee vet at the equine hospital; and Vanessa, the manager of a French restaurant in Swindon. All of these people had been interviewed and asked to account for their presence in the cottage – which they had done, sometimes in more detail than was strictly required. Hunter had halted Colette in full lyrical flow as she had recounted a night of cheerful debauchery the previous month.

This left on the active list at least three more unidentified females whose hair had been found in Freddy's bedroom. Among these was the owner of the long copper-coloured hairs which Russell had brought to Annie's attention.

She was intrigued by these mystery women in Freddy's life. She cheerfully accepted that her interest was partly prurience, the kind that boosted the circulation of the tabloids as they ran daily kiss-'n'-tell stories on the dead jockey. Although it was more than likely, given the distance from which he had been shot, that the murderer had never entered the cottage, Annie couldn't help wondering whether Freddy's all-action personal life might not have a bearing on his death. If she were running things, she'd have concentrated her efforts on identifying these women.

But she wasn't running things. DCI Orchard was in charge and he had a different agenda. As Annie and Hunter entered the incident room on their return from interviewing Kate, he was standing in front of the aerial enlargement, his hands on his broad hips, his bull-like neck thrust forward. He glowered at them, his big pink face knitted into a scowl. Annie would have been terrified of him if he hadn't reminded her so much of a little boy on the verge of a tantrum. She wondered how he had enjoyed such a successful career in the service when he appeared incapable of concealing his emotions. Right now, she could tell, he was in a filthy mood.

'How's it going, guv?' asked Hunter.

'It's not,' Orchard replied. 'I'm being given the run-around by the bleeding Jockey Club. What a shower, I ask you.'

Annie had heard this gripe before. After Freddy's murder, a Jockey Club spokesman had been widely quoted on the subject of 'malign influences infiltrating the Sport of Kings' and had urged the authorities to 'save horseracing as we know it'. In Orchard's opinion, this was equivalent to a drunk waking up to discover vomit on his carpet and blaming someone else. 'I wouldn't care,' he'd announced to the room at large, 'if only they didn't expect us coppers to clean up the mess.'

'What's up now?' said Hunter.

'I've just been on the blower to their so-called Security Department. The snooty buggers won't give me what I'm after until it's been hand-stamped by royalty.' He stuck his hands in his pockets. 'How did you get on?'

'Well . . .'

The glower on Orchard's face was instantly replaced by curiosity. 'Have you got something, Keith?'

Hunter cocked his head towards the door. 'Can I have a word in private?'

Orchard nodded. 'Come into my office.' He headed for the door. 'You, too, Annie,' he added without looking back.

She followed them into the windowless room across the corridor, intrigued. Hunter had told her nothing on the journey back.

'Kate Montague won't admit her brother was on the take,' the DS began.

'Maybe he wasn't.' The remark was out before Annie could stop it.

Hunter shot Orchard a look that plainly said, 'You wanted her in on this.' Orchard grinned and said mildly, 'And pigs might fly, my dear,' which drew a patronising grin from the other man. Annie forced a smile to her lips. The pair of them made her sick.

'While I was in her office she took a phone call from one of the owners.' Hunter took a folded sheet of A4 from his pocket. Annie recognised it as the list of names Kate had reluctantly created on her computer.

Hunter handed the paper to Orchard. 'Guess which owner.'

Orchard scanned the list eagerly. Then the excitement faded from his bright beady eyes. 'I don't like guessing games, Keith.'

Hunter was unfazed. 'This gentleman here' – he tapped a name halfway down the list – 'is the acceptable face of the Triads in Hong Kong. The lot who control the heroin trade in Southeast Asia. Bernard Shen's got legit businesses in HK and in Australia, the US and Canada. Chains of restaurants, car-hire companies, property development, that sort of thing. He started moving into Soho when I was in the Met. There was a certain amount of argy-bargy because some other Mr Big didn't like it. Shen wasn't involved personally, of course.'

'I've heard of him too,' said Annie, undeterred by the failure of her last intervention. 'Mr Shen's mad about horseracing. He's got stud farms in Kentucky and Melbourne. He's a big owner overseas. I didn't know he raced here, though.'

Orchard was looking enthusiastic again. 'So tell me about this phone call.'

Hunter nodded. 'I didn't gather much. Condolences about Freddy, that kind of thing. Sounds like Shen's sending over some character to talk to her about a horse.' He referred to his notebook. 'Cold Call.'

Annie butted in. 'He's lovely. A black four-year-old.'

Orchard beamed. 'What a pair you make. The DS unearths a connection to an international racketeer and the DC interviews his horse.'

Annie was stung. 'Actually, guv, I interviewed Neil Kelly, the lad who found Freddy's body. He said Freddy had a special interest in Cold Call and worked him regularly. He must have been down to ride him.'

Orchard tapped his fingers on the desk top. 'Freddy worked in Hong Kong last winter, didn't he? That must be the connection.'

'Maybe Shen was using Freddy as his way into British racing and someone didn't like it. So bang goes Freddy,' said Hunter.

The two men grinned. Like they'd suddenly solved the case. Annie was irritated.

'But what about the gun?' she said. 'A marksman with a .22 is a funny way to kill someone.'

This was old ground. The peculiarity of the method had been endlessly debated in the days following the murder.

Orchard scratched his jowls. 'Thanks for reminding us.'

'I've been thinking,' Hunter said. 'Suppose the shot through the window wasn't meant to kill him, just to frighten him off.'

Orchard liked that. 'Could be. Let's see what else we can find out about your Mr Shen.'

'But what about the other angle, guv?' Annie said. 'Freddy's personal life.'

Orchard sighed. 'What about it?'

'We still haven't found the missing girlfriends.'

Orchard squinted at her. 'Don't get your hopes up. I agree

we should track down all of lover boy's women but they're just a sideshow. Freddy was bent. I bet you anything you like that's what got him killed.'

Annie nodded meekly. She wasn't confident enough to take the challenge – though she thought about it.

# Chapter Six

The room Laurie used as an office looked out on to the gallops.
On the mornings he did his paperwork, the passage of time
would be marked by the procession of Kate's strings of horses
moving up and down the lane which led to the broad uplands.
This morning, third lot had returned when his eye was caught
by a single horse and rider still up on the skyline, making their
way down towards the yard. As yet they were too far off to
recognise.

Laurie forced his eyes back to the computer screen. He ought
to answer his emails – particularly the latest query from
Marshall – but he couldn't be bothered. He didn't enjoy working
at the keyboard. Perhaps he'd wait till Paul got home from
school and enlist his help.

The door opened and he looked up to see Greta.

'Coffee?'

'Thanks.'

She nodded and disappeared. There'd been an uneasy truce
between them since the drama of last week. Not that they'd
resolved anything. The issue of her pregnancy remained between
them, growing like a cancer in their marriage. To his mind there
was only one way to deal with it but he had not raised it again.
Freddy's murder had called a halt to everything. The day after
their quarrel Greta had been conciliatory and so had he. Their
differences had seemed less significant in the shadow of sudden

death. He'd not carried out his threat to call his lawyer – yet.

Laurie's eyes returned once more to the horseman descending from the gallops. He was closer now but Laurie still couldn't place him, though there was something familiar about the way he rode, a compact figure sitting high and still in the saddle. The tilt of his head reminded Laurie of a jockey he'd once known, years back, in Australia. Someone who'd suffered a horrific accident.

The rider vanished for a moment in a fold in the hillside then reappeared, much closer. Suddenly Laurie recognised the features of Mickey Lee – the man with the metal face. When he'd got out of hospital they'd called him Mickey Tin.

It was like looking at a ghost.

Kate was waiting for Mickey as he rode into the yard and brought Cold Call to a halt.

'What do you think of him?'

Mickey grinned down at her. His expression was scary; one half of his face seemed frozen, without emotion. It was a nasty disfigurement. Kate tried to put it to the back of her mind.

'Good,' he said.

He slipped from the saddle in one easy movement. She took the reins as he dismounted.

Mickey removed his helmet and stepped close to her, hemming her against the bulk of the animal.

'He's better than ever. You've worked a miracle, Miss Montague.'

'Kate,' she said automatically. She didn't like the way his black eyes lingered on her face – and not just her face. There was something intimidating in the way he looked at her. She turned away from him to pat the horse's shoulder. 'I didn't know you'd met Cold Call before.'

'Oh, yes. But he'd broken down last time I saw him. He was a waste of space.'

Kate didn't know how to respond to that. In her book, no horse, however infirm or bad-tempered, could be dismissed so summarily. She swallowed her distaste and said, 'He needs a race. I've got a couple in mind.'

'The Tote Exacta stakes at Sandown,' said Mickey.

'That's a bit ambitious. I thought we'd ease him in gently. There's a possibility at Newbury.'

'No. He runs at Sandown.'

Kate was irritated by the tone as much as the sentiment. 'I really don't think that's a good idea, Mr Lee.'

'Mickey.' He was grinning again, in that strange lop-sided way. And those inquisitive black eyes were still scanning her body, up and down. She folded her arms across her chest.

'He'll be up against it in the Tote. He'll have to carry top weight.'

He put his hand on her shoulder, his grip heavy though the thin cotton of her summer top. 'Kate – what did Mr Shen say to you about me?'

'Not much. He just told me to expect you.'

'And?'

'I can't remember exactly.' He'd taken his hand off her but she could still feel its weight on her skin.

'I believe he said, "Mickey speaks for me in everything." Didn't he?'

Kate remembered now. She nodded.

'So why are we arguing? Cold Call runs at Sandown.'

'If that's what you want.'

151

'It's what Mr Shen wants.' He bowed his head in a strange, formal gesture and said, 'Thank you for your hospitality. You have an excellent yard.' Then he turned towards his hired car.

Kate led Cold Call to his stall for a rub down, relieved to be out of Mickey's presence.

Laurie hailed the squat, powerful figure as he unlocked the door of the car.

'Mickey!'

The man turned at the sound of his name, his face impassive – or was that because Laurie was looking at his bad side, the one with the skin grafts?

Laurie closed on him, as much warmth in his smile as he could muster, his hand extended. 'Do you remember me? We were in Melbourne together with Will Duggan.'

Mickey took his hand and gripped it firmly. 'Of course I remember you, Laurie.' He too was smiling now.

'You were the finest rider I ever saw.' Laurie blurted it out without meaning to.

But it was true – Mickey had been the best. A feather-light bundle of iron nerve and racing instinct who became an extension of the horse beneath him. In one Australian season he'd been a phenomenon – and then he'd suffered his accident. Mickey had changed in many ways since then, Laurie knew. For one thing, the slender youth had bulked up into a solid, well-built man. He wasn't tall but those shoulders were broad and packed with muscle beneath the neat short-sleeved summer shirt.

Mickey accepted the compliment as his due. 'What are you doing here, Laurie?'

'I live here.' He pointed to the house through the trees. 'Come and see.'

*

Tony walked Lifeline towards the horse box. As they neared the ramp the animal slowed.

'Come on, sunshine,' he muttered. 'It's just a big tin can.'

The horse nodded his head and stared at Tony out of his brown golfball of an eye. *A big tin can with an engine, like the one that nearly killed me last time.* Sometimes Tony felt the horse could speak.

He coaxed Lifeline up on to the ramp. His hooves made a hollow thump on the rubber matting. The horse had slowed to a crawl. But he was moving forward into the dim interior, not veering away like the time before. And the time before that. And the countless other occasions over the past few days. Slowly Lifeline was conquering his inner demons.

'You lovely boy,' said Tony, as Lifeline's rear legs stepped clear of the ramp and his whole body entered the box. 'You've done it.' He let the horse eat from the bucket of feed he'd been bribing him with.

He decided against repeating the exercise. Lifeline had had a breakthrough and Tony didn't want to risk a failure that would spoil the achievement. They'd do it all over again tomorrow – maybe he'd be able to raise the ramp next time and close the doors.

It was a slow process, this rebuilding of the horse's confidence, step by step. Why was it, Tony wondered, he was so patient with animals and so intolerant of human beings? Maybe if he'd been more easy-going with Sarah she'd still be with him.

He'd not heard from her since she'd run off a week ago, yet there was a wardrobe half full of her clothes still at his house. Surely that meant she'd be coming back? He'd called her London number and had talked to her mother. She'd been polite but reserved – Sarah didn't want to speak to him for the moment, apparently. Tony had tried again a day later and been told that she was 'away'. Perhaps she was thinking things over and would return the old Sarah, the one who, not so long ago, had told him she wanted to spend the rest of her life with him.

Since she had left, Tony had replayed their time together on an endless loop in his head, analysing the way things had turned out – particularly how they'd turned sour so quickly. He regretted the churlish way he'd behaved when she'd held out the olive branch on their last night. The business with the other man was surely not significant. He'd over-reacted, like he always did. He'd make it up to her.

Tony was well aware of the self-obsessive nature of his thoughts in the light of Freddy's murder. He felt guilty to be gnawing on the hangnail of his loss when Kate was grieving for her dead brother. He wished he'd liked Freddy better so he could feel less of a hypocrite when forced to join in any discussion of his death. It was a terrible thing, all right, for a man to be murdered but what the hell had Freddy got mixed up in? Whatever it was, he had obviously strayed out of his depth.

Tony led Lifeline back to the barn he still shared with Norman the pony. He wasn't in any hurry to put the horse back in the stall he'd occupied before the crash. One thing at a time . . .

Vicky was waiting for them. 'He's making progress, isn't he?' she said, beaming. 'Got to hand it to you, Tony.'

'Thanks.' Since the accident, Vicky had developed a particular fondness for Lifeline. The shared horror of the crash had created a bond. The horse nuzzled her neck.

But she hadn't come over just to say hello.

'Do me a favour, will you?'

'If I can.' Tony had a lot of time for Vicky. The whole place would have fallen apart over the last week but for her.

'Get Kate out of here for a bit.'

'What's up?'

'She's trying to act like normal but it's a heck of a strain for all of us. She needs a break from this place. Even a cup of tea in your pigsty might do the trick.'

Tony thought about it as he settled Lifeline in his pen. 'OK,' he said. 'If she'll come.'

Mickey declined the refreshment they offered him but accepted a glass of water so as not to cause offence. He allowed Laurie to take him on a tour of the old house – or, rather, the part of it that he and his family occupied. He was suitably respectful as Laurie showed him around, though what really interested him were the snippets concerning Kate, who lived in the other half of the Lodge.

It had been no surprise to Mickey to encounter Laurie at Beechwood – Mr Shen's briefing notes had been thorough. Nevertheless, seeing the Englishman again brought back memories of a time in Mickey's life he tried not to think about, his golden season in Australia before the accident. He'd been just a kid then, a kid who'd found his true calling and was making the most of it. Riding had been his route out, away from the criminal life of his family. After the accident, of course, he'd gone back home and forged a different kind of career.

As a jockey of Asian parentage he'd been an oddity. It had got him some attention, made him some friends – and some enemies. Laurie had been at the end of his riding career and, being English, sort of superior and aloof. Or maybe he'd just seemed that way.

Now, over ten years later, this same aloof Englishman was being as friendly as could be. Was it guilt that made him so effusive? Mickey wondered. As if he were trying to make up for what had happened all those years ago. Well, so he should. Mickey hadn't forgotten anything about his accident.

He did not prolong his stay – there would be other occasions. He made polite farewells to Laurie and his family. He could appreciate that the half-Swedish wife was big and handsome but she wasn't his type and she looked as miserable as sin. The son didn't look any more cheerful – maybe he was repelled by the scars on Mickey's face. It happened sometimes and Mickey could live with the insult, though he would not overlook it.

To Tony's surprise, Kate accepted his invitation.

'I want to talk to you about rides,' she said as he opened the front door of his house and grabbed a bundle of mail off the hall floor. A quick glance told him all he needed to know – nothing from Sarah. He dumped the bundle on to a pile of unopened letters and circulars on the hall table.

Vicky was right, the place *was* a bit of a pigsty. Since Sarah had walked out he'd not made much of an effort to keep things straight. At least the kitchen wasn't a complete tip. He'd cleared the place of Sarah's stuff and you can't make too much mess out of fruit and crispbread. He put the kettle on.

Kate sat at the table. 'Actually, it's about Neil.'

Tony sat opposite her. 'Go on.'

'It's a bit difficult but . . . how do you rate him as a jockey?'

'That's not difficult. He's a natural. Tomorrow will be interesting, though.' Neil was riding in an apprentice race at Newmarket the next day. It would be only his third ride for Kate and by far the most important.

156

'If he does well I'm thinking of putting him on Stopgap for the Tote Exacta at Sandown.'

Tony thought about it. 'Good idea.'

'You don't mind?'

'Why should I? No point in holding a kid like that back.'

'I thought you might be hoping to ride Stopgap yourself.'

Tony shrugged. 'I kissed goodbye to that after the King George.'

Stopgap was another of Gladys Lim's horses, perhaps her best. But there was no chance she'd countenance Tony riding – not after his putting up overweight on No Ill Will and losing by a length.

'Won't Mrs Lim want a name jockey?' he asked.

'I'd rather have Neil. I think he'd do a good job for her.'

'You mean he can claim seven pounds.'

She grinned ruefully. 'Yes.'

Apprentices enjoyed significant weight advantages to offset their immaturity. They both knew that this was Neil's real recommendation.

As Tony hunted for some clean mugs, he reflected that the boy deserved a break. 'It'd be great if he won, wouldn't it?' he said.

Kate gave him an unreadable look. 'You might not think so. I want you to ride in the Tote as well.'

That was a surprise. 'I didn't know you had another runner.'

'Cold Call.'

'Surely he's not ready?'

'According to Mickey Lee he is.'

Though Tony hadn't met him, the yard had been buzzing with news of Mickey Lee. His threatening appearance and courteous manner had made quite an impression. The purpose of his visit, however, had not been so clear.

'He owns Cold Call?'

'Not exactly. Freddy . . .' She stopped. The name seemed to stick in her throat. She took a deep breath and started again. 'A couple of years ago, Freddy started riding for Bernard Shen, in Hong Kong and in America. He came across Cold Call in Kentucky where they'd just about written him off. Freddy convinced Mr Shen I could do something with him.'

'Mr Shen sounds like a big wheel.'

'He owns horses all over the world. Not here, though. Cold Call was meant to be a test – if we could get him fit Mr Shen might send us more. I never dealt with him at all. Freddy did all that.'

'And Mickey Lee?'

'Mr Shen's sent him over to' – she shrugged – 'keep an eye on the horse, I suppose.'

'He's come all the way from Hong Kong just to keep an eye on one horse?'

'I don't know. Freddy used to say that Mr Shen had big plans for British racing but he never told me what they were.'

That sounded like Freddy but Tony kept his mouth shut. He considered Kate closely. This talk of her brother made her seem fragile. The skin was stretched tight across her face as if it might tear and the shadows under her eyes were purple, like old bruises.

'I wish he hadn't come,' she said. 'It's like he's been sent to take Freddy's place.'

'Nobody could do that.'

She said nothing and blew into a paper tissue. Suddenly she smiled. 'How long's a woman got to wait around here to get a cup of tea?'

'Sorry. I haven't got any milk,' he confessed.

'A great host you are.'

He stood up. 'Come on. I'm taking you to the pub.'

'What happened to him?' Greta asked after Laurie returned from seeing Mickey out.

'He had a riding accident. Finished his career.'

'Must have been a hell of an accident.'

'It was. He went head first into a telegraph pole.'

'Oh my God.'

'He looks seriously freaky,' said Paul. 'Like Frankenstein's monster.'

Greta frowned. 'That's unfair, Paul.'

'Sorr-ee.' Like all teenagers he could make an apology sound like an insult. 'Like Frankenstein's *Chinese* monster. OK?'

Though Laurie didn't say anything, Paul's response cut deep. To think that Mickey had gone through life being perceived this way was painful – particularly to the man who might have prevented it.

At the time of the accident Laurie had been overseeing a work-out on the gallops. Mickey was on Spanish Dancer, a supple black horse with a neat turn of foot. The horse was new to the lad and he was enjoying the experience, keen to see just how much he could get out of him. They were coming back along the stretch, Spanish Dancer ahead of the string, with Mickey pushing him along. Then, out of the blue, the horse had performed his old trick, ducking sideways through the gate which led back to the stables. Mickey, taken completely by surprise, had been catapulted from the horse's back into a telegraph pole.

Only his helmet saved his life as he crashed head first into the solid upright. It transpired that he'd broken nearly every bone down his left side and half his face had been smashed to pulp.

Laurie remembered the feeling of complete helplessness as the boy lay screaming on the ground. They'd got the Land Rover up from the yard and manoeuvred him into it with difficulty. One of the other lads knew basic first-aid and had sat in the back with Mickey while Laurie drove like fury to the hospital – a forty-minute journey that used to feature in his nightmares. At any minute he'd thought Mickey might die – and it would be his fault.

Laurie knew about Spanish Dancer's habit of suddenly turning through the gate for home. As a rule he made sure another horse was on his inside to prevent it. But Spanish Dancer hadn't misbehaved for months and today, in allowing Mickey to go on ahead, he'd forgotten to take any precautions. Worse still, he'd forgotten to warn Mickey. However he looked at it, Laurie knew the accident was down to him.

He hadn't had the nightmare for at least three years. He had a feeling it would be back again soon.

There were few customers in the pub, it being early in the evening. Nonetheless, Tony found a concealed alcove and bought Kate a gin and tonic. He treated himself to something similar, slimline and without the gin.

'How's it going?' he asked.

'Vicky's got most things under control.'

'I didn't mean that. I wondered how you were managing.'

She considered her answer as she stared down at the bubbles in her glass.

'I'm just trying to keep busy. Mickey Lee turning up is

probably a good thing. Gives me something else to worry about.'

'Instead of thinking about Freddy?'

'Yes.' She sighed. 'But of course I do think about him.' She looked up, her once-serene grey eyes clouded with misery. 'The police are saying Freddy was a crook. They can't come up with any other reason why someone would kill him.'

'It's their job, Kate. They have to look for the worst in people.'

'I suppose.'

He could see she was fighting back tears. He took her hand.

'Look, Kate. It might be better if you admitted that Freddy could be a bit of a rogue.'

Her head snapped back. She tried to remove her hand but he kept hold of it as he pressed on.

'I'm not saying he deserved what happened to him or that he's responsible for his own death – of course not. But he used to bend the rules a bit.'

She glared at him. 'You mean you believe the rumours about Freddy?'

'Kate, they're not all rumours. He offered me money to throw a race.'

'Oh.' Her face fell.

'I'm sorry, but it's true, and you can't run away from it. You must know that Freddy wasn't a saint. Maybe he got mixed up with some real villains and . . .' He stopped himself. He'd said enough.

This time he didn't attempt to hold on as she freed herself from his grip, put her hands over her face and began to sob.

The phone seemed to ring for an age before it was picked up. At least, this time, his father was in.

'Hi, Dad.'

'Oh, it's you.'

'How are you doing?'

There was a long pause punctuated by heavy, wheezing breaths.

'Dad?'

'You don't have to ring me, you know.' The voice sounded slurred.

'But I want to know how you are.'

'Like fuck you do, son. You don't want to know me at all.'

'That's not true.'

'Bet you were disappointed they let me out early. Now you're going to be a big-deal jockey I'm just an embarrassment. You always were a snotty little toe-rag.'

'Dad, have you been drinking?'

'That's right, go all superior on me. Why the fuck shouldn't I have a drink?'

'I didn't say that.'

'I should fucking well hope not. You've got no call to go looking down on me – have you?'

'Of course not.'

'No good reason at all because, you know what? You're just as bad as I am. Worse – 'cos you don't realise what a stupid, ignorant, brainless little gobshite you really are. All right, son?'

Neil stared at the receiver in his shaking hand. Thank God his father had ended the call.

After a bit, Kate stopped crying and pressed Tony for details of Freddy's attempt to bribe him. He told her all there was to tell, which wasn't much. There'd been a simple enquiry followed by a straightforward rebuff. It had been nothing and everything.

'I never listen to gossip about him,' she said. 'But for you to tell me this . . .' She searched his face. 'You're not making mischief, are you?'

'No.' He returned her gaze. The grey of her eyes was ever-changing. Luminous, enigmatic, unique.

He knew he had to move the conversation on. Maybe now was his chance to unburden himself.

'I've got a problem, Kate. I don't want to dump on you but in a way it's related to all this.'

She managed a small smile, lighting up her face. 'Go on.'

So he told her about the money and the note which had arrived on the day Freddy's body had been found. So far he'd done nothing about it, just left it lying on a shelf in the living room, hoping it would magically disappear.

'Why don't you tell the police?' she said at once.

'Because whatever I say about it, it's bound to look incriminating.'

'Take it to a lawyer then. Get some proper advice.'

'I still think it might look like I got cold feet in the middle of taking a bung. The moment it's on the record it's open to misinterpretation. The newspapers would have a field day if they got hold of it. Look at the way Sarah reacted – she just assumed I was on the take.'

Kate studied him closely.

'Has it ever occurred to you that Sarah often had her own reasons for acting the way she did?'

He was surprised. 'What do you mean?'

'I mean not everyone is as straightforward as you are. I always thought Sarah followed her own agenda. That money might have been a handy reason for her to walk out on you.'

Tony chewed on this for a moment. 'Me and Sarah, you and

163

Freddy. I suppose we've all got blind spots where some people are concerned.'

She didn't disagree with him.

'So what are you going to do with the money?'

'I don't know. I feel like burning it, only that would be a waste.'

This time she took his hand, gave it a squeeze.

'Don't worry. We'll think of something.'

Tony certainly hoped so.

Tony had never much liked Newmarket. Maybe it was because he'd been humiliated in his first Classic ride, trailing in last in the Two Thousand Guineas on a fancied horse who'd chosen to take the day off. Maybe it was the all-pervading influence of the Jockey Club, to whom Newmarket was their most important racecourse. Or maybe because the countryside was just too damn flat.

The start of a mile-and-a-half race on either of the two courses seemed in another county to the finishing post. And when the east wind blew and cloud and rain scudded in from the North Sea, it felt even further. On those days it was sometimes difficult to tell where the land ended and the sky began.

Today the weather was cloudy and mild. No breeze ruffled Tony's silks as he popped his horse into the stalls for the start of the race – which was a pity. He could have done with a bit of wind to help clear his head. As ever, his stint in the sauna and his growling stomach had left him in a fog. Not that he dwelt on it – he was used to that.

The irony was that the race ahead was named after racing's most famous casualty of the curse of wasting. Fred Archer, the

Victorian champion jockey, was driven to take his own life by the constant rigours of making the weight. Sometimes Tony knew just how he must have felt.

His mount in the Fred Archer Stakes was an unfairly named five-year-old, Silly Sausage, known in the yard as Crab because of his fondness for having a nip at people whenever he got the chance. In Tony – and Kate's – opinion, Silly Sausage wasn't ideally suited to the rigours of the course ahead, being on the small side and without the long-striding gallop of the best Newmarket contenders. Tony would rather have taken him round a tight course like Catterick or Chester where his balance and neatness of foot would give him an advantage. Here, on what was almost a straight course with just one bend, a thumping great charger was what was required. But Silly Sausage was owned by a consortium of Silicon Valley types from nearby Cambridge who'd lured their staff away from their computers for a day at the races. In the circumstances, that seemed as good a reason as any to give the horse an outing.

The runners set off at a decent clip. Tony tucked in behind a big long-striding chestnut called Jump Start who he fancied was the likely winner. Despite the general flatness of the region, the course was undulating and broad, the six runners could each have taken an acre of space and yet they bunched together on the rail.

Like the more famous Rowley Mile Course – home to the Guineas and the Champion Stakes – the July Course took a righthand turn into the long straight that led to the finish and the crowd gathered in the various enclosures. Tony knew most of them would be glued to the huge screen beside the marquees that gave by far the best view of the race itself.

Jump Start was revving up now, getting into his full stride

and beginning to pull away. Tony pushed Silly Sausage on and the little horse responded gamely, though Tony was aware the others were in position, not far behind.

The straight, which had been flat, now took a dip which suited his mount and he found himself up on Jump Start's shoulder. Tony's hope was that maybe some of the other, bigger types would be unbalanced by the downhill gradient which, he knew well, was followed by an uphill final furlong, a killer for any horse lacking in staying power.

To his amazement Silly Sausage was in the lead as the course began to veer upwards towards the finish. The crowd were roaring and the little horse beneath him was digging deep. It occurred to him that he and Kate had been completely wrong – obviously a crew of computer gurus had more innate horse sense than either of them.

Tony roared encouragement into the horse's ear and the bay went for all he was worth. But the bigger horses were upon them now, superior strength and greater momentum powering them up the gradient. Jump Start cruised past in top gear followed by another horse, then another. Suddenly the winning post was flashing by and they were passing the marquees on their left and the stand on their right. The race was over.

'Jesus Christ!' Tony swore out loud. He liked Newmarket no better. After all these years he was still coming last.

Mickey was enjoying himself. He'd never been to Newmarket before and he felt like he was shaking hands with history. Not that history – especially British history – held much appeal for him. On the other hand, the Panama-hatted Pimm's drinkers and the thatched roofs had a kind of quaint charm. It was like a scene from an old movie – what century did these people think they were living in?

He felt at home in his linen summer suit though he was aware he didn't quite carry it off with the same casual air as the race-goers around him in the champagne bar. He treated himself to a glass as he inspected the throng, particularly the young women in their racing finery. Some of them had more leg than the fillies in the parade ring. Next time, he promised himself, he'd get fixed up with a long-limbed escort of his own. It would cost him but it would be worth it.

He strolled towards the parade ring to cast his eye over the runners in the next. Not that he intended to wager, he rarely did. There were only two circumstances in which he would place a bet – to impress a woman and when he was certain he would win. The first obviously didn't apply and he hadn't been here long enough to arrange the latter. That would come, he reflected. Sooner rather than later.

To his delight, he spotted a familiar figure under the trees near the pre-parade ring. He glided towards her, savouring the fall of her dark shoulder-length hair and the sombre set of her features. Such a full, kissable mouth despite its downturn – how he would enjoy bringing it to life if she would let him. And maybe even if she wouldn't.

'Hello, Kate.'

Her face registered surprise and, just for a split-second, distaste – which, to Mickey's mind, made her look even more desirable.

'I'm sorry to disturb you,' he said.

'That's OK.' Obviously it wasn't but that was too bad.

'I saw you had a runner in the third. Pity he couldn't stay.'

'He did better than I thought. This isn't really his course.'

'Why did you run him then?'

She hesitated. He guessed she didn't want to tell him. 'The owners insisted.'

He laughed. 'So I'm not the only one who's difficult?'

She ducked that. 'I didn't know you were coming today.'

'I'm just doing a little homework on the British racing scene. I feel like a tourist.'

'Then you should visit the National Horseracing Museum here.'

He pretended to consider it. 'If you'd care to show me around?'

'Sorry. I've got a horse in the last. I'd better go and settle my nervous apprentice.'

'How will he do?'

'He'll be fine. I can't answer for the horse, though.'

Mickey watched her walk away through the trees in the direction of the weighing room. He knew he disturbed her and that she couldn't wait to get away from him. He liked that. It was so much more satisfactory than indifference.

Kate fussed over Neil as he weighed out. His face looked drawn and ill.

'Are you OK?' she asked for the second time in the space of a minute. She wasn't normally like this. The encounter with Mickey had thrown her.

'Yes.'

'When we get in the ring, don't be put off by Mrs Lim.' Neil was riding another of her horses, Highwayman. 'She barks a bit but that's just her manner.'

'It's all right, Miss Montague. I've met her.'

Kate remembered that he'd helped out with Pay Back Time at Ascot.

'Just be polite to her. If she gives you instructions, listen closely and say nothing.' Kate had already told him how to ride the race.

'Right you are.'

'Neil – are you sure you're OK?'

His eyes met hers. 'It's not the race really.'

'Go on.'

'It's my dad. I wanted to let him know I was riding.'

'But your mother will tell him, surely?' Kate knew something of Neil's background.

'I suppose. I've left him messages but he hasn't called back.'

'Here's my phone – ring him now.'

He thought about it for a second and shook his head.

'If he won't call, why should I?'

'Then put him out of your mind, Neil. Think about me instead.'

He squinted at her, puzzled.

'I've had two runners today and they've both come nowhere.' Up at Newcastle Last Ditch had tailed off in the Northumberland Plate – they'd watched it together in the weighing room. 'Just get out there and do the business. I need cheering up.'

He perked up. 'I'd better do me best then, hadn't I?'

When it came to it, Gladys Lim had no particular instructions for Neil, beyond a good-natured slap on the back and a cheery 'Good luck!' Some of the other apprentices, Kate noted, had already adopted the fully fledged parade-ring swagger of their seniors. These novice riders indulged in as much whip-twirling and boot-tapping as any star jockey about to ride a Classic. Not Neil, however. As he stood respectfully to attention in front of her, dwarfed by the big frame of Highwayman, Kate wondered if she was making a mistake in letting him ride in this minor race – let alone considering him for the Tote Exacta stakes, the richest mile-and-a-quarter handicap in Europe.

Mrs Lim was obviously thinking the same thing. As Dermot led Highwayman with Neil on board around the ring, she said, 'I'm not happy about Stopgap.'

Kate had already prepared the ground earlier, talking up Neil's abilities and suggesting they consider him for the Tote. The way she'd put it, the matter was entirely in Mrs Lim's hands – which was indeed the case.

'Don't make your mind up yet, Gladys. Let's watch the race.'

Mrs Lim would doubtless have ignored the advice but her attention was diverted elsewhere.

'Do you know that man, Kate?'

Across the ring, among the crowd scrutinising the parade of horses, stood Mickey Lee.

'All the time we've been here he's been staring at you.'

Kate concealed the chill she felt inside. 'Mickey Lee represents one of my overseas owners. Maybe you know him? Bernard Shen is from Hong Kong.'

'I've heard of him.'

'He's got a runner in the Tote as well.'

'You never told me that,' snapped Mrs Lim.

'Don't worry, Gladys, Cold Call can't live with Stopgap.'

Mrs Lim didn't look mollified but at least she dropped the subject.

Kate had warned Neil that his chief danger in the race was likely to come not from competing horses but from their riders. As the starting-stalls opened and the twelve runners began the dead-straight seven-furlong gallop to the line, he could see the truth in that. Some of the other lads had talked a big race in the changing room and Neil had felt a bit intimidated. On Highwayman's back, however, he felt a surge of confidence. As a rider, he knew he wouldn't be found wanting.

Neil had first sat on a horse at the age of six. He and his sisters had been farmed out to various relatives for a few months while his parents had tried to sort themselves out, just before his dad got put away. He'd stayed in Essex with Uncle Dave and Aunt Marge, who kept a pony for their teenage daughter, Mandy. But Mandy had gone off ponies and moved on to boys, which had its good and bad points. The bad was that she no longer had any time for her little cousin but the good was that Neil had her pony all to himself. It had been a great six months – even though he'd missed his mum. Later, when he and his sisters spent their weekends on dismal prison visits, Neil would dream of the golden days he'd spent sitting on Mandy's pony.

He saw that two horses on the inside of him had taken off like trains and were engaged in a private duel. Twerps, he thought. There was no point in riding a finish before you'd gone three furlongs.

Neil's plan – Kate's really – was to get the horse into a rhythm, one he was comfortable with, and build up to a good gallop entering the dip. Highwayman was a big, long-striding type with plenty of puff, ideal for this demanding full-on gallop. He was a bit one-paced, however, without the change of gear that would have lifted him up in class. Nevertheless, provided he could get the horse's momentum going, Neil reckoned he had the beating of most of the field. The grey on the outside looked handy, though. Neil had noticed his rider stretch him out in the third furlong then rein him back in. That was where the danger lay.

Neil dug in a bit as they went past the five-furlong marker and Highwayman began to build steadily to top speed as they headed for the dip. He noticed that the chestnut on his inside, one of those that had gone off like a rat out of a drain, was coming back to him fast. It was also veering off line, straight into Highwayman's path. At the same time, the jockey on his outer seemed to lose control on the downslope and his horse cut inside towards Neil.

For a moment he was in trouble. If he'd thought about it, it would have been too late, he would have been sandwiched on left and right and his horse chopped off. But Neil didn't think. On instinct, he switched his whip from right to left hand and hit Highwayman a sharp crack, shifting his weight high up on the horse's shoulders, urging the big old plodder to find a spurt from somewhere.

As they careered down into the dip, Highwayman responded and Neil shot him through the gap, clear of the danger.

Only the grey was ahead of them now on the rise towards the finishing post. His jockey asked for a change of gear and the horse moved up. But Highwayman was devouring the ground between them, travelling faster than he'd ever gone in his life. Neil felt as if he were riding an Inter-city express. Nothing could stop him winning.

Highwayman caught the grey twenty yards before the finishing post and kept going. It took all Neil's strength to pull him up as they galloped over the line and downhill towards the car-park exit.

There was an ecstatic welcome committee waiting for Neil. Dermot grabbed the horse with one hand and slapped Neil's thigh with the other.

'Great ride, Midget,' he shouted.

Vicky was there, almost pulling Neil off the horse as she gave him a smacking kiss on the lips.

'It's Mighty Midget now,' she cried.

Kate was less ebullient but no less pleased. She kissed him too, when he'd dismounted, and the happiness in her face was perhaps the best thing of all about the victory.

As for Mrs Lim, she gave him a hug that took his breath away and said, 'You ride Stopgap for me. OK?'

And it was.

But he wished, after all, that he'd rung his dad.

Greta was upstairs crying when Laurie and Paul came in. Although she'd been alone in the house, she'd locked herself in the bathroom, just so she couldn't be taken by surprise. She'd had enough surprises recently. Nasty surprises like finding herself pregnant – and seeing her lover killed in front of her.

These crying jags were becoming a habit. She'd hide and force herself to howl soundlessly into a towel, just to get some of the turmoil inside her out into the open. Like a volcano erupting. And when she'd squeezed the last drop out she'd feel better for a while, drained of emotion – until it started to well up inside her again.

The truth was, Greta despised herself. She'd been faithful to Laurie all their married life – more faithful than he'd been, she had no doubt. As their relationship had slipped into the doldrums, both of them trapped in the same old boat with the breeze of mystery and romance long played out, she'd prided herself on sticking it out. Over the years, she'd had offers of adventures on the sly. She'd always said no, despite the temptation. So why the hell had she given in to Freddy? She still didn't know. She hadn't even liked him much – his intentions were so transparent. Maybe that's why she'd said yes. He didn't seem to be offering anything more than a hot roll in the hay – though the intensity of it had surprised her and she'd pulled back quickly. Not quickly enough, as it turned out.

But the way that silly infidelity had led to her present predicament seemed so out of proportion to her offence. Of course, no one else would see it like that. If she went to the police, as her conscience told her she should, then she would be exposed to all manner of indignity, public and private. She couldn't admit to being with Freddy when he was killed. Thank God, no one knew. Except, of course, the killer. Her stomach turned at the thought.

The sound of laughter from downstairs distracted her. She patched herself up and went to see what was going on. Laurie and Paul were in the kitchen. She noted the can of beer on the table – and the two glasses.

'Look at this, Mum,' shouted Paul, waving a wad of money in her face. 'I won seventy-five quid!'

'How?' she said, her voice icy.

'On Neil – he won the race.'

'It wasn't on television,' explained Laurie. 'We nipped into Ladbroke's in the village.'

'You took Paul into a bookie's?'

'So what?' He sounded surprised at her fury.

'He's under age, that's what. I don't want my son hanging around in betting shops. Or drinking,' she said, pointing at the beer can.

'Mum!' cried Paul in protest.

She ignored him and spoke directly to her husband. 'How could you, Laurie?'

'For God's sake. It was harmless fun.'

'When he's old enough he can ruin his own life. He doesn't need you to do it for him.'

She could see he was making an effort to control himself, she'd obviously hurt him. Good.

He spoke in a low voice. 'I don't need any lessons in morality from a cheap slut like you.'

'Oh, fuck off.'

'Very impressive, Greta. Don't blame me for the way you've screwed up our marriage.'

Paul was staring at them in shock. 'Stop it!' he cried and threw the money he was clutching on to the floor. 'You have it – I don't want it!' And he ran out of the door. They could hear his sobs as he blundered up the stairs.

That seemed to break the spell. Her anger had gone.

'Oh shit,' she said. 'I suppose that was my fault.'

Lawrie's expression was unreadable. 'It's too late for apologies, Greta. Just tell me when you're going to get rid of the baby.'

# Chapter Seven

Annie waylaid DCI Orchard in his small office across the corridor from the incident room. She hovered outside while he talked on the phone and then rushed in the moment he replaced the receiver. She couldn't wait to tell him about her own, recently concluded, phone call.

His big mobile face registered curiosity at her sudden appearance. He scared her stiff but she had no choice but to talk to him.

'I've just heard from Jackie Turner, guv.'

He looked puzzled.

She jogged his memory. 'Jonno Simpson's fianceé. He wants to talk.'

'Excellent. Does Keith know?'

'No, guv.' This was the tricky bit. 'Jonno won't talk to Sergeant Hunter. Jackie says he'll only talk to me.'

Orchard didn't seem happy about that. She blundered on.

'I saw him in hospital just after he'd been shot. We got on quite well.' Up to the point where he'd told her to get lost – but there was no need to mention that. 'I took him some grapes.'

The big man pondered.

'Well, you can't just swan off and see him on your own.'

'Of course not, guv. But –'

'Yes?'

'– this could be important.'

'I'm aware of that,' he snapped. He stood up abruptly and eased his bulk with difficulty from behind the desk. 'Let's get on with it then.'

Her apprehension must have been obvious.

'Don't look so worried,' he said. 'I won't jump all over him. He'll think I'm his favourite uncle by the time we're through.'

Somehow Annie doubted that as she meekly followed him out of the door.

Tony had spent most of the morning with Lifeline. After a gentle work-out on the gallops, he'd taken the horse down the back lane to the main road. The idea was to get him used once more to the sound of traffic moving at speed. Then he'd ridden him back to the yard.

Kate came over as he dismounted.

'May I ask you a favour?' She looked uncomfortable.

'What is it?'

'Freddy's cottage. The police say they don't need it any more.' She ground to a halt.

Tony tried to guess what she wanted.

'You'd like some help with Freddy's things?'

'I can't bear to go in there.'

'I understand. I'll pack up his stuff for you.'

She looked relieved. 'Vicky will let you in. She's moving into the cottage.'

'I'll do it now.'

She opened her mouth – to thank him again, he guessed – and he cut her off.

'Kate, I'd be upset if you asked anybody else.'

He could feel her eyes on him as he walked Lifeline to his barn.

*

Jackie Turner lived in a semi on a purpose-built estate. Both outside and in all was neat, new and entirely conventional. Jackie said little as she opened the door to Annie and Orchard and ushered them down the hall. As she showed them into the living room, Annie wondered if the wedding was still on.

Jonno looked in better shape than when Annie had last seen him, grizzling into his hospital pillow. He supported himself on a metal crutch to say hello and held out his free hand for Annie to shake. It felt small in her grasp as she gave it a squeeze and flashed him an encouraging smile. He did his best to return it but his ruddy cheeks drained of colour at the sight of Orchard behind her.

Annie opened her mouth to introduce him but was shouldered aside by her superior. He took Jonno's hand in his great paw and beamed down at him.

'Detective Chief Inspector Orchard, Mr Simpson. It's a privilege to meet you.'

Jonno looked a bit taken aback by this effusive greeting. Unbidden, Orchard settled himself in an armchair, leaving Annie to take a seat on the sofa next to the invalid. As Jonno lowered himself gingerly, the DCI continued in his cheery vein.

'I'm not much of a racing man, Mr Simpson, but you're one of the few jockeys I can put a name to.' He held up three sausagey fingers and recited, 'Lester Piggott, Frankie Dettori, Jonno Simpson.'

Annie gaped at him. Talk about overdoing it. Surely even Jonno – who struck her as a bit slow in the intellectual stakes – couldn't fail to see through such transparent flattery.

The little man squinted at Orchard in disbelief.

'You're having me on,' he said.

'No, sir.' Orchard's grin was face-splitting. 'Last summer I had the honour of placing a wager on behalf of the lads at Farley Road. Proceeds to charity, you know the kind of thing. I looked down the runners and one stood out – Empress Valerie. The Reigate Handicap at Lingfield. You must remember?'

The jockey's face lit up. 'I walked it, didn't I?'

'You did indeed, my son, at fourteen to one. We handed the children's hospital a cheque for over five thousand pounds. My old mum's a Valerie, you see.'

It was corny stuff, Annie thought. But, from the sparkle in Jonno's eyes, effective just the same.

'You wanted to talk, Jonno.'

The sparkle instantly disappeared.

'What is it you'd like to tell us?'

The jockey took a deep breath. 'You've got to promise me I won't get into trouble. I'm not saying anything otherwise.'

Annie looked at Orchard. There were advantages to having the Senior Investigating Officer at hand.

His face was now grave. 'That's a lot to ask, Jonno. I can't make any promises until I know exactly what it's all about.'

Jonno's face fell.

'But,' continued the policeman, 'I'm running a murder enquiry. I'm not overly interested in racing misdemeanours except in so far as they impinge on my investigation.'

Annie could see that Orchard had lost Jonno but he seemed reassured by the general tone.

There was a silence. Annie gave him an encouraging grin and at last the jockey began to speak.

'The thing is – I was offered money to stop my horse in the last on the first day of Royal Ascot. Ten grand. I said no way, and I won by a mile. I reckon that's why I got shot.'

Annie kept the excitement out of her voice as she said, 'It seems a bit extreme – to do that to you just for turning them down.'

'To be honest, it wasn't the first time they'd asked me. I always refused.'

'Were they under the impression, at any point, that you'd said yes?'

'Well . . .' He needed to think about that. His desire not to incriminate himself was certainly holding things up. 'It's possible.'

'And who offered you the money?'

'Freddy Montague.'

'Was he offering you a bribe on his own behalf?'

Jonno laughed. 'You're joking! Freddy was an earner. He took money to chuck races, and if he got someone else to do it he wanted a commission.'

'Who was he working for?' asked Annie.

'I wouldn't know that.' Jonno said it suspiciously quickly.

'No idea at all? A bookmaker maybe?'

'Could be.' He pretended to give the matter some thought. 'Very likely a bookie but I wouldn't know which one.'

'That's a pity,' Orchard chipped in, 'because he might be responsible for the hole in your left foot.'

Jonno shot him an aggrieved look. Annie changed tack.

'Who else did Freddy offer money to, Jonno?'

'Dunno.'

'Are you sure? I mean, you lads are all pretty tight, aren't you?'

'Yeah, but I wouldn't know about something like this. It's private business, isn't it?'

Annie contemplated her notebook for a moment, searching for the right words.

'That wasn't really what I meant. You see, first you're shot, then Freddy's killed. Since you're such mates with the other jockeys, I'm sure you don't want anyone else to get hurt.'

''Course not!' He was indignant. 'But I don't see how I can help.'

She suppressed a sigh. He really was dim.

'Well, if you tell us who else was involved then we'd know who else might be at risk.'

'Oh.'

'Can you think of anyone at all who might have taken Freddy's money? Think hard, Jonno. Someone else's life might be at stake.'

He thought. As he did so, Annie caught Orchard looking at her. He nodded.

'Freddy used to be very thick with Billy Rivers,' Jonno offered.

Annie was unimpressed. 'Billy Rivers went back to America at the end of last season. Isn't there anyone else?'

'Tony Byrne.'

The name took Annie by surprise. 'Why do you say that?'

'Tony's at the same stable, isn't he? With Freddy's sister. The whole lot must be bent, if you ask me.'

'Do you have any specific reason for naming Tony Byrne?'

'Did you see the way he rode in the King George? If he didn't stop that horse from winning, my dick's a kipper.'

When Tony arrived at Freddy's cottage he noticed that the police tapes and warning notices had been removed from the door. He found Vicky already hard at work in the kitchen, the smell of disinfectant thick in the air.

'Hiya,' she said brightly, her arms deep in sudsy water in the sink. The fridge was defrosting and the shelves had been cleared. 'It was foul in here,' she said. 'You can imagine the mess Freddy made and the coppers only added to it.'

'Kate says you're going to live here?'

'I'm fed up with sharing.'

'You don't mind . . .?'

She stopped scrubbing and turned to him. 'No, I don't. I'm not superstitious. And Kate's not asking any rent – she just wants it occupied for now.'

He left her to it and climbed the stairs. He'd half expected to see the chalked outline of a body on the bedroom floor but the room looked quite unremarkable. Only a new pane of glass in the window and a chipped piece of plaster in the bedroom wall bore witness to Freddy's death.

He found some suitcases under the bed and began to pack away the dead man's clothes.

'What do you make of that then, Annie?'

They were heading back to the nick in the car. Orchard was driving – erratically, in Annie's opinion.

'I think Jonno's more scared of Jackie than of us.'

'Exactly. The little bugger's in it up to his bollocks.'

Annie nodded. 'He was hardly forthcoming, was he? He fingered a dead man, an American who's no longer riding and racing's Mr Clean.'

Orchard looked at her. 'Tony Byrne, you mean?'

'According to the press. He once walked out on a trainer when he was setting up a betting coup. That's the rumour anyway.'

'Reputations count for nothing in professional sport. Nobody's Mr Clean.'

'Are you going to pull him then, guv?'

'Not yet. You get a video of that race Jonno was on about – see what you think.'

'Me?'

'You're the expert on the gee-gees – so they tell me.'

'OK.' She was hardly an expert but she wasn't going to contradict him. At least she knew someone who was.

'We'll do a bit of digging on Mr Byrne as well. And there's also that bookie Freddy was seen with in the casino.'

'Herbert Gibbs?'

'You and Keith can have a chat to him. He'll enjoy it even if you don't.'

Orchard cut in front of a lorry on the roundabout and overtook a four-wheel drive on the inside. Annie waited till the drama was over before she spoke.

'Guv, can I ask a question?'

Orchard grunted – probably in surprise. Annie had never asked permission before.

'Where does Bernard Shen fit in? Do you think Freddy was working for both Shen *and* Gibbs? And one of them didn't like it and bumped him off?'

Orchard looked at her in exasperation.

'If you must know, I haven't got a clue. Without a murder weapon or a good inside tip, I think we're probably stuffed. Any other questions?'

She thought for a moment, holding her breath as he shot into the Farley Road car park six inches in front of a bus.

'Just one, guv. Is your mum really called Valerie?'

He chuckled. 'What do you think?'

Tony took a car-load of Freddy's belongings up to the lodge

where Josh helped him unload. Kate directed them to an unused back bedroom. Freddy had slept there as a child, she told them.

Amongst the stuff from the cottage was a carrier bag full of Freddy's post which Vicky had salvaged. She'd placed on top the items which looked as if they might have significance.

'Oh, God,' groaned Kate as she examined them. 'I just hate the thought of having to break the news to people. You'd think they'd know by now – it's been all over the papers.'

She picked up an airmail letter. 'You open it,' she said to Tony.

It was from Australia.

Dear Freddy Montague,

I'm sorry to tell you that our son Jeff died recently in a riding accident. I'm sure this will come as a shock to you as it has to us. He was such a good rider. We can't understand how this terrible thing could have happened.

We know that Jeff was planning to join you in England very soon and you have probably been wondering where he was. We are very sorry not to have written to you earlier.

Sincerely yours,

Bill and Gaynor Collins

Tony handed the letter to Kate.

'Did you know Jeff Collins?'

'Freddy said he was an Australian jockey. He asked me if I could find him a few rides.'

'His trunk's in the shed at the cottage.'

She stared at the letter in her hand. 'Poor things,' she said. 'There's no phone number. I'll write and ask what they want me to do with it.'

'Shall I put it with the other stuff then?'

She nodded unhappily.

Annie didn't bother to make an official request to locate a video of the King George, she knew where to get one – from her dad. Doug James ran his eye along the bookshelf lined with videocassettes in his living room and pulled one out. It was that simple.

Annie's dad lived by himself in a bedsit on the outskirts of Swindon. Annie's mum referred to it as a dosshouse but then she would. Since they'd split up she'd only visited it once and stayed barely ten minutes. Annie didn't think it was all that bad. Doug kept it tidy in most important respects and dedicated the room to his main interest in life: horseracing. It was no coincidence that it took under a minute – even accounting for Doug's bad knee – from his front door to the bookie's down the street.

They watched the King George together once all the way through. Then Annie asked her dad to replay the run-in and he ran it back a couple of times. She'd not told him what she was looking for but Doug was a shrewd observer.

'You want to know if Byrne chucked it, don't you?'

'There's a good chance, don't you think, Dad? They're neck-and-neck right at the death and he stops using his whip. Why would he do that if he really wanted to win?'

Doug nodded. 'I agree it appears that way. But let's take another look.'

He rewound the tape again, back to the two-furlong pole. 'This is where Tony really gets after him,' Doug said. 'He hits him once and the horse is off. Then again as he gets up on the other feller. He's a smart rider, you know. He only uses the whip

186

when he thinks it's going to work. And here' – Doug stopped the tape – 'about fifty yards from the post, he gives the horse a tap and there's no answer. Can you see?'

He reran it a couple of times. It was true: right at the last No Ill Will ceased to respond.

Doug added, 'That horse had never done a mile and a half before. He'd reached his limit and Tony knew it. There's no point in thrashing a horse when you can't improve its position. Much better to send it home happy to race another day. Bloody good riding, if you ask me, though I can understand why your average punter might not agree.'

Annie grinned. 'Thanks, Dad. You're a right clever-clogs sometimes.'

'Not that clever. My selection's still running.'

Neil had not been up on Stopgap before and he could hardly contain his excitement as they skimmed along the turf on the top of the gallops in the cool of the early morning. Kate had suggested he ride the horse out first lot just to get a feel of him before Friday's race at Sandown.

Two ahead in the string, Tony was on Neil's usual mount, Cold Call. That gave Neil a thrill too – to think he'd be up against the pair he knew so well. What's more, he knew just from the short trip up from the yard who had got the better deal. Smashing horse though Cold Call was, Stopgap was in a different class.

Kate's instructions had been precise. Get the feel of the horse. Work him over four furlongs but keep a good hold of him. Don't go flat out. With the race just a few days away all the serious work had been done, now was the time just to keep things ticking over.

Nevertheless, Neil couldn't resist stretching his mount just a little. It was like being given a Ferrari and told not to go too fast – what was the point of that? Heading into the breeze, he asked a few questions with a squeeze of his thighs and nudge of his hands on the reins. The effect was instantaneous, like flicking a switch. He shot past Tony and Cold Call.

'Oh, yes!' muttered Neil to himself, revelling in the power beneath him before reining back in. The horse slowed at once.

Tony came up alongside.

'Enjoying yourself?'

'This feller's got after-burners.'

'I wish mine had.'

Neil nodded. He knew Cold Call's limitations well enough. Sometimes it was like riding an animal who just wasn't interested. He thanked his lucky stars he was on the better horse.

Mickey sat with Kate in the Volvo, assessing Cold Call and Stopgap through a pocket-sized pair of binoculars.

'It's not too late, you know,' she said. 'We can race Cold Call somewhere else.'

'Why should we do that? I think he's going to win.'

Kate shrugged. She could care. This irritating man was no friend of hers. If he was arrogant enough to think he knew best, let him cock it up and report back to his boss. On the other hand, that was hardly fair to the horse or herself. She'd worked hard nursing the animal back to fitness, she didn't want him humiliated in the hurly-burly of one of the toughest handicaps of the year.

'You can see for yourself – he won't finish in the same street as Stopgap.'

Mickey appeared not to have heard her, still gazing through the glasses. 'We'll see.'

'Perhaps if I had a word with Mr Shen myself –'

'That will not be necessary.' He was looking at her now, the binoculars in his lap. 'Mr Shen has every confidence that all the fine work you have put into Cold Call will pay off.'

'OK,' she said quietly. Inwardly she was fuming.

He chuckled. 'You don't like me much, do you, Kate?'

'Ours is a professional relationship. I have no feelings one way or the other.'

'If you say so.' He chuckled some more.

She felt like smacking his ugly smirking face.

The notion of paying Herbert Gibbs an early-morning visit and disturbing him in the bosom of his family evidently appealed to DS Hunter. It improved his mood so much he even let Annie buy him a cup of tea and a doughnut en route. She'd not been in his good books since, as he'd put it, she'd gone behind his back to Orchard over Jonno Simpson.

The bookie lived in a large mock-Tudor pile with a Range Rover parked in the drive and a Merc visible through the open garage door. The front door was opened by a wide-eyed brunette in jeans who appeared to have trouble understanding English.

'Sorry?' she said as Hunter flashed his warrant card and enquired in standard police-speak after the whereabouts of Mr Gibbs.

The appearance of a thirtysomething blonde in pneumatically filled sportswear stopped Hunter in the act of repeating himself.

'All right, Maria, I'll deal with it,' she said. 'Can I help you?'

Hunter said it all over again.

A mixture of irritation and alarm flashed across the woman's face. 'You'd better come in,' she said.

As they stepped into the hall Annie could see a large open-plan kitchen ahead of them. Maria was beginning to clear the table of cereal packets and dirty crockery.

'Wait here,' the woman instructed them and shouted up the stairs, 'Herb, come down.' A small boy popped his head over the banisters. 'You, too, Charlie. Where's your sister?'

Hunter stood awkwardly to one side as the boy bounded past, followed by a fair-haired girl a couple of years older. Both wore smart school uniforms. They grabbed bags and folders that were standing ready on the hall table. Charlie had a blue lunch box covered with football stickers.

Annie winked at him and he giggled.

'Herbert!' roared the blonde in exasperation. 'We're going now.'

A shaven-headed man in his late thirties appeared at the top of the stairs. He was holding a baby. 'Sorry, Liz, I was just changing her.'

'See you later. We're off.' And she turned for the door, pushing the children in front of her.

'Who the hell are you?' said the bald man to Hunter and Annie.

'Police,' said the woman in tones that promised grief later and slammed the door shut.

Hunter went through his introductory rigmarole again, flashing his warrant card.

'Jesus,' muttered Gibbs and turned for the kitchen to deposit the baby in Maria's arms. As he showed them into a sitting room off the hall the infant began to wail.

Gibbs shut the door on the noise, obviously fed up.

'I've got a business address, you know. I work office hours.

Next time leave my family out of it.'

Hunter feigned innocence. 'I thought you might appreciate a friendly word, Mr Gibbs. Rather than a trip to the station.'

'Just get on with it.'

Hunter relaxed back into his seat. Annie knew he was quite capable of spinning this out as long as it suited him.

'I believe you were acquainted with the late jockey, Freddy Montague?'

'Who wasn't?'

'I'll take that as a yes.'

Gibbs did not respond so Hunter continued, 'Am I right in thinking that Freddy worked for you, from time to time?'

'Utter bollocks.'

'We have a videotape of you passing gambling chips to him in a West End casino on the Tuesday evening of Royal Ascot.'

'So?'

'So that might be construed – by a jury, for example – as evidence of your buying a jockey's co-operation in order to fix horse races.'

'As I remember, I lent him twenty quids' worth of chips so he could play a couple of hands. If your tape's any good you'll see he paid me back. This is rubbish and you know it.'

In the distance the baby could still be heard complaining.

'What exactly was your relationship with Freddy Montague, Mr Gibbs?'

'He was a pal. And I'm pissed off that someone murdered him. Why don't you go and catch the stupid bastard who did it, instead of bothering me in my home?'

The baby howled louder and Herbert shifted unhappily in his seat. It struck Annie that the infant was giving him more grief than they were.

'One more thing, Mr Gibbs.' Hunter leaned forward. 'Since Freddy was such a pal, I take it you would make available to us any information that might lead to the apprehension of his killer?'

'I'm not in the habit of grassing people up, Sergeant, but in this case I might be tempted.'

Hunter stood up. He took a card from his pocket and held it out. 'We'll look forward to hearing from you then.'

The bookie took the card and threw it carelessly on the low glass table between them. 'Don't bank on it.'

As Gibbs opened the door the baby's wail hit them in the face. He stormed away from them into the kitchen. 'Maria, where's her bottle? She's hungry, you dozy cow!'

Annie and Hunter showed themselves out.

From inside his car, Mickey observed Josh as he settled Stopgap in his stall. He waited till the lad next to him had moved off before he went over.

'You've done a fine job with this horse,' Mickey commented.

Josh looked up, taken by surprise.

'Thanks,' he said.

'If he wins at Sundown,' continued Mickey, 'I hope everyone will appreciate all the effort you've put in.'

'Mrs Lim always sees the lads right.'

Josh was looking at him suspiciously. Mickey was aware he was the subject of gossip in the yard. Josh would know who he was. Maybe he should change tack.

'Excuse my impertinence but – do you work out?'

Josh stared at him. 'Can you tell?'

Of course he could tell. The lad was twice the size of the others. His biceps stretched the seams of his shirt and he walked with a bodybuilder's swagger. Mickey knew all the signs – he'd been there.

Josh didn't need much prompting. Soon he was telling Mickey about his regime and the difficulties of fitting gym-time into his work schedule.

'I work out a bit myself,' said Mickey.

'Come down the gym. Let me show you around.'

They shook hands on it. It was that simple.

Herbert made his driver drop him off in Prince Albert Road, at the bottom of Primrose Hill. He set off on a steady jog up to the top and his white Adidas singlet was soon wet with sweat. Three-quarters of the way up he was regretting his resolve to make this meet look good. At least the effort burned off some of the anger that had been smouldering in his belly since his early-morning visit from the Old Bill.

He crested the summit dangerously out of breath and brushed clumsily through the crowd of tourists admiring the view. He spotted his target on the grass nearby, performing serious-looking stretches in a sleeveless vest and cut-off denim shorts – Dave Parsons, or China Dave as he was known to his old Army mates. Dave was an interesting mixture of East and West. He had the build of his cockney father, a merchant-navy seaman who had long since sailed out of Dave's life, and the features of his Chinese mother, a Soho waitress and former prostitute. Because of his smooth skin and sculpted lips, Dave's Chinese friends preferred to call him Girlface.

Herbert kept on jogging, relieved he was now on the flat, and Dave fell in beside him. The pair cut across the grass, heading for an isolated bench.

'What's up, H.? I had to reschedule my morning to get here.'

Herbert ignored him till they reached the seat. He slumped down with relief. Dave stayed on his feet and began a series of hamstring flexes with his foot on the bench.

'I had the police round at breakfast time.'

'Yeah?'

'They –' he chose his words with care '– insinuated that I was behind poor old Freddy Montague getting chopped.'

'Yeah?'

'Stop saying that and sit down.'

Dave did as he was told.

'I resent being questioned about this. Freddy was a valued associate. Keeping someone in line is one thing, but this is out of order.'

'Too right.'

'So, Girlface, I'd like you to look me in the baby blues and tell me this has got nothing to do with you.'

Dave's almond eyes narrowed at the sound of his nickname. He was touchy about its use – which, of course, was why Herbert had used it.

'Not me, H.,' he replied.

Herbert glared at the other man, weighing the matter in his mind.

'Naturally, when casting around for likely suspects I thought of you. I wondered if you had possibly misinterpreted the criticisms I made of Freddy just before he died.'

'I swear I didn't. Honest.'

Herbert sighed heavily. 'It's all right, Dave, I believe you. It's a bit out of your league, isn't it?'

'What do you mean?'

'Plugging a sleeping man with a shotgun from three feet is one thing. I bet you couldn't hit a barn door with a rifle in your hand.'

Dave was aggrieved. 'I had weapons training in the Army.'

Herbert pulled a pack of cigarettes from his pocket and lit up.

'Anyhow, there's something bloody funny going on. Someone's bumped off a friend of mine, not to mention a useful business asset, and I'd like to know who.'

Dave ostentatiously waved smoke out of his face.

'I haven't heard anything. There's a million rumours, though.'

'Such as?'

'Disgruntled punter. Pissed-off husband. Or the Mafia – 'cos he's ridden in the States. Take your pick.'

'Rubbish.' Herbert took another deep drag. 'I can't help feeling it's because he was connected to me. In which case, we're all at risk.'

'Blimey.'

'So keep me posted, eh?'


The incident room was crowded for the briefing. Orchard ran through matters quickly. Annie noted that he was wearing the smarter of his two suits – probably because he would be heading straight into a press conference. At the beginning of the investigation, Orchard had talked to the press every day but he'd soon cut it down. It was depressing for all parties to keep repeating the same up-beat platitudes. They were making no obvious progress and everyone knew it.

'How are we getting on,' he asked, 'with Freddy's phone records?' There'd been a delay in tracking them down. It had only recently been discovered that Freddy had had a second mobile phone which he'd kept under the driver's seat of his car.

'Still trying to identify some of the numbers, guv,' said DC Clive Cook, a renowned rugby-player who, Annie knew, would rather have been out chasing an armed psychopath than stuck in the office running a rule over Freddy's phone bill.

'However, we think we've found another of his girlfriends – a dentist's receptionist in Hungerford who admits she had a one-nighter at his cottage six weeks ago. She's only just got back from her honeymoon, though, which puts her in the Seychelles when Freddy got shot. She's definitely in the clear – and so's her husband.'

'Seen the honeymoon photos, have you, Clive?' asked Jim Henderson and everyone laughed.

'I can't tell that to the press,' said Orchard. 'And if I see those photos in the *News of the World* I don't want to hear that someone in here tipped them off.'

Clive spoke up again. 'One other thing, guv. There's a few calls to Tony Byrne's place on the list.'

Orchard's face lit up.

'They were stablemates,' piped up Annie. 'They were probably discussing the going at Newbury or something perfectly innocent.'

Orchard didn't look convinced.

'This Tony Byrne,' said a voice from the back, 'did you know he's got a certificate for a .22 rifle?'

Sergeant Joe Mackenzie was a uniformed officer who'd been co-ordinating the search for the murder weapon. All eyes were on him now.

'As you know, we've been checking all certificate-holders and his name's on the list.'

'And?' Orchard prompted.

'A couple of us called on him to check it out. He was unable to show us the gun. Said it was stolen a couple of months ago.'

'Did he report it?'

'As a matter of fact, he did. Both to the insurance company and to us.'

Annie didn't know what to make of that – nothing, probably. Evidently Orchard felt the same way because he abruptly closed the meeting.


Since the accident that had put paid to his riding career, Mickey had worked hard on his body. At first it had been out of necessity, then out of desire to make the most of his physique by way of compensation. Besides, he enjoyed hard physical work. And building his muscles was one way to attract a certain kind of woman.

Today Mickey didn't overdo it. He put in just enough effort to impress Josh who watched in awe as he bench-pressed three hundred pounds. After that the lad was eager for Mickey's approval, asking for tips and concentrating on every remark he let slip.

He was generous with his expertise, helping Josh run through his paces, encouraging and cajoling as if he were really interested.

Finally they sat on the bench in the changing room, their half-naked bodies gleaming with sweat. Josh frankly appraised Mickey's physique. He was one of those with a body beautiful complex, Mickey could tell.

'I wish I could get that kind of definition,' Josh said. 'Your pecs are just great – look at mine.'

Mickey considered. 'You need to work on them more. More upper body exercises.'

'But I do that. I've been killing myself for months but it makes no difference.'

Mickey pretended to think. 'I can tell you how to get those

muscles in top shape but it's not going to do you much good.'

'Why not?'

'Because you need to build up body mass. That takes supplements.'

'What do you mean "supplements"?'

'I don't think they're legal here. But that's how those guys in the magazines get to look the way they do.'

'Are they dangerous?'

Mickey laughed. 'I'm alive, aren't I? I've been taking them for nearly ten years. If anyone tells you they're damaging that's bullshit.'

'That's what I need.'

Mickey didn't contradict him, just waited for Josh to take the bait.

'Could you get me some?'

'Josh, they're not legal here.'

'Yeah, but if they're safe –'

'If you went into competitions and took a drug test, you'd be in trouble.'

'You think I could go into competition?'

'That's not what I'm saying.'

'Mickey, I'd love some. I'll pay anything.'

He appeared to consider the matter. 'Maybe, Josh, you don't need to pay. You see, I'd like a favour . . .'

# Chapter Eight

Tony sat next to Neil in the changing room at Sandown Park. The lad looked more grown-up somehow in the black-and-green colours of Mrs Lim. He was his usual quiet self but seemed at home among the other jockeys, some of whom had gone out of their way to make him welcome.

'Nervous?' Tony asked.

Neil nodded. 'A bit.'

'You don't look it. When I get nerves it shows. Ask Kate.'

But today Tony was feeling relaxed before the race. For one thing, he had no expectation of getting in the frame on Cold Call. For another, he had no concerns about his weight.

The two factors were connected. Until a horse has three races under its belt the handicapper will not rate it. Consequently, as Cold Call had not run in Britain since his arrival from the States, he had to carry top weight – ten stone.

Tony had no trouble making a weight like that. It had been tempting to indulge himself a little – scrambled eggs and sausages for lunch, for instance – but he knew he dared not stray from the regime that was keeping him straight. At least he'd been able to forego the torture of the sauna.

Annie's father, Doug, loved email. It meant he could keep tabs on all his racing contacts without putting his dodgy knee through the rigours of a day at a racecourse. He could also keep in touch with friends from overseas – like Cliff Templeton, whose mail from San Francisco was currently displayed on his computer screen. Ten years previously, in the twilight of his career, Cliff had ridden in England for a season. He'd returned home to work as a racing journalist and, in Doug's opinion, there wasn't much he didn't know about horses raised in America.

Some days Doug's knee was worse than others and today was one of them. It was tempting to stay in his room. With a television, a video recorder, a phone and a computer he could follow the day's racing all over the country, talk to his contacts and place bets. On the other hand, there was nothing quite like a bit of company when you were on the brink of bringing home the bacon. Besides, Malcolm at Coral's down the road had seen too much of his money recently.

He hobbled into the kitchen and scrabbled inside the teapot he never used. He came up with £150. Good enough.

He moved slowly to the door and the painful descent of one flight of stairs to the street. It was time for Malcolm to give him his money back.

Kate was on hand as Neil weighed out. Stopgap had been given nine stone six in the handicap but because of Neil's novice status that was reduced to eight stone thirteen. Since Neil himself weighed a pound under eight stone that meant the horse had to carry an extra stone of lead in a cloth across his back.

'OK?' she said as she took the saddle from him.

He nodded. 'Yes, Madam.'

'Do you want to borrow my phone and ring your dad?'

She'd wondered whether to make the offer. It wasn't any

business of hers what went on between Neil and his father but she'd hoped relations had improved. Neil shook his head. Obviously they hadn't.

'No, thanks.'

Kate made one more effort.

'Look, next time, why don't we ask him along?'

Neil's mouth turned down. 'I wouldn't bother. He'd never come.'

'Where are you off to, Dad?' Annie was on the doorstep as Doug opened the door, her finger poised over the bell.

'Shouldn't you be at work?' he replied.

'This is work.' She grinned. 'I've come to watch the Tote with you. Bit of a skive but the boss says it's OK.'

'Excellent.' He shut the door behind him and steered her down the street.

'Where are we going?'

'To the bookie's. And you can be my police escort when I relieve them of all their money.'

'Dad!'

'You think I'm joking? Follow me.'

The parade ring was buzzing with trainers, owners and assorted connections but Tony found Mickey in a small circle of isolation in the middle. They'd only spoken briefly up on the gallops the other morning. Notwithstanding the yard gossip about Mickey, Tony had found him polite and sensible. So he wasn't prepared for what followed.

'You have a very simple task, Tony,' said Mickey. 'Follow my instructions precisely and you will win this race.'

Tony began to revise his first impressions.

'I'll do my best,' he said in a noncommittal tone.

'I have no doubt about that but it is most important that you ride the horse exactly as I tell you.'

'I'm listening.'

'First, you follow the pace. You must be up with the leading horses at all times. You have a high draw, that is good. Keep tight to the rail and track the front runners.'

'OK.' Tony doubted that Cold Call could stay with the pace but it was hardly the moment to mention that.

'Second – and this is most important of all – leave your run till late. Do not hit the front until the very last minute. Do you understand?'

'I understand what you are saying.'

'Yes, but you don't believe me, do you? I can tell. Listen, Tony, I know this horse. He's not what you think. He will win if you do as I say.'

'Right.'

'Just don't make a move too soon. If there's no horse in front of him he stops. OK?'

'OK.'

'Good luck then. We shall meet in the winner's enclosure.'

Tony shook his hand – it seemed to be expected – and walked briskly to where Dermot was holding the small black horse. What they'd told him about Mickey was true after all. He was crazy.

'Bloody hell, Dad,' Annie blurted out as she glanced at the wad of notes in his hand.

Doug ignored her and pushed the money under the screen to Malcolm behind the counter. The bookmaker raised his eyebrows.

'I'll take the price,' Doug said and Malcolm noted it on his betting slip.

'How can you afford it?' Annie protested as they retreated from the counter.

'Don't nag,' he said. 'You sound just like your mother.'

Ouch! She took a deep breath and said in calmer tones, 'What are you on then?'

He showed her the slip.

'Cold Call?' The friendly black horse she'd seen at Kate's yard. Bernard Shen's horse. Her heart began to thump.

'What's going on?'

'Look at the price now.'

Her eyes flicked to the odds displayed on one of the screens above their heads. Cold Call 20-1.

'So?'

'It's just come in from twenty-fives.' He pointed to the figure Malcolm had marked on his slip. 'Yesterday he was at thirty-threes. I got some of that too.'

Annie felt a tingle of excitement and unzipped her handbag. Doug chuckled as he saw her bring out her purse.

'Come on, Dad. What's the story?'

'Later,' he said. 'After you've placed your bet.'

Greta chucked the magazine back on to the pile. She couldn't concentrate. She got to her feet and crossed the thick oatmeal carpet to the water-cooler. Not that she was thirsty but it gave her something to do. A young woman in a suit behind the reception desk smiled at her in a practised manner – she probably witnessed all kinds of nervous behaviour in here on a daily basis.

'The Admissions Officer will be down in a minute, Mrs

Somerville,' she said. 'She knows you're waiting.'

Greta nodded. It wasn't their fault. She shouldn't have turned up early. She'd intended to kill time in the Oxford Street shops but, when it came to it, she'd not had the stomach for it. The impulse detour into Mothercare had not been a good idea.

She slumped back into the beige leather Chesterfield and tried to ignore the nausea in the pit of her stomach. She told herself everything was under control. Paul was spending the night with a friend and Laurie had said he might stay in town after he'd been to Sandown. As far as Greta was concerned he could stay away for as long as he liked.

Life was full of surprises. She'd never, ever thought she'd see the inside of an abortion clinic.

Neil was biased but he knew he was not alone in thinking Stopgap the star of the parade ring. His sable brown coat gleamed in the pale summer sunshine and he surveyed all in the ring with an air of regal disdain.

'He looks a picture, Josh,' said Kate as she gave Neil a leg-up into the saddle. 'Well done.'

The lad bobbed his head in thanks and led Stopgap on a circuit of the ring.

Beneath him Neil imagined he could feel the horse revelling in the admiration of the spectators banked on the viewing terrace and massed on the rails. Neil couldn't deny it was a thrill to sit on him.

It wasn't until they got out on to the course and headed for the starting-stalls that he began to have misgivings. There was no spring in Stopgap's step and he was slow to respond as Neil urged him into a trot. Neil couldn't understand it. Compared to

the morning on the gallops, he could have sworn this was a
different horse.

'Come on, boy,' he muttered in the horse's ear and gave him
a tap with his boot. Reluctantly, it seemed, Stopgap answered
the instruction and went on more urgently.

Neil was puzzled. Was Stopgap always like this before a
race? He didn't know. Maybe the horse was nervous but would
perform when the action started.

By the time Neil reached the starting-stalls he was in a
quandary. Here he was on the favourite, moments before the
most important ride of his career so far, and the horse gave
every impression of wading through mud.

On impulse, he avoided the handlers and approached the
starter.

'What's up, son?' Beneath the obligatory bowler hat the
official looked relatively youthful – on the right side of sixty, at
any rate. 'Make it snappy,' he said.

'Does my horse look all right to you?'

The starter gave Stopgap a swift visual examination.

'Looks tiptop. You got a problem?'

'He just doesn't feel right.'

The man frowned. 'Trot him up for me.'

Neil did as he was told.

The starter shrugged. 'He looks fine.' It was obvious the
official wanted to get on with the race.

Neil would have appealed to Tony but he was already in the
stalls. Everyone was waiting for him.

Stopgap was the last in. Perhaps he would be all right once
they started and this bad dream would be over.

Laurie wasn't much enjoying his day at the races. His mind

kept drifting to Greta and what was happening to her. He'd resisted offering to go with her to the clinic – how could he? She'd simply have accused him of being a spectator at the execution. And, of course, she would have had a point.

'Oy, Laurie, top me up, will you?'

He looked up. The extraordinary girl Mickey had brought with him was waving her empty champagne glass at him. He swiftly refilled her glass – he was neglecting his duties. Mickey had not yet returned from the parade ring and had asked him to keep an eye on her.

Not that there was much chance of Caroline going unnoticed. In a shocking pink suit with a gleaming bolt of honey-blonde hair hanging past her shoulders, she was a magnet to the eye. Particularly since half of her six foot height appeared to be made up of bronzed and slender leg.

'What's your fancy now then?' she said, inclining her head towards him so that her hair swung towards him, curtaining them off from the other occupants of the owners' bar. There was an unmistakable double entendre in the enquiry but he took it at face value.

'Stopgap's the one to beat. I've got a tenner on him for my son – though it's hardly worth it at that price.'

'What about Mickey's horse?'

Laurie shrugged. 'Not a chance – but don't tell him I told you.'

Her pretty face fell. 'Wish you'd said earlier. I've just bunged a hundred quid on it.' Then she brightened. 'Never mind, it's his money. Ooh, look, my glass seems to be empty again.'

'Right, Dad, tell me why I've just bet the housekeeping on a horse carrying top weight who hasn't run for a year?'

Without taking his eyes from the television screen ahead, which showed the last horse going into the stalls, Doug said, 'For the same reason other people are lumping money on. Cold Call broke down as a two-year-old in the States but before he got injured he'd gained a bit of a reputation.'

'What kind of reputation?'

'As a lazy beast, not interested in work. But when he got into a race he was a changed personality. He hated to be beaten.'

'So he won a lot of two-year-old races?'

'Only a couple, according to my information, but that's because it took a while to work out how to ride him. You see, when he gets to the front, he stops racing.'

'You mean, he thinks he's won?'

Doug shrugged. 'Something like that.'

'Just as well you didn't tell me before – I'd have kept my hand in my pocket.'

'Well, if we go down, we won't be alone. The starting price has just gone down to eights. Somebody out there has been putting serious money on.'

They'd only travelled a furlong and Neil knew Stopgap was not interested. The Ferrari was stuck in second gear.

Three furlongs into the race, a leading group of five runners had put daylight between themselves and rest of the field. Stopgap was not among them; instead he was lobbing along in the rear, resisting all Neil's attempts to get him up into contention. Soon the position would be hopeless.

Neil thought of his mum watching on the television, and of Kate and Mrs Lim who would waiting for him at the end of the race. What was he going to say to them? As for his dad – well, at least he didn't have to make any excuses to that old bastard.

He gave his lethargic mount a sharp crack with the whip. The horse jerked his head in protest but his legs moved no faster. Neil hit Stopgap again – nothing.

'For God's sake,' he cried in frustration. 'Wake up!'

Greta looked up as a smartly dressed woman stepped out of the lift, followed by a tall girl carrying a small purple ruck-sack.

'Nearly all over, darling,' said the woman in plummy Home Counties tones, adding with feeling, 'Thank Christ.'

The girl did not acknowledge the remark but walked slowly to a large armchair opposite Greta's sofa and slumped into it.

The woman turned to the front desk.

'Thank you so much,' she said to the receptionist.

'Was everything all right, Mrs Chegwyn?' asked the girl in a suit, producing a slip of paper and laying it on the desk in front of her.

The woman put on a pair of spectacles and squinted at the paper. 'You've all been *so* kind,' she announced as she pulled a cheque book from her bag.

For God's sake, Greta thought, you're not checking out of the Ritz.

She looked at the girl opposite her. Tall, slender as a reed, with the same blonde hair as her embarrassing mother, which hung over her face as she sat with her head bowed.

Suddenly the girl looked up and caught Greta staring at her. Her face was as unlined as an egg and white with misery. Greta noticed a brace on her teeth. This girl was young – thirteen or fourteen, maybe. Paul's age.

Greta's heart went out to her. She smiled at her in sympathy.

The girl's face changed as she appeared to notice Greta for

the first time. The blank mask of self-pity was replaced by a glare of anger – and reproach.

Her thoughts were plain: *I* had no choice – but what are *you* doing here?

As he'd gone down to the start Tony had turned Mickey's words over in his mind. His work on Cold Call earlier had not impressed him, and nothing Neil had ever said led him to believe the horse had an unexpected turn of foot. Neil, after all, had been riding out Cold Call for the past few months – he must know him better than anyone. Tony reckoned Mickey's wildly optimistic instructions would raise a smile on the lad's face when this was all over.

From the off the pace was quick. The race had been billed as the most competitive handicap of the season so far and the hundred thousand pounds in prize money was a serious incentive for owners and trainers. Of course, the real money would be made in the betting. Tony had noticed the prices up on the big screen before he'd left the parade ring. It had been a surprise to see that Cold Call's odds had shrunk so dramatically but he was too experienced to pay it much heed. The optimism of gamblers rarely had a great deal of bearing on reality.

For three furlongs Cold Call pulled quite hard and it was an effort to keep him at the rear of the leading group. The little horse was keener now he was in a proper race, that much could be said. Tony kept him tight on the rail as they reached the end of the back straight and entered the sweeping bend that would lead them round into the long uphill battle for the line.

At the beginning of the home straight Cold Call was still in touch. Tony couldn't believe it.

*

It was her mother – Rita's – fault that Sarah ended up watching the racing on the TV. She'd only got back from Nice that morning and was lounging on the sofa in the sitting room, not sure what to do with herself. Rita meanwhile was channel-hopping, pretending to look for a programme like *Ready Steady Cook* or *Countdown*. Sarah suspected she really wanted to catch a daytime soap. In the event she chanced on the racing.

'We're not watching *that*,' Rita stated with some emphasis.

'No,' Sarah agreed hurriedly. Her mother had already had a go at her about 'that episode in your life', as she'd put it, in the car on the way back from Heathrow.

But even as Sarah said it she heard a snatch of commentary that grabbed her attention: '– and Cold Call on the rails is handily placed as they turn for home –'

Cold Call? Sarah knew that name. The horse Freddy was on when they had ridden out that afternoon.

'Wait a minute, Mummy. Turn it back.'

Rita glared at her. 'Are you sure that's wise?'

'*Please*, Mummy.'

Rita handed her the remote control and stalked out of the room.

Sarah switched back to the racing.

The home straight at Sandown Park slopes uphill for all of its four-furlong length until well past the winning post. It's no place for a horse who's short on courage or stamina. And though Cold Call was still travelling well as they came out of the home turn, Tony had every expectation that the little horse would soon begin to tire.

The leader, Lucky Something, was a powerful grey whose

long strides were threatening to take him away from the field. Only Funny Money on Tony's outside and Cold Call were managing to stay with him, though Tony was expecting Stopgap to make a move. He'd not been aware of Neil's horse yet but he'd beaten Lucky Something by two lengths in a late surge last time out so Tony had no doubt he'd be coming.

Two furlongs and the places were still the same. Cold Call showed no signs of tiring and it occurred to Tony that he could hang on to third.

Funny Money was a length and half up on Cold Call and as his jockey began to ply his whip in his left hand the horse moved on to the rail, taking Tony's ground.

With no expectation of success, he switched Cold Call to the outside and gave him a tap, asking the horse the question: *Can you do it?*

Cold Call lengthened his stride and surged to the shoulder of the horse in front. He could do it, all right. Tony urged him on. They cruised past Funny Money and attacked Lucky Something inside the last furlong.

Now they were under the stands and the winning post was flashing towards them. They still had a length to make up.

Cold Call dug deep.

*Is this late enough for you, Mickey?* thought Tony as they took the grey on the line.

'Calm down, Annie,' muttered Doug as his daughter, still caught up in the thrill of the race, whirled him round and round. 'Think of my knee.'

The bookie's regulars stepped back to give them room and looked on in amusement. They wouldn't forget this in a hurry. They'd be ribbing Doug for months.

Annie finally let him go. 'Dad, you're a genius!' she cried. 'You should have been a professional gambler. We could have lived in luxury.'

'I thought you were meant to be observing the race with a detached professional eye.'

'Oh.' In the excitement she'd forgotten she was meant to be working. 'You know, Dad, I'd be interested to see if Mr Shen is in the winner's enclosure.'

'I thought you might. Let's go home and have a look. I've got the video working.' He headed for the door.

'Aren't you forgetting something?' He looked puzzled. 'Our winnings,' she added.

'How silly of me,' Doug muttered and turned towards the counter where a grinning Malcolm was waiting for him.

'He looks happy,' said Annie, 'considering you've just taken him to the cleaner's.'

'A big pay-out's good for business. Besides, most of the money was on Stopgap and where did that finish?'

Good question, thought Annie.

Sarah was in turmoil as she watched the scenes of jubilation on the TV screen. Tony was acknowledging the crowd, a grin of delight and disbelief on his face. Other familiar faces were all around. Vicky, hanging on to Cold Call's bridle with one hand and thumping his gleaming black coat in congratulation with the other. She could see Laurie in the crush, next to a smartly dressed Asian man. And there was Kate, tearful and smiling, as the commentator spoke in glowing terms of her courage in soldiering on despite her brother's murder.

A memory of that wonderful afternoon up on the gallops came back to Sarah with full force. The way Freddy had schooled Cold Call with such skill and patience. How pleased he'd been with the little horse. Freddy should have been riding Cold Call at Sandown this afternoon. The victory belonged to him, not Tony.

Sarah blinked back the tears and came to a decision. She couldn't carry on hiding for ever. She owed it to Freddy.

'Is that him, do you think?' Annie pointed at the Oriental face behind Kate Montague's shoulder as she faced the TV camera.

'He looks too young,' said Doug. 'I think Bernard Shen is even older than I am.'

They watched the presentation ceremony in the winner's enclosure. The Oriental gentleman was introduced as Mr Lee, who accepted the winner's trophy on behalf of the owner who would, Mr Lee said in a brief statement, be 'very happy'. He added that this was Mr Shen's first winner on British soil but he predicted it would be the first of many.

Annie pressed on. 'Do you think Mr Lee fixed the race?'

Doug scratched his head. 'I don't know – probably. I bet somebody somewhere made a lot of money out of it, but you'll never prove a thing.'

'Thanks, Dad. I'm sure that's just what my guv'nor wants to hear.'

Kate found Neil close to tears in the weighing room.

'I'm sorry, Miss Montague. I tried everything but he wouldn't run. He was completely different to before. I don't understand it.'

'Neither do I, Neil.'

'You won't want me to ride for you any more now. I've let everyone down.'

'I don't believe that and you mustn't either. This game will always bite you once in a while.'

But he would not be consoled.


Rita was on her knees in the kitchen when Sarah came in. She had on a pair of yellow Marigold gloves and was scrubbing out a cupboard.

'Why are you doing that, Mummy? Leave it for Eva.'

Eva came on Mondays and Thursdays. Sometimes there was nothing for her to do.

Rita ignored her and redoubled her efforts.

'I've come to ask for Joe Shapiro's number.'

That brought the cleaning to a halt. Rita got to her feet.

'So you've come to your senses?'

Sarah nodded. They'd talked long and hard about it before she'd fled to join her sister holidaying in the South of France. Sarah had been adamant about not going to the police. She'd said she couldn't face it.

Her mother stripped off her gloves and found a number in her address book.

'That's his direct line.' Joe – a partner in Shapiro & Jacobs – was Sarah's cousin. He'd drop everything for Auntie Rita.

Sarah hesitated in front of the phone.

'There's going to be such a lot of fuss, Mummy. I'm really sorry.'

Rita put her arm round her. 'So there's a fuss. You've got to do what's right.'

'I know.' She picked up the receiver. 'There's just one thing –'

'Don't worry, darling. I'll deal with your father.'

Sarah made the call to the solicitor.

*

Jill Carlton, the Admissions Officer of the Lambton Clinic, tapped her pencil impatiently on her clipboard as the lift took an unaccountable journey up to the sixth floor. The door pinged open to reveal an empty landing. This was typical of how her day had gone so far. The only good thing about it had been getting shot of the Chegwyns. And now she'd left Mrs Somerville cooling her heels for an extra twenty minutes.

Finally the lift plunged down to reception and Jill exited briskly with her I'm-*so*-sorry expression firmly in place.

The room was empty of patients.

Jill turned to the receptionist. 'Where's Mrs Somerville?'

The receptionist looked back blankly. 'Isn't she with you?'

'No.'

'She was gone when I got back from the loo. I thought you must have fetched her.'

Jill chucked her clipboard on to the desk. It wasn't the first time someone had got cold feet while sitting in reception. Well, stuff it. At least now she had time for a cup of coffee.

Like everyone else on the course, Vicky was curious about Stopgap's failure to perform. She looked at him with concern as he stood in his box, guzzling a pail of water.

'How do you account for it, Josh?'

The lad shrugged his shoulders. 'That's horses for you, isn't it?'

'Not this horse.' Stopgap was one of the yard's most reliable performers. In any weather, on any course, you could set your watch by him. He'd never been known to give less than a hundred per cent in his life.

The horse lifted his big brown muzzle from the bucket. Vicky could see he'd drained it of every drop.

'He seems pretty thirsty.'

'He's just had a race, hasn't he?'

'Not by his standards. He hardly broke sweat.'

Josh grinned inanely. There was something odd about his manner. As if he didn't care. Vicky thought of something he surely did care about.

'Aren't you a bit pissed off? I'd have spent my win present already in your position. He was a cert.'

'What's a hundred quid?'

This was a different tune from the one Josh normally sang – particularly the night before payday. He was really beginning to get up her nose.

'Don't you want to know why your horse did bugger all?'

He stared at her insolently. 'I think you've already asked me that. The answer, Vicky, is that I couldn't give a stuff.'

She turned on her heel and left, finding it deeply suspicious that the one person who didn't want to know why Stopgap had failed was his lad. Maybe that was because he already knew the answer.

Kate's post-race confrontation with Mrs Lim didn't run along the lines she had expected. Gladys didn't shout and badger her and demand explanations which she could not give. She simply fired her.

'I am truly sorry, Kate. I think you are an outstanding trainer and I value the time you have devoted to my horses and also to me. I particularly regret having to withdraw my string at a time when you have suffered a personal loss.

'However, I believe there is something bad going on at your yard and you do not seem able to stop it. Pay Back Time dies, your leading jockey is killed, Stopgap forgets how to run – who knows what will happen tomorrow? Well, I can guess. This Bernard Shen is a criminal. Now you are doing business with him, I can no longer do business with you.'

'Gladys, I have only one horse of Mr Shen's . . .'

But Mrs Lim's mind was made up.

Annie's colleagues at Farley Road seemed less impressed with her analysis of the Tote Exacta Stakes than with her windfall at the bookie's. Apart from DS Hunter.

'Are you telling us that your father knew the race was going to be fixed?'

'No. Dad had perfectly good reasons for fancying Cold Call and when the price started to drop it confirmed his judgement. He's just a gambler who got lucky – for once.'

'Nevertheless,' said Hunter pompously, 'if the race was rigged, then your winnings have been unlawfully acquired.'

In the event, she volunteered to put £50 behind the bar at The Goat that night and they turned their attention to her dad's recording of the race. No one recognised 'Mr Lee' but they took stills off the video. There was a good chance someone in the Met or the Hong Kong police would be able to identify such a distinctive face.

Orchard had retired next door to talk to the Jockey Club about testing Stopgap, the under-performing favourite, to see if the horse had been doped. He returned with the information that a vet had already taken blood and urine samples though the results wouldn't be available for a few days. The vet had also examined the animal and found him to be perfectly sound.

Of more interest was a phone call he'd just received from London.

'Any of you ever heard of a woman called Sarah Cooper?'

They all looked at him blankly. 'No, guv.'

'She's Tony Byrne's ex. Lived with him for six months and walked out on the morning after Freddy was killed.'

That was a bit of a bombshell.

'How come we didn't know about her? No wonder we're not getting anywhere with this enquiry. You'd think we'd know who all the key personnel have been shacking up with.'

Annie had a question. 'Do you know what colour her hair is, guv?'

Her male colleagues groaned.

'No, I don't. But you'll shortly be able to see for yourself. Her solicitor is driving her up from North London as we speak to make a voluntary statement. And you, DC James, will be one of the officers staying behind to interview her.'

'Oh.' That put the mockers on her evening.

'Since you've spent the afternoon at the races, as it were, I'm sure you understand. I would also of course value your feminine insight into the mysterious Ms Cooper.' He turned to Hunter. 'Keith, do you mind listening to what this woman's got to tell us? They'll be here in about an hour I expect, depending on the traffic.'

Annie pulled a £50 note from her purse and handed it to Clive Cook. 'Leave something on the tab for me,' she said though she knew there was little hope of that.

Kate needed someone to confide in. Vicky was the obvious candidate – she'd doubtless start making lists of prospective new owners before Kate had finished talking. But she wanted a different kind of sympathy, from someone who would tell her everything was going to be all right. It hurt to admit it, but she wanted a man.

Tony listened to the news of Mrs Lim's defection as they sat in his car before leaving the racecourse.

'Exactly how many horses does she have with you?'

'Twenty-one. That's nearly half.'

For a second his face told her what she knew all too well. This was a calamity.

'Jesus. That's a bit of a shock. How're you feeling?'

She shrugged. She'd thought she was taking it well but suddenly she wasn't so sure.

Tony put his arm around her shoulder. 'Come on, Kate. You're a great trainer. You won't have a problem finding new owners.'

'Do you mean that?'

'You bet. You're the best trainer I've ever worked with.'

That was exactly what she needed to hear.

'Thanks, Tony.'

All the same, Kate realised it wasn't going to be easy. She knew there was prejudice against her in some quarters simply because she was a young, attractive woman. Until she had a few big winners under her belt it would be hard to convince the biggest and the best owners. What she needed was someone from outside the British racing establishment. Someone not impressed by reputation alone. And, of course, there was already one at hand.

Before this afternoon's racing, Kate would quite happily have severed her relationship with Mr Shen, even at the expense of losing Cold Call. It would have been a relief to have Mickey's menacing presence out of the yard. But now the situation had been turned on its head.

'Mickey wants me to go to his party tonight,' she said. He was hosting a celebratory buffet supper at a house in Surrey, not far from the course. He'd mentioned it to her before the race. At the time she'd thought talk of celebration was a bit premature but, as it turned out, he'd been right.

'I said no but perhaps I ought to go. I can't face it on my own, though.'

Tony grinned. 'I can take a hint, Kate. It will be my pleasure.'

Most of the team were in the pub drinking at her expense as Annie spied the navy blue BMW nose into the car park three floors below.

'They're here,' she called and Hunter and Orchard joined her at the window.

They watched as a balding fellow in spectacles and a blue suit got out of the driver's seat. They waited expectantly for the off-side door to open. There was a flash of movement in the windscreen as, Annie guessed, the passenger checked her makeup in the driver's mirror. Then the door opened and legs, shapely feminine legs, protruded from the vehicle.

'Aye-aye,' muttered Orchard.

Ms Cooper was in full view now, also dressed in a dark suit which did nothing to hide her well-turned figure. But her crowning glory, particularly from this viewpoint, was her long curling copper-coloured hair.

'So there you are,' said Annie to herself with undisguised satisfaction. 'You're Freddy's redhead, aren't you?'

Annie had never seen Hunter so affable. He positively twinkled with amiability as he ushered Sarah Cooper and her solicitor, Joe Shapiro, into the interview room. Annie had not thought him capable of small talk so it was a surprise to hear him tut-tutting over the traffic on the M25 and remarking on the disappointing weather, just like any bar-room bore.

By contrast, Sarah and her brief were noticeably quiet as they took their seats. After introductions had been performed and refreshments offered, Shapiro cleared his throat and launched into a rehearsed speech. He laid great emphasis on the voluntary nature of the statement his client was about to make and her overwhelming concern to help the police enquiry in any way she could.

Annie was keen to hear what Sarah had to say for herself and examined her closely as Shapiro banged on. She was quite a looker, the sober suit couldn't conceal that, and her gleaming suntan was of the kind that had obviously not been casually acquired in the course of a day's work. In fact Annie would have bet that Sarah Cooper didn't do too many days' work from one week's end to the next.

At last the interview got underway and Sarah began to talk in a cultured drawl that, Annie guessed, was the product of an expensive independent education. At her own school she'd sometimes played netball against the fancy North London teams and those girls had talked just like Sarah.

At a glance from Shapiro, Sarah began her story, confirming that until recently she had been living with Tony Byrne and was acquainted with Freddy Montague.

'Acquainted?' queried Hunter.

'We were lovers actually,' she said, holding her head up and looking him straight in the eye.

Well, of course they were. Annie had already guessed as much but it was nice to have the matter out in the open.

Hunter smiled encouragingly and, sufficiently prompted, Sarah resumed.

'Tony and I hadn't been getting on too well. To be honest,

the relationship was coming to an end. That's when Freddy and I became close.'

'So how long was it before Mr Montague died,' Hunter asked, 'that you and he started, er, seeing each other?'

'About a fortnight.'

'But you were still living with Mr Byrne?'

'Yes.'

That would explain the phone calls to Tony's place listed in Freddy's phone records.

In the short pause that followed Shapiro spoke up. 'Perhaps, officer, it would be a good idea if Ms Cooper gave you her information in full before you ask her any more questions.'

Hunter nodded. 'By all means – fire away, Ms Cooper.'

Sarah opened her mouth to speak but, before she could begin, Hunter interrupted again. 'Just one more thing – did Mr Byrne know about your friendship with Mr Montague?'

'No.' There was a shrill edge to her voice now. 'At least, I didn't think so at the time.'

'And now?'

'Now I think he must have. And that's why he did it.'

Hunter looked puzzled, as if he'd lost the thread of the conversation. Annie knew just how he felt.

'I'm sorry, Ms Cooper – that's why he did what?'

'That's why he killed Freddy. That's what I've come to tell you.'

Hunter looked the way Annie felt: flabbergasted. They'd not expected this.

Sarah's voice sounded even shriller than before. 'It's all my fault. Tony killed Freddy because of *me*.'

And she laid her head on her arms and burst into tears.

# PART THREE

PART THREE

# Chapter Nine

Tony turned to Kate as they waited in a line of cars snaking into the Sundial Mansions private estate. 'You know that money? I'm going to give it away to charity.'

'That's what I hoped you'd say.'

'The trouble is, there are so many deserving causes.'

'I suggest you get rid of it quickly, Tony.'

He nodded. 'First thing tomorrow.'

Ahead they could see a knot of security men in fluorescent yellow jackets. Occasionally a car would shoot down the outside lane and be waved through, to the annoyance of those in the queue.

'I notice,' observed Kate as a Mercedes saloon with tinted windows swept by, 'that the really fancy cars go straight in.'

'They're the family bosses,' said Tony. 'Can't keep Vito Corleone waiting.'

She chuckled. 'I'm not sure that's funny. Gladys Lim says Bernard Shen's a crook.'

'And you believe her?'

'No. I think she was trying to justify herself.'

The line of cars moved up a space.

'Just stay by my side, Tony.'

'It's a party. Suppose I get lucky?'

Her face fell.

'I'm only joking, Kate,' he added hastily. 'How could I get luckier than squiring the Goddess of the Gallops?'

Eventually they reached the knot of yellow jackets by the security barrier and, after some walkie-talkie communication and much studying of lists, they were allowed to proceed.

The grounds of the Sundial Estate seemed to roll on for miles. They gazed on neatly husbanded woodland and lush green acres of lawn interrupted by tennis courts and croquet lawns. In the distance could be discerned the fairways of an extensive golf course.

'I don't see any houses,' muttered Tony after they had travelled for about five minutes. He'd been instructed to 'follow the arrows' – fortunately there were plenty of them pegged in the roadside verges.

As he said it, the arrows directed them down a branch road through a set of towering wrought-iron gates set into a high dense hedge. They drove into a landscaped vista of more woods and lawns, like a park within a park.

'There's the house,' said Kate, pointing to a two-storey redbrick pile that sprawled disappointingly in a dip at the end of an avenue of birch and beech. 'It looks modern to me. I bet they knocked some wonderful old building down to put it up.'

'That's so they could install the laser cameras and the infrared security systems.'

More yellow-jacketed attendants directed them to a concealed meadow half full of parked cars. They left the car and strolled across the grass to the knot of people surrounding the marquee in front of the house.

'I promise I'll try and make this quick,' said Kate.

'No need to rush,' Tony replied. 'This looks like more fun than I've had in a long time.'

It had taken a while for Sarah to get going after her outburst. Annie had suggested the weeping woman take a few minutes to recover. Sarah had retired to the loo for nearly a quarter of an hour.

Just when Annie was on the point of fetching her, Sarah had returned and begun her story in low, matter-of-fact tones. For the moment her emotions were well under control. She gave a brief resumé of her romance with Tony and how she'd recently become involved with Freddy, the result, she claimed, of an argument.

'Tony and I had a row because he wouldn't take me out. We stayed in a lot because he was always watching his weight. God, people think women are fussy about their diets. They've got nothing on men like Tony. At least a woman will go to a pub and have a Perrier.'

Annie nodded in sympathy. She'd been through as many slimming regimes as the next girl but she'd never hung around indoors – though maybe that's why her diets had never worked. She forced her mind back to the point. Sarah was recounting her first night with Freddy.

'I went to the pub on my own but a lot of people from the yard were there. I got a bit drunk – because I'd had a row with Tony, I suppose – and Freddy offered to drive me home. Only we ended up at his place and, you know . . .'

She looked at Annie for support and the policewoman grinned back, anything to keep the river of information flowing.

'Anyhow,' Sarah continued, 'I didn't get back to Tony's until three in the morning and he wasn't even there. There was some drama with Lifeline, his mother's horse, and he got back later than me. He spent all next day saying sorry. Pretty funny, when you think about it.'

Annie didn't think it was funny at all but she smiled nonetheless. It made sense to let Sarah believe she was on her side.

'Freddy and I saw each other a lot after that – as often as we could, in fact. Even Tony began to notice that things had cooled off between him and me. Freddy and I were in love. He asked me to move in with him.'

'When exactly was this?' Hunter asked.

'On Thursday afternoon. I was meant to be at Ascot watching Tony but I stayed behind to be with Freddy instead.'

'That was the afternoon of the day he was killed?'

'That's right.'

'You spent all day with Freddy?'

'From lunchtime till about half-past five. Just before the last race on the television.'

'And that was the last time you saw him?'

Sarah hesitated. Her bottom lip was trembling again. 'Yes – and no,' she replied.

'What do you mean, Miss Cooper?' Hunter couldn't contain the eagerness in his voice.

'That was the last time I saw him alive,' she replied. 'When I went back to his cottage the next morning he was dead.'

And the tears began to flow again.

To Kate and Tony's surprise, they recognised a number of people amongst the crush on the lawn, many of them well-known racing faces. They found themselves surrounded by owners, trainers and jockeys, and a few of the larger-than-life rails bookies who weren't always made welcome at receptions of this nature. It looked as if Mickey had issued a blanket invitation to the entire racecourse.

A waiter appeared by their side with a tray of drinks. As Kate reached for an orange juice, a familiar voice said, 'For God's sake, woman, have a decent glass of fizz for once.'

Laurie looked as if he'd already had one or two himself but Kate said, 'Why not?' and took a glass of champagne.

For two pins, Tony would have done the same but Tim Shaw, one of Kate's owners, was standing at Laurie's elbow. Since Tony was down to ride Shaw's entry in the Commonwealth Handicap at Sandown the next day, it would hardly have been prudent. Instead he asked, 'What's Mickey Lee's connection with a place like this?'

'It belongs to Bernard Shen.' Shaw's Bostonian twang put the emphasis on the second syllable in 'Bernard'. 'He's got a ranch in Kentucky and I don't think he goes there much. Say, Kate,' he turned to her with hardly a pause, his bulk shutting Tony and Laurie out of the conversation, 'is it true Gladys Lim's taking her string off you?'

Kate gave him a rueful grin. His small colourless eyes gleamed with curiosity in his pink moon face. Though inherited wealth put him on the boards of a dozen companies in New York and London, the sharp intelligence that maintained his position was all his own.

'You're quick off the mark, aren't you, Tim?'

He didn't beat around the bush, it wasn't his style. 'What you gonna do? That's half your income up in smoke.'

Kate made an effort to smile. To appear downhearted before a man like Shaw would be a mistake. 'I'll find some new owners,' she said with more confidence than she felt.

'I wish I could help but I'm fixed up right now.' Shaw owned more than the two horses he kept with Kate, his others were with one of the most celebrated – and the most expensive – trainers in the land. Technically, Kate's two belonged to Shaw's daughter and both had passed into Kate's hands because they had a history of illness. 'Of course, things could change if Evening Shadow wins tomorrow.' And he laughed. Kate joined in politely – in her experience owners never missed an opportunity for special pleading.

Shaw moved closer and laid a big square hand on her arm. He dropped his voice. 'Seriously, I might be able to do something for you next season, though we'd have to take a close look at your facilities.' Kate knew this was a reference to the top-of-the-range amenities Shaw's horses currently enjoyed. Private gallops and a swimming pool were not available at Kate's yard.

'In the meantime,' he continued, 'you might try and do more business with Bernard. You did a heck of a job on that little horse of his today. And Mickey likes you. Believe me, these guys are serious players.'

Kate didn't doubt it.

'This is an extraordinary set-up,' Laurie told Tony. 'Half of Chinatown's been bussed in.'

Tony looked around. It was true that there were a lot of Chinese faces on show. Apart from the serving staff, who were handing round food and drink, there were smartly dressed Oriental figures everywhere, most of them male.

'Take a look inside the house,' Laurie added. 'There's some kind of gambling in every room. From roulette to Mah-jong – you name it.'

Mickey caught this remark as he eased through the crowd to join them. 'Chinese people love gambling,' he said. 'Tonight we're having some fun. Of course, everyone is welcome to join in.'

Mickey was as affable as Tony had ever seen him – and there was a hint of smugness in his eyes too. They'd not spoken in the excitement following the afternoon's race. Tony couldn't put it off any longer.

'I owe you an apology, Mickey. Cold Call did everything you said and more.'

'And so did you.' Mickey's lop-sided smile stretched wide. 'He followed my instructions to the letter,' he explained to Laurie, 'even though he thought they were crazy. So, next time, Tony, are you going to believe what I tell you?'

The duck pond was almost square in shape, with a crumbling brick wall around three sides and a thicket of brambles on the other. Even on a golden summer's evening like this one it was not the most picturesque spot. The disused greenhouses nearby, with their shattered glass, Keep Out notices and head-high riot of nettles, were an eyesore. The surface of the pond was murky and oil-streaked, probably from the rusty Ford Anglia that the Benson kids had chucked in it back in the eighties. And of ducks there was no sign.

But Alan Sykes and his son Daniel were not bothered by nettles or broken glass. And the clouds of midges that drifted across the still black water, providing a moving feast for the skimming swallows, were only a minor irritant. They had other things on their mind: fish.

It had taken Alan a month of campaigning to get to the point where he and the lad were setting up their equipment by the wall of the duck pond, on the spot he'd last fished as a ten-year-old some twenty-five years ago. The farm had changed hands at that point and Franklin, the new owner, had embarked on a tomato-growing venture that had finally come to a sticky end – hence the dilapidated greenhouses. In the intervening time, fishing had been forbidden at the pond and trespassers effectively discouraged by the greenhouse guard-dogs.

But Alan had never forgotten the pond and the handsome carp it had occasionally yielded to him and his pals, and when Daniel had taken up fishing he'd sometimes spoken about the monsters that, unmolested by man for a quarter of a century, must surely be breeding in the unknown depths of Ed Franklin's pool. Naturally Daniel had been captivated and Alan had tracked Ed down at his local. It had taken him a month to wring permission out of the surly old sod, a month of misty reminiscence and regular trips to the bar. But here they were at last.

Fish were feeding just below the surface, as evidenced by the occasional ring rippling through the scummy skin on top of the pool. But father and son had long fixed their minds on fishing the bottom of the pond – if there were big carp to be had, surely that's where they would be.

'The best fish I ever caught here,' said Alan, 'was under the wall in that far corner. A beauty. Six or seven pounds, I reckon, but my mate Billy's scale only went up to five. We put him back, of course. I wonder if he's still there? Carp live a long time, you know.'

But Daniel wasn't paying much attention. He was casting towards the far corner of the pond.

Sarah Cooper was quite the coquette, Annie decided. The way she was feeding them tit-bits about the drama of Freddy's death was probably an indication of her technique with the men she managed to hook. A snippet of sensation here, a glimpse into her secret store of information there – her statement to the police was like an extended striptease.

After her second trip to the loo to recover and repair her make-up, Sarah resumed her bravest face for the continuing ordeal. Annie had no doubt that, at some point in the future, she'd be reading about it in the tabloids.

Hunter was eager to follow up Sarah's admission that she had returned to discover Freddy's body. However, Shapiro suggested that, for the sake of clarity, they stick to a chronological version of events. Hunter reluctantly agreed and Sarah continued her story.

'When Tony got back from Ascot he was angry with me for not going to the races. I thought the only decent thing was to own up so I told him I'd become involved with someone else. We had an argument. Well – you can imagine.'

Sarah shot Annie a conspiratorial smile. Annie returned it. She could imagine there would have been quite a bust-up following Sarah's revelations.

'How did he react?' asked Hunter.

'He got kind of clingy and weepy. How could I do this to him? You know the sort of thing. Then he said he had to get out and clear his head. He took off – I don't know where he went.'

'What time was that?'

'About eight, I think.'

'What did you do after he'd gone?'

'I was pretty upset. I thought about going straight round to Freddy but I didn't. I couldn't leave Tony in that state. It was like, unfinished business, you know? So I waited for him to come home. He must have returned about ten-thirty. I know it was after dark.'

'How was he when he returned?'

'He seemed quite together but I knew he was keeping it all buttoned up inside. He's like that, very intense, but this was worse than normal. He begged me to stay. Said he still loved me and we had to sort all this out. I said I was sorry but it was over and the right thing was for me to leave the next day. Then we went to bed.'

There was a pause before Annie asked, 'Did you go to bed . . . together?'

'He wanted to but I said no. It wouldn't have been fair on either of us.'

Hunter nodded, as if in approval of her sensitivity. Annie could only imagine what he was thinking.

'So I slept upstairs and Tony slept on the sofa in the front room. I didn't see him again until the next morning. I went downstairs just as he was opening the post and all this money fell out. Thousands of pounds.'

'Money?' Hunter sounded as surprised as Annie felt.

'I was amazed. He was opening a brown envelope, A5 size I'd say, and inside was a big roll of fifties and one of those yellow stickers with a note on it.'

Another pause – whether consciously or not, Sarah was milking her big moment for all it was worth.

'Did you read this note, Miss Cooper?' Though the tone was matter-of-fact, Annie knew Hunter well enough by now to detect a hint of impatience.

'It was about the King George – that's one of the races Tony rode at Ascot the day before. He'd stolen the ride off Freddy, actually. The note said something about him riding a great race.

It was obviously a bribe. I tell you, it was a hell of a shock.'

'Why was that?'

'Because I'd always thought Tony was as straight as a die. He wouldn't even cheat at Snap. And I'd been feeling like a complete bitch because of the Freddy thing and suddenly I'd caught him taking a backhander. It's only in the past week I've seen through Tony properly but that moment, when I saw him with the money, was what opened my eyes.

'Anyway, I'd packed a few things in a bag the night before so I just slung it in my car and drove round to Freddy's. When I got there the front door was open so I just went in. I called out for Freddy but got no reply. The TV was on and so were the lights. I turned them off and went upstairs. Well . . . you know what I found. I knew at once that he was dead. I felt for a pulse but – nothing. Then I ran back to the car and drove to London. I know I should have stayed and reported it but I wasn't thinking. I just panicked.'

Annie made a mental note to ask about the tyres on Sarah's car – she'd bet they were Firestones.

Hunter had a different question. 'Why didn't you report Mr Montague's death when you got to London?'

'He'd been found by then. I heard it on the radio. It was terrible. I went to my mother's and she could see I was in a state. I told her I'd just left Tony and she thought it was because of that. She suggested I went away for a bit so I joined my sister in the South of France. I only got back this morning.'

It was years since Alan had been fishing and he'd been all fingers and thumbs with his line. He still used his old schoolboy rod and did everything the old-fashioned way. He didn't, for example, have a fancy bite-indicator like Daniel. Instead, he hung a piece of breadpaste on a loop in his line below the top ferrule of his rod, which Daniel thought hilarious. An hour or so had gone by with no action and Alan was reunited with that long-ago feeling, familiar to every fisherman, that the fish – should they even exist – were laughing at him. Not that he gave a stuff.

He'd resigned himself so completely to the fact that he wouldn't catch anything that he didn't notice he'd got a bite.

'Dad, look at your breadpaste.'

Alan saw that the loop in his line had disappeared and the little white ball of paste was bumping against the barrel. He lunged for the rod and struck. Oh, yes! There was something live and solid trembling at the other end. The sensation of playing a fish shot through his fingertips for the first time in twenty years.

'Steady, Dad,' said Daniel, the voice of experience these days in the fishing department, 'let him play himself out.'

But Alan didn't have any choice in the matter. The fish was big and powerful with a mind of its own. It shot from one side of the pond to the other, rising to set the surface boiling, then plunging downwards almost at their feet. Alan reeled in frantically to keep the line tight but now as he fought there was a change in sensation. There was a weight on the other end all right but not the pulsing and jerking of a living creature running for freedom. This was a dead weight.

'I'm snagged on something,' he said. 'The ruddy fish has done me.'

He yanked hard on the rod and the weight on the other end grudgingly yielded. He reeled in a few inches and yanked again. The weight shifted once more.

'Have you got the landing net?' he asked Daniel.

The lad eased it into the dark water as Alan raised the rod tip.

'Bet you've caught an old boot, Dad,' said the boy.

But he hadn't. He'd caught a gun.

'The South of France?' Annie could see Hunter was struggling to control his irritation. 'I suppose that explains the suntan.'

'It wasn't much of a holiday,' replied Sarah. 'I couldn't think about anything except Freddy's death. And Tony. Now I knew what he was really like, what a hypocrite he was with that money, I realised he'd be capable of anything. While I was asleep he could have gone out and killed Freddy.'

'I thought he didn't know who your, er, new friend was?'

'Well, of course he must have known. He's not dim. I mean, Freddy and I hadn't exactly been discreet. He probably put two and two together. And you know he had a gun, don't you? A .22 rifle like the one in the newspapers. He kept it in a brown canvas bag.'

'Mr Byrne reported it stolen in a burglary.'

'So what? We reported other stuff missing that turned up later. The place was such a mess we kept finding things we thought had been stolen. His golf clubs turned up in the garden two days after the robbery. It could easily have been his gun, too.'

'Did you see the gun after the robbery?'

'I can't say for sure, but I was squeamish about it. I bet Tony found it and put it out of my sight. In the garden shed or something.'

'Miss Cooper, do you have any evidence to suggest that the gun was not stolen as reported by Mr Byrne?'

Sarah reflected. 'Not evidence – that's your job, isn't it?' She

237

leaned forward to make her point. There was no sign of frailty now. 'Look, until recently Tony had a .22 rifle. He was jealous of me and he was jealous of Freddy because he had all the best rides. And on the night of the murder he could have got to Freddy's cottage and back without anyone knowing.'

She tapped the desk for emphasis as she continued. 'That's means, motive and opportunity. You're the detectives – work it out for yourselves.'

Kate would not have said she was really enjoying the party – the implications of Mrs Lim's departure and the loss of her brother cast unavoidable shadows. But the sympathy of the racing fraternity gathered around her was like a shot in the arm, and Cold Call's unexpected victory in the day's big race provided a focus for their feelings. Congratulations rained down upon her, followed by commiserations and expressions of support that, she could see, came from the heart. For once, she didn't mind being hugged and patted by all and sundry – as if she were a horse herself, she thought. And amidst the warm-hearted sentiments were promises of horses to train and introductions to influential parties which might – who knows? – lead to lucrative work at some point in the future.

Mickey almost had to drag Kate away from a retired jumps trainer who, inspired by the champagne, was embarking on her own tale of triumph over tragedy for the second time.

'Please follow me,' he said, gesturing towards the house. 'There's someone I'd like you to meet.'

'Who?'

'You'll see.' It was obvious he wasn't going to tell her.

Kate looked round for Tony. He'd promised he'd stay with her but she couldn't see him in the crush. Damn!

'What's up, Kate?'

She felt a flood of relief as he materialised at her side and she seized his arm at once.

'Come on. Mickey's taking us to meet some mysterious VIP.'

For a moment it seemed as if Mickey might make some objection; instead he smiled and ushered them towards the house.

Annie could see that Hunter's basic instinct was to interrogate Sarah all night – preferably in a basement dungeon with a dripping tap and a spotlight shining in her eyes. She'd once or twice reflected it was his misfortune to be a policeman in the wrong time and the wrong place. Czarist Russia would have suited him well – or any regime not hamstrung by the niceties of the democratic rule of law.

However, Hunter was holding himself in check. Since Sarah was making a voluntary statement she was at liberty to leave whenever she wanted – unless they could find a reason for arresting her. Unfortunately, they didn't have one, since failing to report the discovery of a dead body was not a crime.

In the event, there was no need to worry that Sarah might walk out. It was plain she wasn't going anywhere until she'd said her piece.

Hunter asked her about the last night she'd spent at Tony's house, when they'd slept apart. Was she aware of him leaving the house after she'd gone to bed? Had she heard his car start? Did she remember anything at all of that night? To each of these questions she'd replied no – she'd taken a sleeping pill to be sure of getting a good night's sleep and had gone out like a light.

'You said Tony was jealous of Freddy because he had the

best rides. Would you care to tell us more about that?'

Sarah thought for a moment. 'It was just the way it was. Freddy was the star jockey and, even though Tony had more experience, he was number two. Tony always had weight problems, for one thing, and so there were rides he couldn't do. And, of course, Freddy was Kate's brother.'

'Was Tony very cut up about this?'

'He didn't go on about it, if that's what you mean. But I know he hated it. It must have been eating away inside him all the time. I mean, with Freddy out of the way he'd have the best horses, wouldn't he? Like today. Freddy would have ridden Cold Call at Sandown, I know that for a fact.'

'But you're saying this went beyond professional rivalry? That, in your opinion, Tony Byrne would kill another jockey to get better rides?'

Sarah chewed on that for a moment. 'Given the way he felt about me, I think he might. Tony's ambitious and obsessive. When I saw him on the television today, celebrating on Freddy's horse, I knew he'd got what he really wanted. Freddy and I could have been so happy . . . The bastard's cheated both of us.'

The house was a warren. Mickey led Kate and Tony along a hallway through a labyrinthine living complex. They passed rooms packed with people – the gaming rooms Laurie had mentioned to Tony. Most of the participants looked Chinese, playing noisily, smoke from their cigarettes thick in the air. They left the gamblers behind as Mickey plunged down a narrow corridor that took them past the clatter of the busy kitchen and out into the open air.

Two burly men in dinner jackets flanked an arch of climbing roses. They stood aside to let Mickey pass and he ushered Kate and Tony down the leafy path. In the middle of a lawn, a small Chinese man of mature years sat on his own at a garden table. He got to his feet to greet them. His bony face creased into a smile, the skin around his eyes feathering into dozens of tiny lines.

'Miss Montague and Mr Byrne, I presume.' His handshake was warm and firm. 'Please take a seat.'

Kate hesitated. The mystery had gone on long enough. 'And you are?'

The old man laughed. 'Haven't you told them, Mickey?'

Mickey did not join in the laughter.

'This is Mr Shen,' he said.

'What do you reckon, Sarge?'

Annie and Hunter had finally finished with Sarah and were on their way to the incident room.

'Women like that,' he said, 'are about the only good reason I can think of to abolish the death penalty.'

'You've lost me.'

'What I mean is, Sarah Cooper is all set to see her ex-boyfriend swing. She'd put the noose over his head herself, I suspect.'

'So you think she's lying?'

'Did I say that?'

They found DCI Orchard in the incident room with Jenny, one of the PCs who manned the twenty-four-hour phone line. He was beaming like a fat boy let loose in a tuck shop.

'Have fun?' he said the moment they set foot in the room. 'No, don't tell me yet – listen to this. Jenny?'

She too was looking pretty cheerful. 'We got a call on the hotline about forty minutes ago from a guy in a pub near

Lambourn. He reported finding a rifle in a duck pond earlier this evening.'

'What duck pond?'

'On a farm owned by a Mr Franklin,' said Orchard. 'It's a couple of miles away from Freddy's place.'

'Didn't Mackenzie check it?'

Orchard's smile evaporated. 'Obviously not. Though it's bloody impossible to check every hole in the ground as you know so keep off Joe's back. I've sent him over to Lambourn to see what it's all about. He should be calling me on this line' – he pointed to a nearby phone – 'any moment now.'

On cue, it began to ring.

The civilities took a little while. Mr Shen asked after Kate's well-being in the light of her brother's death and spoke warmly of Freddy himself. He told her of the glowing recommendation Mickey had given him of her skill in restoring Cold Call to health, and he applauded Tony's proficiency in producing a winning ride. It appeared he had watched the race on television.

'Why weren't you there?' asked Kate.

'Mr Shen rarely goes out in public,' said Mickey. 'In fact, I'd rather you didn't tell anyone you have seen him here.'

The old man addressed Kate. 'So you have lost the custom of my compatriot Gladys Lim? That must cause you difficulties.'

Kate bristled but kept her feelings in check. 'Only temporary ones. I shall replace her horses before long, I'm sure.'

'I have some other horses I would like to race in England. Would you be interested?'

'How many?'

He looked at her coolly. 'Fifty maybe.'

'Fifty!'

'If I'm going to race here I would like to do it properly.'

'I could only take half that number.'

He smiled regretfully. 'That's a pity. I would want them all to be in one place.'

'I just don't have the room.'

'Is that accurate, Miss Montague?'

'I'm sorry?'

'I believe you have the room but not the facilities. In which case, would you be interested in a further proposal?'

Kate nodded. Things were running away from her here. She regretted the champagne she'd drunk earlier.

'I much prefer,' Mr Shen said, 'to have a proper stake in any operation I do business with. I would be happy, for example, to make an investment in your yard. More stables, extra staff, a swimming pool –'

Kate's thoughts were whirling. This was everything she'd ever wanted on a plate but . . .

'What do you mean by "a stake"?'

'I would like a share in your yard, Miss Montague.'

'Oh.'

'I believe I could offer the kind of backing that would assure you of the success you deserve.'

'I would never relinquish control of my yard.'

'Of course not but – excuse me if this is insensitive – you have just lost a partner. I know your brother had a share in your enterprise. I'm not suggesting I could replace him but, maybe, with the kind of connections and finance I can provide . . .'

Kate got to her feet.

'I don't know,' she said with more emphasis than she'd intended. 'I mean, I've got other people to consider.'

'Mr Somerville?'

'That's right.'

Mr Shen nodded. 'Very well. All I'm asking is that you sell me Freddy's share in your business. I think you'll find I can be very generous.'

Kate held out her hand. She just wanted this meeting to be over so she could think.

Mr Shen rose slowly to his feet and accepted the handshake. 'Just let Mickey know what you decide.'

Orchard put the phone down with a flourish. His colleagues looked at him expectantly – they'd not been able to gather much from his side of the conversation.

'About time something went right,' he announced.

'Come on, guv,' said Annie. 'Don't keep us in suspense.'

'Well . . .' He scratched his stomach thoughtfully and grinned. 'Looks like we've got the murder weapon. Joe hasn't had a close look – he's packing it off to Forensics sharpish. Apparently, about eight o'clock this evening, a man and his son were fishing for carp in some out-of-the-way pond. Dad got a big bite and pulled out a brown canvas guncase containing a .22 rifle.'

'Brown canvas?' Hunter's lugubrious features lit up.

'That's right.'

Hunter looked at Annie. 'You know what that means, don't you?'

It took a second for the penny to drop. She was annoyed that Hunter had got there before her but she remembered now. Sarah's statement clearly said Tony Byrne had kept his gun in a brown canvas bag.

'Out with it then.' Orchard wasn't too pleased to be kept in the dark.

'Right then, guv,' said Hunter with relish. 'Our turn, I think.'

*

Mickey led Kate and Tony back to the reception on the lawn. As they retraced their steps from the rose garden, a small group of Oriental men were waiting to take their place with Mr Shen. Evidently they were the next in the queue for an audience with the great man.

The party was still in full swing. The noise level had moved up a notch or two during their absence as the drink took hold and guests shouted to make themselves heard.

Kate put her mouth to Tony's ear. 'I'm not in the mood for this.'

'I'll take you home.' He grabbed her hand and manoeuvred her through the crush and back to the car.

'Are you all right?' he said as he put the key in the lock.

'I'm not sure.' She looked at him across the top of the car. 'I used to think Mickey was creepy but Bernard Shen leaves him standing.'

Tony put a finger to his lips and she smiled. 'Get me out of here, quick.'

Without his yellow jacket on, Dave Girlface Parsons was hard to spot in the twilight of the car-park field. He'd slipped it off as he noticed Kate and Tony leave the party and followed them at a crouch, ducking down behind the parked cars. Dave often picked up good stuff by earwigging punters as they left a party. As a rule, they'd still be jawing loudly and loosely. Often they'd be dead keen to share some gossip or other they'd just picked up. Sometimes they left with people they shouldn't and that could be useful, too. Information – that was the name of the game.

In this case he was well aware who Kate and Tony were. His

association with Herbert Gibbs required him to keep up to speed on the personalities of the racing world. And, of course, these two were key players in the Freddy Montague business.

But he'd not expected the little tit-bit about Bernard Shen. Everyone in Soho's Chinatown knew of the legendary Bernard Shen, a man so jealous of his own mortality that he rarely left his power base in the Far East.

Fancy finding him so far from home.

By the time Tony stood on his front doorstep it was dark. He'd dropped Kate at the yard and she'd invited him in to continue the discussion they'd had in the car.

So they'd debated Bernard Shen's offer some more. Tony had not tried to persuade her one way or the other, though he'd suggested she at least clarify what exactly Mr Shen had in mind.

'He was very vague. You need details, Kate, otherwise it's just so much hot air.'

'I suppose so. But I don't want to be stuck haggling with Mickey and I know that's what it would come down to.'

She looked small and tired as she sat in the middle of the large chintz-covered sofa. They were in her front room – Tony had not sat in here before. It had an old-fashioned feel, cosy but under-used. He guessed it looked pretty much as it had done in her parents' day.

Eventually he'd got up to go. 'Sleep on it, eh? And see what Laurie says.'

'I suppose so.'

She'd sounded uncertain, which was most unlike Kate, and hugged him warmly as he left, taking him by surprise. She fitted snugly in his arms – as if she belonged there, he thought as he drove the short distance home.

So his mind was elsewhere as he opened his front door.

Two figures came out of the dark, taking him by surprise.

'Mr Byrne?'

'Yes.'

The bigger of the two held up what looked like a badge. 'Detective Chief Inspector Orchard and this is Detective Sergeant Hunter. I don't believe we've met.'

Tony's first impulse was to tell them to get lost. He was dog tired.

'If this is about Freddy, I've already answered a load of questions.'

The policeman ignored his remark. 'It is my duty to place you under arrest for the murder of Frederick Montague.'

'What?'

'You do not have to say anything. But it may harm your defence if you do not mention when questioned something which you later rely on in court. Anything you do say may be given in evidence.'

Tony listened in a daze to the caution. Though familiar to him through countless episodes of TV police procedurals, it made no sense at all.

'I've got nothing to do with Freddy's death,' he protested.

'Would you like to come this way, sir?' said the second officer, indicating a car parked on the other side of the road.

Though it was phrased as a question, Tony knew he had no choice.

# Chapter Ten

The Custody Sergeant was obviously a racing fan.

'Bit of an up-and-down day, eh, Mr Byrne?' he said as he booked Tony in.

Tony didn't trust himself to reply. Though he had a reputation for being nervous and short-tempered – particularly before a race – he knew that, in a real crisis, he had as cool a head as anybody. A man who earned his living riding racehorses could not afford to give way to emotion.

This, however, was a different challenge from anything he had ever faced on a racecourse. It was utterly preposterous to suppose that he had anything to do with Freddy's death but there had to be a reason why the police thought he did. He forced himself to take deep slow breaths as he turned out his pockets and handed over his personal possessions.

'You're entitled to a phone call, Mr Byrne.'

The first person who came to mind was Kate but something held him back. How could he wake her to say he'd been arrested on suspicion of murdering her brother? She'd have to be told but not yet.

He shook his head.

'What about a solicitor?'

His family solicitor was in Yorkshire and not much use to him right now. He mumbled words to that effect.

'We'll rustle up the duty brief for you then. He'll put his skates on, I shouldn't wonder.'

They put him in a cell to wait. There were two wooden benches fixed to the floor, a plastic mattress on each propped against the wall. Behind a small alcove was a toilet bowl without a seat, the porcelain stained and chipped. The room was as bleak as his worst expectations.

Tony wondered how many innocent people were rotting behind bars. The thought that he might soon be one of them terrified him.

He closed his eyes and concentrated on his breathing. He had to keep calm if he was going to survive this nightmare.

It was less than an hour before the duty solicitor appeared but it felt like an eternity. Just when Tony most wanted to shut out his surroundings and take refuge in sleep, he'd never felt more awake. The complaints of a Friday-night drunk in the next cell, the tramp of boots in the corridor, the smell of pee and disinfectant that hung in the air of the grubby room, all played on his senses. So when he was summoned to meet the solicitor he could have wept with relief.

He was taken to a small and shabby interview room containing two chairs, a table and a dirty ashtray. The solicitor was a sandy-haired fellow of thirty in a crumpled suit, who did indeed look as if he had scrambled out of bed in a hurry. However, his handshake was firm and his brown eyes full of concern. He introduced himself as Gus Jones.

Having assured himself that Tony had been treated according to the rules, Gus produced a pad and pencil.

'The police haven't told me much beyond the charge and

that they'll be interviewing you once they've completed a section eighteen search.'

'What's that?'

'Section eighteen of the PACE code of practice for the searching of premises. They're having a look round your house for evidence.'

Tony digested the information. It made sense, given that he was under suspicion, but it was painful none the less.

'They won't find any evidence of me shooting Freddy,' he said. 'Because I didn't.'

Gus nodded and made a note on his pad. 'Have you got any idea why you're under suspicion?'

Tony shook his head. 'It's all I've been able to think about since they arrested me. And I haven't got the foggiest.'

Kate wasn't surprised when the phone rang in the office at 6.45 a.m. Many people were aware that she put in twenty minutes' paperwork before first lot rode out at seven. On the other hand, most knew not to disturb her except in emergencies. She lifted the receiver half expecting trouble.

She replaced it a few minutes later, her expectations fulfilled – though she never could have anticipated what she had just heard. Tony arrested for Freddy's murder – it was a joke, surely? Except that she knew Gus Jones of Jones & Whitaker in Swindon; his firm had once acted for a neighbour in a boundary dispute.

Gus had tried to play down Tony's arrest, stressing that no charge had yet been made against him and that he was simply being held for questioning. However, the solicitor had not been able or perhaps willing to shed any light on the police case. He'd laid stress on Tony's assertion that he was completely innocent and his concern that Kate be informed as soon as possible that he would not be able to ride that day.

She had spent most of the night in a stew over Bernard Shen's offer for the yard. Despite its obvious attractions, her gut instinct was to walk away. When she'd talked it over with Tony the night before he'd been at pains not to influence her decision. In the small hours, she'd realised she really wanted to know how he felt. His feelings mattered to her. She could trust him. And she could still feel his arms around her, holding her up, giving her strength.

Now this phone call had thrown everything back into the melting pot.

The idea that Tony had killed her brother was crazy – why would he do that? And, if he had, how could he offer her a shoulder to cry on? How could he invite her to his home, take her out, escort her to Mickey's party? How would that be possible? Unless he was cynically after Freddy's place in her yard and a place in her heart as well. Which would make him some kind of psychopath. A cold-blooded killer.

Of course, if the police were right, maybe that's exactly what he was.

She couldn't believe it.

Out in the yard she could hear first lot assembling. Through the window into the barn she could see Neil preparing Summer Storm. She reached for the phone. At least she knew what to do about replacing Tony on Evening Shadow in the Commonwealth Handicap. Tim Shaw wouldn't enjoy being woken at this time in the morning, especially with the hangover he'd been working on the night before, but that was the least of her problems.

*

Kate wasn't the only one who'd been losing sleep. Vicky, too, had been chewing on a puzzle that had kept her awake.

Following her unsatisfactory conversation with Josh after the Tote, she'd kept a close eye on Stopgap. She'd never seen the horse drink that amount of water before.

When the horse box had arrived back at the yard the evening before, she'd dismissed Josh and taken Stopgap back to his stall herself. She'd spent some time settling him in and chatting to him. The horse had behaved in his usual offhand manner, he wasn't the sort to lavish affection on his minders.

'You mucked it up today, didn't you?' Vicky said. 'I wonder why?'

She found a clue as she went to fill his feed box – a scattering of white particles in one corner. She dipped a wet finger into them and held it up to the light. The powder looked remarkably familiar. She sniffed it. No smell. She touched it to the tip of her tongue. Salt.

Now Vicky was itching to tell Kate her theory about Stopgap's poor performance and was pleased to see her boss sitting at her desk in the office. She just had time to catch her before they rode out.

She opened the office door. 'Got a moment?'

Kate looked straight through her, as if she'd not heard her speak.

Vicky shut the door behind her. 'Are you all right?'

'Sit down, Vicky. I've got some news.'

By the time Kate had finished, Vicky's theory had gone completely out of her head.

Neil was excited when he called his mother. Despite Kate's reassurances, he'd been convinced he'd blown his chance of

further good rides after his disappointing performance on
Stopgap. Yet here he was back at Sandown on Eclipse day with
a decent chance of winning the Commonwealth Handicap on
Evening Shadow.

He hoped he'd sounded sufficiently grateful when Kate had
told him. 'Why isn't Tony riding him?' was all he could think of
saying.

'Change of plan,' she'd replied, as if it wasn't any business of
his, and Neil hadn't pursued it. He was just thrilled to get the
opportunity to redeem himself so quickly.

He could tell his mother was pleased even though all she
said was, 'I hope it runs better than the last one. All this is
costing me a packet.'

'Mum, you don't have to put money on a horse just because
I'm riding.'

'Of course I do. Otherwise you might go and win and then
I'd be kicking myself.'

He'd moved the conversation on swiftly to the topic that
really concerned him.

'Have you seen Dad?'

'Once or twice.'

His parents had divorced during his father's last stint in
prison but Neil knew his dad was living close to his mother.
Trying to get back in her good books, he suspected.

'I've left messages for him but he never rings back.'

'You know your father.'

Neil could tell by her tone that she didn't want to get
involved. He persisted nevertheless.

'Have I done anything to offend him?'

There was a pause on the line. 'Only you would know that,
son. Have you?'

'Of course not,' he replied though it wasn't entirely true.

Gus had warned Tony to expect a long wait. It would take the police a while to complete their search of his house and to make sense of whatever they might find there. The solicitor explained that they had twenty-four hours in which to question him before laying a formal charge – and that period could be extended to thirty-six hours.

'In other words,' said the solicitor, 'just be prepared to sit it out. Don't expect to get out of here before Sunday. Play it cool.'

Tony had no doubt it was good advice, though easier said than done. The night dragged by. Despite Gus's words he expected at any moment to be taken off for questioning and almost relished the prospect. Then, at least, he'd have some idea why he was suspected of murder.

He didn't sleep.

The moment Vicky saw Josh's bulky figure riding out, everything came flooding back to her. She managed to get her word with Kate after second lot.

The trainer heard her out and then said, 'Why?'

'You'd better ask him.'

Kate invited Josh into the office for what turned out to be an acrimonious five minutes.

The lad was indignant. 'I never touched the bloody horse!' he shouted.

Vicky accused him of putting salt in Stopgap's food. 'He was drinking too much, Josh. I noticed it after the race but I bet he was drinking before, too.'

'Bollocks!'

'He couldn't run because he had a bellyful of water.'

'You're off your head.'

'When I got back last night I found salt in his manger.'

'You're a lying bitch,' he yelled at her. 'You'd make up any story to protect Neil, wouldn't you? Face it, he'll never make a jockey as long as I've got a hole in my backside.'

'Just tell us why you did it, Josh,' said Kate. 'Did someone pay you?'

'The pair of you are barking mad.'

But Kate was not convinced by his protests, she could see the guilt in his face. She kept her voice low. 'I'd like you to leave immediately, Josh. I'll give you a month's salary and strongly suggest that none of us speaks about the matter outside this office.'

He turned at the door for a parting shot. 'You two make a right pair. One's a fat nympho who can't get a man and the other's a raving dike. You deserve each other.'

They waited in silence till he'd crashed out of the building.

'What a great guy he turned out to be.' Vicky dropped into a chair.

'Not daft though. That salt trick's clever – it won't show up on the tests.'

'Josh is not that bright. I wonder who put him up to it?'

Kate said nothing, just rubbed the back of her neck. She felt exhausted. She'd bet any money Mickey was behind this – but she'd never prove it.


Herbert met Dave Parsons in a greasy spoon on the other side of the river, a safe distance from his office. Herbert wasn't keen on entertaining Girlface in the smart glass-and-chrome environment of the H.O. Gibbs Group.

'Got some news for you,' said Dave.

Herbert grunted. Of course Dave had news – why else had he been dragged over here?

'Big excitement in Soho. You know – the Hong Kong connection.' Dave winked. On another day Herbert might have found this amusing but he wasn't in the mood right now. He'd been up with the baby since five and, instead of going back to bed when Maria clocked on at eight, he'd had to get down here. What a way to spend Saturday morning.

'You can say Triads to me, Dave. As far as I'm concerned they're all the same.'

'Well, that's where you're wrong. In the London Chinese community there's two important factions —'

'Just keep it simple.'

'OK. Let's say there's Team A. They've got all the important action here and things are pretty hunky-dory for them. But back in Hong Kong there's Team B, their big rivals. The A team live in fear that B will move in on their London turf.'

'Gotcha.' Herbert sipped his tea and felt a bit better.

'Just recently, the head of Team B sent over his main fixer, Mickey Lee. And now Team A are shitting themselves in case the main man himself turns up. A guy called Bernard Shen.'

Herbert banged down his cup, slopping tea into the saucer. 'What? Bernard Shen the racehorse owner?'

'The very same.'

That was food for thought, Bernard Shen not being Herbert's favourite man that morning. Yesterday's betting-shop figures were way off target due, so he was told, to Cold Call's unexpected victory at Sandown. Herbert's high-street chain of shops – soon, of course, to be eclipsed by his internet betting scheme and his property enterprise – was based in the big urban areas, Manchester, Birmingham, Glasgow. It appeared that a lot of small bets had been placed on Cold Call at long odds and his people had been slow to cover the position. Even the failure of the favourite, Stopgap, hadn't been as profitable as expected. Someone, doubtless Bernard Shen, had pulled off a bit of a coup. As a sporting man, Herbert wasn't against that – except when he wasn't in on the scam.

'Thank God he doesn't race here often,' he said.

'Haven't you heard? He's moving in big-time. Mickey Lee said so on TV.'

Herbert pulled a face. He didn't like it, but who said life was going to be easy? 'Is that it then?'

Dave's plush lips curled into a smile. 'Don't you want to know who slotted Freddy?'

'Get on with it, Girlface.'

'My information is that Freddy rode for Mr Shen in Hong Kong last winter. One of Shen's angles is to fix the Pick Six bet at Sha Tin. It can be done, you know.'

Herbert knew it well enough. For the Pick Six you had to find six winners on a race card. If you nobbled enough riders and picked the right card *and* laid out enough money on tickets it could be done. It helped, of course, if you were a Triad drugs baron with a fortune in dirty money to clean. Enormous sums changed hands on the Pick Six.

Dave continued. 'A mate of Freddy's called Jeff Collins pinched the winning ticket off one of Shen's runners. Mickey Lee caught up with Collins in Australia but by then he'd shifted the ticket to Freddy here in England. They were in it together, see?'

Herbert nodded. 'And?'

'Mickey Lee flew to England. Landed the day before poor old Freddy died.'

'So you're saying this Mickey bloke took care of him?'

Dave shrugged. 'He was on the scene. He washes Mr Shen's dirty laundry. I'm not saying any more than that.'

'How did you hear all this?'

'I just happen to know that Mr Shen is in the country. A pal of mine is working for him and he picks things up. He's getting a bit greedy though.'

Herbert pulled out his wallet and put six fifties on the table.

'I'll leave you to settle up then,' he said as he got to his feet.

There was a spring in his step as he walked to his car. If Freddy had got himself popped in some freelance lark then it was none of his business. No further action was called for. Then he remembered Uncle Yip.

Laurie woke late in an unfamiliar bed. A curtain had been drawn and summer sunlight fell in a strip across the pale peach Axminster, on to a straight-backed mahogany chair piled with clothes. Laurie recognised his own linen suit, draped carelessly over the seat and, on top of it, something violently pink – a skirt of pocket-handkerchief proportions. And there on the floor, by the chair leg, a scrap of black – a tiny pair of women's briefs that he remembered only too vividly. He had lowered them down Caroline's unending legs at some point in the early hours of the morning.

There was an indentation in the bed next to him and, from behind the bathroom door opposite, he heard the hissing of a shower.

He picked up the phone by the bed. Greta answered on the second ring.

'Yes?' Her voice was flat.

'It's me.'

'Where are you?'

'In Knightsbridge. At Mickey's hotel.' There was an awkward silence. 'How did it go?'

'I'll tell you when you get back.'

The bathroom door opened and Caroline emerged with a towel wrapped around her.

'You are coming back, aren't you, Laurie? I promised Paul you'd take him to Sandown.'

'OK. I'll see you later.'

He cut the connection.

Caroline raised her arms to unpin her hair. The towel fell to her feet. 'Oops,' she said, making no attempt to cover her incredible body.

Laurie gazed on her high, sun-dappled breasts and the beckoning vee of her perfect thighs, and felt – nothing.

'Mr Byrne, have you ever deliberately lost a horse race?'

Four of them, the two weary-eyed policemen who had arrested him the night before and Gus Jones, sat in a grim and airless interview room with a tape-machine recording every murmur of their conversation.

The first question took Tony by surprise and his reply came quicker than he had intended.

'No.'

Hunter, the policeman asking the questions, looked unconvinced.

'Have you ever been offered money to lose a race?'

'All jockeys get approached at some time.'

'Have you ever accepted?'

'No, I haven't.'

'Isn't it difficult to turn down all that easy money?'

'I've never found it difficult.'

'Good.' That seemed to please Hunter, who grinned to himself. He was already getting up Tony's nose.

'So when was the last time somebody tried to bribe you?'

'A few months ago. At the beginning of the season.'

'Who was it?'

Tony thought for a moment. He'd have been reluctant to incriminate anyone but, in this case, didn't see how the truth would hurt.

'Freddy Montague.'

The policeman nodded as if that were no surprise. 'How did he approach you?'

'I don't remember the exact words. Something like, "Do you fancy some easy money?" '

'That's all?'

'It was obvious what he meant. I told him I wasn't interested.'

'So you've never taken money from Freddy Montague to throw a race?'

'Absolutely not.'

Hunter was having trouble controlling his obvious satisfaction as he produced a folder from beneath the desk. Inside were two clear plastic sleeves. The top one contained a brown envelope.

'We found this on the bookshelf in your front room. How do you account for it?'

Tony stared through the shiny surface. He knew at once what it was: the envelope he'd received in the post the morning Sarah walked out. The other sleeve held the envelope's contents – banknotes and a yellow Post-It note.

How could he explain the problem this package had caused him? Kate had understood his dilemma but he couldn't expect any sympathy from these two cynical policemen. They were looking at him keenly, waiting for his answer. Anything he said was bound to land him in it.

'I can't account for it at all,' he said uncertainly. 'It arrived in the post but I don't know why. I was going to give it away.'

'You were going to give away three thousand pounds?'

'Yes, I don't want it. It was obviously sent to me by mistake – or as a joke. I don't know who by.'

Hunter grinned. 'Let me enlighten you then. The envelope, the note and the rubber band around the money all match materials we discovered in Freddy Montague's writing desk. The same desk, incidentally, also contained a large amount of cash.'

Tony was puzzled. He could only think Freddy had done it to cause mischief and had succeeded all too well – though doubtless not in the way he had planned.

'I don't understand it,' he maintained. 'But I can assure you I had no knowledge of this money before it turned up and I did nothing irregular to earn it.'

Hunter changed the angle of his attack.

'Do you know Jonno Simpson, Mr Byrne?'

'Of course I know him.'

'Do you value his opinion as a fellow jockey?'

'Not much.'

'What would you say if I told you that, in his estimation, you deliberately prevented your horse' – he consulted his notebook – 'No Ill Will, from winning the King George V handicap at Ascot? The race that's mentioned in the note that came with this money.'

Tony was exasperated. 'Jonno's a Monday afternoon jockey.

If he'd been riding No Ill Will he'd have flogged him half to death and he still wouldn't have won.'

'You have to admit, Mr Byrne, that there were many other people who shared his view.'

Tony shrugged. 'They weren't on the horse.'

The other policeman, Orchard, spoke for the first time. 'How do you feel about being short-changed?'

Tony wasn't sure how to respond. 'I don't follow you.'

Orchard continued. 'My point is that three grand doesn't seem much for pulling a horse. Jonno Simpson told me Freddy offered him ten to throw a race.'

That was news to Tony though it didn't surprise him. 'What's that to do with me?'

'Suppose you agreed to fix a race for Freddy but then he paid you seven grand less than the going rate. Don't you think you'd be a little fed up with him?'

Suddenly Tony saw where this was heading.

'You're not seriously suggesting I'd kill Freddy if he owed me money, are you?'

'You said it, Mr Byrne.'

Tony grinned and shook his head. 'You people must be desperate.'

Laurie left Caroline in the hotel room performing unnecessary magic on her face. He couldn't wait to get away from her. He'd not been unfaithful to Greta for eight years, since a messy affair with a stablegirl had almost torpedoed their marriage. He'd learned his lesson then, he'd thought. He'd only stepped out of line last night for revenge and this morning regretted it. It was strange – he felt as if he'd not only betrayed Greta but Paul as well. It had been stupid of him.

Mickey was at a table on his own in the breakfast room, so Laurie could not avoid him. Mickey was responsible for the previous evening's entertainment – he'd left the party with a svelte brunette, making it clear that Caroline was Laurie's for the night. Now, Laurie assumed, he'd expect to be thanked – one way or another.

'Did I tell you,' Mickey began, 'we've spoken to Kate?'

'About?'

'Mr Shen's interest in the yard.'

Laurie poured himself a cup of coffee. 'What did she say?'

'She said she'd talk to you.'

'OK.'

'You will be positive, won't you?'

'Up to a point.'

'You owe me, after all.'

'Come off it, Mickey. One night with a whore in a fancy hotel doesn't put me in your pocket.'

Mickey leaned forward, his face sombre. 'Our debt goes further back than that. Or have you forgotten?'

Laurie's stomach contracted. He thought of playing innocent. Or denying what had taken place. Instead he said, 'I still have nightmares about it.'

The piercing black eyes bored into him. One half of Mickey's face was smooth and immobile, the other drawn into a mirthless smile. 'How terrible for you.'

'I promise,' Laurie said at last, 'I'll do my best to persuade Kate.'

In the circumstances, what else could he say?

Hunter and Orchard lost no time in wiping the smile off Tony's face.

'Where were you at approximately eleven-thirty p.m. on the night Freddy Montague was shot?'

'At home in bed.'

'Where is your bed exactly?'

'Upstairs in the bedroom. Where else would it be?'

'Were you alone?'

'No. My girlfriend was with me.'

'And her name is?'

'Sarah Cooper. Actually, she's now my ex-girlfriend.'

'So if we asked Miss Cooper she would confirm that the pair of you spent all night in the same bed?'

'Yes.' They hadn't, of course, but Tony was damned if he was going to discuss the details of his personal life with these two.

'As a matter of fact, Mr Byrne, we have already asked Miss Cooper that question and she has given us a different version of events.' Hunter couldn't disguise the triumph in his voice. 'She says that she slept in the bed upstairs and you slept downstairs. So who's telling the truth, Mr Byrne? You or her?'

Silence descended in the stifling little room. Tony felt a complete fool, caught out in a fib like a naughty schoolboy. If he hadn't been so tired he'd have figured out there was a good chance they'd spoken to Sarah.

'She is. We'd just decided to split up and I thought I'd better sleep on the sofa. But I can't see what business that is of yours.'

Hunter was smiling broadly. 'Surely you must see the significance of someone providing you with an alibi for the time of the murder?'

'This is stupid.' Tony heard the note of fear in his own voice. 'Why would I want to murder Freddy?'

Time for Orchard to chip in. 'Your winner yesterday, Cold

Call – he was down to be ridden by Freddy Montague, wasn't he?'

'I suppose so.'

'Are there other rides that have come your way as a result of his death?'

'I've taken some, yes.'

'So you get better rides now Montague's out of the picture?'

'Yes, but ... I wouldn't. I mean, that's no reason to kill somebody.'

Tony glared at the pair of them. They'd been steadily cutting the ground from beneath his feet. He feared that now they were about to push him over the edge.

'It's not just the professional rivalry though, is it?' Hunter spoke this time, his voice sly and suggestive. 'I've got a lot of sympathy for you, Mr Byrne. Miss Cooper's a very sexy woman.'

'What are you talking about?'

'I'm simply saying I appreciate how you must have felt when you discovered she was sleeping with Freddy Montague. Jealousy's a very powerful emotion. A lot of men can't handle it.'

'Sarah was sleeping with Freddy?' Tony's voice sounded shrill, a nerve plainly exposed.

'That's right. It must have been tough to bear. Why don't you tell us about it?'

Tony barely heard him. Suddenly a lot of things were tumbling into place. Freddy of all people.

Just as well the little shit was already dead.

Laurie made good time returning to Lambourn which was fortunate, given that he was going to turn round and head back to Sandown with Paul. He found Greta in the kitchen, chopping carrots.

'Hello, darling,' he said, coming up behind her to put his arms round her waist. He suddenly thought that, to an observer, they would look like any other devoted husband and wife.

She stopped chopping but did not turn her head. 'I didn't do it.'

'What?'

'I didn't have the abortion. I couldn't go through with it.'

He froze. Aware of his hands on her belly, where another man's seed was growing inside her.

'I'm sorry,' she said.

He turned and walked out of the door. He couldn't trust himself to do anything else.


'Is there something you want to tell me, Tony?'

He was on his own with Gus, following the interview with Hunter and Orchard. The solicitor had requested time out from their verbal pummelling and the policemen seemed happy enough to back off for the moment. However, Tony was under no illusion that his ordeal was over.

'I didn't do it.'

Tony met the other man's probing gaze. He could see Gus was trying to decide whether he was guilty or not.

'I didn't do it,' he repeated. 'They've got it all wrong.'

Gus tapped his pen thoughtfully on the table top. At last he spoke. 'At least we now have some idea of the way they're thinking. I'd like to avoid too many more nasty surprises, though.'

'Like the money, you mean. And Sarah.'

'She doesn't sound very found of you, Tony.'

'She told me she was screwing someone else but she never said it was Freddy.'

'Unfortunately it's her word against yours.'

'I can't believe she'd deliberately stitch me up.'

Gus sighed, a world-weary sound that belied his years. 'Look, in legal terms she's a hostile witness. Think hard, Tony, what other damaging statements could she have made?'

In his heart Tony knew Gus was right. Sarah had never had a good word to say for her former lovers and now he had joined their number. But as for what further damage she could do, he hadn't a clue.

Kate found it strange to be driving to Sandown by herself. She'd got used to riding with Tony and missed his company – a disturbing thought, given the present circumstances. She'd imagined that the arrest of a suspect for her brother's murder would be cause for celebration – but how could she be pleased that it was Tony?

She'd had a call from the sympathetic policewoman, DC James, before she'd set out.

'We're beginning to make progress.'

'I can't believe you've arrested Tony.'

'We've also found a gun.'

'The one that killed Freddy?'

'Possibly. Forensics are fast-tracking it through the system. We'll be calling a press conference later. Can you keep it to yourself till then?'

'Of course.'

Kate was grateful for the call. Apart from anything else, she was better prepared when a couple of news reporters tackled her outside the weighing room. They'd obviously got wind of Tony's arrest.

'I'll only talk to you about racing,' she said firmly – which made for a short conversation.

*

Neil wasn't so fortunate. Ian Thomas, a broadsheet racing correspondent, collared him before he'd made it to the changing room.

'Got a moment, Neil?' he asked.

The apprentice flushed with pleasure – he wasn't aware the reporter even knew his name.

'How does it feel,' said Thomas, 'to get Tony Byrne's ride in these circumstances?'

'What circumstances?'

'Come off it, you must know about him.'

'No. Miss Montague asked me to ride the horse, that's all.'

'Really?' Thomas leaned closer, his voice a conspiratorial whisper. 'According to our crime desk, Tony was arrested last night.'

'What for?'

'Freddy Montague's murder.'

Neil felt as if he'd been kicked in the guts. It took him a moment to get his breath. The reporter was watching him closely.

'Have you any comment to make?'

Neil knew he shouldn't say anything at all but he couldn't help it.

'That's rubbish! Tony didn't do it. I know he didn't.'

'Why's that, Neil?'

But he got no reply. The boy had fled.

Laurie spotted Tim Shaw and his daughter, Cameron, casting an eye over the runners in the first. Cameron was a precocious teenager of about Paul's age, reed slim, a beauty in the making.

'Don't say I never do you any favours,' Laurie muttered to

his son as he hailed the pair and asked if Paul could keep them company for a few minutes. Then, congratulating himself on killing two birds with one stone, he set off to find Kate.

He found her in the owners' and trainers' bar, drinking coffee. It seemed she knew what he was going to say before the words were out of his mouth.

'You know about Mr Shen's offer, don't you?'

'Mickey told me.'

'And I suppose he asked you to twist my arm?'

'I'd never do that. Though it does seem an interesting proposal – if he's going to put money into developing the yard.'

Kate sighed. 'When people put money into your business they like to tell you how to run it.'

'Not everyone. I've never interfered, have I?'

'That's true.' She took his arm. 'You worked with my father – what do you think he'd do?'

Laurie laughed. 'He'd make damn sure he stayed in control. But he'd also consider the human cost of the alternative.'

'What do you mean?'

'Well, you're set up to train around fifty. Without the Lim horses you won't need so many people. Unless you can replace her business quickly, half your lads will have to go, won't they?'

Neil changed in silence, ignoring the banter of the other jockeys. The revelation of Tony's arrest had distressed him. When one of the others asked where Tony was, he simply claimed ignorance. News of the arrest had not yet got this far, though it was only a matter of time.

Neil could hardly even bear to talk to Kate as he handed her his saddle and number cloth after weighing out. What could he say? Luckily, she was too concerned to make her points about the race before the ritual rhubarb with the owner in the parade ring.

Since the owner – technically – turned out to be a fourteen-year-old girl, this made a lot of sense. As Neil approached the knot of people gathered round Kate in the parade ring, he was surprised to see Paul among them. He stood next to a slender young woman in a navy jacket, looking irritatingly pleased with himself. Neil glared at him. Here was someone he *did* want a word with.

Kate introduced him to Tim Shaw and the girl, his daughter Cameron. She had full pink lips and blonde curls, and was obviously enjoying her role as racehorse owner.

'So here's my handsome warrior!' she cried in a loud American rasp at odds with her angelic appearance.

'Got any instructions for him, honey?' said her father. 'It's your call.'

'Neil's a genius in the saddle,' Paul chipped in.

Neil didn't look at him. If Paul thought that kind of remark would make things OK between them, he was wrong.

'I bet he is,' said Cameron, stepping close, fixing Neil with her sky-blue eyes. 'Just win it for me, genius.'

Her father laid a hand on his shoulder. 'Stay in touch and pull the trigger two furlongs out, son.'

Kate helped him into the saddle with an amused expression on her face. Neil was grateful she'd already given him her instructions. Just before Vicky led him into the circle, he called Paul over.

The boy could hardly control the grin on his face. 'What do you reckon to her then?' he said.

Neil ignored the question and bent low in the saddle to

whisper in his ear, 'Tony's been arrested.'

Paul's grin vanished in an instant.

As he cantered to the start, Neil tried to wipe his mind clean of all distractions. At least he felt better about one thing: Kate had told him how Josh had sabotaged Stopgap the day before. Neil was relieved that the horse's failure had not been his fault. And here he was with an unexpected opportunity to put that bad run behind him. He only wished it wasn't at Tony's expense . . . He forced himself to focus on the race ahead.

He'd never ridden two miles before. It meant maintaining his racing concentration for longer than he was used to, a good three and a half minutes, in fact. It was also likely to be more physically draining. However, neither of these factors bothered him. He relished the prospect of a circuit and a half around a glorious track like Sandown, and Kate had pointed out that a longer race would give him more time to recover should he make a mistake.

What concerned him most was Evening Shadow. He'd never ridden the big grey. All he knew was that the horse was one of Kate's 'Lazarus' jobs – an animal brought back from the dead. Evening Shadow's career looked to have come to an end as a three-year-old when he broke down at York. He'd arrived at Kate's yard in January and she'd got him in shape for the new season, raising hopes that he'd finally realise his potential. He'd had one run out over two miles at Warwick, in a Class E race where he'd had things pretty much his own way. He'd beaten a poor field by five lengths and Kate had been well satisfied. This, however, was a sterner test.

Kate had walked the course with Neil beforehand. On the far side she'd made him stop and look across to the winning post.

'Fix that lollipop in your mind. It's almost a mile uphill so don't start racing from here. Save your petrol.

'There's no doubt he'll get the trip,' she'd added. 'And some of the others might not because they're stepping up in distance. However, Tim Shaw tells me that this horse had an extra gear before he got injured. He's shown no sign of that with me. He didn't need to turn it on at Warwick so this race will find him out.'

Neil kept Evening Shadow in the middle of the ten runners as they sped past the stands for the first time and headed downhill, around the bend out into the country. The horse hugged the rail, devouring the ground beneath him in an easy stride. Kate had warned Neil that he pulled to the right but on a clockwise course like this that was hardly a disadvantage.

Heading downhill into the back straight the front runners picked up the pace. Neil held Evening Shadow back and slipped to the rear of the field. They were still over a mile from home and, provided he kept in touch, he was happy to bide his time. In his mind he was constantly updating just how far he was from the winning post.

By the end of the flat back straight some of the others began coming back to him. He urged his mount on as they entered the turn for home, a long sweeping bend which would leave them a final uphill half-mile to the winning post. At this point, Neil guessed, those horses making the step up from a mile and a half would find themselves answering some tough questions.

The curve of the bend was extended by temporary fencing which, Kate had told him, was used to preserve the inner ground for meetings later in the season. Evening Shadow tracked the rail, closing now on the leading bunch of six horses who were beginning to spread across the track.

Suddenly, as they came into the mouth of the home straight, the temporary fencing came to an end. The lead horses headed in a direct line for the old rail some half a furlong ahead and Neil saw his opportunity. If he could exploit the gap on the inside created by the temporary fencing then he could get his horse in front.

He used his whip, urging Evening Shadow into the opening on the inner. The line of horses ahead of him were three lengths up and taking a direct route. This was a gamble.

Evening Shadow responded. Neil could feel the horse stretching, racing for the opening that could give him the race.

But even as his mount quickened and gained ground on the leaders Neil knew he wouldn't get there. The gap ahead was closing fast as the inside horse blocked off daylight on the rail. Asking Evening Shadow to make up the distance was expecting too much.

There was now a wall of horses in front of him as they galloped up the rise towards the stands. Neil flicked his eyes to the left. If he was to get up in time he'd have to go round the outside. He hit Evening Shadow on his right flank, urging him to switch over.

The horse didn't like it. The pair lost momentum as Neil manoeuvred him to the left.

With a furlong to go, Evening Shadow was at last in position and he still had plenty to give. The grey was in sixth and eating up the ground. But time was running out.

They picked off two labouring horses and crossed the line in fourth place. Evening Shadow finished like a bullet, going far better than those in front of him. To Neil, it was no consolation.

\*

Kate watched the race in the company of the Shaws, which turned out to be an uncomfortable experience. Despite her tender years, Cameron was a loud-mouthed young lady who shrieked throughout the whole encounter, mostly with displeasure at Neil's performance. As Evening Shadow kept up the rear down the back straight, Cameron urged her jockey to 'get your ass in gear' and then, rounding the home turn, to 'Go, go, GO, you dumb-ass motherfucker!' When Neil's bid to pinch the inner ground failed, the air turned blue around her and even her father, who had watched in silent discontent, urged her to 'cool it'.

'Some fucking genius,' she'd muttered in Kate's ear as Evening Shadow just failed to get in the frame.

'Your boy screwed up,' was Shaw's parting shot as Kate hastily excused herself to see to the horse and, more importantly in her opinion, the jockey.

As she rushed to the unsaddling enclosure, her mobile rang. She cursed and scrabbled for it in her bag. She didn't dare leave it unanswered. Annie James had promised to call if there were new developments at the police station.

It was Greta.

'Make it quick,' muttered Kate as she pushed her way through the crowd.

'I'll explain later but – can I stay at your place tonight?'

'Of course.'

'Thanks. I'll let myself in, if that's OK?'

'Do you want me to give a message to Laurie?'

'No. Pretend we didn't have this call. Please.'

Puzzled, Kate broke the connection. What the hell was going on? She put it to the back of her mind. First things first.

*

275

Neil sat miserably in the weighing room as Kate pointed out that he had simply misjudged Evening Shadow's capabilities.

'When you go for a move like that, you have to be certain your horse is quick enough. It's like overtaking when you're driving a slow car – you've got to get your momentum just right.'

'I still blew it, though,' said the boy softly. 'He was the best horse in the field and he didn't even get a place.'

'Look at it this way, then. We've all learned something from this. And when you ride him next time, you've got a great chance of winning.'

But he wouldn't be consoled. 'There's no chance that Cameron girl will let me near him again, is there?'

Kate denied it but she feared he was right.

Mickey had been keeping an eye open for Kate all afternoon. He'd caught sight of her once or twice in the crush but on each occasion it was evident she was busy. He finally ran her to ground outside the weighing room as the excitement built before the Eclipse.

'Why don't we watch this with a drink in our hands?' he suggested. He knew she didn't have a direct interest in the race.

She allowed herself to be steered into a corner of the Champagne Bar, where Mickey had had the foresight to order some refreshment. He pressed a glass upon her which she held tightly without sipping.

'Who's going to win this?' he asked as, on the big screen above their heads, the horses settled in the starting-stalls.

She shot him a piercing glance. They both knew that wasn't why he had sought her out.

'Don't ask me.'

The runners were off.

Mickey pressed on. 'Put it another way. Which of these horses do you wish you were saddling?'

She thought for a moment. 'Nutmeg.'

Nutmeg was the third favourite. A lightly raced three-year-old trained in America.

'Why?'

'Great pedigree. Big, rangy frame. Looks happy in himself. It's a gut feel, really.'

'You fancy working him at Beechwood?'

'Chance would be a fine thing. He cost three million dollars as a yearling. My owners don't have that kind of money.'

'Not your current owners maybe.'

Above them, Nutmeg was making the running, increasing the pace as the runners reached the home turn.

Mickey said, 'Mr Shen bought a colt for five million at the Kentucky sales last July. He's thinking of racing him in Britain next year.'

In the home straight, Nutmeg's rivals were bunching on his shoulder, ready to launch their charge.

'It's very tempting, Mickey.'

'So give in to temptation for once, Kate.'

Nutmeg's jockey rousted him with two furlongs to go. Mickey and Kate watched the finish in silence as, around them, voices were raised in a barrage of excitement. Nutmeg burned off the competition and won by two lengths, having led from start to finish.

'We could be standing in the winner's enclosure together this time next year,' said Mickey.

'No.' Kate turned and faced him. In the whooping crowd she was still and intense. She was the most beautiful woman he'd ever seen. He ached for her.

'I'm sorry, Mickey. Mr Shen's offer is most generous but I can't accept. I value my independence too much.'

So, she was going to play hard to get.

Mickey put his hand into his inside pocket and produced an audio tape.

'Don't shut the door just yet,' he said. 'Take this.'

She looked at the tape suspiciously. 'What is it?'

'A little souvenir – of your brother.'

He had always suspected it would come to this. If he were honest, he preferred it this way.


The self-service shop was busy, it being Saturday afternoon, but that was probably no bad thing. Herbert had pulled on a dirty denim jacket he kept in the car and changed into trainers. At first glance he looked as down-at-heel as the rest of the customers in this scruffy store. All the same, as he plonked a pint of milk in his wire basket – just for the sake of appearances – he wondered if he wasn't off his rocker coming here.

At the rear, by the deep freeze, he asked a Chinese boy in a white overall if Mr Yip was available. The boy looked at him blankly. Herbert pulled a twenty from his pocket.

'Uncle Yip?' he said. 'Tell him Mr H. wants to see him.'

The boy grinned and snaffled the note. 'Oh, *Uncle*,' he said and disappeared through a door at the back of the shop. Herbert pretended to study the frozen veg. The boy was back within thirty seconds, pointing the way up a steep flight of uncarpeted stairs.

Mr Yip was waiting on the first floor landing. A small thin man of unfathomable age, his eyes rheumy and skin the colour of straw, he smiled at Herbert's approach and offered his hand. His fingers were like dry twigs in Herbert's meaty paw. In his crumpled shirt and worn carpet slippers he did not look like the owner of a restaurant chain, an Oriental-foods distribution business and two mansion blocks in the West End – to name just his legitimate interests.

Yip ushered the bookmaker into a room piled high with boxes of crisps and other produce. In the corner, a Western played in black and white on an antique television. Yip turned off the sound as he offered Herbert a choice of the two rickety chairs next to a stained Formica-topped table.

'I hope there's no problem with Hospital Street,' the old man said.

'It's going well – thanks to you.'

Hospital Street in Wapping was the location of a former garment factory which the H.O. Gibbs Group were, even now, turning into Millennium riverside apartments for rich young singles, a project which had caused Herbert endless hassles. At first it had looked like a windfall; he'd picked up the building for a song as settlement of a long-standing debt. But nothing is ever that good, as Herbert often reminded himself. Only after he'd acquired the property did he discover that the existing tenant's lease extended for a further five years. And Mr Wo, the tenant in question and owner of the garment business, turned down all reasonable offers to surrender the lease. Furthermore, with a cadre of knife-wielding factory workers at his beck and call, he'd not proved susceptible to threat. It looked like Herbert would have to pay a crippling price to get him out – or go to war.

At this stage in the drama, Mr Yip had appeared in Herbert's office and offered to make the problem with his countryman go away. Herbert had naturally smelt a rat, suspecting that he was being set up. But on his next visit to the factory, Mr Wo agreed to sell the lease for the first sum Herbert had named and, within a week, the Gibbs Group had vacant possession.

Of course Herbert had offered to recompense Mr Yip for his services but the old man had turned him down, giving Herbert a different kind of problem. By now he'd learned a little about Uncle Yip and discovered that he was both respected and feared in the Chinese community. No one said the word 'Triad' but it was bloody obvious to Herbert. He didn't like the idea of owing such a man a favour – maybe what he had to tell Mr Yip would erase the debt.

The boy brought them tea in a large pot which he poured into funny little cups without handles. At least these days Herbert knew enough not to ask for milk.

'I was wondering,' Herbert began, 'if you'd come across a bloke called Bernard Shen.'

'Of course. He is an important businessman.'

'So he's a friend of yours?'

Mr Yip's face didn't change as he sipped his tea. 'I didn't say that. His concerns are in Hong Kong.'

'So what's he doing here then?'

Mr Yip slowly put down his cup. On the television screen a man in a stetson fired a soundless pistol.

'Are you sure Bernard Shen is in this country?'

'Positive. I've got a friend who says he's here right now, taking care of business.'

'Your friend knows him?'

'In a manner of speaking. He knows where he's staying at any rate.'

'Herbert, do I know your friend?'

'His name's Dave Parsons. Some people call him Girlface. I can tell you where to find him, if you like.'

\*

'Where did he finish?' Tony asked Gus as they shuffled back into the interview room at Farley Road.

The fate of Evening Shadow had been on Tony's mind. He'd given Gus strict instructions to follow the Commonwealth Handicap and report on the result. It had seemed a trivial thing, in the context of his present situation, but Gus hadn't been fazed. 'That's the most interesting thing a client's asked me to do this year,' he'd said.

Now, as they took their seats across the tobacco-scarred table, he turned to Tony.

'Fourth, I'm afraid. He should have won, according to the radio, but the jockey was a bit green.'

That would be Neil. Tony cursed under his breath. He should have been there. He'd let everybody down.

'When you've quite finished the racing bulletin, perhaps we can get started?' Hunter looked even smugger than when Tony had last seen him. He wondered what new revelations were about to be sprung on him.

'Mr Byrne, I believe you are the owner of a .22 rifle.'

'I used to be. It was stolen in a burglary at the beginning of April. I reported it missing at the time.'

'Just like you reported that a set of golf clubs were missing.'

'That's right, they were.'

'But they didn't stay missing, did they?'

Tony sighed. The police must have got this information from Sarah.

'I found the golf clubs under a bush in the garden a few days later, after we'd supplied the insurance company with a list of what had been taken. I rang them up and told them to take the clubs off the list.'

'Are you certain you didn't find your gun under the same bush?'

'No, I didn't.'

'I'm sure you understand our concern, Mr Byrne. You own a weapon which is conveniently stolen before a shooting takes place. Since other items which were reported missing subsequently turn up – why not the gun?'

'Because it didn't.'

'As a matter of interest, why do you possess a gun, Mr Byrne?'

'I got it to shoot rabbits on my mother's farm in Yorkshire. She asked me to take it with me when I moved here. Since the house came with a big garden, I thought I might need it.'

'And why wasn't the weapon properly secured when you were burgled?'

'I thought it was. They managed to get into the gun cabinet.'

'What precisely did they take?'

'My .22 rifle and a carrying case.'

'Can you describe the case?'

'It was brown canvas.'

'Any ammunition?'

'I didn't have any. But if I had it would have been stored separately – that's the regulation, isn't it?'

Hunter pressed on. 'Would you be able to identify your particular weapon?'

'The stock's made of beech. It's a bit scratched. Apart from that the serial number's on my firearms certificate. Why?'

Hunter grinned. 'We've got something we'd like you to take a look at, Mr Byrne.'

*

There wasn't much conversation in Laurie's car on the way back to Lambourn.

He was brooding over Greta. He'd have to make her see sense. Have to. She couldn't have this child and expect him to be its father. A woman couldn't ask that of a man, could she?

Paul was staring glumly out of the window. He'd been out of sorts ever since the second race and Laurie thought he knew why. The American girl, Cameron Shaw, had latched on to him at first and then dropped him for an older boy who'd whisked her off to tour the bars. He couldn't blame Paul for being pissed off.

'Never mind, son,' he said. 'That's women for you.'

The boy looked at him.

'What you on about, Dad?'

'Oh, nothing.'

Laurie could understand if Paul didn't want to talk about it. The wound was probably a bit raw right now. In a couple of days maybe. He turned on the radio.

They caught the news. The item on Freddy's murder was at the top of the bulletin.

*'As racegoers left the Eclipse meeting at Sandown Park this evening, they were greeted by the sensational news that jockey Tony Byrne has been arrested on suspicion of murdering his stablemate Freddy Montague.'*

'Good God,' said Laurie.

*'At a press conference this afternoon, Detective Chief Inspector Ronald Orchard, the officer in charge of the murder enquiry, also revealed that police have retrieved a .22 rifle from a pond in Ashbury.'*

Laurie glanced across at Paul who stared back at him, his face drawn in anguish. He had seen a lot of Tony recently, helping out with Lifeline. He was obviously in shock.

'Don't worry, son,' Laurie said, switching off the radio. 'I guarantee they've got the wrong guy.'

First they showed Tony the gun case. It was still wet and the canvas was stained with mud and weed.

'That could be mine,' he said. 'I couldn't say for sure.'

'What about this?'

Hunter produced the gun, wrapped in clear plastic sheeting. It, too, showed signs of water damage; the wood of the stock was mottled and the steel barrel was dull. Tony recognised it at once, however.

'That's my gun,' he said.

The two policemen exchanged a look. Their relief was tangible.

'Where did you find it?' he asked.

'Exactly where you put it, Mr Byrne, after you shot Freddy Montague.'

Tony took a deep breath. He assumed Hunter was trying to make him lose his cool and say something incriminating.

In a carefully controlled voice, he said, 'Are you saying Freddy was shot with my gun?'

'That's exactly what I'm saying. We've conducted a test firing and we're a hundred per cent sure that the bullet that killed him came from this gun.'

Tony absorbed the blow.

'I'm sorry to hear that, officer, but it doesn't mean I fired it. The gun was stolen from me weeks ago.'

'So you say.'

'It's obviously been in someone else's possession. They've fitted it with a different gun sight.'

That surprised them. They looked at the telescopic sight on the rifle.

'I just used the standard fitting,' Tony said. 'Maybe that's why I'm not much of a shot.'

Hunter leaned forward. 'Let me get this clear. You're saying the gun is yours but you didn't fit this gun sight?'

'Precisely. You want to find out who did. That's the person who killed Freddy – not me.'

# Chapter Eleven

There was no sign of Greta when they got home. Laurie found a letter on the mantelpiece, saying that she was staying with Kate and that supper was in the oven. She asked Laurie to keep away from her for a few days.

Paul read the note over Laurie's shoulder.

'So she's buggered off then,' he said.

'She'll be back soon.'

'Oh, yeah?' Paul shrugged. 'Anyway, why the fuck should I care?'

He turned for the door.

'Paul, come back.'

But he was heading up the stairs.

Laurie called after him, 'Don't you want some supper?'

The only reply was the slam of Paul's bedroom door.

Laurie slumped into a chair. He'd talk to his son later.

Gus had already warned Tony to expect another night in the cells but the news still gave him a jolt.

'I tried to argue that they'd had plenty of time to decide whether or not to charge you but it cut no ice.'

'Do you think they will charge me?'

Gus didn't prevaricate and Tony liked him all the better for it.

'Yes,' he said. 'They're desperate for a suspect and they think you fit the bill.'

Tony felt like laughing. This was some kind of preposterous joke.

'Sarah's responsible. I can't believe she'd stitch me up like this. She said she loved me.'

Gus made no comment.

As Kate opened her front door she remembered that Greta had invited herself to stay. Her heart sank. All she wanted to do was to sit quietly and listen to the tape Mickey had given her. She'd put it on in the car but the moment she'd heard Freddy speak she'd turned it off. She couldn't trust herself to drive with her dead brother's voice in her ears. So she'd left it till she could listen without any distraction. Now she realised she'd have to wait a little longer.

Greta appeared in the door of the kitchen. She looked drawn and unhappy.

'I've left Laurie.'

'What?'

Greta's eyes filled with tears. Kate put her arms round her and felt her friend's whole body reverberate with sobs. She let her cry, holding her as she soaked her blouse with tears. In a strange way she was envious of the other woman's ability to surrender to her emotion. It was the kind of release she herself needed.

At length the crying ceased. Kate guided Greta to the sofa in the front room and found her a box of tissues.

'I'm sorry,' Greta said.

'Don't apologise. I wish I could let it all out like you.'

Greta blew her nose loudly.

'Look,' said Kate, 'you can tell me about it, if you like. It's up to you.'

Greta looked more composed now. 'I'd rather not.'

Kate was relieved, she'd prefer not to be piggy in the middle between Greta and Laurie.

Greta looked her in the eye, her face pink and raw. 'Can I just stay for a few days?'

'Of course.'

'Oh, Kate, I don't know what to do.'

Her face crumpled again and she reached for the tissues as the tears started to roll again.

Kate said nothing. What a bloody mess.

It was midnight by the time Kate had the privacy she needed. Though Greta had stuck to her word and not discussed her quarrel with Laurie, that still left plenty of ground to cover. Where was she going to live? How was she going to manage on her own? What about Paul? And many other questions with no easy answers.

Finally, Greta had stumbled off to bed, leaving Kate drained and exhausted. Nevertheless, her thoughts kept returning to Mickey's tape – she had to know what it contained. She slipped it into the machine by her bed and pushed the Play button.

At first it was hard to make out what was going on. Freddy's voice sounded loud and distorted, as if he were too close to a microphone. He was asking someone – Jeff – if he wanted another beer. Kate had heard this in the car before she'd turned the tape off. She'd had time to think about 'Jeff' and assumed he was Jeff Collins, the jockey who'd sent Freddy his trunk.

An Australian voice cut across the hiss of the tape. 'Yeah. Chuck us another tinny, would ya?'

Kate guessed the recording had been made while Freddy had been away last winter. There were background noises. The distant rumble of traffic and the sound of a police siren. She pictured a small, stifling hotel room in Hong Kong, the windows open high above the teeming city streets. The two jockeys talking the night away.

'So, is it worth me coming to England, Fred? Am I gonna make my fortune?'

'You'll coin it, mate. Nobody can ride a loser like you and it's no different in England.'

Laughter. Then the Australian spoke again.

'I was thinking of riding a few winners, actually.'

'You can try that first but if you're not in the top league the only real money's in stopping 'em. If you combine the two, it's even better. I've been doing it for years.' There was more laughter.

'Are you sure your sister will let me ride?'

'If I ask her, she will. Just play it straight with Kate, though. She's a hundred per cent legit.'

'Really? How does she put up with you then?'

' 'Cos she doesn't bloody know, that's why. I'm her sweet and innocent baby brother and she trusts me.'

More laughter.

Jeff spoke again, his voice full of sly curiosity.

'I've seen photos of your sister. She's a hell of a looker.'

'Dream on, Jeff.'

'No, don't get me wrong. I'd never touch a mate's sister, it's just that –'

'You were wondering if there's another kind of riding vacancy in her yard. I know you.'

'Well, she *is* a looker.'

'You're a few years too late, sunshine. She used to shag like a bunny but now she's turned herself into a Vestal Virgin.'

Kate couldn't believe what she was hearing. How could Freddy talk about her like that? And, as she listened, her anger mounted.

'I used to cover for her when she first got into boys. I'm a couple of years younger, so she'd pretend to be keeping an eye on me while she was trying out the local lads in the back of their crummy Sierras. And I'd back her up with our mum and dad. I couldn't wait to get someone in the back of a Sierra myself.

'Then, when she turned sixteen, she really blotted her copy book. Mum and Dad had gone out to some dinner dance and she was minding me. She asked this biker boy who'd caught her eye over and I had a girl round from my class. We raided Dad's drinks cabinet and had a bit of a party. Then Kate and her boyfriend disappeared into her bedroom, leaving us to snog on the sofa. Bugger me if Mum and Dad didn't come back early. The two of us downstairs were OK, we pretended we were watching the telly. But Kate and the biker were going at it like the clappers upstairs, making a hell of a racket. Dad threw a fit.'

Kate's face burned with embarrassment at this crudely reported snapshot of her past. The lad Freddy was talking about was hardly a greasy leather boy. He'd been an art student with brown soulful eyes and wild hair. At the time she'd thought it was love and had paid a heavy price for this escapade – her parents had despatched her to a draughty boarding school in Northumberland where she'd failed her A-levels just to spite them.

On tape Freddy was still talking about her. This was a special kind of torture, hearing her brother gossip about her past to a stranger. With the ghoulish twist that both of them were now dead.

'I thought she'd given up men after that. She never seemed to have boyfriends once she began working in the yard. Then she started getting me to cover for her again. Dad had got me apprenticed over in Newmarket and she'd say she was going to see me and, of course, never turn up. And she'd use an old schoolfriend in London the same way. In fact, she was having her end away with one of Dad's owners, a City bloke twice her age with three kids and a cracking-looking missus tucked away in Kent. When the wife found out, the shit hit the fan. Poor old Katie thought he'd leave his family for her but of course he didn't. He dumped her and Dad, too – took a dozen horses out of the yard. Thank God, I wasn't around at the time. The funny thing is, two years later this Henry Wheatcroft ran off with another woman and the wife blew the whistle on him. It turned out he'd embezzled millions in the City. Ended up inside.'

'Jeez! Sounds to me like your sister had a lucky escape.'

Kate turned the tape off. She couldn't stand any more. Not that there would be any more. There'd been no lovers in her life since Henry. The shit. He'd conned her like he'd conned so many others. She wasn't running the risk of being conned again.

But, wary or not, she realised she'd been caught. The tape was a pistol to her head. Unless she cooperated with Mickey she had no doubt it would find its way to the newspapers. And then they'd be after her, turning her Ice Queen image on its head, dragging in her brother's admissions, rehashing his murder – and playing the Wheatcroft angle to the hilt. Was she strong enough for all that?

She didn't know.

Was Mr Shen responsible for the tape – or was it just down to Mickey? She didn't know that either. She didn't want to go into partnership with a blackmailer but the alternative was too dreadful to contemplate.

Surely Mr Shen just wanted her to train his horses?

She wished she had someone to turn to.

The image of Tony took shape in her mind and, with regret, she shut it out. How could she trust the man accused of her brother's murder?

Hungover, Laurie blundered around the kitchen making breakfast. There was no sign of Paul and he still had no idea what he was going to say to him about Greta. He could stall, say she'd be back soon – or he could prepare the ground for something more permanent. He shrank from that. He'd have to talk to Greta first. Whatever their personal disagreements they had to present a united front for their son.

It was time Paul got up. Laurie wandered into the hall and called for him but there was no response. He trudged up the stairs and knocked on his son's door.

'Paul.'

There was no reply. Laurie opened the door and stepped inside. As usual the room was a tip. He skirted a jumble of clothes on the floor and pulled back a curtain. Sunlight lanced into the gloom.

Paul lay motionless on the bed, his face turned to the wall.

'Come on, mate. I've got breakfast going.'

The boy still didn't move and Laurie took in a detail of the scene that, in a split-second, turned him to stone. On the bedside table, next to a clock and a scuffed paperback, lay a scattered jumble of white and silver – blister-packs for Paracetamol. Each small plastic indentation was empty.

Laurie lurched to the bed and reached for the shoulder turned towards him. The boy rolled over on to his back, floppy as a doll, his eyes closed.

Dead to the world.

'Thanks for coming in, everybody. I'm sure you'd all prefer to be in church.'

DCI Orchard was addressing half a dozen of his troops, Annie James among them, who had surrendered their Sunday to further the enquiry. Not that they minded – after all, who couldn't use the overtime?

'I'm convinced,' Orchard was saying, 'that we've got the man who killed Freddy Montague but there's still work to do. Tony Byrne admits he owns the murder weapon but claims it was stolen in a burglary two months ago. He also says the gun sight is not his.'

DC Clive Cook spoke up. 'Were there any fingerprints on the gun, guv?'

'No. Either it had been wiped or else they'd rubbed off on the canvas case. And I don't suppose sitting on the bottom of the duck pond helped either.

'So,' continued Orchard, 'I'd like to tie our man to this gun sight. Jim, have you found Byrne's financial records?'

Henderson laughed. 'Dunno about records, guv. He had bits of paper all over the house. Half his post wasn't even opened. We took away a pile of stuff – Don and I are trying to sort it out.'

'While you're going through it, keep an eye open for payment for a telescopic gun sight. It might be fairly recent – within the last couple of months. And look out for paperwork on other sporting goods – he might use the same supplier.'

'You can buy shooting accessories over the internet,' said Annie.

'We couldn't find a computer,' said Henderson.

'Go back and double-check,' said Orchard. 'Make sure there's not a laptop tucked away somewhere. Annie, I'd like you and Clive to visit all local outlets for shooting gear. See if they sell sights like this one. Maybe they'd remember a customer like Tony Byrne. Who knows – you might get lucky.'

She noted down the make and specification of the gun sight – a Mercury Riflescope. She'd check Yellow Pages but doubted if there were more than three or four shops within a fifty-mile radius who might sell such a thing. And they wouldn't be open till tomorrow.

'How much time's Tony got left?' she asked Orchard. She knew he had already extended the jockey's arrest period by twelve hours.

'Till midday. But don't worry, he's not going anywhere. I'm about to go and charge him with murder.'

Paul's eyes flicked open. He looked at his father with sleepy confusion.

'Dad?'

Laurie's heart was still pounding even as relief flooded his veins. He held up an empty blister-pack.

'How many did you take?'

'Uh . . .' The boy was still half asleep. Laurie could see him adjusting to the waking world and its nasty realities.

Paul pulled himself into a sitting position. As he did so, something small and white tumbled to the floor. A pill. There were others on the floor too and more scattered all over the bed.

'Did you take any of these?'

'No.'

Laurie's fear evaporated, to be replaced by anger. 'What the hell are you playing at?' he shouted.

The boy stared at him, sullen and mute.

Laurie took a deep breath and sat on the edge of the bed.

'I'm sorry. You scared me, Paul. When I saw the empty packets I thought you'd taken them.'

'I should have done but I didn't have the nerve.' His voice was low and tremulous. 'This is all my fault.'

Laurie put his hand on the boy's arm. 'Paul, what's gone wrong between your mother and me isn't your fault.'

'It's not just Mum. It's the gun . . .'

For a moment Laurie was lost. What was he talking about?

'The gun in the duck pond that killed Freddy. I found it first – months ago.'

Laurie gazed at him in shock. 'You know about the gun?'

'Yes.' Paul's voice was almost inaudible.

It took Laurie a while to coax the story out of him. When he had finished, Laurie didn't know what to say. He stared at his tearful son. He hadn't thought this situation could get any worse – but he'd been wrong.

'I reckon it's because you're left-handed, Jack. There's very few top golfers who are southpaws.'

DI Jack Fletcher considered his foursome partner, Tom Harris, with amusement. They were engaging in their usual Sunday morning ritual – analysing the deficiencies in the detective's game over a drink at the club bar. Fletcher had only recently taken up golf and, if truth be told, he preferred the post-game pint to the game itself.

'That's a comforting thought,' he said. 'Does that mean I can claim some extra strokes if I'm playing a right-hander?'

A man on the other side of the bar was trying to catch his eye. For a second, lulled by his surroundings, he couldn't place him. Then it clicked: Duncan Hamilton of Hamilton & Cosgrove. He'd last seen him across the table in an interview room at Farley Road nick, advising a local pusher of his rights. He'd forgotten the solicitor was a member of the golf club.

Hamilton was making unmistakable signals and Fletcher cut his friend short.

'Excuse me, Tom. I've got to have a quick word with someone.'

Hamilton saw Fletcher coming and pointed to the door. They met up overlooking the eighteenth green.

'Sorry to talk shop, Jack, but I need a moment.'

'You could have called me at the station, couldn't you?'

'Then it would have to wait till tomorrow, wouldn't it?' Hamilton lowered his voice and continued, 'Look, I'm just a messenger boy here. I don't really want to get involved but . . . Jerry Priestley wants to talk to you in confidence.'

Jerry Priestley – a career criminal whose career was about to be interrupted for a lengthy spell thanks to Fletcher's efforts. Priestley was due in court shortly on multiple burglary charges. Fletcher made the obvious assumption that Priestley was offering information in an attempt to reduce his sentence.

'What's he got? It'd better be good if he wants to influence the judge.'

'I told him that but he's adamant. It's regarding the Montague murder.'

That took the inspector by surprise. 'What's that got to do with him?'

Hamilton grinned. 'You'll have to ask Jerry that, won't you?'

*

Greta nearly shut the door in Laurie's face. She'd specifically asked him to wait for her to get in touch with him.

'Go away,' she said.

'We have to talk.'

'Not yet. I'm not ready – please, Laurie.'

'This isn't about you and me.'

There was something in his tone which made her look closely at him. His voice was flat, without emotion.

'It's Paul,' he said. 'I don't know what to do.'

She let him in. Kate was in the yard so they had the house to themselves. Greta led him into the kitchen and poured him a cup of coffee. She added a spoonful of sugar and placed it at his elbow.

'Go on,' she said.

'A couple of months ago, he found a gun.'

This wasn't what she'd expected to hear. The words came out of nowhere. 'What?'

'He was cycling to school and saw a long brown canvas bag by the side of the road. He says he thought it was a fishing rod. Inside the bag was a .22 rifle.'

'Why didn't he say something to us? We could have reported it.'

'Just listen, Greta.'

She nodded. She knew she was not going to like what followed but there was no point in interrupting.

'Paul hid the gun in a hedge and collected it after school. Then he showed it to Neil and the pair of them decided to keep it.'

'Why?' Greta couldn't help herself.

'They're boys, Greta. They wanted to shoot at things. Paul says they kept the gun in an old shed by Itchinfield Wood and took pot shots at cans and bottles.'

'But what with? Did he find bullets as well?'

'Neil got those from some relative, apparently. And he bought a telescopic sight as well. They'd go out at night with a flashlight and try for rabbits.'

Laurie paused and drank. He seemed more animated now, as if sharing his burden made him feel better. It was having the opposite effect on Greta.

'Then they discovered that the gun sight was good for other things as well. They started looking into people's windows at night. Specifically, Freddy Montague's. And don't ask me why, Greta. Most adolescent boys would give their right arms to watch people fucking. I'm sure it was an education to watch Freddy at it.'

Greta sat down, numb with shock, as Laurie told her the rest of the story.

'Paul says that he felt bad about snooping like this so he stopped it. But it became an obsession with Neil once he'd seen Freddy with Sarah Cooper.'

'Freddy was screwing Sarah?'

'Apparently so, in the week or so before he got shot.'

'Jesus Christ.' Greta didn't know what to think. She was appalled to find within herself a spark of jealousy but suppressed it quickly. Freddy had been entitled to bed whoever he liked once she'd told him their affair had no future.

'Paul doesn't know exactly what happened the night of the murder except that Neil went off to see if he could catch Freddy with Sarah again. Neil had this thing about her, didn't he?'

Greta nodded. It had been a bit of a joke around the yard. 'You're saying that Neil shot Freddy?'

'Yes.'

'Why?'

'I can think of a few reasons.' Laurie ticked them off on his fingers. 'One – Neil couldn't stand seeing Freddy with Sarah. Two – Freddy treated him like shit. Three – with Freddy out of the way, Neil gets some rides. And, four, it's in the blood – Neil's father's been inside for manslaughter.'

Greta took all this in. 'We've got to take Paul to the police.'

'There's something I haven't told you yet.'

What could that be? Greta couldn't believe things could get any worse.

Laurie looked her squarely in the eye. 'Paul says if all this comes out he'll kill himself.'

'He wouldn't do that!' Greta cried, her hand covering her mouth.

'He nearly did,' Laurie replied. Then he told her about the pills.

'Grub up, mate.' The copper in the doorway holding a lunch tray was a cheerful soul. 'Sunday dinner. Got to be some compensation for getting banged up on a weekend.'

Tony was going to send him away but the smell of roast lamb spoke directly to his tastebuds. He'd not eaten since he'd been arrested. He could see the plate piled high with meat and two veg; a pudding of jam stodge sat next to it.

'Thanks,' he said.

Until an hour ago he'd expected to be released and back in the saddle for the coming week. Then DCI Orchard had charged him with Freddy's murder and the prospect of imminent release had disappeared. The chances of being bailed on a murder charge, Gus had told him, were slim unless he could put up some serious money. He didn't have it and wasn't about to go cap in hand to his friends and family to try and raise it.

So, in these circumstances, what was the point of starving himself?

He cleared his plate – both plates – and lay down, bloated with food. Was this the slippery slope? he wondered. The end of a fasting regime that had put him back on some top horses and given a new lease of life to his career.

He didn't know and, for the moment, he didn't care. The past thirty-six hours were catching up with him. He made himself as comfortable as he could and fell into a deep sleep.

'He's still not rung me, Mum. What have I done?'

Neil heard a deep sigh on the other end of the line. He knew she didn't want to discuss it.

'It's not my problem, son. It's between you and your father.'

'What's he said to you?'

'Nothing.'

Neil didn't know whether to believe her.

'There is one thing,' she added. 'When did you last see him?'

It had been a while, Neil thought. A depressing prison visit about a year ago.

'It's not easy to get away,' he mumbled.

She didn't bother to reply to that. It sounded feeble even to himself.

While he waited, Laurie pretended to work in his study. But work was impossible. It suddenly didn't matter much.

At last he heard Greta close Paul's bedroom door and come downstairs.

'How is he?' Laurie asked anxiously.

'He cried a lot,' she said. 'He's just a baby really.'

'But what did he say?'

'What he told you, I imagine. How he and Neil used to fool around with the gun.'

'So he's agreed to talk to the police?'

She stood over Laurie. 'Paul's not going to the police.'

'But he has to! For God's sake, Greta, an innocent man's been arrested. He has to come forward.'

'No. Being mixed up in something like this would ruin his life. It mustn't come out.'

'What about Tony?'

'If he's innocent then they'll set him free.'

'What do you mean, *if*? We know he is.'

'We know nothing of the sort. The police obviously have a case – hasn't it occurred to you that, if Freddy was sleeping with Sarah, Tony's the obvious suspect?'

Laurie stared at her, perplexed.

'Anyway,' she continued, 'all that's an irrelevance as far as we're concerned. What matters to us is Paul. Do you want him to be called as a witness in a murder trial?'

'No, but —'

'But nothing. Freddy's dead and we can't change that. We *can* protect our son.'

'How?' It occurred to him that she'd taken charge. She was the backbone of their marriage. It was one of the reasons he loved her.

'I'll take him to stay with Aunt Sonja.' Greta's aunt lived outside Stockholm. 'It's almost his summer holiday anyway – we'll leave as soon as we can get a flight.'

'OK.' Then something occurred to him. 'Are you sure you're all right to fly?'

'What do you mean?'

'The baby.'

She smiled. 'You can fly up to twenty weeks and more.' The smile vanished. 'Anyway, what's it to you?'

She turned for the door.

'Greta —'

'Yes.'

'You're not going to stay at Kate's any more, are you? We need you here.'

Kate was examining Big Dee's slow-mending hip when she heard a voice calling her. She looked out of the stall to see the policewoman Annie James crossing the yard.

'I've been ringing you,' Annie said.

Kate nodded. She'd switched her mobile off so she wouldn't have to speak to Mickey Lee.

'Who's this?' Annie asked, looking at the horse.

'Big Dee, a six-year-old gelding with a dodgy hip. I'm afraid his best days are behind him.'

Annie stroked the horse's muzzle. Big Dee basked in the attention. 'He's lovely. Can I take him home?'

'Come back when his hip's better and you can ride him.'

Annie's face lit up. 'Can I really?'

Kate laughed. 'You like horses, don't you?'

'I'm sorry. I should be more professional and keep my enthusiasm under control.'

'So this is an official visit.'

Annie's smile faded. 'I wanted to let you know we've charged Tony Byrne with Freddy's murder.'

Kate didn't know how to react. Poor Tony. She could hardly believe it.

She wanted her brother's murderer caught, of course. But since last night she'd been thinking hard about the tape and Freddy's casual admission to fixing races. That surely had to be the reason why he'd been killed. She remembered her conversation with the obnoxious Sergeant Hunter. The police had clearly been thinking along those lines themselves.

'I don't understand. Why would Tony kill my brother?'

'Freddy was having an affair with Sarah Cooper.'

'What?' But Kate wasn't really surprised. She remembered the afternoon when Sarah had turned up to ride and had gone off with Freddy. That liaison made perfect sense, even if nothing else did.

'So what happens to Tony now?'

'He'll go before a magistrate in the morning. He'll probably be remanded in custody – bail will be sky-high.'

Kate was pondering this information when she heard the sound of footsteps. Greta was crossing the courtyard towards them, her face sombre.

'Sorry to interrupt,' she said. 'I just want to say that Laurie and I have patched things up. I'm going back home, Kate.'

That was good news at any rate. Kate smiled at her. 'I *am* pleased,' she said.

Greta nodded, then turned and made her way back to the house.

Annie watched her go. 'It's a shame she's so sad, given her condition.'

'What condition?'

'She's expecting, isn't she?'

Kate stared at her. It had been her first thought, weeks back, before she'd realised it was impossible.

'She's not pregnant.'

'Really?' Annie frowned. 'I've never been wrong before.'

'She can't be. They're not able to have children.'

'I thought they had a son.'

'They adopted Paul when they discovered Laurie's fertility problem. So, you see, Greta can't be having a baby.'

Even as she said it, Kate realised how blind she had been. Annie said nothing.


'Come on, Neil. Have another bit of treacle tart.'

'No, thanks, Mum.'

'Go on. You're nothing but skin and bone, ain't he, Mary?'

'Leave him alone, Mum. He knows his own mind.'

Neil's mother shrugged and bit back the words that Neil knew were on the tip of her tongue. She couldn't accept that being a jockey meant turning down second helpings – even for a featherweight like him. She picked up the remains of the tart and carried it off to the kitchen.

Neil shot his eldest sister a look of gratitude. 'Thanks.'

'If you came home more often she might not fuss so much.'

Neil reflected that he hardly deserved the welcome he'd received since he'd turned up unannounced at his mother's door.

'You're right,' he said. 'I'll try harder in future – I promise.'

'Not that we're not proud of you,' she said. 'We'll have a bit of a party round here when you're riding on the telly. Any excuse, you know.'

'Does Dad show up?'

'Of course. He grabs the best seat.'

'He won't talk to me now. He puts the phone down on me when I ring up.'

Mary stood and began stacking dirty plates. 'Well, you know where to find him, don't you?'

'The Coal Hole?' A bar on Kilburn High Road where, it was said, Liam Kelly had served almost as much time as in the Scrubs.

'Yeah. And, since you're here, you can put him to bed tonight.'

'What do you mean?'

She dug in her handbag and held out a keyring with two keys. 'He's on the ground floor, thank God. Forty-eight Clovelly Road, first right, down from the bar.'

'But I'm supposed to get back tonight, Mare. I've got to be at work by half-five.'

Her mouth thinned and her eyes clouded, hardening her pretty face. 'Every night me or Brenda, or Maeve on a Saturday when she comes over, dig the old man out of that flea-pit and get him home. If your sisters can do it, so can you.'

Neil stood up. 'I don't understand. Why does anyone have to look after him?'

Mary's face softened. 'He's not what he was, Neil. You'll see.'

He saw his mother watching from the doorway as he pocketed the keys.

Kate let the phone ring and heard the click of the answerphone as the caller's message began to record. She knew who it would be, the same person who had been calling all evening – Mickey.

She'd pick up when he rang again, she decided. She couldn't put it off for ever.

Neil was preoccupied as he made his way through the maze of narrow terraced streets to his father's drinking club. He'd not been able to get hold of Kate so he'd left a message saying his father was ill and that he'd be back as soon as he could the next day. He hoped that would do.

The Coal Hole did not advertise itself. The entrance was through the back of a mini-cab office sandwiched between an Asian self-service store and a dry-cleaner's. Neil had been there a couple of times with his mother but that had been before his father's last prison term and he'd been so young he'd had to wait outside.

Now he rang the bell and waited for the door to be opened. A sandy-haired bruiser in a short-sleeved shirt appeared and looked down at him.

'Sorry,' he said without apparent malice.

'I'm looking for Liam Kelly.'

'No one of that name here, son. Piss off.'

'He's my father.'

The door shut in Neil's face. He stood for a moment, at a loss. He was about to ring again when an older, red-faced man opened up. 'Jesus,' he said, peering down at him.

'Hello, Uncle Fergus.'

The man's face split into a grin and he seized Neil's hand.

'Sorry about Padraig,' he said as he ushered Neil down the narrow staircase. 'He's good at keeping people out.'

The room was much as Neil had expected: small, foul and smoke-ridden. The bar was jam-packed and voices were raised high over piped Celtic chords. Fergus pushed him through the throng. His father sat at a crowded rear table smoking a hand-rolled cigarette and smiling.

'Liam,' called Fergus, 'someone to see you.'

'Oh, yeah?' said his father cheerfully as he turned his head towards them.

'Hello, Dad.'

The smile vanished from his father's face in a flash.

Mickey didn't bother with preliminaries when Kate picked up the phone.

'Have you had a chance to reconsider Mr Shen's proposal?'

'I've given it some thought.'

Kate was determined to make no reference to the tape-recording. She hoped Mickey was of the same mind.

'So what can I tell Mr Shen?' he prompted.

She took a deep breath. 'I'm prepared to give it serious consideration.'

'Excellent.'

'On one condition. You must arrange bail for Tony Byrne.'

There was silence at the other end of the line.

'Don't tell me that's beyond your capabilities,' Kate added.

He chuckled. 'Of course not. I'm sure Mr Shen would be eager to assist one of our stable jockeys.'

That 'our' irritated her but she let it pass. 'Good. I'm going to give you the home number of Tony's solicitor. You've got to talk to him tonight – is that clear?'

Irrational though it was, when she put down the phone Kate felt as if she had scored a minor victory.

Though Neil was sitting next to his dad, it was not possible to have any kind of conversation. His drinking companions were noisily hospitable, treating Neil like a minor celebrity and quizzing him on every aspect of the racing scene. Drinks appeared in front of him despite his protestations and, whenever he tried to pay for a round, his money was ignored.

Throughout all this, Liam Kelly sat silent and morose, steadily working his way through pint after pint of Guinness, chased down by tots of Jameson's. When he got up to go and relieve himself he supported himself on the shoulder of the man sitting on his other side.

Neil watched him move slowly through the crush, his thin frame bent like a dowager's, his feet uncertain. He was a long time returning.

'You've made his day,' said one of the men around the table. The others nodded.

'All he talks about is you,' added another.

Neil found that hard to believe but it was not as unlikely as discovering that his domineering, forceful father had turned into a frail old man. Had the last year in prison been that bad? Or was it the booze he'd been pouring down his throat since his release?

After that, Neil tried to take him home but Liam ignored his requests. Neil could see that while drink was still on the table, his father wasn't to be budged.

Just after eleven, Fergus came over. Neil had the impression he'd been watching his attempts to persuade his father to leave.

'I'll give you a hand,' he muttered. 'One of the girls usually gets him about now.'

To Neil's surprise, Liam responded to Fergus's commands and together they manoeuvred him through the bar and up the stairs. Out in the street, Neil gripped his father's arm tightly and steered him slowly along the pavement. Thank God they didn't have far to go.

Forty-eight Clovelly Road was part of a Victorian terrace, built on three floors with a porch. The pair of them stumbled up a flight of steps to the freshly painted front door.

Liam had said nothing as they'd blundered along the road. Now, as Neil pulled the keys from his pocket, he said, 'You silly little twat.'

'Come on, Dad,' he protested mildly, opening the front door.
'You stupid fucker!'
'Dad, please.'
Neil pulled his father inside and looked for the door to his
room – according to Mary's directions it was the first on the
left.
'A stupid, stupid fucker, I said!'
The room could have been worse. Though the wallpaper
was a grimy pink-and-primrose stripe, the furnishings were
functional – bed, table, TV, a sink and cooker in an alcove, and
a door which led, Neil guessed, to a toilet. It was clean, too – no
doubt his sisters' doing.
His father wobbled inside and Neil quickly shut the door
behind him before his inebriated ramblings brought unwanted
attention down on them.
To his surprise, Neil was seized and slammed against the
wall. Suddenly energised, his father had him pinned in an
unbreakable grip. He glared into his face.
'I never thought you'd end up like me.'
'Let go, Dad.'
'I've been talking to Frankie Taylor.'
'Uncle Frank?'
'He's not your fucking uncle. None of them are your uncles.
They're just shites like me who've fucked up.'
'Dad, put me down.'
'I've heard about the bullets, son. Frankie told me. I never
thought you'd be such a fool.'
So he knew.
'It was just for a laugh, Dad. I never meant any harm.'
'But that wasn't how it turned out, was it? I'm not a complete
bloody idiot, you know. I read the papers. Are you telling me

one of those bullets didn't end up inside Freddy Montague?'

Liam's grip relaxed, the fire dying as suddenly as it had flared.

'Once I could have helped you,' he muttered. 'Now it's too late.'

The pair of them stood swaying in each other's arms, both of them holding on tight.

# Chapter Twelve

Neil sat gloomily on the 8.15 from Paddington to Swindon, his body stiff from a night spent in his father's armchair. He felt far from rested. Sleep had been kept at bay by his dad's phlegmy snores – and by the thoughts buzzing round his head. Now he knew why he'd been in his father's bad books: Frankie Taylor had spilled the beans. He regretted approaching Uncle Frank but where else could he have got ammunition for the .22? He'd sworn the old boy to silence but, on reflection, he could see that secrecy might have been difficult for Frankie to extend to his father.

Why on earth had he wanted to muck around with that gun anyway?

He cursed himself for being such a fool.

Annie was waiting at the door of Tudor's Sporting Goods as it opened for business on Monday morning. She flashed her warmest smile along with her warrant card at the podgy, balding gentleman who unlocked the front door. For a shop dedicated to outdoor combat with fish and fowl and other forms of hairy-chested endeavour, Mr Appleby looked distinctly weedy. However, he was clearly keen to be helpful. His eyes slid all over her as she explained the purpose of her visit.

'We don't keep those in stock,' he said, referring to the Mercury gun sight she asked for.

Annie wasn't surprised. Nothing was ever that easy. She thanked him and headed for the door.

'I can order it, though,' he added. 'Forty-eight-hour delivery.'

She turned back. 'Have you ordered one recently?'

'I'll get Terry's book,' he said and disappeared into the rear of the shop.

'Terry deals with firearms and shooting accessories,' Appleby explained as he returned holding a hardbound volume with ruled pages. 'He's not in today, though. Long weekend with his new girlfriend.' He gave Annie a knowing leer.

She pointed at the book. 'The gun sight,' she prompted.

He flicked through the pages and ran his eye down neatly drawn columns of names, addresses and goods ordered.

Even upside down, Annie spotted it before he did: 'May 10th, Mercury 3–7×20mm Riflescope'. Followed by a name, not Tony Byrne but 'Neil Kelly, Beechwood Yard, Upper Lambourn'.

Well, well, well.

'Did you deal with this customer, Mr Appleby?'

'Oh, no. Like I said, Terry does guns and he's on a dirty weekend with—'

'His girlfriend. You mentioned it. May I borrow this book?'

'Well' – his eyes lingered on her chest for a split-second – 'if you promise to return it in person.'

'Of course.' Annie beamed at him – the creep. It might be necessary to retain the book as evidence, of course, but she wanted to show it to Orchard straight away.

'Thanks, Mr Appleby. You've been most helpful.'

'It's a pleasure, officer. Do you fancy a coffee?'

Annie was dying for one but she shook her head vigorously. She couldn't get out of there fast enough.

*

Fletcher saw Jerry Priestley in an interview room at Farley Road station which, apart from saving the DI a trip to prison, was essential for Priestley's own security.

'I'm not here to grass anyone up,' the burglar said at once. When it came to negotiating a reduced sentence, informing on a third party was the most reliable method of getting a result.

Fletcher ignored this remark and went straight into a preamble of his own to establish (a) there were no guarantees a word from him would have any effect on the judge in the forthcoming burglary trial, and (b) Priestley had better not be buggering him about.

The burglar waited for him to finish, unmoved. He was a whippet-thin individual in his mid-thirties with a face worn and creased beyond his years. He was no fool and had the reputation of being a pretty straight fellow – for a crook. In Fletcher's opinion, he could have done more with his life than fetch up here looking at another five years inside.

'As you know, Mr Fletcher,' Priestley began, 'I made a mistake in working with Billy Robinson.'

Robinson was a teenager whose inability to keep his mouth shut was a sore point. Fletcher grunted, familiar with the whole saga.

'A couple of months back, we did a house in Upper Lambourn. In Uplands Road.'

Fletcher perked up. Tony Byrne's house was in Uplands Road.

'It was easy pickings. No security to speak of. No dogs. We got a couple of nice pieces – an antique carriage clock, some jewellery. I did upstairs and left Billy downstairs. He doesn't have much of a clue but he knows what a TV looks like. We were out in about ten minutes.'

'Why didn't we hear about this one, Jerry?'

'You don't know everything, Mr Fletcher.'

That was certainly true. In making a case against Priestley, Fletcher thought he'd considered every unsolved burglary in the county in the past two years. Obviously this one had slipped through the net. 'Get on with it then,' he muttered.

'As we were driving off, Billy was gabbing on about a set of new golf clubs he'd found in the back room. I couldn't remember loading them in – turned out we'd left them behind. Any road, I turned in my seat and looked into the back of the van. We'd covered the stuff up in case we got stopped but, right next to me, sticking up was a long brown bag. "What's that?" I asked Billy and he said, "Aha – surprise," like he was talking to some kid. So I reached over and grabbed it. I don't like surprises when I'm working.'

He paused and grinned at Fletcher. 'I don't suppose there's any chance of a cuppa, is there?'

The policeman grinned back. 'When you've finished, Jerry. Maybe.'

Priestley shrugged. 'Anyhow, I unzipped this bag and inside was a rifle. I did my nut. I never have anything to do with guns. They're big trouble.'

Fletcher nodded. He wasn't going to argue with that.

'Billy was going on about how he'd found the key to this steel cupboard in a jar on the mantelpiece. He thought he was a right clever clogs. I made him stop the van and chucked the ruddy thing out of the window. Should have seen the look on his face.'

'And?'

'And nothing. That's the last I saw of it. But when I heard you'd pulled a rifle out of a duck pond in connection with that jockey's murder, I got on to my brief. Interrupted his dinner party on Saturday 'cos I reckoned this was important.'

'Did you get a good look at the gun?'

'Good enough.' Priestley leaned forward. 'Are you sure you can't help me out, Mr Fletcher? My brief says you could write the judge a letter. Tell him how helpful I've been.'

'I might. I'm still considering.'

'The gun was a .22.'

'Would you recognise it if you saw it again?'

'Try me.'

Fletcher got to his feet. 'I'll see about that tea.'

When the taxi dropped him off at the hostel Neil dashed in to wash and change into his working clothes. By the time he had rushed down to the yard, second lot was returning.

'Where the hell have you been?' snapped Kate, getting out of her Volvo. 'I expected better from you, Neil.'

'But I've just got back from London,' he protested.

She stepped close to him, her voice low but firm. 'If you want rides you've got to act like a professional. I was going to give you a ride tomorrow but you don't deserve it. I'll find another jockey.'

She turned on her heel and left him standing open-mouthed.

DCI Orchard was at the magistrates' court for Tony's hearing so it was Hunter who accompanied Fletcher as he resumed his interview with Jerry Priestley. Fletcher carried a cardboard cup of tea and a cellophane-wrapped pack of ginger nuts; Hunter held a large plastic bag.

They didn't waste time. Hunter placed the bag on the table. The rifle was plainly visible through the transparent covering.

'Is that the gun?' he asked.

Priestley considered it for a moment then nodded his head. 'Yeah. Could well be. I remember that little diamond mark.' He pointed to a motif on the butt. 'On the other hand . . .'

'What?' said Hunter impatiently.

'The gun we nicked never had no telescopic sight.'

Sitting in Gus Jones's office, Tony felt light-headed and euphoric. For a man who had just been brought before a magistrate and charged with murder that was a bizarre way to feel. But he wasn't yet ready to contemplate the ordeal ahead of him – a trial, ruin, maybe even a life sentence. Until a few minutes ago, he had been steeling himself to be remanded in custody and now, out of the blue, he was free on bail. In the short interview before the proceedings, Gus had said there was a chance he'd get it but Tony hadn't believed him. Yet here he was, bailed for the staggering sum of £100,000 thanks to, of all people, Bernard Shen. It was unreal.

Gus was discussing practicalities. Tony had difficulty in taking them in.

'The press will be after you, Tony. Have you got an agent or a PR representative?'

'You're joking.'

'I know some of you sportsmen have a host of advisers.'

'Not me.'

'OK. Then, if you're agreeable, I suggest you issue a statement through me, professing your innocence and saying that if this misguided charge should come to trial you look forward to clearing your name.'

'You write it. I just want to go home and get to bed.'

'Ah.' The tone in which Gus uttered this syllable forced Tony to pay attention. 'That's what I'm getting at. You won't get any peace there at the moment. You'll have reporters banging on the door and hassling you on the phone.'

Tony's euphoria disappeared in an instant.

'Don't look so alarmed,' Gus continued. 'I suggest we hammer out this short statement which I will issue to the press. Then I'll whisk you out the back and round to my house where you can catch up on your sleep. In the meantime, I'll drive one of the lads over to your place, grab some clothes and things, then bring your car back.'

Tony stared at him, speechless with gratitude. 'I don't know how to thank you, Gus.'

He grinned. 'You obviously don't realise it, Tony, but you're the most important client I've ever had.'

Annie was aware that the case against Tony Byrne suddenly wasn't looking so strong. Orchard had returned from court irritated that Tony had made bail despite police objections. The intervention of Bernard Shen had surprised everyone and, as a side issue, reminded Hunter that he'd not had any response from Hong Kong to his enquiry about Mickey Lee.

More to the point, Jerry Priestley's statement had thrown a spanner in the works. If Jerry was telling the truth about the gun then so, surely, was Tony. Officers were despatched to interview Jerry's accomplice, Billy Robinson. Since Robinson had never mentioned the Tony Byrne robbery – and he'd blabbed about everything else – there was a chance he might cast enough doubt on Jerry's story to discredit it.

Now Annie was about to drop the bombshell of Appleby's order book.

The incident room fell silent as Orchard considered the entry for a full minute. Finally he said, 'So we might be barking up the wrong tree with Tony Byrne.'

'Yes, guv.'

'Kelly's the boy who found the body, isn't he?'

'He's also got a father who's done time for manslaughter,' chipped in Hunter. 'Not that I'm suggesting it's more than a coincidence.'

'Suppose,' said Annie, 'Neil found the gun after Jerry Priestley chucked it out of the van and kept it. Then he bought the telescopic sight and—'

'Shot Freddy.' Orchard finished the thought for her. 'And why would he do that?'

'Because he didn't like him – he told me so. And, like Tony, he's got good rides now Freddy's dead.' Something else popped into Annie's head. 'And because of Sarah Cooper.'

'You're not saying this kid was knocking her off too, are you?' said Hunter.

'Oh, no. It's just that he went very funny when I asked him about Freddy having a redheaded girlfriend. Suppose he knew about their affair – he might just have been jealous.'

Orchard gave her a ruminative stare. 'I'd say you were a mile off beam, Annie – except you seem to have a better idea what's been going on up there than the rest of us. Anyhow, you and Keith had better get on with it.'

'Bring him in, guv?'

'As quick as you can.'

The wind up on the gallops blew the stiffness and fatigue from Neil's body and the cobwebs from his head. He was up on Susannah's Secret, a sweet-tempered filly recovering from a bad cough.

Kate's dressing-down had shocked him and he was mortified to miss out on a ride. He hoped he hadn't blown his chances for good. How stupid of him to have stayed overnight in London – yet what choice did he have? If he could just ride some winners, in a year or so, when he was old enough, he should be able to buy a car. Then he wouldn't be dependent on trains and taxis – he'd be free.

But as third lot ambled back into the yard and Neil spotted the two detectives, he knew he'd been kidding himself. Even before they began to caution him, he knew that his freedom was no longer guaranteed.

Tony groaned as he weighed himself in Gus Jones's bathroom. Since he'd rediscovered his appetite he'd eaten everything that had been put in front of him and already he could see the effect. He'd have to get back to his starvation regime quickly if he had any hope of riding in the near future.

But was riding even on the cards? He didn't yet know where he stood with Kate but she could hardly be expected to use him when he was charged with her brother's murder.

He dried himself vigorously and pulled on the bathrobe Gus's wife had made available to him before she'd taken her two small children out for the afternoon. Now, after a couple of hours' sleep and a bath, he felt revived though he had no idea how he was going to get through the next few days. He was innocent, the victim of a terrible misunderstanding, but how was he going to prove it?

He heard the sound of footsteps on the stairs.

'Tony? Are you in there?'

He opened the door to Gus.

'A couple of reporters turned up at your place while we were there. I told them you wouldn't be back for a few days. They hung around for a bit then drove off.'

'So can I go home now?'

'You should be safe. Your car's outside. Have you any friends who can keep an eye on you?'

Tony thought. Till he worked out how to approach Kate, there was only one other place he wanted to be at present. Time to get some kind of normality back into his life.

'I'll be fine, Gus,' he said. 'I'm going to spend some time with my horse.'

From his father, Neil had acquired a robust disrespect for policemen. In his mind, some were bent, some were bullies and some were out-and-out bastards. This Hunter character, for example, with his shiny domed forehead and beaky nose, was obviously one of the bastards. Neil could tell he was dying to slap him around a bit just so as he'd say whatever Hunter wanted him to. But, of course, he couldn't do that. Neil had a solicitor on his side, a square-set grey-haired woman, Miss Jenkins, who reminded him of a schoolmistress. Nobody could lay a finger on him with Miss Jenkins looking on. Hunter would have to trick an admission out of him and Neil was confident he had the answer to that.

'No comment,' he said for the umpteenth time to Hunter's questions, enjoying the spark of frustration that flickered for a split second in the policeman's eyes.

It wasn't Hunter who bothered Neil, it was the female policewoman – 'Annie' she'd called herself when they'd first met up at the yard. He'd let slip far too much when they'd talked back then. She was warm and open with big brown eyes that looked right into you. She'd embarrassed him up at the yard when she'd talked about Freddy's girlfriends, putting her finger right on the spot that made him squirm. He knew that once Hunter had got fed up with asking about the gun sight, she'd be in there with her questions. But he was ready. If she started on about redheads again, he'd simply say, 'No comment.'

It was funny, Tony thought, but his place looked tidier after the police had turned it over than before. He resolved to make an effort to keep things straight from now on.

He listened to the messages on his answer machine – most were from racing reporters. Many of them wished him good luck while at the same time imploring him to ring them back. His mother had called, the concern clear in her voice. But he'd already spoken to her from Gus's house to tell her he was OK and it was just a misunderstanding. He wasn't sure whether she was persuaded but she'd heard him out in her usual phlegmatic style.

There was one other message, from Kate, just a simple enquiry about how he was and suggesting they should talk soon. Tony resisted the impulse to ring her at once. That conversation ought to take place face to face. It was important to convince her he had nothing to do with Freddy's death.

One thing puzzled him. Kate's message was timed at ten that morning, just when he was appearing in court. How had she known he would be set free? Unless, of course, she had persuaded Bernard Shen to put up his bail money.

What a bloody fantastic woman she was!

Kate, too, was checking the messages on her phone. She'd left them from the night before, when Mickey had been on her back. Now she was surprised to hear Neil's voice, apologising for being stuck in London on a visit to his dad. She felt a stab of guilt. Maybe she'd been too harsh with him that morning – though his subsequent arrest had rendered her criticism irrelevant. She was perplexed by the police interest in him. Considering what had happened to Tony, it seemed they were determined to pin Freddy's murder on one of her other jockeys. She was beginning to doubt their competence.

The doorbell rang. She was half expecting – indeed hoping – it might be Tony and was dismayed to find Mickey standing on the doorstep. He carried a bottle of champagne and a briefcase.

'Let's talk,' he said.

She'd have said no if she hadn't been taken so completely by surprise. As it was, her protest was feeble.

'It's not convenient, Mickey, I was about to . . .'

He took in her jeans and T-shirt – the clothes she'd worn all day.

'Go out? Or are you expecting company?'

'Well, no.'

She'd never been good at lying and, in any case she couldn't put this conversation off for ever.

'Come in,' she said unnecessarily. He was inside already.

'How's it going?' asked Orchard as Annie and Hunter took a break from quizzing Neil.

'He's a tough little sod,' said Hunter. 'Guilty as sin, though.'

Orchard turned to Annie.

'He's been up to something, guv, but he's not saying a thing.'

'He might have softened up by morning,' Hunter added.

Orchard grunted. 'Let's hope so. Or maybe we'll turn something up at the yard. He must have kept the gun somewhere.'

'How's Clive getting on?' asked Annie. Clive Cook and Jim Henderson had been questioning the other lads who shared the hostel with Neil.

Orchard pulled a face. 'They don't know much about him. He doesn't go drinking with them, just hangs round the horses all the time. A bit of a loner.'

'That's suspicious in itself, guv,' said Hunter. 'He's guilty as sin, bet your life.'

Tony was surprised – but pleased – to find that Lifeline had been moved back to his old stall in the courtyard stables. He'd mentioned to Kate he was going to try it and obviously she'd gone ahead in his absence. He guessed that was a good sign – at least Lifeline's recovery hadn't been held back by his troubles.

There was no one about as Tony saddled him up, for which he was grateful. He didn't want to run the gamut of awkward explanations and embarrassing pauses. God knows what everyone was thinking about him. At least Lifeline's pleasure at seeing him was untainted by suspicion or fear or sly delight – or any of the other complexities that cast a shadow over human relationships.

The horse knew his way up the hill on to the gallops and Tony let him jog along at his own pace. It was a bright summer evening with a fresh breeze blowing into their faces on the top. After his claustrophobic imprisonment in the basement of Farley Street nick, Tony luxuriated in the open space, the sky as limitless as the ocean.

'Come on, old feller,' he said to Lifeline, 'let's give your legs a stretch.'

The horse responded at once, lengthening his stride, enjoying himself as he felt the turf beneath his feet.

*

'I'm sorry about the tape.'

Kate was caught off guard. She stared at Mickey as he sat opposite her across the kitchen table. He'd opened his briefcase and was in the act of passing her a folder of papers.

'Believe me,' he continued, 'it wasn't my idea.'

She didn't know whether he was telling the truth, though there was a look in his eyes she hadn't seen before. An appeal for sympathy maybe.

Well, he wouldn't get any from her.

'I should have listened to Gladys Lim,' she said angrily. 'I'm being blackmailed and my horses are being sabotaged. You got Josh to fix Stopgap, didn't you?'

He shrugged. 'Mr Shen likes to influence events.'

'Then why should I do business with him?' she replied.

He gave her his lop-sided grin.

'Because you have no choice.'


Tony was amazed by the strength of the horse beneath him. It seemed the colt had energy to burn and Tony wondered what kind of work he'd been putting in lately. He didn't want to disrupt Kate's regime but it was tempting to get a glimpse of what the horse could do.

He turned Lifeline down wind, remembering the excitement of thundering past the winning post at Ascot. He was curious to know if the colt was back to that kind of form, fully recovered from the road accident and all the traumas that had followed. There was only one way to find out.

'Go on then,' he shouted, crouching in the saddle and shortening the reins.

*

Mickey watched Kate as she concentrated on the sheet of paper in front of her. It contained a summary of Mr Shen's proposals: the number of horses he was committed to train at Beechwood, a guaranteed cash sum should he fall short of that figure and suggestions for upgrading the yard's facilities. It was a very generous proposition – though the reality might turn out to be rather different.

While Kate read, Mickey indulged himself in a fantasy that would have revolted her had she known of it. He imagined that this was his home and she was his woman. That he could lean across the table and kiss the corners of her mouth. That the most important thing in her life was to spend the night in his arms.

He could dream, couldn't he?

He had ways of making dreams come true.

Tony put the brakes on slowly, sitting back down in the saddle and easing Lifeline out of top gear. For a few seconds, all his present anxieties – the police interrogation, the court appearance, Sarah's persecution – had been forgotten. The horse had swept him away in a heart-stopping blur of speed that had obliterated his sense of self.

He caught his breath, awed by this glimpse of Lifeline's capabilities. The colt had come through the fire and emerged fitter and faster. If only Tony could say the same for himself.

'How about some champagne?'

Kate had agreed to the outline document, it seemed the right moment to propose a toast.

She shook her head. 'You go ahead but I'd prefer tea.'

'I'll join you,' he said. Frankly he didn't care what they

drank – provided some liquid was served. How else was he going to get what he wanted?

She boiled a kettle and made the tea. His eyes devoured her as she stood with her back to him. The pale blue T-shirt clung to her, outlining the thin strap of her bra and line of her spine. Her waist was narrow, emphasising the swell of her hips. She was slender and delicate, not fleshy, and her gentle curves thrilled him. He loved her kind of understated sexuality. She reminded him of Amy Ho – though Amy had been more obvious in every respect. He wouldn't make the same mistakes he had with her.

Kate placed the two mugs on the table.

'Do you have any sugar?' he asked.

Without answering, she turned to the cupboard behind her. It was all the time Mickey needed. He had the liquid – gamma hydroxybutyrate, the date-rape drug – in a small vial. As Kate reached for the sugar bowl he tipped it into her tea.

'Thank you,' he said, helping himself to a spoonful of sugar.

After that, it was just a question of watching Kate drink up.

To distract her, he produced some photographs of the five-million-dollar colt. They, at least, put a smile on her face.

Tony dismounted and led Lifeline the last mile downhill to the yard. The horse had done enough without carrying an over-weight jockey for longer than he had to.

The sun had set and the light was fading fast. Swallows and house martins skimmed the fields on either side of the bridle way. The house and stables below nestled cosily in the crook of the hillside, peaceful and idyllic. But appearances, Tony reflected, could be deceptive.

After he'd settled the horse – taken off his tack, rugged him up and given him a drink – he'd drop in on Kate. He'd not seen her since Friday night, which seemed an age away, and he missed her. But he was anxious about his reception. In the circumstances, she could hardly be expected to welcome him with open arms. On the other hand, if she'd fixed his bail, then she must still believe in him – and he owed her a profound vote of thanks.

It was about time he found out exactly how things stood.

The effect of the drug on Kate was dramatic, Mickey noted. Whereas Amy had fought its influence, resisting sleep and rallying just when he'd thought the battle was won, Kate surrendered suddenly. One moment she was asking him about Mr Shen's horses, the next her head was pillowed on her arms.

Mickey gazed at her. The hands of the clock on the wall opposite moved on. Five minutes passed. Her shoulders rose and fell with every breath.

'Kate?' He spoke loudly. 'Kate, can you hear me?'

There was no response. He stood up and looked down at her. The nape of her neck was visible beneath her fine dark hair. He extended a finger and gently stroked the smooth white stem. The skin was warm to his touch, soft like silk. He bent his head and placed his lips to the milky column. His kiss was tender. All the women he bought remarked how tender he could be.

Only a man who has taken life, he thought, can truly savour its fragility.

Josh stopped his motorbike on the road fifty yards past the turning that led up to Kate's yard. He wheeled it over the grass verge and concealed it behind a sprawl of hedge and hawthorn. It wouldn't do for the bike to be spotted during the next hour. As a car approached, heading for the village, Josh ducked down into the bushes – he didn't want to be picked out in the headlights either.

He couldn't wait to be shot of Lambourn. He'd only stayed on over the weekend because he couldn't bear to leave without getting back at those bitches who'd dismissed him. It wasn't so much that Kate had kicked him out, it was the way she'd done it. After all, it was his word against Vicky's but Kate had not been interested in giving him a fair hearing. Maybe he should have explained about him and Vicky instead of losing his temper. Vicky had always had it in for him. Especially after that night in The Black Plough when he'd offered to slip her one so she wouldn't die a virgin – not his best joke, thinking about it, but there'd been no need for her to throw such a wobbly.

Anyway, what the hell? He was off to pastures new but not before he'd left his mark. A dignified retreat under cover of destruction. He believed it was called a scorched-earth policy.

Mickey moved Kate's chair backwards then knelt in front of her, his arms around her limp body, glorying in the stolen intimacy. He licked the hollow at the base of her throat, then moved his tongue upwards, leaving a snail trail of saliva across her silky skin. Her lower lip pouted, pink and swollen and irresistible. He kissed it gently, then harder, hugging her compliant torso close, revelling in the soft pressure of her breasts against his chest.

This was the real reason he'd come to England. Not because he was running from trouble at home, nor because there was a fortune hidden here waiting for him to pick it up, but because he had to have this delicate English beauty. He'd felt that way ever since Mr Shen had shown him her photograph in Paris.

He fought back the urge for instant gratification that gripped him. He must have her soon but not here. She was his for the night and there was no rush. First he would carry her upstairs to bed.

He leaned back on his haunches, allowing her body to topple forward over his shoulder. He stood carefully, hoisting her in a fireman's lift, her soft weight borne comfortably by his muscular torso. Her denim-ed hip rubbed against his chin as he carried her out into the hall.

Then the doorbell rang.

Mickey froze. He waited.

The bell rang again.

Who the hell could it be?

Mickey stepped into the front room and laid Kate on the sofa. He stole softly to the window and looked through a crack in the curtains. Tony Byrne was standing on the path, staring at the house. The bell rang again. There were lights on upstairs and down – Tony would know someone was at home.

Trouble.

Mickey stepped into the hall.

'Tony,' he cried as he opened the door.

The jockey was obviously surprised to see him – stunned, in fact.

'Good to have you back,' said Mickey. 'I suppose you want Kate.'

'She left a message for me.'

'The thing is, Tony –' Mickey moved closer, dropped his voice ' – she can't talk to you tonight.'

The jockey stared at him.

'To be honest, she's asked me to send you away. That's why it took so long to open the door. I'm sure you understand. Leave it till tomorrow, eh?'

'OK.' Tony didn't sound convinced but it looked like he might swallow Mickey's story all the same. He wasn't moving though, but peering over Mickey's shoulder into the house.

'We're just finishing up a business meeting.' Mickey pointed down the hall into the brightly lit kitchen. His briefcase stood open on the table and scattered papers and mugs were in view. It looked a plausible setting. 'Kate's in the bathroom. I'm afraid she really doesn't want to see you.'

Tony nodded and took a pace back.

Thank Christ for that.

'Tell her I'll be down tomorrow,' he said.

'Cheers, mate,' said Mickey and shut the door.

Tony didn't know what a lucky bastard he was. If he'd insisted on coming in, Mickey would have had to kill him.

The hay in the three-sided outhouse next to the open barn was bone dry. Nonetheless Josh took a jerrycan of diesel from his back-pack and doused two bales just to make sure that the fire would stay alight. He stuffed the empty can back in his sack – he'd chuck it miles away from here. With luck no one would suspect arson. There were always fires in the hay and a fire extinguisher was kept at the ready on the wall.

He lit a match but it was immediately blown out by the breeze. He took more care with the next one, stepping under cover to apply the tiny flame to a tuft of straw. It crackled into life at once, sparking along the stalk. He moved to another bale and struck another match.

Within a minute he had half a dozen little conflagrations kindling merrily, their flickering lights dancing in the gloom.

Satisfied, he turned away into the dark.

\*

Tony stood on Kate's doorstep for a full minute. The news that she didn't want to see him was a blow. But the more he thought about it, the less sense it made. There was the message on his answer machine, for a start. 'Come and see me when you get back' was unequivocal, wasn't it? Also, it was hardly her style to avoid an unpleasant confrontation – if that's what it was to be. Kate Montague talked straight, everyone knew that. And to send Mickey to put him off was puzzling to say the least. He'd thought she couldn't stand Mickey.

He walked round to the Somervilles' front door. Maybe they could cast some light on Mickey's supposed business meeting with Kate. But they weren't at home and Laurie's car wasn't in the drive.

Tony stood in the shadows, his mind racing with indistinct but frightening images.

Something strange was going on in that house and he wasn't going home just yet.

# Chapter Thirteen

After his temporary employment on the Sundial Estate, Dave was well aware of the security systems in place at Mr Shen's mansion. There was a protective outer ring around the house and gardens, manned by uniformed estate staff. The house itself was protected by an infra-red system, which was switched on at night and, of course, by Mr Shen's private guards who covered all entrances to the property. But once inside there were only Shen's business associates and domestic personnel – house-keepers and kitchen staff. Of these, one cook remained on duty all night in case Mr Shen wanted anything. The guards were required to fend for themselves in a separate kitchen area.

Dave had discovered all this from Tommy Feng, the cook on the night shift he'd made it his business to meet. This was undoubtedly a stroke of luck though Dave prepared to think of it as fate. His time was now. Time to step up a league and prove he was worthy of better things – and fatter fees. He'd get a lot more for Mr Shen's neck than Jonno Simpson's foot.

What's more, it was his first real job for his own people. He'd been surprised when he'd been summoned to meet Mr Yip. He knew of Uncle Yip, of course. Everyone in the Chinese community did. And after they'd talked and Uncle Yip had made his proposal, Dave's heart had jigged with excitement. This was his passport to the big time and a ticket home all rolled into one.

Of course, a job like this required more brain power. Dave liked that. He always responded well to an intellectual challenge. This was a proper hit and he had devised a proper plan. The key to it was the yellow fluorescent jacket worn by all the estate's security staff. He had taken the precaution of not handing in his jacket and cap after last Friday's party.

Now he approached the two security men kicking their heels by the gate at the top of the Shen mansion's drive. He gripped a clipboard in one hand and held a walkie-talkie in the other. He looked the part, all right.

One of the men recognised him from the night of the party.

'Cor, you back again? Thought we'd seen the last of you.'

'No such luck, mate. Kenyon made me an offer I couldn't refuse.' Bill Kenyon was the supervisor who'd hired the temporary staff for the party – Dave had noted the name. 'Now,' he consulted his clipboard, 'is there a Tommy Feng back there?'

The other man consulted a list and nodded.

'He's filled in his parking renewal form all wrong and I've got to get it sorted.' Dave made to step between the two of them down the drive.

'Oy,' said the second man, 'where's your pass?'

'Haven't got one yet. The photo machine's bust so they can't do it till tomorrow.'

'Sorry, mate. Can't let you through then.'

Dave shrugged. 'Suits me. I don't want to fill in some form with a Chinese guy who can't write English. Can you go through it with him when he comes out?'

The man frowned. 'That's not my job.'

'Oh, for God's sake, Pete, let him through,' said the first man. 'He's all right.'

'Cheers,' said Dave and headed down the path to the house.

\*

Mickey kept an eye on Tony from the crack in the curtain. He watched him walk across to Laurie's door. The angle was such that he couldn't see him knock but, a few moments later, he reappeared in front of the house, looking at the room in which Mickey now stood. At last he turned and began to walk away.

Mickey held his position for a long time but Tony did not come back.

Eventually he turned to Kate, lying in a chemically induced slumber on the sofa. He should take her upstairs but, for the moment, the spell was broken. Tony's interruption was too fresh in his mind. Besides, there was something else he had to do.

Josh had told him he'd helped Tony move Freddy's belongings from the cottage into the Lodge – including a trunk. Surely that had to be the one Jeff Collins had sent from Australia – the trunk that contained the Pick Six ticket. All Mickey had to do was locate it.

He found Freddy's stuff in a room at the back of the house on the first floor, just where Josh had said it would be. Suitcases and boxes were piled high, blocking the doorway. Mickey began to drag them into the hall. He forced his way through the clutter, searching for the big black box with metal corners that Josh had described to him. He couldn't see it.

After ten minutes of hauling bags and cases around so he could peer into every corner, Mickey realised it wasn't there. He angrily shoved the last of the boxes back into the room and shut the door. It had to be somewhere. He'd just have to search the rest of the house.

Tony stood at the rear of the Lodge staring at Kate's living quarters. He'd gained entrance from the Somervilles' side, through a gate in the fence which divided the old Lodge garden. A conservatory encroached on Kate's portion and, through it, Tony could see into her kitchen. Though seen from the opposite direction, the view of the table with the open briefcase and the strewn papers was the same – exactly the same. Whatever had been going on in the house since Mickey had closed the door, it had not taken place in the kitchen.

Tony's attention had long since shifted to the first floor where another light shone from the back of the house. His bewilderment increased. He knew that back room well as he had recently lugged Freddy's stuff up there. What were Kate and Mickey doing?

Suddenly the light went out. Tony stepped closer to the conservatory. He was sure he couldn't be seen from inside. He waited.

After what seemed like an age – maybe ten minutes – he saw Mickey appear at the bottom of the stairs. He went into the front room then emerged again almost immediately. He disappeared from sight into the dining room, then returned to the hall. It looked like he was searching for something.

Mickey cursed. The place had a million hidey-holes where even something as bulky as a trunk could be shoved out of sight. He was starting to get seriously pissed off.

Then he found it, in about the last place he looked. Off the main hall a corridor led to a side entrance to the house, opening into an old-fashioned cloakroom, cluttered with riding tack, wellington boots and neglected fishing gear. There, by the side of the door, beneath a wooden bench, sat the trunk.

Mickey tugged it into the open and was relieved to see the name 'Jeff Collins' on the label. He saw that Jeff's name had been crossed out and a new label pasted next to it: 'Bill & Gaynor Collins, 27 Eucalyptus Apartments, Croydon, Victoria 3136, Australia'.

So that explained it – Kate was shipping the dead man's belongings back to his family. He'd found it just in time.

Mickey looked at the locks. He could get inside, no problem, though it might take a little while if he was going to avoid damaging the trunk. He wanted to leave as little evidence of his activities as possible.

Now he'd found the trunk he wasn't so anxious – everything was under control. He'd come back later and pick the locks.

Time for his rendezvous with Kate.


The Chinese guards at Mr Shen's house turned out to be easier to handle than those at the gate. They took in Dave's coat and cap and simply said, 'What you want?' He asked for Tommy and the cook was summoned.

Tommy, already richer by £300 and on a promise of more, subjected the guards to a barrage of Cantonese and then led Dave into the kitchen.

'They said you could stay five minutes,' Tommy said when they were alone.

'Fine.'

Dave took off the coat and cap while Tommy unbuttoned his white chef's tunic. They swapped uniforms. The cap was big on Tommy.

'I don't look like you,' he said.

'You'll be fine. Go through the door and just keep walking. Put your hand up, like you're being polite, but don't stop.'

'It's too dangerous.'

Dave had suspected this might happen. He took a wad of

notes from his pocket and peeled off £300. 'That's what we agreed.'

Tommy looked at the bundle in Dave's hand. 'More.'

Dave added another £200. 'Hide the clothes in the bushes and drive out as yourself.'

'I know,' said Tommy. 'Five hundred is not enough.'

Dave added more notes. He was getting annoyed. 'Here's seven. That makes a grand and it's your lot.'

The money disappeared into Tommy's pocket. 'What if they ask about you at the gate?'

'Say I've met a friend from the other night and we're having a chat. They're going off shift soon, in any case.'

Tommy grinned at him, debating no doubt whether to demand more money.

'Don't push your luck, mate,' Dave snarled. 'Get going.'

Tommy went.

From the garden Tony saw Mickey walk into the kitchen, run his hands under the tap and splash water on his face. Now, surely, he would gather his papers, pick up his briefcase and leave.

Instead he turned once more for the hall and disappeared into the front room.

Tony's heart was thudding in his chest. The sight of Mickey strolling around the Lodge as if he owned it was sickening. And where was Kate?

Lying somewhere with her throat cut?

Kate lay stretched out on the sofa, still deep in peaceful sleep. Mickey picked her up, carrying her in his arms as if she were a child. There would be no more waiting. He stepped into the hall, hugging his delicious burden close.

\*

In the garden, gazing through the conservatory window, Tony stood transfixed as he watched Mickey step into view, cradling the unmistakable form of Kate in his arms, the dark mop of her hair resting on his shoulder. Tony's heart missed a beat. His worst fears were being confirmed in front of his eyes.

As Mickey reached the bottom of the stairs and moved out of sight, Tony's fingers closed on the handle of the conservatory door.

The handle turned but the door wouldn't open. He pushed hard and it yielded a fraction but something was holding it fast at head height. Through the glass he saw the metal glint of a sliding bolt.

What the fuck was he going to do now?

Mickey dumped Kate on the bed like a sack of coal into a cellar. She bounced, her limbs flailing. Mickey was breathing hard and not just from his exertions. It was time to get to work.

He pulled the hem of her T-shirt from her waistband and skinned it up her torso. Her creamy flesh glowed in the half-light. He had to take her clothes off carefully – no ripping, no tearing. He mustn't leave any clear evidence. Not that there wouldn't be suspicion on her part when she woke in the morning, naked in her bed, maybe a little tender in places, wondering why she had no memory of the night before.

But he had the audio tape. That would keep her in line. Especially if he didn't get *too* carried away.

From downstairs came the sound of glass smashing.

The earthenware plant pot disintegrated in Tony's hand as he shattered the glass in front of his face. He felt a shard of glass slice into his thumb as he reached through the broken door and slid back the bolt. In a second he was in the house, his heart pumping and a voice sounding in his ears – his own.

'Kate! Are you all right?' he shouted as he rushed through the kitchen and into the hall.

'Tony – what do you think you're doing?'

Mickey was descending the stairs fast, surprise and bewilderment on his face.

Tony didn't stop. He charged at Mickey as he reached the bottom of the stairs, catching him in the ribs with his shoulder and spinning him round.

'What the fuck!' cried Mickey as he stumbled against the wall.

Tony hit him, grazing the other's face as he dodged to avoid the blow. Tony struck again but Mickey ducked inside the swing and grappled with him.

'Have you gone mad?' Mickey shouted in his face.

Tony didn't answer, just jabbed upwards with his knee.

Mickey rolled to the side and Tony was thrown against a door. It opened behind him, pitching him on to the floor of the sitting room. Mickey fell on top of him and the pair of them wrestled in the dark, banging against half-perceived furniture.

Mickey was the heavier and the stronger. He pinned Tony's arms to the floor and brought all his weight to bear.

'Jesus, Tony,' muttered Mickey, 'what the fuck are you playing at?'

'Have you killed her, you bastard?'

'Killed her?' Mickey began to laugh. 'You're barking up the wrong tree, mate. For a moment I thought you were pissed because I was in bed with her and you weren't.'

Mickey's words went through Tony like an electric shock.

'You mean you're . . .' The words stuck in his throat.

'Screwing her? Bit of a turn-up, eh? I know I'm an ugly sod but there are still things I can do for a woman.'

Tony was in shock. He rapidly reviewed events: the length of time before Mickey answered the door, the unconvincing explanation of Kate's failure to show, the vision of Mickey carrying her upstairs – obviously not a victim at all but a compliant and sated lover.

And he was the silly bastard who'd intruded on a lovers' night of fun and games. He felt like a fool.

But his over-riding feeling was jealousy.

As Mickey grappled with Tony on the floor he knew he would have to kill him. But he couldn't just bludgeon the fool to death. It had to look right. And it couldn't happen here.

Telling Tony he was bedding Kate had been a master stroke. It had sucked the wind right out of the other guy's sails and bought Mickey time to figure something out. It had always been obvious to him that Tony was smitten with the mistress of Birchwood. Now the silly bastard would be so eaten up over his loss that Mickey could get away with anything – like murder.

He pulled Tony to his feet. 'I'll show you out.'

As he shepherded the jockey to the front door he came to a decision.

Suicide. It would play very well given the circumstances. String Tony up in the barn near his beloved horses. No note. Balance of mind disturbed. Mickey liked it.

Tony had his hand on the door. He turned back. 'Look,' he began but he didn't finish the sentence. As he opened the heavy door a blast of hot air rolled across them like a blanket, together with a tide of noise that, Mickey realised, had been a murmur in the background as they'd rolled around on the floor. Now it was a full-scale roar – of wind and crackling and banging and thumping and an inhuman screaming.

'The barn's on fire!' cried Tony.

They both stared at the yard, lit by the dancing glow of flames shooting high in the air. The outhouse and the barn beside it was a ball of orange. Sparks, borne on the stiff breeze, showered on to the wooden stables. The pitch of the screams intensified.

'The horses!' shouted Tony, running towards the yard. 'Come on!'

The heat was like the breath of a hot oven as Tony reached the old stables. Black smoke from the blaze was flung into his face by the swirling wind and he tried not to breathe it in.

The stables were built around three sides of an ornamental green, etched with painted white stones: they contained stalls for some twenty horses. The burning barn was immediately behind the central block and Tony could see that flames were already licking along the ridge of the stable roof, driven on by the wind.

Tony made for the middle stalls, which were directly in the path of the fire. He slipped the bolt on the first door and stepped aside as a panic-stricken grey bolted from the smoky interior. He moved on to the next, which was empty. The removal of Gladys Lim's string of horses meant that some of these stalls were no longer occupied. Nevertheless, they would all have to be checked.

The big chestnut in the next box was trying to kick his way out.

'Steady, boy,' cried Tony as he reached for the bolt. It stuck for a moment. The horse whinnied in terror and threw itself against the door. Tony gritted his teeth and managed to throw the bolt. The horse blundered into the smoky yard with such force that the door hit Tony a jarring blow on the shoulder.

The first stall that he had liberated was now properly alight. Flames shot from inside it as the bedding began to blaze. The stall on the other side was now under threat.

Lifeline's stall.

The evening had gone pretty well, all things considered. Laurie had taken Greta and Paul to the boy's favourite restaurant, The Ox on the Roof, out on the Swindon road. It was their farewell meal before the flight next morning for Stockholm and there had been many feeble jokes, as they tucked into steak and chips, about surviving on a diet of open sandwiches and pickled herring. And on their way back in the car, Laurie and Greta had sung their way through Abba's greatest hits, to the accompaniment of Paul's pantomime retching. No one made any references to their troubles.

On the way up the lane, halfway through a stirring version of 'Fernando', they saw the first indication of the fire. A gap in the trees disclosed a view of flames in the night, of smoke billowing and buildings burning.

'That's our house,' cried Greta and Laurie put his foot down.

But as they got closer they could see that it wasn't the Lodge but the stables which were burning. The fire looked like it had been raging for some time.

The road ahead was blocked by loose horses and Laurie stopped the car.

Greta had the mobile in her hand. 'Fire brigade,' she said urgently as Laurie and Paul leapt out.

*

Even as he urged horses from their stalls, Mickey was reassessing his own situation. He was keeping an eye on Tony, too. There was no need now to worry about fake suicides. If he played his cards right, Tony would be a casualty of the fire. 'Murder suspect's heroic death' was preferable to 'Accused takes his own life'. Tony should be grateful to him.

He could see the jockey was having trouble getting a horse out of his box. The panic-stricken animal was rooted to the ground. Mickey ran over.

Tony saw him coming. 'Lifeline won't budge,' he shouted. 'Get me a head collar with a long lead rein.'

Mickey had seen tack hanging neatly in a shed across the courtyard. He returned quickly with the gear – now surely was his chance.

As Tony fitted the collar on the traumatised horse, Mickey looked round for a weapon. He seized one of the stones which bordered the lawn and brought it down hard on the back of Tony's head. The jockey's legs buckled and Mickey hit him again, the blow landing on his shoulder as he slumped sideways.

Mickey dragged the limp body into the next stall, where flames were already curling round the roof beams and the straw on the floor was smouldering. He pushed Tony into the dark space behind the door where he could not be easily spotted and stepped away, leaving the door wide open. From the outside, the stall looked empty.

A voice sounded above the roar of the flames. Mickey whirled round.

Laurie was running through the smoke. 'Are all the horses out?' he called.

Mickey grabbed the rein that Tony had fitted to Lifeline.

'Just this one left,' he replied and gave the horse a tug. 'I've got him.'

'Good man.' Laurie clapped Mickey on the back. 'The fire brigade's on its way.' To Mickey's relief, Laurie ran back across the green to the stalls on the far side which were now beginning to smoulder.

Lifeline was half in and half out of the box, whinnying softly.

'Let's go,' Mickey urged, wrapping the canvas webbing of the lead rein around his arm and yanking hard.

The horse resisted, planting his feet.

Mickey tightened his grip and pulled. 'Come on!' he shouted.

At that moment, the roof of the next stall fell in, showering the pair of them with flaming debris. Lifeline leapt forward into the yard and Mickey pulled back on the rein. But the horse had no intention of stopping.

Mickey tried to untangle the canvas lead from around his forearm but Lifeline was moving too fast. Suddenly Mickey was flat on his face, his arm stretched above his head, the entire length of his body being dragged and scraped over the grass and then the dirt of the path as the horse galloped beneath the stable arch.

As his clothes were sliced from his body and the flesh was scraped from his bones, Mickey was anaesthetised by disbelief. He wasn't meant to die like this.

In the seconds before his head smashed into the stone buttress of the main gate, he cursed Tony Byrne and his crazy horse.

Lifeline ran as fast as he could away from the heat and smoke and noise, trailing Mickey's corpse behind him down the lane like a tin can tied to the back of a runaway car.

\*

Tony hurt. There was smoke in his lungs and fire all around him and he couldn't move. I'm going to die, he thought without panic. He didn't care.

The big hoses played on the flames, containing and then controlling the conflagration. The Lambourn fire-fighters were a well-drilled and professional team. Laurie and Paul had now been joined by Vicky and some lads who'd just returned from the pub. They rounded up the loose horses, tending to them in a paddock behind the American barn, well away from danger.

In front of the burning stable block, fire-fighters in breathing apparatus searched the burning buildings. One shouted, his voice tinny and distorted by his headgear. Another joined him and, despite their bulky suits, they moved swiftly into the heart of the blazing stables to pull out the body of a man.

He was still alive.

Dave had brought no weapons into the house. For one thing, he'd thought it possible he might be searched by Mr Shen's guards though that hadn't happened. For another, he liked the idea of going naked, as it were, into the house of the enemy and completing his mission with bare hands. Like a holy warrior.

He waited till midnight before he made his move. Tommy had told him Mr Shen usually went to bed at ten and slept till two or three, when he would ring down for tea. Though sometimes, he said, the old man would wake earlier and call for refreshment around one o'clock. Dave didn't want to risk that. He wanted his victim asleep.

He crept up the stairs. This was the dangerous part. If someone should appear now he would be totally exposed. He could do with his shotgun. He rejected the ignoble thought – he would fight the enemy with his bare hands if he had to.

Mr Shen's bedroom was on the second floor, the first door on the right – he'd made Tommy draw him a map.

His fear was that he'd climb the stairs and discover a guard sitting outside the room. But the corridor was empty.

Dave stood at the door, his fingers on the handle. The knob turned silently. He took a deep breath, consciously relaxed his body and summoned his energy.

He slipped like a shadow into the big square room. A flickering light danced across the ceiling. He looked for the source. A small squat candle sat in a bowl on a low table. The old man had a night light, like a child. Fancy that.

The bed was on the far side of the room, across an acre of carpet. Dave crept closer.

Mr Shen lay on his back, a small mound in the middle of a vast double bed. He lay with his mouth open, the regular whistle of his breath echoing round the room.

Dave planned his move. He could snap that scrawny neck like a chicken's. Or strangle him. Or – a spare pillow was just inches from his hand – simply put him to sleep . . .

He picked up the pillow and straddled the old man's body, pressing down on his head with all his strength.

The effect was like flicking a switch. Suddenly the inert, frail-seeming bundle beneath him was alive, wriggling like an eel, kicking and punching and flailing.

But Dave was implacable, a force that could not be resisted. This was how the pros did it. Hard and quick. There was mercy in no mercy.

He must have been holding Mr Shen down for a full minute – it seemed like much more. The man beneath him was still fighting but there was a sluggishness in his resistance now. The blows were feeble. Dave smiled to himself. The old boy's light was going out.

It was easier now but Dave was taking no chances. He could feel himself bathed in sweat – even his thigh was sweating. That was strange. There was a stinging sensation in his right thigh. How weird. He looked down past the pillow to the tangled bedding and the blue-striped nightshirt the old man wore and saw sheets stained and wet.

Blood. Thick and dark. Puddling on the sheet.

The strength went from his arms and he pulled back, shaking and suddenly enfeebled. The stinging had turned into an ache, an icy numbing pain seeping into his guts. He looked in disbelief at his torn and stained trousers. And in the dead man's hand he saw the reason. A knife. Small, pointed, glistening red.

Dave clamped his hands over his gushing femoral artery and watched his lifeblood dribble through his fingers.

The candle guttered and went out.

Annie's head was in a spin as she sat in her car outside the sports shop. She'd just paid another early-morning visit and this time, thankfully, she'd avoided the creepy Mr Appleby. Terry, his assistant, turned out to be a much more persuasive advert for the sporting life – tall and lean with a mischievous spark in his brown eyes. As befitted a man with a new girlfriend, he appeared not to share Appleby's interest in Annie – unfortunately. On the other hand, he was eager to help.

'I remember Neil Kelly,' he said. 'He's getting a few rides now, isn't he?'

Without prompting he had gone on to say that Neil had

indeed bought a telescopic gun sight which Terry had had to order.

'To be honest,' he continued, 'Neil didn't say much. It was the kid with him who knew all about the gun sight. He had a ton of questions about shooting. He was the keen one.'

'Can you describe him?'

'A well-built lad, bigger than the other one. Looked about fifteen. Sandy hair.'

'I don't suppose his name came up?'

'Oh, yes. Neil called him Paul.'

Now Annie was assessing the situation in the light of this new information. The Somervilles had been interviewed at the outset but she'd only spoken to Greta the other day at the yard. Paul was her adopted son.

She flicked through the notes she'd made on the forensic discoveries at Freddy's cottage, two lists of names headed 'Non-combatants' and 'Live Ones'. They'd not considered the first group to be of significance. She pulled out her mobile – she had to talk to Russell, the SOCO officer. Fortunately he was at his desk.

'You know you found samples of Greta Somerville's hair in Freddy's cottage? Were there any upstairs?'

'None in the bedroom, if that's what you're getting at. There were some on the upstairs landing though.'

Annie reflected on this. Now she had to talk to Orchard.

She found Hunter and the rest of the team in the incident room.

'Nice of you to join us,' the DS sniffed as she walked in. 'Billy Robinson has backed up Priestley's story about the gun. So we're dropping the charges against Tony Byrne.'

Clive Cook grinned at her. 'That should help him pull through.'

Annie was puzzled. 'Pull through what?'

'Haven't you heard about the fire?' said Clive.

She shook her head so he filled her in on the Beechwood blaze and the news that Tony Byrne was recovering in hospital. And that Mickey Lee was dead.

'How?' she asked.

'It seems he was trying to get a horse out of the stable on a long canvas rein. When the horse bolted he couldn't untangle the canvas because it was wound too tight around his hand. They found him in a field half a mile away, still attached to the horse. He must have hit his head on something and shattered his skull.'

Annie winced. 'Poor man. What a horrible way to die,' she said.

Hunter gave a dry laugh and pushed a piece of paper under her nose. 'You won't be shedding any tears when you read this.'

'What is it?'

'Fax from Hong Kong. They finally identified Mr Lee for us.'

Annie ran her eye down a resumé of Michael Chung aka Mickey Lee and several other aliases. It contained a small but impressive list of convictions for extortion and drug-dealing, together with offences suspected but not proved. The Hong Kong police were currently keen to interview him in connection with a complaint of date-rape.

'Funny thing is,' said Hunter as she finished reading, 'Kate Montague slept through the whole thing. She woke up on her bed with half her clothes missing and claimed the last thing she could remember was drinking tea with Mickey Lee.'

'Oh, no!'

'Don't worry, Annie. It looks like she had a lucky escape.'

Annie ran Orchard to ground in his office. He heard her out in silence.

'You've got a thing about hair, haven't you?' he said when she'd finished. 'From the start you've gone on about Freddy's girlfriends' hair.'

'I was right about Sarah Cooper, wasn't I?'

He nodded. 'You know, just because Mrs Somerville was on the landing doesn't mean she was in the bedroom. She might just have gone to the bathroom.'

'I bet she didn't.'

He grinned. 'I'm not betting with you, young lady.' He stood up. 'Come on. You and I had better get over to the yard.'

'But I'm supposed to be interviewing Neil in a few minutes.'

'Hunter can find someone else. It's bound to be a "no comment" interview anyway, going by yesterday.'

'Right, guv.'

They left the room together.

'Just one thing,' added Orchard. 'This is your idea, so you do the talking.'

'Thank you, sir.'

'Don't get me wrong. I'd rather it's you making a fool of yourself and not me.'

Beechwood was a sorry sight after the fire. The old stable block at its centre, together with the nearby outhouses where the fire had started, were in ruins. Fortunately, the Lodge itself was untouched.

Annie and Orchard knocked at the Somervilles' door but there was no response.

A well-built woman with unruly blonde hair was talking to a man in uniform – a fire brigade officer, Annie deduced. Breaking off her conversation, she headed towards them and Annie recognised her – Vicky the head lad.

'They're not at home,' she said. 'They've gone to the airport.'

That was a surprise. Vicky filled in more details.

'Greta's taking Paul to Sweden to stay with his great-aunt.'

'You don't know what flight they're on, do you?'

'BA to Stockholm, one-forty, Heathrow, terminal one. Anything else you need to know?'

'No. That's excellent.'

'Good. Because I've got a dozen horses to rehouse, the trainer's sick, half the yard's in ruins and I've got runners at three different meetings this week and no jockeys.'

'Impressive girl,' muttered Orchard as he started the car.

They'd phoned ahead to Heathrow and Greta and Paul had been placed in a separate lounge to await their arrival.

'What the hell is going on?' Greta demanded, springing to her feet as Annie and Orchard stepped through the door. 'We've got a plane to catch.'

'We'd just like you to answer a few questions, Mrs Somerville,' said Annie.

'Can I refuse?'

'If you do, we'll arrest you and take you back to the station.'

'I haven't got much choice then, have I?'

Greta allowed herself to be ushered into a separate room by the two police officers. An airport official remained outside with an anxious-looking Paul.

Annie began hesitantly, conscious of Orchard's eyes on her.

'I apologise in advance for these questions, Mrs Somerville. They are of a personal nature.'

Greta glared at her impatiently. 'Just get on with it.'

'Are you pregnant?'

There was a pause. Evidently this was not what she had expected.

'Yes.'

'Who is the father of your child?'

'I'm a married woman, officer.'

'Are you saying your husband is the father?'

'Why wouldn't he be?'

'Our information is that your husband is not capable of fathering children.'

'Who told you that?' Greta was indignant.

'Is it correct?'

'You'd have to ask Laurie about his medical history. Not me.'

'But Paul's adopted, isn't he?'

'Yes. We had trouble conceiving. But who knows how nature works? This baby is a miracle as far as I'm concerned.'

Annie shifted tack.

'When I saw you at the yard on Sunday you told Kate that you and your husband had made up.'

'So?'

'What did you fall out about?'

Greta shrugged. 'It wasn't serious.'

'It was serious enough for you to move in with Miss Montague, though, wasn't it? Does Laurie know who got you pregnant?'

Greta stared at her, not with anger or defiance but with another emotion that Annie couldn't yet place. She pressed on.

'It was Freddy, wasn't it?'

Greta blinked at her and Annie identified her emotion – fear. It swirled in the depths of her milky blue eyes as she said, 'No.'

'So you've never slept with Freddy Montague?'

'No.'

'Never been in his bedroom?'

'No.' Spoken hesitantly.

'We've found hair on the carpet upstairs in his cottage that matches the sample you gave us at the start of the investigation.'

Greta thought hard for a moment. 'Look, I'll do a deal with you. Let Paul get on the plane by himself and I'll return with you and make a full statement.'

'That won't be possible, Mrs Somerville.'

'Why not? This has nothing to do with him. Let me see him off and then I'll tell you everything. I was with Freddy when he was murdered.'

Excitement surged through Annie. She'd been right! She said nothing as Greta leaned forward urgently.

'Please. Let Paul go to Stockholm. Then I'll tell you what happened when Neil shot Freddy.'

'Neil?' Orchard spoke for the first time.

'You must know that – you've got him under arrest. He used to spy on Freddy, hoping to see him in bed with Sarah. Neil had a crush on her. I suppose he just got jealous.'

'But Freddy wasn't with Sarah on the night he was shot,' said Annie. 'He was with you – you just told us.'

Greta looked confused. 'But who else could have shot him?'

'I'm sorry, Greta,' said Annie. 'You do see why we can't let Paul get on that plane, don't you?'

\*

Paul's statement wasn't lengthy. Once he'd been assured that his mother would not be detained, he made it freely in the presence of Gus Jones, Annie and DCI Orchard. Unburdening himself was obviously a relief.

'After I found the gun in the road, Neil and me used to go out in the evening and go shooting, up in the woods. We'd aim at the rabbits but we never hit one once. So we got a proper telescopic gun sight and it made a hell of a difference. You could see stuff really clearly from quite a distance.

'We first started watching Freddy by accident. We were up on the field opposite his house one night and he had the lights on. When we took a peek we could hardly believe it – he was on the bed with a girl. They had no clothes on and they were doing it. I'd never seen anyone doing it before. We kept an eye on him after that. He always had women up there and he never drew the curtains.

'Then he started doing it with Sarah and Neil went all funny. He wouldn't go up there with me any more. He didn't want to see her with Freddy. I did, though. She's bloody good-looking, fitter than half the women you get in *FHM* or *GQ*.

'The night it happened, Mum and Dad had been rowing and he'd smashed up the living room. I heard him say he wanted a divorce. I was in a bit of a state. Not that them splitting up matters much in the long run, I suppose. I wasn't adopted till I was six so I've always known, deep down, that it might all turn out to be temporary. I can understand why Mum might want a proper child of her own. It just sort of took me by surprise. And I felt for Dad. Well, I felt for them both but if anything I was on his side.

'So, I sneaked out later, just to get out of the house. I wanted to take my mind off it – like a diversion. And watching Sarah and Freddy screwing was that all right. I'm ashamed to admit it but that's the truth. So I took the gun from the old shed where we kept it and cycled up there. I loaded it just in case I got lucky with a rabbit or a pheasant. I didn't normally load it but that night I was angry – you know I wouldn't have minded blowing the head off a rabbit or two.

'At first I didn't think anyone was in. Then I saw the lights of a car in the lane. It stopped at the cottage and I assumed that Sarah had turned up. Then the light went on upstairs and I got the window in the sight. I could see into the room clear as day. Freddy was there with a woman all right but it wasn't Sarah, it was my mum.

'I couldn't believe it. I kept telling myself that this was some other girlfriend of his and I was seeing things. But there was no doubt it was my mum. She was wearing the clothes she'd worn to the races. I remember telling her how good she looked in them. And he was standing behind her with his hands all over her. He unbuttoned her blouse and slid it off her shoulders and she just stood there and didn't do anything. And he was pawing her, you know, squeezing her tits and she's my mum and she's letting him.

'Then I thought about what I'd heard Dad say and it all made sense. Mum was going to leave home to live with Freddy and have his baby. I so much didn't want that to happen. It was just wrong.

'So when Freddy came up to the window and started to draw the curtains, I pulled the trigger. I didn't think about it, I just did it. And he fell over. I thought he'd just slipped or something, then I saw Mum bending over him and blood on the carpet.

'I don't know how I hit him. I'd never shot anything before. Just lucky, I guess – if that's what you call it.

'Anyway, I knew I had to get rid of the gun. First of all I took off my shirt and wiped it all over. You know, to get rid of fingerprints. Then I put it back in its case and cycled over to Franklin's pond and chucked it in. I was terrified someone would see me but they didn't. And when I got home it was all quiet. The car was there, like normal. So I slipped in the back way and went to bed. When I woke in the morning I just went off to school as usual and tried to pretend it was all a dream.

'It still seems like a dream. The worst I ever had in my life.'

# After

It rained all night in York – as it had done most of the week, according to the waitress in the hostel canteen.

'What kind of a summer d'you call this?' she said to Neil at breakfast, as if it were his fault. 'The middle of bloomin' August and it's tippin' it down. It's not good for business, I tell yer. Not unless you're in the umbrella business, of course.' And she'd laughed energetically as she'd cleared away his plate and strode off without expecting a reply. That suited Neil just fine, cheerful banter – especially with chirpy young women – not being his forte.

He had travelled up the night before in the horse box from Lambourn with a crew of lads and horses, including Lifeline. Today was the second day of the Ebor festival, the third race being the Ebor Handicap itself, one of the big betting occasions of the year. But Neil's real interest lay in the Gimcrack Stakes which followed, one of the top events in the racing calendar for two-year-olds – and Lifeline's comeback race.

As it happened, Neil was also concerned about the weather. So far Lifeline had performed best on firm ground. And though he had yet to be tested in a race on the soft, Neil knew from working him in all weathers that the wet didn't suit him. He peered anxiously through the window at the thick grey cloud and the steady downpour. If this kept up, the horses would need water-wings to get round.

He returned to the room he was sharing with three other lads and pulled on his rainwear. His room-mates had all gone into town. Neil had already seen to Lifeline. For once, Vicky had not travelled with the lads and he'd felt his responsibilities keenly. He hadn't been able to sleep so he'd fed the horse and mucked him out at six. He'd put some tack on him and trotted around at half-seven. The rain had been just as insistent then and, though Lifeline hadn't complained, Neil could tell the horse had been keen to get back to his dry box for a rub down.

With the hood of his anorak pulled over his head and wellington boots on his feet, Neil stepped out into the rain. Despite the wet, now was as good a time as any to walk the course. Perhaps he could pick up some useful information for Tony – it was his comeback race too.

The weather was just as bad on the motorway as Tony and Kate drove north. As ever on a weekday morning, the M1 was chock-a-block with traffic, domestic and commercial, all of it in a hurry.

'It's like driving under water,' muttered Tony as the rain bucketed down, plumes of spray shooting up from the wheels of the heavy lorries.

'Would you mind pulling over at the next services,' said Kate.

The idea was appealing – he suddenly felt dog-tired. But they didn't have all that much time to spare. 'We should push on.'

'No, Tony. I've got something to say to you.'

That sounded ominous.

When Kate had visited him in hospital two days after the fire she'd obviously been shocked by the extent of his burns.

'Are you in pain?' she'd asked.

'It's good pain,' he told her. 'It means the nerves are still working. They say I'll be out before long.'

'How are you going to manage?'

'Somehow or other.'

'Vicky's staying with me in the Lodge. You'd better move in too so we can keep an eye on you.'

He'd opened his mouth to make a token protest but she wouldn't listen.

'Tony, you saved me from Mickey. You pulled my horses out of the fire. Now it's my turn to take care of you.'

So since he'd got out of hospital he'd been living in a spare room at the Lodge. His injuries – second-degree burns to the arms and legs – had made it difficult to fend for himself and Kate had insisted he remain under her care. It had been a good arrangement as, after her near-rape, she couldn't bear the thought of living in the house by herself. But now his wounds had healed and she had 'something' to say to him – maybe she wanted him to move out?

Or maybe she wanted to discuss the yard, which was still in chaos after the destruction of the fire – or 'the case', which was how Tony had come to think of Freddy's murder, the complications of which had taken over so much of their lives. The day after the fire the police had dropped the allegation against Tony and charged Paul instead. His trial was due in the autumn and would not be pleasant for any of them.

Tony and Kate found a seat in a corner of the service-station restaurant.

'So.' He searched her face for clues. She looked, as she so often did, grave and tired. And very beautiful. He closed his mind to that. The last thing she needed after Mickey was unwanted attention from a man.

'It's about you,' she began.

His heart sank. She wanted him to back off and get out of her life. All his failures in previous relationships paraded before his eyes.

She took a deep breath.

'I don't want you to ride Lifeline.'

He was stunned. She rushed on.

'You're the most bloody-minded individual I've ever met. I've watched you for the past two weeks, pushing yourself to the limit, starving yourself, ignoring your injuries. I want you to stop riding.'

Tony said nothing. This had come out of nowhere. It took him a while to readjust his thinking. It was true he had been obsessed with getting back for this race.

She pressed on, obviously taking his silence for dissent.

'Take a look at yourself. You're a sick man still getting over a serious accident. You're two stone below your natural weight and the stupid thing is, you're still too heavy to do the job.'

It was true. Despite his wasting diet, Tony had three pounds to lose before the race that afternoon. His main problem was a legacy of the fire. It was worse hell than ever now to go into the sauna where the heat played a symphony of pain on the nerves in his recently burnt flesh.

'Please, Tony.' Her hand was on his, squeezing his fingers. 'Please stop now before you really hurt yourself.'

Tony pushed aside his first thought, which was to tell her to mind her own business. This *was* her business. Perhaps he should finish this everlasting battle with his weight – the painful, mind-over-matter challenge that only got tougher as time went by.

Could be she was right. Since the night of the fire, everything about Kate had seemed right.

'You're the boss,' he said eventually. 'If you don't want me to ride then I don't ride.'

'Tony –' She seemed at a loss, which was unlike her. Kate the trainer was always in control. 'I'm not giving you orders. It's not like that any more.'

'Really?' He looked into her magical grey eyes. She was still holding his hand. 'What is it like then?'

She said nothing though her lips parted slightly.

A motorway service restaurant is not the most romantic setting for a first kiss. But Tony didn't care.

Just when Neil had reconciled himself to the rain lasting all day, it stopped. He lowered his hood and looked up. The clouds seemed higher and the sky was brighter. Though he stood on his own at the start of the six-furlong Gimcrack straight, he could imagine the relief that would be felt all over the course. His gloom lifted with the weather as he looked around and imagined the throng that would soon be gathered for one of the finest days' racing of the summer. Neil liked York best out of all the courses he'd visited. So far he'd only performed a lad's duties and he longed for the day he'd get the chance to ride a race.

He pushed those thoughts aside and focused on Lifeline's task that afternoon. He adored all the horses he worked with but he loved Lifeline best of all. Maybe it was because he'd spent so much time with him, especially during the past month while Tony had been recovering from his brush with death. After Neil had been released from custody, having frustrated all Hunter's attempts to get him to incriminate himself, he had devoted himself to the horse.

He'd known from the first that Paul must have shot Freddy but he'd sworn to himself that he wouldn't be the one to grass him up. And he hadn't, though that didn't make him feel any better about his part in the matter. If only he hadn't given way to Paul's pleading and found a way to get some bullets . . . but he had and Freddy's death had followed.

To cover his guilt he had thrown himself into his work at the yard and Vicky had allowed him to spend as much time with Lifeline as he wished.

'That horse is a hero,' she'd said to him. 'He ought to get a medal for the way he dealt with Mickey Lee.' Neil couldn't agree more.

So the Gimcrack this afternoon was more than just a race to Neil. It was a chance for Lifeline to show his true face to the world and emerge a champion. He couldn't bear the thought of the horse being beaten.

Neil squelched over the first furlong, sticking close to the rail on the stand side – where Lifeline had been drawn. It was like walking on a sodden green carpet, the water oozing up the sides of his boots with every step. Even though there were six hours to go before the race, it was unlikely the going would ever be better than soft. These heavy conditions certainly wouldn't suit Lifeline. What was worse, they might be good for Board Six, a small grey with a rounded action who would love some give underfoot. He'd won in the wet at Newmarket a month ago by half a length from Putmedown, a filly who raced in a nose band and who was also on the Gimcrack card. It looked like Lifeline would have his work cut out.

Neil looked across the course. It didn't appear any better on the far side but he walked across all the same. He saw at once that there would be no advantage in the low draw. Water had pooled on the surface in places and, though it would drain away, there was no chance of the ground properly drying out.

The middle of the course, on the other hand, seemed a lot firmer under his feet. With rising excitement Neil walked a narrow strip in the centre of the course from the five-furlong pole to the stands. By the time he had finished, he was feeling pretty pleased with himself. The centre strip down the middle wasn't dry by any means but it was a lot less wet than the ground elsewhere. Now that was a piece of information worth passing on to Tony.

'I'm not hungry,' Tony had said but Kate insisted he had something to eat. He ate a doughnut just to please her. It tasted fantastic. There was something unfamiliar in her expression as she smiled at him. For the first time in months she looked happy.

'I wouldn't give up Lifeline to anyone but Neil,' he said.

'I know. But it makes sense, doesn't it?'

He nodded. He realised he'd just kissed goodbye to his life in the saddle and all he could feel was relief. 'So what do you suggest I do now I'm an ex-jockey?'

'Help me turn a burnt-out, undersubscribed yard into a winning concern.'

'Who says I can train?'

'I do. You're knowledgeable, patient and dedicated. You'll have to leave the owners to me, though.'

He grinned – that made sense.

'You've thought it all through, haven't you?'

'Do you mind about that?'

'Mind?' He stroked her cheek. 'I love it.'

*

It was quite like old times. Annie and Hunter had been summoned to Orchard's office.

'How are you two getting on with the Jonno Simpson enquiry?' he barked.

Annie shuffled guiltily in her seat and looked at Hunter.

'What progress have you made recently?' continued the DCI.

'It's gone a bit cold, sir,' said Hunter at last.

'You mean you've forgotten all about it. Too many other fish to fry, is that it?'

Orchard's words hung in the air for a moment before he continued. It occurred to Annie that he was enjoying himself.

'Fortunately not all of us are asleep at the wheel. I've just taken a call from a Mr Raphael, who is representing Mr Simpson. It seems that, during his long convalescence, Jonno has been reflecting on his past and decided, not before time, to tell us everything he knows about fixing horse races. You'll be taking a statement from him shortly but I got his brief to give me some highlights. We are promised specific details of dates, races, monies – and names.'

Orchard paused – for effect, Annie assumed – and Hunter jumped in. 'What names?'

Orchard grinned. 'Herbert Gibbs. It seems Herbert has been a one-man industry in this regard. Mr Raphael promised lots of leads that could be followed up by an industrious team like you two. So,' he added, 'no more sitting on your arses, eh?'

Annie spoke for the first time. 'Did he say why Jonno's decided to come clean now?'

'Not in so many words but he implied it's down to that pretty little fiancée of his. It seems the wedding won't be going ahead unless Jonno stands up to be counted. Sometimes a small blonde can be a sight tougher than a six-foot villain. Wouldn't you agree, Keith?'

But Hunter didn't rise to the bait. 'I'll get on to Raphael right now, sir,' he said and left the room in a hurry.

Annie seized her opportunity. There was a matter she wanted to raise with Orchard on her own.

'Speaking of Jonno Simpson, guv – when we interviewed him you said you once won five grand on one of his rides.'

'I wish I had, Annie. The Blackthorn children's ward could have done with it.'

'Well, could they use three thousand pounds instead?'

He looked at her quizzically.

'Only that money we found at Tony Byrne's place – he doesn't want it back. He's asked me to find a good cause.'

'You're kidding.'

'No, sir. I wouldn't fib about something like this.' She paused – her turn for a touch of dramatic emphasis. 'Unlike some people I know.'

Liam Kelly had not stopped grumbling all the way from London but Mary and Vicky were deaf to his complaints. As for allowing him to walk down the train to the buffet car, that was out of the question. Mary even shadowed him to the toilet.

'It must be twelve hours since he's had a drink,' she said to Vicky. 'That's the longest he's gone since he got out of prison.'

'Can you keep an eye on him at the racecourse?' asked Vicky.

'I'll keep him sober till the race is over, if that's what you mean. Though I can't answer for what'll happen if Neil wins.'

Vicky laughed. 'Who cares? If Neil wins we'll all get plastered.'

*

Kate and Tony found Neil in Lifeline's box, muzzling him up so he wouldn't nibble the straw of his bedding before the race. The lad looked alarmed as Kate asked him to step outside. He didn't take it in when they gave him the news.

'You're riding in the Gimcrack,' Kate told him.

He gazed at her in confusion.

Tony put a hand on his shoulder. 'You're riding Lifeline.'

'Why?' The lad looked anxious. 'Are you all right?'

'I've decided to retire.'

'You can't do that.' The boy was upset.

'Someone's just pointed out a few facts of life to me, Neil. I can't make the weight any more.'

'But—'

'But nothing. He's a fine horse and he deserves better than a clapped-out rider like me. He's got a much better chance of winning with you on board.'

Neil was lost for words. 'Thanks,' he managed, clearly overwhelmed.

Kate stepped in to save his embarrassment. 'You'd better get changed. I've brought your kit.'


Vicky was thankful the train wasn't late. She and Mary had carefully timed Liam's arrival at the racecourse to minimise the temptations of the many watering holes eager to accommodate a man of his unquenchable thirst. The taxi dropped them at the entrance at 2.45 with just an hour to go before Neil's race. At least, Vicky hoped it would be Neil's race. When Kate had outlined her plans, she'd been confident she could get Tony to see sense. But suppose he'd refused to step aside? Vicky would feel foolish if she'd persuaded Liam and Mary to make the trek north and Neil wasn't in the saddle.

So she approached the stables with some trepidation. As she walked along the line of boxes she spotted Tony stroking Lifeline's muzzle, talking softly into the horse's ear.

He spotted her coming and his face froze. He waited till she was close before he spoke.

'You were in on this, weren't you?'

'I was.' She'd prefer not to have a row with Tony but she'd not back down.

'I think,' his eyes bored into her, 'that you're as tricky as she is.' Then he grinned.

Vicky gave him a big smothering hug.

'Put me down,' he said at last. 'What other cunning plans are you hatching?'

So she told him about Neil's father.


Lifeline's starting-stall was on the stand-side rail where traffic from earlier races had done much to churn up the already heavy ground. Despite Neil's tight grip on the reins, the horse jumped out faster than he would have liked, charging for the inside berth. Neil fought to hold him back – this was not his plan for the race.

The twelve runners packed on the stand side, skidding along the slippery turf, their hooves hurling chunks of topsoil into the air. Before they'd travelled a furlong, Neil's goggles were half obscured by mud and debris.

Beneath him Lifeline was straining to find a rhythm, the heavy going hampering his stride, gluing his feet to the ground. Neil took a pull on the reins. He had to get the colt out from the inside – and quickly, or the race would be lost.

\*

In the owners' and trainers' bar Liam Kelly's attention was focused on the screen above him. His second Guinness of the day was in his fist, already half drunk though Mary had presented it to him only a minute before.

'What's the eejit doing?' he complained to his daughter. 'He's going backwards.'

To Neil, it did indeed feel like he was travelling backwards as he switched the colt to the middle of the course. The pack charged ahead as he urged Lifeline across to the dry strip he'd spotted earlier. The colt was now at least six lengths behind the next horse. To an uninformed observer it looked like a disaster.

'What the hell are you doing?' Paul yelled at the television set. He turned to his parents. 'Neil's mucked it up, hasn't he?'

'Looks like it,' said Laurie. They were watching the racing together because Paul had suggested it.

'He's looking for better ground,' Greta said. 'It's too heavy for Lifeline on the inside.'

'But the others are miles ahead. He'll never catch up.'

Greta was tempted to say, So what? She was touched that Paul appeared to care so much about Neil, the boy he'd gone shooting and spying with. In her eyes Neil was as culpable as Paul for what had happened. He was older than Paul – he should have prevented it somehow. Neil was just as guilty as her son.

Though not as guilty as she was.

She reprimanded herself as these thoughts – the ones that preyed on her night and day – flashed into her mind. She mustn't think like this. Negative thoughts were bad for the baby. She caught Laurie's eye and lifted her head. He was watching her with concern.

Laurie had been brilliant, she had to admit. He'd assembled a first-rate legal team to defend Paul – God knows how many favours he'd had to call in. As a result she felt much less gloomy about the boy's prospects. Given his age, and the fact that the killing had not been premeditated, Laurie had said a judge might consider the death simply a tragic accident. So there was a good chance he might not receive any kind of custodial sentence.

One thing the whole terrible business had done was to bring the family together. The expanding family.

'I suppose I ought to be grateful to Freddy,' Laurie had said after he'd heard the truth about her pregnancy. 'We'll get the baby we've always wanted.'

'You're not just saying that, are you?' she'd replied. 'You told me you couldn't bear to bring this baby up.'

He'd looked rueful. 'I've been thinking. I'm going to be the only father this kid ever has, aren't I? I reckon I can live with that.'

Thank God she still had Laurie.

'Look, Mum,' yelled Paul in excitement, breaking into her thoughts, 'you were right!'

The effect of the firmer ground beneath Lifeline's hooves was instantaneous. His stride lengthened and his rhythm returned as he stretched out, building into a steady gallop.

Neil breathed a sigh of relief. This was more like it! He was a long way back but at least he'd given himself half a chance. He'd never have got up on the inside.

There were three furlongs left in the race and the pack were ten lengths ahead. It was impossible.

Neil didn't care. He urged Lifeline on with the whip just once and felt the renewed surge of power as the colt responded to his call.

The pack began to come back to him.

The Guinness in Liam's hand was forgotten as Neil and Lifeline began their inspired dash for the line.

'Mother of God,' breathed Liam, 'he'll never do it.' But there was optimism in his voice and a light in his eye as he yelled, 'Go on, my son. Go on!'

By the furlong pole Lifeline had overhauled the back-markers on the rail. Out of the corner of his eye Neil could see the two favourites, Board Six and Pickmeup, fighting it out in the lead but it looked like they were now going up and down on the spot . . .

He rode the kind of finish he'd always imagined, balanced high on Lifeline's shoulders, head tucked low, hands and knees urging, pushing, cajoling the horse on to the line.

And Lifeline gave it everything, expending all his energy in a lung-bursting drive for the winning post that flashed past them in a sudden blur. Neil eased the horse down, pulling off his mud-spattered goggles and taking in gulps of air. He could swear he'd forgotten to breathe on that last wild gallop for the line. He had no idea where he'd finished.

There was a muffled announcement over the loudspeaker system as he turned the horse round, back towards the unsaddling enclosure. Board Six and his rider, Aidan Gillespie, were just five yards off.

'Who got it?' he called.

374

'Photo,' yelled Gillespie. 'You, me and Breezie.' Jimmy Breeze was on Pickmeup.

A three-way photo, that was something.

When they announced the result of the photo, Liam Kelly was beside himself.

'He *is* my son,' he explained to a nearby group of spectators who'd watched his frantic performance, urging Neil home.

And then he rushed from the bar, abandoning his half-empty glass without a second thought.

For a second Neil didn't recognise the middle-aged man in the suit and tie who charged into the winner's enclosure and lifted him bodily from Lifeline's back.

'Dad!' he cried in amazement.

Liam crushed him to his chest. 'I'm proud of you, son,' he breathed into his ear. 'And I'd be just as proud if you'd finished last,' he added.

Neil was overwhelmed. Behind his father he saw Kate, Tony, Vicky and Mary avidly watching the pair of them.

'Thanks, Dad,' was all he managed to say.

A familiar figure managed to thrust herself into the crowd around the winning trainer.

'A bloody fine horse,' shouted Mrs Lim in Kate's ear, 'and young Neil too. I always said so.'

Kate allowed herself to be grabbed and kissed.

'Are you OK?' demanded the small woman. 'No more Mickey Lee. No more Bernard Shen.'

'That's all finished, thank God.'

'Excellent. So I can bring my horses back next season?'

'Are you serious? You've been doing so well.'

Kate had been aware of many recent winners now Mrs Lim's horses were with Sir Philip Avery, the most successful trainer in the country.

'Pooh! Sir Avery doesn't know my horses like you. This year you had bad luck, next year will be different. And, you know what?' She charged on without a pause for breath. 'I have a new horse you will adore. His previous owner died tragically and I've snapped him up. It's an ill wind. Can't you guess his name?'

'Tell me.'

'Cold Call.'

Kate was speechless.

'So.' Mrs Lim's face was earnest now. 'Do we have a deal?'

'Of course. Oh, Gladys, you don't know how much I've missed you.'

Jeff's trunk sat in Bill and Gaynor Collins's hall for a couple of days after it arrived from the shippers. They didn't have the key and Mark, Jeff's elder brother, was out of town. But he came over the night he got back and attacked the locks with a selection of tools. By the time he'd broken inside, the trunk wasn't much good for anything though no one cared about that. Bill and Gaynor had no use for it anyhow – it contained too many memories.

Mark went through Jeff's stuff with his dad, his mum couldn't handle it. It was mostly clothes and Mark kept what he could get into as Jeff had had pretty good taste. It was a pity he was so small around the waist though.

There were CDs and photos and other personal stuff. And one book, *The Lord of the Rings*, which Mum and Dad had given Jeff for his sixteenth birthday.

Tucked inside the book was an envelope. It contained a ticket. Mark thought it looked like a betting slip. He promised to check it out. After all, if Jeff had put it in a separate envelope it might be worth something.

His father disagreed. It was probably just a souvenir of Jeff's days in Hong Kong. 'But if it's worth anything, son, let's go fifty-fifty.'

They shook hands on it – just for fun.


The day after the Gimcrack Stakes, Laurie found Kate and Tony together in the office.

'I've just had Gavin Marshall on the phone,' he said. 'You'll never guess what he wants.'

They looked at him expectantly.

'He's been talking to the syndicate about Lifeline. They offered to buy him once, remember?'

Tony nodded. 'I remember all right. You withdrew the offer after the car crash.'

'Well, it's back on. Only the money's gone up. What do you say to five hundred thousand pounds?'

Tony stared at him, then at Kate. They could do a lot with half a million quid.

'What do you think?' he said to Kate.

She held up her hands. 'Leave me out of it. It's your call.'

Tony pretended to think about it, just to look businesslike, but there was no point. He knew in his heart the right thing to do.

'Sorry,' he said. 'Tell Marshall, Lifeline's not for sale.'